Tin Can

by Colin Noble

4th Floor Press, Inc.

www.4thfloorpress.com

This book is a work of fiction. Names, characters, places, and the scenarios depicted are meant to be fictitious. Any resemblance to actual persons, living or dead, establishments, locations, or events is entirely coincidental.

Library and Archives Canada Cataloguing in Publication

Noble, Colin, 1953 May 5-
Tin can / by Colin Noble.

ISBN 978-1-897530-35-1

I. Title.

PS8627.O186T55 2012   C813'.6   C2012-907235-4

4th Floor Press, Inc.
www.4thfloorpress.com
Printed in Canada
1st Printing 2012

Dedication

To my family and my closest friends who have shown me the power of motivation and the necessity of making connections.

Chapter 1

September 2048—Florida, Earth

Amber lamp-like eyes were fixed on the two boys tussling on the floor. The small cadet with a green woolen cap stretched over his rather large, lumpy head was busy entangling himself in between the other boy's legs as the older cadet tried to get to his feet. A turbine whine started up somewhere, sending vibrations through the floor, walls, and alloy furnishings that were bolted in place.

Clutching his big brother's left leg, the small cadet pleaded, "No, Jacob, stay! Stay with me! I've never launched before."

"I have to go, Billy," Jacob shouted, peeling his brother off his baggy blue pants. "Mom and Dad need me at the bridge for liftoff. It takes three of us to manage the controls—you know that. Quincy will stay with you, so you'll be okay. I'll come back as soon as I can."

"I want you to stay with me, too!" Billy wailed in a panic. Jacob pulled himself away and made for the door of their bedroom. Hesitating, he turned and ordered, "Take care of him, Quincy. I'll be back as soon as I can. Promise." Then he left, pulling the door firmly shut behind him.

The watchful Ring-tailed lemur leapt across the room to strap the young deformed boy safely into his bed. Howling hysterically, Billy allowed himself to be secured for liftoff. The bawling slowed to profound sobbing, Billy snorting and gagging as he made ineffectual swipes at his runny nose. Quincy gently nestled close, strapping himself in with the quaking child. Curling his long black-ringed tail in front of Billy's tear-stained face, he blocked out the bright interior light, warming the boy and perfuming the air with his distinctive scent. Billy's hiccupping whimpers

1

became muffled until at last he was restored to a dejected composure. Quincy and the exhausted boy lay together, waiting quietly.

"You're late, Jacob. Your mother and I have been trying to make do shorthanded." Hunched over a console, Jacob's father, Dave Edwards, spoke curtly, not bothering to look up as his son crossed the bridge.

"Sorry, Dad, I got tied up for a few minutes. But I've practiced. I know what to do."

"Tied up?" queried his mother, Lucy Edwards. She gave Jacob a knowing look. "Quincy looking after him?"

Soberly, Jacob nodded. Focusing on his liftoff responsibilities, he jumped into his ergonomic captain's chair. At least his mother understood.

The bridge deck faced out towards a large parabolic screen with banks of instruments lined up beneath. Skimming silently over the metal plate floor by reverse magnetic propulsion, Jacob's parents were already whizzing about the room in their chairs. Every time a hovering chair arrived at a desired control panel, it clamped down onto the floor with a thud. Dave and Lucy raced up and down the long banks of controls, operating them manually or through the use of the chairs and head visors.

Jacob joined his parents, gliding from console to console. Each was responsible for one system, but their tasks needed to be coordinated for takeoff. Lucy managed life support and interior systems, Dave looked after navigation, while Jacob was in charge of rocket propulsion, the simplest of the systems to orchestrate but also the most vulnerable and volatile. Two hundred metric tons of liquid hydrogen-oxygen, a crude but effective propellant, was going to blast Jacob and his family off on their journey to Europa, one of Jupiter's many moons.

This was a last-minute, hastily cobbled together exploratory journey. While the computer systems and navigation tools onboard their spaceship were top of the line, the craft itself was an older model, relatively inexpensive and lacking in safeguards. Every technician had vacated the underground launch site. The Edwards family was on its own.

Just above them, on the Earth's surface, one of the endlessly recurring hurricanes was waging destruction across a desolate landscape. Separating the rocket ship from the raging storm, a huge metal alloy lid-shaped panel was buffeted by the wind and pounded by falling debris. Echoes of the upper onslaught resounded through the underground cavern like a drum.

Dave shouted through the growing din, "Commence the ignition sequence, Jacob! Clear sky will be directly overhead in ten minutes." Dave had forecasted the departure time, and had roused his family with uncharacteristic jubilance at three in the morning, just an hour earlier. A fortuitous combination of events was set to occur. The calm eye of the hurricane would pass over the launch site during a momentary lull in the solar storm out in space, giving them a rare opportunity to make a run for Europa.

Jacob cranked up the thermal couples and the two ignition ducts caught fire, burning hot until they shimmered crimson red. Jacob then released the fuel ballasts, draining hundreds of pounds of ice-cold liquid hydrogen-oxygen into the superheated ignition ducts. Detonation occurred with a deafening roar. Dave instructed the launch station's computer to begin the liftoff sequence. Massive restraining bolts held the ship down as the metal ceiling slowly began to retract. Not until adequate heat and thrust were achieved would the bolts abruptly disintegrate and release the ship.

"We're off to a good start," Dave said resolutely. Lucy and Jacob knew they had better be—with full ignition they had passed the point of no return. The free flow of rocket fuel could not be shut off until the liftoff containment tanks had been emptied.

Suddenly, the ceiling panel came to a halt. Then, before the disbelieving eyes of Jacob and his parents, it started to reverse direction.

"What's going on?" Dave shouted, thinking he had made a mistake. Cursing under his breath, he worked frantically at the controls. Releasing their chairs, Lucy and Jacob glided over to Dave. Lucy began working alongside her husband to try to reverse the process while Jacob looked on in horror. With the panel closing over them, the ship would blow like a grenade in a pressure cooker. Two hundred tons of rocket fuel exploding in a contained space would wipe out miles and miles of the labyrinthine tunnels used by Space Command.

"I can't break into the program," Dave fumed. "It's an anomalous code running in a self-enhancing loop, but I need to crack into it and reverse it."

"It's a vortex program, Dad. There's no way to dismantle it from the outside," declared Jacob grimly. "It's already begun to spiral its way through Space Command's entire computer system. The program will destroy every software program in Space Command before it blows itself out."

"Is there nothing we can do?" Dave asked Jacob. His face, ghostly pale, mirrored the white, still faces of his son and wife.

"Once we're sucked into the vortex, there's no defense, Dad. We'll be eliminated."

Eliminated. The devastating finality of that word triggered a thought, and all at once Jacob's face lit up. He flipped the flashing screen in front of him back and forth. "That software, there's something familiar about the signature ... " he muttered. "It's almost exactly like the signature on Earth Shaker!" Ignoring the questioning looks of his parents, he feverishly began typing into the console. "Hail Viacron. We be Gamilins and mean ye no harm. Our quest is simple. We wish to search deep space. Exploration and habitat transformation is our mission. Victory is yours. Release us and we shall honor thee." For a moment, he held his breath. It was a risk. "That vortex, its signature program is the same one Trickster, the elite gaming cult, uses," he tried to explain to Dave and Lucy.

Jacob stopped and waited, but there was no response from his monitor. Dave and Lucy stared aghast at their screens, not knowing what to do. The whirling program crisscrossed systems while the charged rockets outside deafened them.

"We are not a spy satellite. Five of us are onboard this ship. Please help us," Jacob typed quickly.

"Understood. Will try, but not much time. Sorry," was the anonymous response on his screen.

"What do we do now?" Dave hollered, seeing the same message cross his monitor.

Turning to his parents, Jacob shouted back, "Buckle yourselves in and wait it out."

The rising burn drew in more and more fuel so that the escalating roar of the rockets drowned out any remaining conversation. There was no way the twenty-inch thick metal slab could retract in time. The pressure inside the launch chamber was building exponentially from the discharging heat and exhaust. Smaller, weaker hatch doors were already exploding out into the tunnels.

Any second now and the whole thing is going to blow—and take us with it, thought Jacob. KABOOM!

Jacob winced, but his parents kept their eyes glued to the instrument panel.

KABOOM!

The ship shuddered, then broke away from the launch pad. Jacob watched, fixated, as the nose of their ship barely grazed the alloy panel. With only minor scrapes, the ship rattled and shook, accelerating in fits and starts and leapt towards the open sky. Every organ and muscle in Jacob's body felt dragged down to the floor, and the deafening roar blocked out every thought. Jacob clutched the armrests.

In twenty minutes, an eternity, it was over. Completely drained, the liftoff fuel tanks fell away silently in space. Jacob's dragging sensation disappeared with the onset of weightlessness. They had succeeded. Jacob turned to his parents in shocked disbelief, then, seeing them alive and well, started to laugh uncontrollably. His parents' stricken faces took longer to go back to normal, but as their color returned, they too broke into nervous giggles. Back in the sleeping quarters, Billy, unaware that he had messed his pants, sniggered and snorted so uncontrollably against his restraining straps that he peed himself as well. Quincy quickly released himself. He batted Billy's nose once with his ringed tail before launching himself across the room, bouncing off the walls and ceiling.

"How did we break free in time?" Jacob asked incredulously.

"Your friend," answered his father appreciatively, "blasted the running rails off the steel roof and the fifty-ton panel popped off like a champagne cork. All the pressure that had built up in the launch chamber simply blew it out of our way. And with the sudden chamber decompression, the restraining bolts gave way." He added, "I thought we were goners."

Jacob sat visibly perplexed, digesting the information before answering shyly, "I've never met him before, Dad. But he must have also been the one who sabotaged our launch. An Anarchist."

"An Anarchist?" Lucy asked incredulously. "How did you know an Anarchist would help us, Jacob?"

"The whole scenario just made sense. Our launch isn't on Space Command's schedule. No one else was working in the tunnels. Then, without warning, in the middle of the night, there's an unscheduled launch. Pretty suspicious."

"Suspicious?" his mother queried.

"For someone on the outside, yeah. It would have looked like a high priority spy or military satellite launch," Jacob explained. "I mean, c'mon—no one has dared to go in space for over a year. With all the solar storms raging, it's been too dangerous. Whoever set the sabotage sequence didn't know we were on the ship. It would have looked like a ready-made opportunity for an Anarchist—total destruction of Space Command's primary launch site and computers, without any fatalities, using their own rocket fuel to boot."

"Who are these Anarchists, Jacob, and what's Earth Shaker?" Lucy was intrigued. They all lived under the same roof, but, more and more, Lucy understood her children's perspectives and knowledge were a paradigm shift away from hers.

Animated—realizing he had some specialized information to contribute—Jacob bubbled forth. "It was the assailing software–I recognized the vortex. The program was similar to Earth Shaker's, the latest game being played out on the grid. The creators of the game, Trickster, use a code so intricate it can't be broken. But, I'd bet any money that whoever hacked into Space Command has tried. There were nearly identical markers in the matrix. He must be a huge fan of the game."

"How can you be sure these creators, Trickster, aren't the ones who tried to attack us?" Dave asked, quite concerned all of a sudden, about the company his son was keeping online.

"No way a Gamer would do something like that, Dad. While Gamers might have political beliefs that don't mesh with our government's, they'd rather spend their time escaping Earth's problems, living through their imaginations, creating games. Anarchists, on the other hand, are trying to disrupt the 'establishment' at every turn. While an Anarchist might be a fan of computer games, they still have strong political goals that keep them very much grounded in the here and now."

"Anarchists, Gamers, political unrest?" Dave asked skeptically. As he leaned over the console to fingerprint a holograph, he brooded, *how did I become so out of touch?* Drawing his index finger across a holograph of the bridge deck, both the flooring and captain's chairs slid out towards the perimeter wall. The panoramic wall screen moved out of the way and shifted upwards, towards the rocket cone. Automatically, every apparatus in the room slid into its designated position for travel in space. With brushing strokes on a series of holographs, Dave reconfigured every compartment on the ship, from the storage bulkheads to the sleeping quarters.

"Billy and Quincy, this is Dad," Dave said loudly, so the internal communications system would register his voice. "I can see you on the

7

monitor. I'm going to change your berth around to make the ship ready for space." Billy's bed, bolted to a floor panel, glided smoothly to the periphery of the room, while Quincy, ecstatic about being in zero gravity, continued to jump from wall to wall. During the final phase of the conversion, the upright rocket repositioned itself, becoming a horizontal rotating cylinder to give them a sense of gravity and the ability to walk again. Quincy abruptly tumbled down the cabin wall, landing hard on his pointed black nose.

Over the monitor, the crew on the bridge heard Billy exclaim, "Ouch. That's gotta hurt, huh, Quincy?" The lemur jumped up hastily, clucking to himself irately while patting an obviously tender nose.

Jacob went on, wanting his parents to understand about the Anarchists. "According to the government, the Anarchists are a dangerous sub-cult that harasses the grid. The authorities are always trying to hunt them down, but they rarely catch them. They're way too computer savvy to be ambushed."

"Billy and Quincy, stay where you are. We're on our way," interjected Lucy, unbuckling herself and heading for the door. Jacob and Dave followed close behind, with Jacob persisting.

"The Gamers aren't seen as much better. The games they design and release on the grid are highly illegal and difficult to get in on," Jacob stopped dead in his tracks as his parents skidded to a halt and spun to stare at him, their mouths agape. "Oh, c'mon, it's not that bad. I bet you've done worse things in your day than play a few illegal games … "

"You're 'in on' these illegal games? But how?" Dave slowly started walking again.

"It's the same for everybody. I started playing the simpler games and making a name for myself by winning. As I got better and better, other competitors would drop me hints on where to find even more action— bigger games with better graphics, more complex plots. It's kinda like an initiation. The players have to prove themselves in each game. Other Gamers will ask subtle questions to scope out who's who. The Anarchists spot each other easily, as well. Through the games, everyone sorts out who everyone else is and communicates in code with each other. They know who's real and who isn't. Anyone who tries to infiltrate their ranks gets scrambled on the grid."

As they turned the corner to the corridor leading to the boys' room, Lucy and Dave just shook their heads in disbelief. They had never once suspected that Jacob saying he was going to play his game meant that he was rubbing elbows with criminals, talking in code, and potentially listening in on political plots being developed. He was just a kid!

"The battle cry of the Anarchists is 'screw the establishment!' But it's considered a mark of failure if anyone gets physically hurt. They're such tech wizards that a lot of them end up working for the establishment. They argue the ethics of it fiercely, but pretty well everyone knows that in these tough times, you gotta do what you can to survive. To disrupt the establishment is the goal, but no one is to get hurt. The one you harm in a sabotage strike might have been your partner in a previous game."

Dave put the pieces together. "So that's why you called out to the Anarchist to release us. You relied on the directive that no one is to be hurt."

Jacob nodded, "Yep, but I also wanted him to know I recognized the signature he was using—that I'm a fellow Earth Shaker player, so he'd know that I wasn't a member of Central Command."

Getting a glimpse of her fourteen-year-old in a new light, Lucy spoke wryly, "Let me get this straight. You wanted to acknowledge and honor this person, someone who was actively sabotaging our flight, for his achievements in this game?"

Jacob blushed, hearing it put that way. "It's not as silly as it sounds. Whoever hacked into Space Command's computer system didn't know we were onboard. It wasn't his fault. If you ever played Earth Shaker, you'd know what a strong moral code the Anarchists have and how difficult it would be to replicate Trickster's programming. He wouldn't be out to hurt anyone. I knew he'd try to help us if he could."

"Well, we're lucky your intuition turned out to be correct," Dave said with an edge in his voice.

Opening the hatch into the children's berth, Lucy found that Billy and Quincy were right there, standing at the door, waiting. Billy rushed to Lucy, and she swung him up into her arms and held him tight. Beaming broadly, Dave and Jacob unconsciously stepped back, noticing a strong odor. Quincy performed for all of them, executing a series of backward somersaults. Only when the family celebrations finally settled down a little did Jacob notice the message on the room monitor.

"Mistakes were made. Sorry."

Rushing to the console, Jacob excitedly typed in, "No harm done, we're all safe. You couldn't have known. We left in the night in a hurry because the conditions were right."

"What's your mission, exactly?" appeared on the screen.

"To explore Jupiter's moon Europa and see if life is feasible there," Jacob typed without thinking.

There was a ten-second pause and then the screen showed, "Interesting. Remember us back on Earth. Namaste."

"I hope our paths cross again," Jacob typed. Then, after some thought, "Earth Shaker rocks!"

"I suspect we will—either back here on Earth or in the game. You'd be a great opponent."

The writing vanished and the screen went blank. Jacob looked up to find his mom, Billy, his dad, and Quincy gathered around the monitor. A smile broke out on his face, then everyone started to grin.

The Edwards family was finally on its way. The space voyage had begun.

Chapter 2

"Move over. I'm cold," Billy demanded. Jacob, not quite awake, pulled his little brother into his bed. Shivering, Billy burrowed in, his feet rhythmically pedaling against Jacob's thighs as if he were running. Jacob held his little brother close, and slowly, Billy began to relax. Jacob could feel the clammy skin on his brother's thin, crooked back and on the sweaty forehead pressing against his chest: his little brother wasn't cold; he was hot. He had been running and fighting in his dreams again. Jacob pushed off the blankets and covered himself and his brother with a single sheet. Three nights in space had passed, but Billy was no different than he was on Earth. Jacob cursed his naivety, for vainly hoping Billy might stay in his own bed now that they were in space.

Eventually Billy settled into a fitful sleep, leaving his brother awake, lying in an awkward position, feeling hot and uncomfortable. When Jacob moved away, Billy cried out and moved back into his brother's arms. And so there they lay, bundled up together until morning, with Jacob eventually drifting back to sleep. For Billy, just another bad dream—for Jacob, yet another night's sleep disrupted.

Dreams haunted Billy, dreams he could never adequately describe. Billy wasn't good with words, perhaps because he didn't see the world the way the others did. He saw the world only through his own unique crystal prism.

"Get off me, fathead," Jacob mumbled, trying to untangle himself from his brother's clinging arms. Billy obligingly rolled away. His older brother was always a grouch in the morning when Billy found himself in his bed. He remembered nothing of the previous night, so he felt it was unfair that his older brother was so cranky. It wasn't as if Billy wet Jacob's bed anymore.

"You're a fathead, Jacob."

"That's pretty original for a fathead," Jacob sneered.

Billy let it go—he never won arguments with his older brother. And Billy did have a big head—a big, misshapen head. All the brain scans, x-rays, and lab tests said anybody with such a deformed head and abnormal brain should not be alive. Billy's brain was incompatible with life. But against the odds, Billy was still there, irritating his brother on a regular basis.

Just over eight years before, his parents had been doing field research, mapping the Sun's magnetic coronal field. Without warning, a colossal magnetic wave had arced far out into space before breaking down and releasing radiation. Discharging like a cannon, it scored a direct hit against the Edwards' tiny research vessel, orbiting a hundred thousand miles from the Sun's perimeter.

The story of the young couple's survival—repairing, then navigating their disabled ship back to Earth while enduring horrific radiation sickness—made headline news worldwide. Not until after the accident did Lucy realize she was pregnant with Billy. Medical doctors gravely agreed a live birth was improbable. Billy proved them wrong.

However, the radiation poisoning and the absence of gravity drastically influenced his development, preventing Billy's gestational compass from following a normal growth blueprint. His brain grew rapidly, chaotically, budding like a mushroom, while his inner white brain matter became honeycombed by islands of gray cortex.

Billy ended up with a vast excess of thinking gray cortex cells inside a maze of abnormal, and what should have been lethal, neural interconnections. Afflicted with repetitive neural echoing, his senses perceived the world as a wavering mirage. Feeling ill at ease in the physical world, Billy compensated by having a very active inner life, and envisioned many scenarios in a vain attempt to explain the phenomena occurring around him. As Billy was never sure what was real, his imagination stepped in to fill the vacuum.

"I'm going to wake Quincy since you're such a grump, Jacob. Quincy likes to play with me. I'm the *only* one who can catch him," Billy boasted.

"You won't catch him this time. He'll be awake from all the noise you're making."

"Ha! Just watch me." With minimal gravity to hold him down, Billy launched himself though the air from the bed, reaching high. He caught the vertical nine-foot pole in the corner with his left hand and pole-vaulted his feet over his head. Though small for his age, Billy had the strength, and when he concentrated, the spatial coordination of a spider monkey. He intended to arrive just under Quincy's platform perch and, with a free hand, grab the lemur's luxuriant, and temptingly dangling, tail.

Too late. With a flick of his tail, Quincy shot away, leaping back towards Jacob's bed. Jacob grabbed the zero gravity safety railing and hastily rolled off his bed to watch. Billy followed Quincy's trajectory flawlessly, landing on Jacob's bed exactly where Quincy had touched down. Unfortunately for Billy, the lemur had since bounced on to the room monitor and ricocheted back to land one second later—on Billy. Jacob jumped on the two of them, crying, "Pile on!!"

The three rolled over and over on the bed, wrestling and tickling each other viciously, laughing and crying. Not until they bounced as a ball to the floor did they stop to catch their breath. The morning was in full swing.

After disentangling their limbs, Jacob and Billy got up and began preparing for the day, with Quincy following them and jumping up onto his perch on a special stand at the sink. Washing up and brushing their teeth, there was the usual jostling for space at the sink. Jacob, being bigger, won, finishing first unscathed. The other two gave a good account of themselves, but in the end a tender spot was left on each side of Quincy's rib cage and there was a welt on Billy's forehead from when he had unthinkingly bent over to rinse the soap off his face and had his head forced into the sink by a tiny paw.

When the voyage was hurriedly being arranged, Quincy, an experimental prototype, had been added to the mix. Every member of the crew was ultimately expendable, but clearly, picking an animal for an undertaking where survival was unlikely was easier. The dilemma, however, was that to complete the required tasks, an intelligent and physically capable creature was needed. In Quincy's case, the answer lay in genetic engineering. Scientists had decided years before, in anticipation of such a journey, to create a lemur laced with multiple genes for intelligence, genes picked from some of the most intelligent people available—but not the genes needed for speech. An animal with human intelligence that could also talk might prove difficult. They also added the human gene for growth hormone, causing Quincy to top out at twenty-five pounds, making him capable of operating spaceship controls.

The planners were proud of Quincy, impressed with their technical achievement. Created to serve on space missions, no one ever considered that Billy might adopt Quincy as his friend.

The two boys and Quincy marched into the ship's conference room, which doubled as a dining area adjacent to a tiny galley. By necessity, living quarters were cramped, set in the outer revolving sleeve of the space ship. The rotating drum's centrifugal force gave those aboard the ship enough outward pressure to keep their feet on the floor and maintain their health.

"Morning," Jacob said, stepping into the galley. Lucy and Dave smiled and finished preparing breakfast.

Sitting down to eat, Jacob asked, "Anything new happen on Earth overnight?" He knew his parents would have been up for some time, busy running checks on the ship and scanning communications relayed around Earth by satellite.

"Last night's reports from Earth confirm our tests here in space," Dave answered. "The Sun's instability is more advanced than we feared."

The Edwards were not on a simple exploratory trip. The Sun was swelling and becoming progressively unstable and tipping, scientists suspected, into a red giant, a dying star. Frequent solar flare breakouts were releasing enormous amounts of radiation that burned through Earth's atmosphere, keeping people underground during the day for the past two years. Weather patterns had been destabilized, causing increasing numbers of hurricanes, tornadoes, floods, and droughts to occur. Food production was dwindling in spite of the industrial fermentation projects going on in abandoned mines. The programs instituted to keep people sheltered and fed were proving to be only temporary maneuvers. Earth was in a decline.

"That's why we're heading for Europa, right, Dad?" Jacob responded as he swiped a hand through his light brown hair and fixed an optimistic smile on his handsome face.

"Yes, that's our mission," Lucy interjected, leaning across the table to wipe a splatter of reconstituted milk off Billy's chin. Billy barely noticed as he shoveled another overloaded spoonful of cereal into his mouth. "To scout out Europa and see if it's possible for us to colonize its ocean, lying beneath two miles of pack ice. Space probes indicate there may even be primitive life forms present in the ocean, like plankton and small crustaceans that we could eat. You boys remember the time we had freeze-dried shrimp for your father's birthday, don't you?"

Jacob and Billy grinned. The shrimp had been a real treat saved from bygone years, from before the sea had been fished out and the oceans poisoned with toxic metals.

"Unfortunately, we won't know anything for sure until we burrow through the ice and find out for ourselves," their mother went on pragmatically. She ached to give Jacob and Billy better prospects, but didn't want to get her sons' hopes up too much. Their father, forever the optimist despite his serious demeanor, reached over, turning on the large screen monitor, bringing up a view of the icy moon. They could see a promising picture of the ice sheets cracked by Jupiter's gravitational pull and the ocean's underwater tides. "And if it is habitable, we'll need to send

15

a report back and set up a preliminary base to house the missions coming from Earth."

Jacob piped up excitedly, "How many people do you think can make it from Earth?"

Lucy turned away, hiding her expression from the boys and Quincy. Dave answered, speaking slowly, determined to stay honest with his son, "Maybe a thousand, Jacob, but that's better than none."

"But if Europa turns out to be uninhabitable, we can't make it back to Earth, can we, Dad?"

Lucy shot a grim look at her husband and pulled Billy into her arms for a cuddle. Quincy jumped down from his chair to sit at Lucy's feet, his tail wrapping around her ankle. Crestfallen, Dave answered Jacob, "No, we won't have enough fuel or supplies for a return trip. But if we had the means, by the time we made it back, your mother and I believe there might be little we would want to see—maybe only a few million survivors living underground, competing fiercely for dwindling resources. And, over time, the toxic effects of radiation, problems with the food supply, or some unforeseen disaster will destroy them all."

Steadfastly returning his father's gaze, Jacob's face became wooden. At fourteen he prided himself on knowing the facts. The reality was, Earth was turning into a vicious, uninhabitable place. Food supplies were already dangerously low. The entitled still relied on hydroponically grown grains, fruits, and vegetables from underground laboratories, but the vast bulk of the population survived off genetically manipulated fermentation products. Central Command maintained control of all the major stores of raw ingredients needed to manufacture basic supplies. Fortunately because of the Edwards' social standing, Billy still had access to some of his standby favorites, like peanut butter, but others weren't so lucky.

Settling Billy, who was wriggling in her arms, Lucy broke in. "Europa isn't the final answer, Jacob. It's just that it's that much farther away from the Sun and protected by ice. The ocean could potentially be full of life, able to sustain us in the way that Earth's seas once did. It might even contain large ocean caves we could fill with air to live in. We'd have a refuge and there'd be a place for more people from Earth—provided they can make it there. Still, it will only give the human race a little more time to come up with a better solution."

Dave continued where Lucy had left off, filling in the gaps, intent on getting the whole story out on the table. "As a red giant, our Sun will eventually release so much heat, it will torch Earth. Our planet will become a barren, scorched rock like Mercury. Farther out, on Europa, we'll have a little more time. The ice cover will eventually melt, but at least we'll be able to investigate other possibilities for settlement, far beyond Europa. When our Sun finally collapses in on itself, imploding as a supernova, it will wipe out our solar system and everything else for light years in every direction. Europa and all the planets and their moons will be long gone when our Sun finally shrinks into a small, dark, hyper-dense neutron star.

"Before the cataclysm occurs, the few remaining on Europa will need to find a habitable planet in another solar system. We haven't found a secure solar system yet, nor do we have the technology to reach it. But as a species we have to try.

"Even if we fail, your mother and I believe it's better to die out here in space, trying to complete our mission, than back in the squalid subterranean enclaves on Earth. But we think Europa is habitable. We petitioned very hard to get this mission off the ground. It's the only hope for our family."

"Thanks for staying straight with us, Dad," Jacob said, giving his father a reassuring hug, while Billy, for once, sat very still in his mother's arms. Listening in on the conversation, Quincy stared at the four of them with his wide eyes.

Uncomfortable with emotion, Dave waited a minute before stiffly saying, "Your mother and I have to go reset the navigation parameters, so finish your breakfast and meet us up front. We'll continue your lessons on flying procedures."

"Quincy," Lucy said, looking down to the lemur. "You keep an eye on Billy this morning, okay? We'll all meet for lunch at twelve hundred hours." Quincy reached for Billy's hand and nodded to Lucy. She smiled warmly as the two walked past Dave towards the doorway. Turning at the last minute, Billy smacked his head into the wall. He paused, raising a hand to the lump he was sure would soon be forming, and smiled lopsidedly at his dad. "Lunch, right?"

"Yes, Billy, we'll see you at lunch," Dave said, shaking his head at his son's constant clumsiness. A day didn't go by when Billy wasn't injured in some small way, or another.

"Dad doesn't think me and you are very smart, does he, Quincy?" Billy asked the lemur as they started clearing the dishes in the galley. They made an odd pair, the barrel-chested, spindly-legged boy and the oversized lemur, but they had become comfortable almost instantly upon meeting.

Quincy stared back, motionless.

"I know how smart you are," Billy said earnestly. "And Jacob sort of knows how smart both of us are. And Mom knows more than Dad, I think, but she listens to Dad too much. Just because some people and animals don't think like everyone else and can't talk so good, doesn't mean they don't know things. Maybe we know important stuff. Maybe we understand stuff in different ways."

Billy let out a big sigh. Quincy released an even bigger, theatrical sigh, and they broke out into giggles.

"Whatever," Billy said. "Let's go to the zero gravity room and I'll show you some moves I dreamed through last night."

Quickly gathering up the last of the breakfast dishes, Quincy and Billy outdid each other, stacking the dishes in the most dramatic, precarious manner. Rarely would they drop a dish, for to do so would disgrace the revered family tree of lemurs. In the days leading up to the launch, as the two were becoming acquainted with one another, Billy had formally asked to be accepted as an honorary member of the prosimian order. Only after he had diligently completed the requisite jumps, learned arcane grooming rules, and shared in bizarre food rites was Billy inducted. Quincy, as the only available spokesperson, conducted an elaborate secret ceremony.

They quickly tidied up, and then the two amigos were on their way to the zero gravity room, bouncing off walls and each other.

Chapter 3

In the central core of the spacecraft was a long cylindrical room. Isolated from the outside revolving sleeve, it remained motionless. This zero gravity space was required for the recalibration of precise navigational instruments and experiments that needed to be performed in isolation from the centrifugal force of the outer periphery. The cylindrical room was large, in order to stabilize the outer rotating drum.

Speaking into a wall panel, Billy called on the ship's computer to unlock the isolation portholes. "Request acknowledged," came the reply, and the ceiling hatch slid back, exposing a steel wall, the massive hub around which the ship rapidly revolved. Rotating in the outside tumbler Billy and Quincy waited, watching painted numbers on the steel drum pass by above them. Close to the hub of the ship, they stood in a low gravity environment, which assisted Billy as he jumped toward the painted number five. When Billy reached the ceiling the numbers decreased to what should have been zero, but instead of the digit a large round opening appeared.

Billy torpedoed through, pulling his feet up tight so the rotating sleeve didn't cut them off. He went into a high-speed spin, landing like a cat in a crouch on the far wall. On the second rotation Quincy came plunging through the orifice. Scrambling to the side, Billy avoided having Quincy land on his head.

Since the launch three days before, they had played in the room frequently and secretly—no need to inform the others of what they were doing just to be told not to do it.

"Hello, Billy, it is good to have you back," stated the disembodied voice of a woman.

Billy gave a screwball smile to one of the room's cameras. His eyes bugged out and his tongue hung to the left. Space Command demanded that the computer record all activities onboard the ship. In the event the crewmembers were found dead, this would enable Space Command to analyze everything that had gone on before. In case of death, Billy was intent on having a catalogue of his own for them to retrieve–no two facial expressions were to be the same and none normal.

"Computer, I want to run through last night's dream with you and Quincy. I'm sure it must have been a scary one. Jacob looked like I kept him up most of the night."

"Would you like music?" asked the ship's computer.

"Sure. Something slow, sad. It'll help me get into a trance and retrace my steps."

Six of the eight cameras spun around to Billy, while the two remaining focused on Quincy. There were no unmonitored secrets on ship. Billy didn't like it, but there was nothing he or anyone onboard could do about it. He just had to trust that his parents wouldn't snoop.

"Quincy, you spot me, so I don't get hurt."

Quincy acknowledged Billy with a perceptive look. He seemed to have the knack of knowing just what to do. He knew when to pair up with Billy in a dreamlike dance; when to be a fierce adversary (and after putting up a tremendous fight, lose, because it was Billy's dream they were acting out after all); and how to perform a spectacular gymnastic stunt, getting Billy out of a sticky situation in the nick of time. Watching Billy's facial and body movements, Quincy anticipated his needs, possessing powers of concentration that never seemed to waver or wander.

They sprang to their starting places. Billy went to the center of the wall and Quincy crouched thirty yards to the side, ready. The lights went down and Spanish guitar music began playing softly. Billy closed his eyes and soon fell asleep. He turned pale and began to tremble, then his eyes opened into an opaque stare. Bending forward, he blindly pitched himself

21

off the wall, somersaulting in a free-fall, as if jumping off a cliff on a moonless night. The computer cut the music and there came the sound of rushing wind and distant waves crashing onto rocks, the two forces melding into a fearful symphony.

Billy's trance had begun. Quincy dove to catch Billy before he smashed upon an imaginary rocky shore and hauled him away from the rock face out into deep black water and big waves. They were swept out to sea, drawn under and dragged along by the riptide. Billy tried to grasp the passing kelp as they tumbled through a swaying undersea forest, but was forced to give up–the current was too strong. In the open ocean he surfaced, gasping for air. The fury of the wind whipped up thirty-foot black waves, the tips cresting and crashing into a saltwater froth and roar. Lightning flashed and thunder echoed over the wind and the waves. Struggling to keep his head above water, Billy floundered. Choking on the brine, he felt himself drowning.

An immense barnacled wall rose up in front of him, scraping his chest and legs as it went by. Then, the unblinking eye of a Gray Whale stared at him as it, too, passed by. Blowing out a great blast of air from its blowhole, the whale sank back down into the black water, pulling Billy down with it. The pitch-black seawater was broken by bright fluorescent green patches as the whale's flukes shocked the phytoplankton. A luminescent path of a billion intricate vortexes trailed the massive mammal, swirling down towards the ocean depths. Billy's eyes traced the flowing patterns into the darkness.

As waves crashed above him, Billy sank into the stillness, following the shimmering green path. From the depths of the ocean, a curtain of bubbles rose up to encircle Billy, then was gone. In its place, a pod of Gray Whales appeared, swimming around and around him. Flukes gliding over him, the whales summoned Billy to listen, calling out to him in their language of musical notes and rhythms, mathematical configurations without numbers.

I think like that, Billy realized, stunned. He floated, suspended in the midst of the pod, and listened raptly as the whales told him their story: their beginning, their journey, their now.

Once, a long, long time ago, the whales' ancestors had lived on land in the enormous triangle of India. But, one day, impelled by forces they could neither name nor understand, their ancestors left the safety of land, slipping into the water. They languished in the big river estuaries of India, hemmed in by the ocean until they evolved. Once they had adapted to drinking salt water and become great swimmers, they set out into the open ocean, colonizing every corner of the globe.

Billy's unconscious and conscious minds responded to the story. *I was conceived in outer space and perceive what goes on around me through a strange spatial prism*, he thought. *Was I meant to return to space and evolve?*

Billy let go, sinking further into his trance and the dark depths of the ocean. The gray whales escorted him until it was too deep even for them, then silently returned to the surface. Billy drifted downward into the murky darkness, his eyes adjusting to the gloom. Approaching the ocean bed, he saw a faint luminescence radiating up from sulfurous sea vents. Shipwrecks twisted and torn apart loomed toward him, and large hideous fish with great shining eyes and gaping jaws rushed up, starving, from the bottom. The ocean floor trembled, and a shock wave struck Billy as an underwater volcano tried to shake off its mantle. Sea vents collapsed and opened up again, vomiting scalding water rich in methane, sulfur and other minerals. Oozing lava poured over the ocean floor, rivers of ruby-red fire. Alien-looking sea creatures, undisturbed by the fresh surge of lava, continued scouring the terrain in search of food or shelter. Life and death clashes ensued. Billy hung above the nightmare landscape, horrified and transfixed.

As his dream finally came to an end, Billy uttered a soft, short cry and went slack. Quincy quickly swept up his quivering, damp body, and the computer started playing gentle spiritual music, before slowly turning up the lights. The weary boy lay spent and unconscious in his friend's arms.

Quincy, waiting for Billy to wake up, peeled the green cap away from Billy's head and tenderly groomed his matted brown hair.

Everyday their private ritual was repeated. The ship's computer, programmed to record all encounters, was asked to keep the records of the encounters out of sight in an undisclosed file.

***

While Quincy and Billy played out the dream, Jacob had headed directly for the bridge. He knew his dad would be waiting for him impatiently. Except for the stabilizing central core room, the bridge was the most spacious room on the ship. It was round, like a huge barrel, with what appeared to be a massive, curved window stretching across and lining the front cone of the ship. In reality, the window was a three-dimensional holograph. Sensors outside the ship absorbed the complete spectral range of electromagnetic radiation and could formulate a color-enhanced picture on the screen, illuminating the whole spectrum in visible light for the ship's occupants. The holograph was the Edwards' view into space, and the ever-changing scene was mesmerizing.

The floor lay three hundred and sixty degrees around the revolving perimeter, and the screen turned parallel with the floor, giving the crew a sense of stability. Jacob entered through the rear hatch and saw his father and mother up front above him. Sitting upside down at the ring console, they were busy going through their daily instrument checks. Behind and below the window were the massive instrument bank and the adjoining circular console. The immediate flight controls were adaptable, and constituted part of Jacob's educational program as he learned how to fly the ship. The ship was meant to be primarily an exploration vessel, but in the event of an emergency, its flight guidance system was configured to respond like that of a meteor reconnaissance ship.

Jacob looked longingly at an elaborate chair imbedded in a three dimensional gyroscope—that hung freely suspended and unencumbered in the weightless center of the room. There, a pilot strapped in could single-handedly fly the ship, providing the pilot had the required skill set and lightning reflexes. Every small movement by the pilot's hands, feet, and eyes, monitored by the flight computer within the revolving gyroscope, directed the ship's flight path, weapons, and shields. In that chair Jacob could expand and make use of all the know-how he had gained from years of playing high-end computer games—for real.

"Here at last," said Dave. "Lucy, let's go back to our navigation updates. We haven't gotten very far with them yet, and I want Jacob to have a thorough understanding of the subtleties in navigation."

"Dad, space navigation is an advanced course at the academy. Why not let me practice piloting the ship today? It's really cool and I'm getting good at it. You said so yourself," declared Jacob.

"You're the best fourteen-year-old pilot I've ever seen," Dave laughed. "But your mother and I have been talking . . ." Dave hesitated, unsure of how to continue.

Lucy took over. "We've decided that you need to know everything about running this ship, not just the fun stuff. You're the oldest. If your father and I weren't here, you'd need to step in and run this ship. It would be up to you to complete the mission and, more importantly, to look after Billy, Quincy, and yourself."

Jacob frowned. "Whoa, I'm not old enough to command the ship! Learning to fly is one thing, but I'm not ready to study the other stuff yet—there's way too much to know and most of it's really boring."

Lucy looked at him sternly, but her soft brown eyes were moist. "Did you know that two hundred years ago, teenagers not much older than you commanded sailing ships across open seas, because they were the only ones onboard who could read and navigate? Your brother and Quincy can help with the simpler day-to-day operations on the ship, but you're the only one able to captain."

Uncomfortable with the confrontation, Dave jumped up and spun Jacob around to face him. "Listen. Your mother and I love you very much and we're here to help you. But if something should happen to us, we know you're smart enough and responsible enough to look after Billy and yourself. Your brother is smart in his way, but he doesn't think like other people. He couldn't look after himself in space, on Europa, or back on Earth with strangers.

"You must be as prepared as possible to fly this craft and set up base on Europa. Then you would be able to radio back to Earth and wait for the other ships to arrive. Do you understand?"

"I get the message, Dad. I also get that there's something you're not telling me," Jacob shot back. His parents winced, but ignored the last remark.

"Let's begin with the essentials of navigation, Jacob," Lucy began. "We have a lot of ground to cover. You'll see. It's not all boring." She smiled encouragingly. Giving his mother a resigned grin, Jacob settled into his chair.

Gazing at her eldest son now dutifully listening to his father, Lucy thought, *please remember we love you. It's just that sometimes we don't like the choices available to us—but we go on, and make the best decisions we can.*

While Jacob was kept busy working alongside his parents, Billy's responsibilities included only a few menial chores, ones he could perform by himself without screwing up too badly. Left on his own with a great deal of free time, Billy played with Quincy or amused himself on the ship's computer. When the bridge became free, because his parents and Jacob were off elsewhere carrying out ship maintenance or other duties, he and Quincy often crept up for the panoramic view of deep space.

"Take a look at that asteroid cluster," exclaimed Billy. "Aren't they fantastic? Computer, please magnify the image by a thousand. Watch them move, Quincy, each one of them in its own flight pattern."

Enthralled, Billy took in the careening forms flying across the floor-to-ceiling screen, jostling for position, smashing into each other, breaking apart or glomming together, before going off on new trajectories. Quincy sat beside Billy, eyes glued to the screen.

"Computer, can you put the complete electromagnetic spectrum reflected back from the asteroids on top of this?" Billy asked excitedly. The screen lit up in iridescent colors as the tumbling, crashing asteroids spewed incandescent debris across the black sky.

After a time, Billy saw something more than a chaotic free-for-all. "Look! Look, Quincy! The dark green asteroid is going to pulverize the third asteroid towards the front, spin around, and charge directly into that purplish thing. Then, boom! It'll blow off the back corner and be blown to smithereens by that neon blue asteroid coming up the center. Bam! It'll explode everywhere!"

Over the next twenty minutes, the scenario played out exactly as predicted. Quincy stared at Billy. But his back was turned, and Billy just sat there oblivious—engrossed, as each impact flowed into the next.

Even with its mathematical capabilities, the ship's computer could not accurately analyze the movements of more than ten asteroids at once tumbling through three-dimensional space. At best, it could predict only the overall direction of an asteroid pod. Billy's vision, however, was not restrained by mathematical deductions. He saw a fluctuating universe of shapes, shadows, and colors, flowing in their own rhythm. The dendrite connections in his brain registered the trajectory of each asteroid and then foresaw the oncoming collisions and resulting fragments spinning off in new directions. Here was something exciting, something that made sense to Billy, and something he could be good at. The bridge became an even greater draw than the zero gravity room for the little cadet and Quincy.

Chapter 4

Over the following weeks, life on the ship fell into some semblance of routine. For the first part of the voyage, the ship was to fly outward but always within the cover of Earth's shadow, protected from the solar storms. Dave and Lucy spent most of their time tutoring Jacob, and together the three of them worked on flying and maintaining the ship.

Billy and Quincy had very different routines. Mornings, right after breakfast, were still reserved for working through Billy's previous night's dreams in the zero gravity room, but in the afternoon Billy now spent much of his time studying space phenomena, inspired by his time on the bridge, attempting to push the boundaries of his predictions forward in time.

During these slack afternoon hours, Quincy wandered off to amuse himself. With at least one computer station in every room, it was natural that Quincy found himself eventually goofing around on a terminal. All sorts of interesting pictures popped up on the screen. Hunched over on a stool, feet drawn up under him, with his tail lying across the floor, Quincy's small, agile digits were soon tapping away on the keyboard.

For as long as Quincy could remember he had understood what humans were saying. He never considered this unusual—people were always talking over his head and Billy chatted to him incessantly. His innate curiosity had even caused him to memorize the spelling of a few isolated words. From there, with pictures and adjoining text juxtaposed on the computer screen, he had put two and two together and taught himself to read. Fooling around each afternoon, he didn't consider it any great feat that he became computer savvy. He had spent some time as a lab animal. The skills were the same—press, response, press, response. Moving from site to site was similar to remembering your way around elaborate mazes. Actually, it was easier. No one was jabbing him with a taser to go faster, which made it easier to concentrate.

Naturally inquisitive, Quincy found himself on the grid. When he realized what it was about, he began a search. Surfing through digital libraries, he researched his lemur roots. Watching archived computer clips of lemur troops stirred him horribly. Seeing twenty Ring-tailed lemurs on the move, leaping through the trees, hollering back and forth, made him cry out. Each one held its tail straight up as a flag so no one lost their way and fell behind. Quincy felt their joy. In the empty ship's lounge he'd leap from chair to chair, tail held high, but it wasn't the same.

From outdated satellite films he searched the island of Madagascar, the land of his ancestors. Finding a few stands of primeval forests that still remained, Quincy wondered, *Are the trees still there today? Is my troop roaming through those forests right now? Would my mother recognize me? What would she say?*

Rummaging further through the library files, Quincy found that Ring-tailed lemurs lived reasonably simple lives. They looked for fruit or small prey to eat, kept an eye out for predators, slept in the shade during the heat of the day, and sunbathed on their backs when it was cooler. They were proud of their special scent, using it to mark their territory. The males even flung stink bombs with their tails to win battles with their enemies. Quincy understood these notions; his lemur genes made this all very clear for him.

But over time, watching the lemurs on the film clips interacting with each other, Quincy realized he was different. It wasn't just that he lived in space and they roved freely through forests. Their behavior was—there was no getting around it—much more basic and simple than his. And although his markings and features were the same, he couldn't ignore the fact he weighed twenty-five pounds when a normal Ring-tailed lemur weighed seven pounds or less.

Why am I so different? I know I was raised in a lab, not in the wild, but can that really be the only reason? Quincy wondered, staring at the screen. *Do the Edwards all know why I'm different?* Questions about his pedigree unnerved Quincy, undermining his confidence. He didn't even want to confide his secret to Billy, ashamed at not fitting into a normal species classification. Obsessed with investigating his roots, he eventually found out what he thought he wanted to know. The high priority given to the voyage gave the ship's computer automatic access to restricted files. Buried deep in Space Command's classified section under "Ongoing Genetic Research," he found a report with his birth name: "Neither Animal nor Human—Quincy, a Genetically Engineered Lemur."

The report read: "A member of the prosimian family, diverging from the human species fifty million years ago, was conceived in a Petri dish. The embryo's cloned genome was successfully embedded with human genes for intelligence and injected with long-acting growth hormone precursors. The gestation was completed in a glass jar instead of a womb, the few remaining lemurs being required for further experimentation. Having the fetus' placenta grow into a polymer membrane bathed in dissolved oxygen and essential nutrients appeared to satisfy its nutritional requirements. Scientists at Space Command's laboratories triumphantly "announce" that after a number of unsuccessful attempts, we have created a unique animal, one that is smart enough and has the necessary size and strength to perform tasks for a complex mission on completion of which there is no chance of survival."

Quincy sat at the screen, feeling hollowed out, completely empty inside. Chaotic thoughts buzzed in his head like bugs about a sparker trap.

I'm a changeling, no more a lemur than human, just some disposable hi-tech gear for Space Command. I'm a sacrificial lamb. No wonder they won't let me talk! If I'm speechless, they can picture me as a dumb lab animal. It won't be murder when they send me on a suicide mission—just mission completed, too bad about the expense. Expendable equipment.

"Hey, Quincy," Billy said as he walked into the room.

Quincy scrambled to flick the screen in front of him off and spun around in his chair.

"Whatcha doin'?" Billy asked through a mouthful of peanut butter sandwich. The evidence of the snack was smeared across his chin and in the fingerprints on his orange shirt. With a loud smacking sound, he smiled at the lemur and tilted his lumpy head.

Quincy stared at Billy blankly. He was still reeling with anger at the humans. Images of lab coats and experiments swirled in his mind and he wanted nothing more than to hate them all. Looking at Billy though, he knew he couldn't.

"You okay, Quincy? You look a little … I don't know … uh … stunned?" Billy asked as he sat down in the seat next to Quincy and offered him a bite of his nearly-mashed sandwich.

Quincy shook his head, snapping himself out of it, and looked at his friend. *Friend,* he thought to himself. *Billy is my friend. There's no way he knew about what the other humans did. Perhaps I need to think about this some more. Keep it to myself for a while and see what Dave and Lucy ask of me.*

"C'mon, let's get out of here. You wanna play?"

Quincy reached out a small paw, grabbed the last bite of Billy's sandwich and jumped off his chair. With a challenging look over his shoulder, the game was on.

With a slight head start, Quincy bounded down a series of hallways losing Billy, before silently stationing himself in a half-open doorway that looked out into the empty hall. Crouched in the room, his hind legs coiled up like metal springs, his long tail twitched back and forth in anticipation.

Sensing a trap, Billy stopped short of entering the corridor and peered around the corner. Quincy's telltale pointed black nose, stuck out just past the doorframe.

Aha! The fur ball is waiting for me to innocently walk past, thought

Billy, *how stupid does he think I am? Hmmm ... he's too far away to ambush, and I can't sneak up on him without him seeing. I'll have to take a run at him from here, and hope he makes a mistake*, Billy thought, lunging in the microgravity.

Hopping out into the open hallway, Quincy faced Billy flying towards him. Pulling his black lips back tightly, brandishing his canines, the lemur smiled at Billy triumphantly. Doubt crossed Billy's mind. *Is this a trap?*

A split-second before collision, Quincy launched himself upwards, disappearing through the zero gravity portal just above. When Billy regained his footing, the entry had closed. Billy was furious. *I've been had! I didn't even notice the darn porthole!*

Billy yelled at the rotating drum, "Two can play at this game. Ready or not, here I come!"

Billy blasted through the hatch on the next revolution, shooting straight into absolute darkness. The lights were off and refused to come on with Billy's voice command. Quincy had jigged the controls. *Worse and worse,* Billy thought. He floundered in the darkness before doing a face plant directly into the opposite wall with a sickening whack. Crumpled, he fell back into free space. Sensing his advantage from the opposite wall, Quincy snapped his head and front paws back, arched his back, and pushed off hard with his hind legs. He spun backwards like a boomerang.

They collided with an audible crunch, the back of Quincy's head accidentally striking Billy squarely in the nose. Fountains of blood streamed out of both of Billy's nostrils as he shrieked in surprise and, a moment later, pain. Clutching his face, he twisted about like an animal in its death throes, howling. Quincy swung around and grabbed Billy in the pitch black, before making a crying yip, code for the computer to turn on the lights. Trying to help, the two ended up spinning about, rotating inside a thickening cloud of red droplets. Eventually Billy began to snicker and snort in between his wails. "Nice hit, Quince. Geez, you had to go right for the nose, didn't you?" The ridiculousness of the situation wasn't lost on him.

Quincy looked briefly to the floor and shrugged.

"Ah, it's not a fatal wound, don't worry about it," Billy assured him. "But yuck, we better get this cleaned up before the blood spreads out and stains the walls and stuff. Mom'll freak if she sees this … "

They stopped the game to vacuum the dispersing mist of red droplets floating in the chamber. But on finishing the task, they paused for only a moment longer—to realize the game wasn't over. With two quick yips, the lights went off again.

A soft grunt came from the far right. It was Quincy leaping. Billy pushed off, somersaulting forward in the air a dozen times, and heard Quincy land hard where he had just been. The game was on. Billy dove back to where Quincy was last heard, but he was gone. No surprise. They played the new game out at stellar speeds like two accomplished gymnasts. Quincy had the advantage and eventually hammered Billy from behind, fair and square. They tumbled in a ball before hitting a wall, laughing wildly. The game was over but a new sport had begun. Quincy had found a clever solution to the mounting boredom.

The two played the game tirelessly, but in the end Billy always lost. In the beginning, they entered the room one at a time, with the first one initially holding the advantage. When they became more accomplished, they jumped through the portal together, then tried to shove or throw the other off into the distant end of the room, to formally start the game.

Energized and determined to beat Quincy, Billy felt himself becoming better, bit-by-bit. But after losing to Quincy for a week, something changed. Billy stopped thinking in terms of up, down, right, left, forward, and backward. Caught up in the excitement of the game, a large piece of his dormant mind became active and his approach altered. Meditatively, his mind mapped the dark three-dimensional cylinder and logged in his current flying position, freeing him up at last to focus in on small details and the slightest changes.

In the absolute darkness, Billy's and Quincy's flying bodies created subtle air currents and gave off a slight scent. Ricocheting off the walls, they created minute harmonic vibrations. These lingering traces of air movement, smells, and sounds became residue. Billy's mind turned the moving molecules into swirling fluorescent color. Now, Billy found he could identify Quincy's location by tracking his spatial footprints, and anticipate his trajectory by the fluorescent trail left streaming behind.

On the morning of the eighth day as they played their game, Billy managed to stay clear of Quincy's flight path for twenty minutes. Quincy was acutely aware that something had changed. They should have collided long before. But Billy stayed out of the lemur's way, formulating a strategy. Quincy's approach was always to crash and grab. Using his long tail to help steer, Quincy held his four, strong paws out in front to grab Billy or land and launch himself off to the next wall.

When the time was right and Billy felt he could accurately trace Quincy's trajectory, he shot off on a flight course parallel to the lemur's course. Reaching out in the darkness, he grabbed hold of Quincy from behind and hung on. Twisting and turning, Billy managed to land feet first on the upcoming wall. Quincy's feet were left dangling helplessly in the air. Springing off, Billy continued to bounce around the room holding on to Quincy tightly to protect him from contact with the smooth, hard walls.

In the total darkness, Billy experienced a spatial epiphany, an awakening. "Quincy, do you feel it too?" Billy asked excitedly. He stopped at one end of the cylindrical room and called out to the computer to turn on the lights. "It's like passing through a dream. Flying in zero gravity without sight, without instruments, you can imagine you've slipped into another place. Or another dimension … "

Realizing how silly he must sound, Billy stopped himself and looked into Quincy's yellow eyes and admitted, "I'm a freak, too."

Quincy gaped at the trembling boy, taken aback by his confession. Billy could have no knowledge of his manufactured origin or purpose.

Billy simply told the truth as he sensed it. Wrapping a furry arm around Billy's shoulders, Quincy tried his best to comfort him, one freak to another.

Chapter 5

Lying in his bunk, Jacob stared at the digital clock over the door. The clock cast a soft red pall over the room, doubling as an exit light in case of an emergency. To his left, in the dim light he saw Billy squirming under the covers. Listening to his brother's agitated snuffling sounds, Jacob knew Billy would soon be making his nightly trek over to his big brother's bed. Looking up over to the far corner, Jacob could see Quincy's crow's nest, but from this angle he wasn't able to see the lemur. Still the muted snoring, like a distant teapot, told him that Quincy was sound asleep. The faint high whistling sound recurring through the night usually settled Jacob, soothing and reassuring him, so that he was able to fall asleep as well.

But not tonight. Instead, Jacob found himself obsessively going over and over emergency maneuvers in his mind. He was exhausted and found it hard to concentrate all the time. But his dad drove him, reiterating that he had to stay alert and keep learning, that he had the ability, and, being the oldest, he had to be responsible.

Jacob rehashed the afternoon.

I totally blew it, behaving like a kid. Having a meltdown over nothing in front of Dad. What was I thinking?

Long past the breaking point, Jacob had been expected to memorize yet another advanced and boring procedure. He broke down without warning. "I'm not that smart, Dad! I can't do all this stuff and I shouldn't have to. And I don't think it's fair that I should have to take care of Billy all the time, either. Why couldn't I have a normal brother? Somebody to do stuff with, somebody who could help me out for a change, instead of someone I always have to look after. Billy's just a freak and always will be!"

Silence. Jacob knew he had crossed the line.

"That's enough!!" his father shouted, grabbing Jacob with both hands and shaking him. And then just as suddenly he stopped, the fury quickly contained, bottled up so no one would be hurt. Previously his father had always tolerated a little whining, as long as Jacob got right back to his studies. But he was never to call Billy names, especially names like "freak," "weirdo," or "loser."

Lucy watched but said nothing. To get into it now would only make it worse between them. She held her breath and waited.

Dave took a couple of quick gasps, but appeared to collapse in on himself. Jacob saw his dad crumple, and knew he was hurt. Slowly, pulling himself together, Dave repeated his mantra, "The family comes first, Jacob. We'll only get through this if we do it together, as a family." Jacob knew this meant his dad wanted him to try harder. But the picture of his father, a powerful man, shaken and suffering, seared his consciousness.

Eventually Jacob slipped off into an uneasy doze, but flinging himself side to side, he shouted, over and over, "Dad, it's gonna be alright, I can do better!"

"Move over," cried Billy, pushing his way into Jacob's bed. Billy was soaking wet with perspiration and trembling. He burrowed deep into Jacob's side.

Jacob woke suddenly, unprepared, seething with anger. He wanted to scream, "Billy, you're eight years old. Sleep in your own bed, you freak!" But he didn't. After a moment's reluctance he rolled over to make room for his fearful brother, attempting to make the two of them a little more comfortable. Perhaps Billy would settle down quickly and they could both get some sleep.

"It's okay, Billy, it was just a dream. You're all right now." Looking up at the clock Jacob was shocked to see it was already five in the morning. "Try and get some sleep, Billy. We only have a couple of hours until we have to get up."

Billy shivered for another twenty minutes with Jacob spooning him until eventually, he settled and dozed off.

"You are so very special, my little brother. Don't you ever forget that," Jacob whispered as he too drifted back to sleep.

***

Dave lay flat on his back, his mind in turmoil. He felt absolutely wretched. Never in his life, even when he was poisoned with radiation, had he ever felt so sick.

What a fool I am, taking my frustrations out on Jacob. Jacob, who will be twice the man I am, if I haven't killed him on this suicide mission! Always thinking I could make things work if I tried harder. Smug, that's what I've been. How could I be so pig-headed as to think we could outrun the Sun's gauntlet to Europa and not be scorched? Stupid, self-serving vanity blinded me to the obvious. Made me such an idiot.

"Dave, are you still awake? What's wrong? Why aren't you sleeping?" Lucy murmured, stirring beside him, forcing herself to wake up.

"I'm fine, Lucy, go back to sleep. I just woke up for a couple of minutes—I'm going back to sleep now."

Lucy pulled herself from the deep sleep of exhaustion. "No, you're *not* fine." Lucy sat up, pushing herself upright with both arms and turning on the light. "You've been worrying that we might be killed and blaming yourself."

"Well, it's true, isn't it?" said Dave, propping himself up on his elbow.

"No, it's not true—at least the part about you being the only one making the critical decisions around here. We decided to make this journey together and I insisted we take the children. Hiding underground with the human race perishing around us is not the place for our family. If we die, it's better we die here in space than waste away on Earth. It was the best decision available to us."

"Lucy, you are always so damn clear and definite in your opinions," Dave said, irritated. "Forgive me, but this time I'm not so sure you're right."

"I'm not finished with you yet, my loving but overly sentimental husband," chastised Lucy, getting up and walking around the bed to stand over him. "You've changed and I don't like it. No matter how bad things got, I've always been able to count on your wry sense of humor and positive attitude. We need that now more than ever, and the children and I aren't getting it. Instead you're coming down on everybody, including yourself, when your unqualified support is more essential than ever. What's going on?"

Dave looked up into her beautiful brown eyes and knew she was right. "I'm sorry," he said wearily, rolling over to sit hunched at the edge of the bed. "I've tried to make everything work, but I'm afraid we're finished. It was only blind luck today that we happened to be in Venus' shadow when that solar storm erupted. If we had been in open unprotected space, we would have ended up like fried egg whites. The Sun's magnetosphere is breaking down faster than scientists thought it would. Massive solar eruptions are occurring with increasing frequency and little warning. I don't think we can make the run through unshielded space to Europa. There's bound to be a massive discharge of solar wind when we are exposed and vulnerable. I don't see any hope in us completing this mission, and we're past the point of no return."

"Then we'll do the best we can. We must pull together. In our darkest hour is when we need to be the bravest and show compassion for one another. Remember the core of a civilized human being is someone who, even in adversity, continues to make the best choices left to them and remains kind."

"Didn't you hear me? We are going to be in unprotected space when the next solar storm suntans our stomach linings!"

"All I know is that we have to start appreciating each other's strengths. You and I were on space missions before we ever met, and now we're a team, a good team—with a dozen missions performed together since. We've always made our decisions jointly and split the work equally. You don't have the luxury of becoming a sullen space cadet right now, feeling hard done by because you're the one responsible for saving us. You haven't failed, *we* haven't failed–not yet, anyway."

Lucy sat down on the edge of the bed and slipped her arms around her husband. "Your heart is in the right place, but it's misdirected. Try to show the kids more of the dad they knew before this mission. We both need to lighten up a little and spend some good times with them.

"And don't worry about Jacob–he's getting on. He's meeting your challenges and he's modeling himself after you, I might add." She leaned forward, pressing her forehead against his, and smiled.

"And Billy and Quincy are capable of a lot more. I think they could participate in more of our daily work. They've been left alone to their own devices for too long. We hardly ever see them now. If it ends up that we don't have much time left, then we should all spend it working together."

"Billy and Quincy?" said Dave, taken back. "How can they help in any meaningful way? Quincy is capable of performing simple tasks, but this is an emergency, and Billy, he has trouble reading even a simple text. He isn't up to the task of following complicated scientific manuals. I even find him difficult to talk to. Most of the time I have no idea what he's thinking.

"I love him, though, I really do. He is so gentle and unaffected. Around him, I feel joy and very protective."

"Then start by spending more time with him. Let him know you love him, as he is, without conditions. Billy believes you care more for Jacob than him. He can't help but notice you spend most of your time briefing Jacob on running the ship."

"Lucy, we're in a critical situation here, one I don't think we'll get out of. Jacob is our only back-up should something happen to one of us," Dave shot back, frustrated by his wife's prodding.

Undeterred, Lucy pressed on, "I don't deny Billy is a different bird, but he is clever. You saw his exam results. He perceives space in a unique way. Without the use of numbers or words, Billy solved all the questions involving space by manipulating shapes and volumes from different orientations. The examiners were forced to run computer simulations to test his answers. He even offered up his own ideas for questions about alternative dimensions—a theoretical concept still not proven. He has some valuable talents for a family hurtling through deep space. You need to stop seeing Billy only as a child with special needs."

"Okay, okay, I get it, Lucy. I'll include Billy in some of my simpler maintenance routines. But what's this wild talk about Quincy? He's just a lemur jazzed up with some human genes so he could be useful to us. And now Billy's gone and made him into a pet. What a mess. Now, if we're forced to enlist Quincy in a suicide mission, Billy will never forgive us."

"There'll be no suicide mission for Quincy, Dave. I would rather go first than knowingly send him to his death."

Dave pushed Lucy away, stood up to his full six-foot-two-inch height, and stomped off several paces before whirling around to face her. "Have you gone completely daft? Quincy's a lab animal, bred to be killed if needed. Have you gone goo-goo eyes over what has become the family pet?"

"Goo-goo eyes" was too much for Lucy, but she held her anger in check, barely. Dave realized what he had said, and to whom he had said it. Unconsciously, he stepped back. When Lucy resumed the discussion, it was very civil. "Dave, I believe there's more to Quincy than meets the eye. Quincy isn't behaving like Billy's pet. Watching Billy and Quincy, always joking around, pushing and jumping on each other but still quite protective of each other, made it clear to me. They're behaving like brothers. I was misled at first because of Quincy's external appearance and because he can't speak. But then I thought, Billy's strengths are nonverbal, so they're natural together."

"That's insane! Are you trying to tell me Quincy is our youngest son, or have you decided to measure his age in lemur years?" scoffed Dave.

Lucy got up and retrieved her housecoat from the closet. "Come with me. I have some sealed transcripts encoded on the bridge computer. It's time for you to see the liberties Space Command has taken, supposedly on our behalf."

Walking through the halls, Lucy was careful not to dash ahead. She took her husband's hand. They were a team and in this together. Besides, she loved him. Entering the bridge, both of them stopped, struck by the panoramic vista of deep space. It was gorgeous. The star-studded sky lighting up the wraparound screen dominated the room, reminding them why they belonged out in open space. Standing, staring out at the view together, Dave felt compelled to slip his arm around his wife's trim waist. Lucy leaned into his side. They belonged together, even more than they belonged to their children.

"Come, sit with me at my terminal. I'll open up the file I've been saving for you," Lucy finally said. They split apart reluctantly and sat down close to one another at the console. "Right, here's your genetic map from the medical archives." Long lengths of DNA from Dave's twenty-three pairs of chromosomes rolled across the screen like a winding train of boxcars. Through blood samples, Space Command always mapped its astronauts' genes to ensure none of them harbored genetic diseases that might impact a mission. "Aren't you a pretty thing seen up close like this, eh? Now watch, I'll do the same for me. We're different, as you would expect, which proves of course that opposites do attract. And I am definitely attracted to you."

Dave groaned, making a ridiculously childish face for her benefit. When Lucy teased him, he knew to go along with it. It made him feel as playful as she was.

"Now, look here at the genetic maps of our two stellar boys. Compare their paired chromosomes at the individual gene locations—like this, and you get a perfect cross between you and me. A fifty-fifty split. You are definitely the father and I'm their mother. No surprise there, I hope." Lucy gave her husband a nudge, pretending to push him off his chair.

"Now, look at Quincy's chromosomal pattern. Doesn't look at all like ours, does it? He is a lemur after all, and we know the prosimians separated from our human ancestors some fifty millions years ago."

"My point exactly," Dave said decisively.

Ignoring his remark, Lucy carried on. "When Space Command first told me about Quincy, something didn't feel right. Their explanation as to why he'd be such a perfect fit for our mission seemed off, somehow. So, I wrote and ran a program to analyze and dig out all the human genes inserted in his genome. Look what I found. Two thousand and thirty-eight human genes encoded in his genetic material. Very important genes, I might add, because when you compare those genes with yours and mine, and Jacob's and Billy's, what do you think you get?"

Dave shrugged. He didn't much like Lucy's tone or where this was going.

"A perfect match. Not only that, they split each gene pair between you and me, fifty-fifty, just like what happened naturally with Jacob and Billy. The question you have to ask yourself is, are two thousand and thirty-eight genes known to account for human intelligence enough to make Quincy our son? You tell me, Dave." Lucy settled back comfortably in her chair.

Chapter 6

Dave couldn't fall asleep. Lucy had given him too much to think about, and she had been right about her husband's obsessiveness. All his life Dave had been driven. He had always felt personally responsible for every mission he had been on, right down to the most minor details. This compulsion had made him one of the most successful scientific astronauts in the space program. It had also made him the loneliest, until Lucy stepped in. Once she entered his life, Dave felt a tremendous lightness come into even the dreariest tasks. So maybe she was right about the boys and Quincy. He had been working on the premise that Jacob was the only one capable of continuing with the mission if something should happen to Lucy and him. Solely responsible, Jacob would have to be so thorough, so careful. Dave understood Jacob and the cost of responsibility. His eldest would be left emotionally numb and isolated.

But if Billy and Quincy could help, their chances of success would improve immensely. And, closer to the heart of it, Jacob wouldn't feel so alone. He and Billy and Quincy could depend on each other.

Dave finally drifted into a light sleep, comforted by the thought that Jacob's legacy wouldn't be to live as he had lived, forced to endure the same bone-crushing emptiness for so long. Gradually, his analytical mind relaxed, as it had not relaxed for quite some time. Descending into REM sleep, his mind was unshackled at last, and fresh approaches, inventive scenarios to solve the problem of passing through space unscathed, drifted in and out of his head. Slowly and indistinctly, an impression, an inkling of a possible plan, took form. It was maddeningly vague and fragmented, but appeared to be a workable solution. Guardedly holding on to the subtle intricacies, filled with fear he would lose essential nuances and details,

Dave slowly lifted the entire idea up to his conscious cortex.

He shook himself out of his slumber, feeling drained and drugged. He hadn't thought this deeply for years. A billowing cloud pulsed and shimmered in his mind. The answer was there, in the storm, but how to realize it? A collecting funnel would be necessary, difficult to picture, because it somehow must turn over on itself.

Dave slipped out of bed, excited but agitated. His head ached as he tried to hold on to the quickly dissolving memory of the bizarre structure. He padded softly over to his desk and under the nightlight tried to sketch the shield's design layout onto paper. Unfortunately, attempting to define his dream caused the details to vanish from his memory. Determined, Dave moved to the computer terminal and slogged through potential mathematical formulas, trying to recreate the configuration graphically. But his vision was gone.

"What's wrong now, Dave?" Lucy said, leaning over his shoulder and startling him.

His disappointment barely contained, Dave barked, "Lucy, I had the solution to the problem, but I lost it. It's gone and it would have worked, I know it."

"Solution to what problem?"

"I dreamt of a shield that would protect us from a solar storm. I tried to draw its layout on paper and then reconstruct it with mathematical formulas on the computer, but it's vanished."

Lucy inquired, "Are you sure it wasn't just a fleeting dream that felt real at the time?"

"Yes, it was a dream," Dave responded curtly, "but it would work. I remembered enough of it when I woke up to know it was possible." But even as he spoke he started to doubt himself. It did seem real, but he couldn't keep it in his head. Dave's eyes dropped, "Maybe it was only a dream, but I think it was our only chance, Lucy."

"Then we'll try to get it back." Lucy sat down at the adjoining terminal, trying not to think about how tired they both were. "Show me what you've done so far, and we'll see if we can figure it out together." Within Lucy was an unquestioning belief that her husband possessed profound talents that he was never fully aware of.

Over the next two days, when they weren't involved in the day-to-day operations of the ship, Lucy and Dave worked on the design for the shield. Mathematical constructs could recreate something of what Dave pictured, but they were unable to formulate a funnel that turned over on itself repeatedly. It was Jacob, peeking at the computer screen, who came up with a suggestion. "Why not ask Billy? If you explain the problem to him in a way he can understand, he might be able to help."

Frowning, Dave ignored Jacob's suggestion, but Lucy, acknowledging the fruitlessness of their endeavors, asked, "Would you please go and get your brother, Jacob?"

He found Billy alone in the galley, fixing himself a snack. Billy stood there, concentrating hard at applying the peanut butter and jam evenly over the bread, careful not to allow the knife to slip over the edge and smear the countertop. Walking in unannounced, Jacob surprised Billy. "Mom and Dad want to talk to you right away, up on the bridge." The knife slid off the bread, leaving a long streak of jam and peanut butter across the counter before falling out of Billy's hand to the floor with a clatter.

Disgusted, Billy looked up, "What do they want, Jacob? I swear I haven't touched anything important, neither has Quincy."

"They need your help, Billy."

Glancing back at his mess, Billy tilted his heavy head and scratched at his green cap. "Me? Help? I can't even make a sandwich … "

"I told them you might be able to, so Mom asked me to get you."

"What'd you do that for?" Billy asked angrily, retreating a little.

"Come on, Billy, they won't bite." Jacob caught Billy's sleeve, pulling him towards the door. "They're your parents, too, ya know."

Billy fidgeted and squirmed in his seat as his father told him his dream. It made him anxious whenever his father focused his attention directly upon him. Billy heard nothing of what he was saying.

"Hold on, hold on," Jacob, watching Billy's eyes glaze over, interrupted. "Let me try, Dad."

"Sure, why not?" Dave shrugged, not expecting much to come of it. He watched as Billy nearly tipped off his chair and shook his head.

"Billy, Dad is asking you about a dream he had. It was about a shield for our spacecraft, a shield that's an unusual shape. This isn't a test or anything." Billy looked up at him with his big, brown eyes and exhaled deeply. "We just need you to think about it for a while and see if you have any ideas that could help," Jacob finished with an encouraging smile. "Try again, Dad."

"Right, from the top," Dave said, leaning in close to retain Billy's attention. "I dreamt of a shield. In order for the shield to be effective, cosmic rays would need to be captured, deflected, and then streamed through a multitude of ducts. The charged particles would need to flow down the path of least resistance, as though they were always traveling downstream, forever falling. Entrained into the looping channels the energy would circle repeatedly … " Dave paused, hoping Billy would show him some sign that he understood, but found no comfort as Billy diverted his eyes and stared at the drawing on the console screen. "As more and more energy is absorbed, the walls would become energized, turning the shield into a great electromagnetic magnet suspended in space. Once the walls absorbed a critical quantity of pure electromagnetic energy, the ducts would ignite in a maelstrom. High-energy particles would alternately split or fuse, flip from matter to anti-matter and back again. Super-charged particles would begin tunneling independently throughout the metal maze and the solid superstructure would transform, converting itself into pure energy. The positive feedback loop would create a giant solar dynamo absorbing more and more radiation until it lit up the sky like a small sun.

"Tucked inside the storm's epicenter, the ship would remain unscathed, as if it were standing sheltered inside the eye of a hurricane.

"And it should hold, just as long as the swirling electromagnetic radiation doesn't build up to the level of a quasar. If that happened we'd be forced to dump the energy out into space. But if the shield held up, and we didn't have to drain off the energy, we might survive the coming solar storm."

Listening closely and examining the models his father had constructed on the holographic computer screen, Billy's ears perked up when Dave explained that the charged particles needed to flow down the path of least resistance, as though they were always traveling downstream, forever falling.

Forever falling, falling forever ... Without conscious thought, Billy began sketching something across the touch-screen. In his head, he slid into the gaping sail-like funnel his father had started with. Around he spun and down he went. By the time he reached the narrow constriction, he was spinning wildly. The tube made a hard turn to the right and light was left behind. Prickling ion particles, condensed by the funnel, scraped past him like nettles.

A cry welled up inside him and he was gone. Jacob and his parents saw Billy close his eyes and turn waxen. His finger raced across the screen, tracing out long and convoluted three-dimensional pathways.

"It looks like a souped-up zero gravity waterslide!" Jacob said uneasily, watching his little brother. Billy drew channels that branched out and converged, opening and closing sporadically, splitting, diverting, and multiplying the flood of energy. Suddenly, the image split a thousandfold, a millionfold, fanning out a spray of ions. The liberated ions surged forward, transforming themselves into a howling, circling wind. The funnel and ship disappeared inside the storm cloud. Escalating turbulence billowed out into the sky before being pulled back in magnetically.

Absorbing the oncoming cosmic rays, the raging cyclone encircled the ship like a cocoon, but in the process powered itself up to terrifying levels. Jacob and his parents watched the simulation, awestruck but apprehensive. The tempest built on itself for what seemed an eternity, then, just as suddenly, an extension projected itself far out into the sky, so full of turbulence it couldn't be pulled back into the central core. The thunderhead released its energy in a bolt of gamma rays, dissipating the storm's energy out into wide-open interstellar space. The ship lay unharmed in what was now quiet, empty space. The simulation was exactly as Dave had dreamed.

Billy fell back into his seat, gasping for breath. Lucy quickly told the computer, "Save," then leaned over Billy, tilting his chin up and forward to allow him to take the enormous breaths he seemed to require. In a few minutes Billy woke up and became responsive. Everyone relaxed a little. Lucy let go of his chin to wipe the sweat from his forehead. "Billy, you just had a dream, but you're awake now. Are you feeling okay?" she asked in a reassuring voice.

"Yeah, I'm alright, Mom." Sitting up straighter, Billy craned his neck around, looking for his father. "Did your dream scare you, Dad?"

Shocked, Dave answered automatically, "No, not really … I mean, it was about a shield."

Billy nodded—how could a dream frighten his father? His father was a hero. He wouldn't be scared of something like that. Only Billy, who was eight and not like other kids, would have recurring nightmares. "I dream about stuff like this all the time," confessed Billy. "Sucked down dark tunnels that open in front, then close behind me. I can never find my way back, ya know? Always falling, while some kind of weird stuff seems to build up inside me? Then, wham! Nothing, or something new, I'm not sure."

His father listened, astonished. The dream had frightened him. But not knowing why and afraid of it, Dave had pushed the fear out of his mind upon waking. In so doing, he had unwittingly lost the dream's essential character: the crucial insights were organized around the fear they caused. Denying his fear cut the anchor rope, releasing the ideas, allowing the nuances to drift away and the dream's meaning to be lost.

"Billy, would you let me have a closer look at your computer simulation?" Dave asked. Helping Billy out of his chair, he gave Billy a quick, distracted hug and sat down in his place. Lucy was already on the console next to them, hot on the trail, preparing to run the simulation through some rigorous mathematical models. Dave went to work packaging the data, preparing to download the information to Earth so Space Command's scientists could run their own tests. This was going to take a huge collaborative effort and there wasn't much time.

"Jacob, stay here and help us on your console," Dave said. "Your experience with space games might help us in formulating some of the computer simulations required.

"Billy," he added, "you've been a tremendous help. Somehow you managed to give us the breakthrough we needed. Thank you." Looking over from her screen, Lucy congratulated Billy as well, but he hardly noticed. Feeling a little bit lost; Billy was heading towards the door to find Quincy. Maybe the two of them could play in the zero gravity room some more.

Chapter 7

Billy's visualization of the shield was analyzed through hundreds of computer simulations. Lucy called on her close friends at Space Command to help out, while Dave enticed university departmental heads to explore this first-time approach to shielding. Curiosity piqued a small army of researchers who pored over the diagrams. At the end of the day, no one knew if it would work. All that could be said was that it met the test of remaining mathematically consistent. The concept was so novel it needed to be proven experimentally, but there was no time for that.

Undeterred, Jacob and his parents began preparing the materials inside the spacecraft, but only Dave and Lucy went outside to construct the scaffolding for the shield. Unprotected in open space, they received mild radiation burns from some minor sun flares and had to treat themselves with radiation chelating agents and genetic regeneration catalysts. They were left weak and nauseated, but time off for recovery was impossible. They were fighting for their family, knowing the Sun would give no quarter when it struck with force.

After a week's work, Lucy and Dave were pleased. That the Sun had remained relatively quiescent for so long was surprising, but it had. In four hours, after a short nap, they would pull the remaining covering sheets over the scaffolding and that would be that. The shield would be completed. Privately, Dave was especially glad to see his dream had become a reality. He hadn't led his family on a suicide mission. He believed the shield would protect them for the duration of the trip.

The two of them hugged and tucked their children into bed. Then, after Lucy had given her two boys their customary goodnight kisses and said goodnight to Quincy, Dave and Lucy prepared to go. "We'll all be okay, won't we, Dad?" asked Billy. Nighttime was always difficult for him.

"Yes, I believe we will. You found the answers we needed to get us out of a very difficult situation. I feel very fortunate to have you as my son." Billy squirmed beneath his blankets at hearing such praise from his father. The excessive delight Billy displayed surprised Dave. Tomorrow morning, once work on the shield was completed, Dave decided he would spend time with Billy, alone.

Sealing Jacob and Billy safely in their cabin with Quincy, Dave and Lucy did their final rounds, resetting the ship's numerous night monitors. Then, exhausted but satisfied, they went to bed for a short rest before the last big push.

It was two in the morning when the alarm sounded in Lucy and Dave's room. "Satellites orbiting the Sun predict a colossal coronal mass ejection of plasma," the console screen flashed. "A coronal arc reaching millions of miles out into space is breaking down, and expected to hurl billions of tons of toxic ions out into the solar system at speeds of five million miles an hour … "

Dave's finger traced the trajectory image racing across the screen. "We're sitting in the line of fire!"

A glance at their room monitor confirmed their children and Quincy were still fast asleep. Without further hesitation, or another word, Dave and Lucy suited up and launched themselves out into open space. The shield had to be finished. They worked with desperate intensity to finish pulling the membrane over the scaffolding.

The work was exhausting. Hundreds of yards of cloaking still had to be spread over the articulated frame. The covering sheets needed to be dragged out from the ship's containment compartment in correct sequence, unraveled centrifugally using the energy from the spinning ship, then positioned manually in an intricate three-dimensional puzzle. Winches and pulleys were hastily set up and the cloaking stretched skintight across the ship's newly built exoskeleton before being permanently secured.

Everything was done in zero gravity, and because of the shortage of time, Lucy and Dave took chances, often releasing their lifelines for extended periods of time before reattaching them on a distant girder. Dave leapt from rafter to rafter, pulling the covering sheets with him, hooking them on as he went. Measuring out the distance, he fearlessly flung himself into space, catapulting across empty nothingness, landing violently at the targeted post beam. Lucy stayed close to the ship, winching the sheets tightly, fastening them securely to the base.

There were only three more sheets to bind to the exterior scaffolding when Dave launched himself into space yet again. This time, his lifeline tethering him so that he swung around in a graceful arc, like a spider swinging from its dragline. A blinding flash flared across the scaffolding and Dave's head and body snapped backwards, his spinal muscles locking up as if he had been electrocuted. Immobilized, Dave swung about and smashed into a metal column. Two more flashes came in quick succession, but Dave dangled motionless, suspended by his line. In a moment, Lucy had unbuckled her harness and was clambering free of the hub struts to hurl herself towards her husband.

"Are you all right, Lucy?" Dave gasped, trying to recover.

"I'm coming to get you. Hang on!"

"No, no, if you're okay, stay where you are! I have three sections left to clip on the outside dome. I need you to tighten them up with the winches or they'll never hold. The storm must be heading straight for us—it's the big one."

"I'm hit, too, but I'm okay," Lucy answered, hiding her pain.

"Then let's finish the job so we can get inside and watch the fireworks."

Lucy retreated to winch down the sheets as Dave, moving slowly, methodically, tried to finish attaching them. She could see he was badly hurt.

Rocked by waves of nausea, Dave saw his hands fumbling uselessly on the cover catches. *Focus!* Dave tried to rally himself. *But my muscles feel like napalm jelly. They're burning inside. I just want to curl up and die.*

Don't you dare! Three to go and they'll be safe. Two to go now. Don't vomit in your face shield; you won't be able to see.

One more to go.

Batten down the hatches, mission accomplished.

"I love you, Lucy," Dave murmured, but the transmitter in his suit had burnt out. Releasing his grip on the scaffolding, he fell away.

"You're not slipping off without saying goodbye," Lucy said, suddenly in front of him, pressing her face visor against his so she could be heard. Looping one arm around him, she gripped her lifeline with her free hand and started pulling them in toward the ship.

"Lucy, let go. You have time to make it back to ship. It's too late for me, just go! Take care of the boys," Dave pleaded, his face twisted in torment.

"It's over for me as well, Dave. The boys will have to look after themselves. With the shield up they'll have a chance now. I would rather die out here with you. I don't want to be inside knowing you're floating alone in space."

Dave's face relaxed a little and he smiled weakly for Lucy.

"Let's watch the fireworks together," Lucy said. She tucked them into a recess between the fuselage and a strut holding one of the ship's rockets, then unclasped her lifeline and tied the two of them together before binding them to the strut. Lucy wrapped Dave's arm around her, and then she did the same. Together, the two of them peered out through the funnel into pristine space, the Sun in the distance.

"Are you cold?"

"Yes. The electromagnetic shock must have knocked out all the circuits in our suits. The heat-generation properties are gone. We won't last long out here without them.

"Are you sure you don't want to make a break for the ship's loading dock? You could spend your last bit of time with the boys. I'm lashed to the ship. You can come and get what's left of me after the storm," Dave urged.

"No, I'm fading fast. We'll end it with just the two of us–like in the beginning. The children have each other, they'll sort it out." Lucy began to gasp as her lungs filled with fluid.

"I'm scared," whispered Dave, his voice breaking. "I've let my family down."

"You've been an optimist all your life, Dave. Don't quit on me now. Jacob, Billy, and Quincy will manage. They'll pick up where we left off. It was just plain bad luck that the storm struck a few hours early. No one's at fault, definitely not you. Hold on, Dave," Lucy said, tightening her arms around him.

A hazy halo appeared, pulsating and blurring the Sun. In response, the outer membrane around the ship started shimmering with soft fluorescent colors that spread down the frame, brightening into an incandescent flame. A throbbing harmonic hum rose, vibrating across the stretched sheath. Streaks and sheets of ultraviolet energy crackled off the solid surfaces. Lucy and Dave felt their hair and skin tingling and their insides become light. Forgotten memories surfaced as living experiences, then disappeared as neon blue electromagnetic waves washed over the membrane above them.

Lucy tugged at the lifeline, pulling the two of them further into the recess of the ship. If her children found them, she didn't want them to see their parents visibly burned by the radiation. She wanted them to see their parents as they were, locked together in love, even in death.

Dave murmured, "So much energy captured with so much potential, Lucy. A real waste to just discharge it into empty space."

"I thought you were gone."

"Almost. I'm so cold …

"Lucy, I love you. Goodbye."

Lucy started to cry.

Chapter 8

Jacob woke suddenly at the sound of a heavy pulsing drone. His hair was standing on end and a tingling sensation was running over his skin. His sheets and blankets crackled with what looked like static electricity, but he hadn't been moving. Looking over the side of the bed, he saw that Billy's and Quincy's sheets and blankets crackled and glowed as well. The entire room was lit with a pale blue-green glow from the sparks.

"What the … Billy, Quincy, wake up!" Jacob shouted. Billy responded by jumping in one bound onto his big brother's bed. Quincy swung down from his aerial quarters, reaching the bed just as Billy pressed himself in beside Jacob.

The bed coverings sprayed firefly light across the room. Not sure what to do, Billy, Quincy, and Jacob huddled together. The intercom didn't seem to be working. There was no response to their calls. Why had their parents not come to make sure they were okay?

An ominous notion took shape in Jacob's mind. He said grimly, "Mom and Dad must be in trouble." *Or they're dead*, he thought.

Running through the corridors, looking everywhere for Lucy and Dave, the boys and Quincy found their way lit by the flickering, eerie blue-green light. When they reached the bridge, they could see the ship's shield was alive with translucent yellow-green ultraviolet emissions. They were witnessing a solar dynamo from the inside, safe in the eye of the storm. The revolving energy was terrifying. But as Dave's dream had predicted, the ship, held in the recesses of the cyclone, lay protected and unharmed.

"Look you guys, Mom and Dad have been outside finishing the shield," Jacob said as he noticed that the shield's remaining panels had been set in place. "They're probably still out there. We've got to find them."

Most of the exterior cameras had been damaged and registered only a speckled gray interference. The brothers ran back through the ship, Quincy bounding beside them, calling out for their parents, but this time they stopped and looked fearfully out of each porthole they passed.

The question was, had their parents been blown off into free space, vaporized by the radiation, or were they alive and needing help? Jacob didn't know and he didn't know what to do. If he stepped out of the escape hatch would he be vaporized instantaneously? Would the cosmic rays flow into the ship and kill Billy and Quincy? Standing in the corridor staring through a porthole, Jacob felt trapped and helpless in a situation for which he had had no preparation. Looking at the maelstrom and the canopy seething with plasma, anguish flooded across Jacob's face. Billy knew his older brother. He knew what he was thinking. They both wanted to save their parents. But Jacob was trying to be responsible, to come up with a plan to look after everyone at the same time.

And Billy knew that he alone could envision the tempest, flow with the storm, understand its energy. He stepped forward and touched his brother's shoulder. Speaking hesitantly at first, he gained confidence as he went along. "Jacob, we can open the hatch and go outside. It's okay if we crawl along the side of the ship, but we have to stay beneath the scaffolding. We're inside a solar hurricane, but the shield is working. If we can hold on to the ship, we shouldn't feel anything worse than the static we're feeling now, maybe a lil' more. We just have to hold on super tight, or we'll be magnetized by the energy and pulled into the plasma."

"Hold on to what? There's is nothing out there to hold on to!" Jacob shot back despairingly.

"Ropes. We can scale the ship with ropes, they won't magnetize. Like rock climbers, we can tie ourselves to outside instruments and support structures. Only, instead of stopping ourselves from falling down the side of a mountain, we'll have to keep ourselves from being lifted off the ship

… Or we'll be vaporized," finished Billy with a sickly smile.

For a split second, Jacob glimpsed the irony of his father's face, in Billy. It raised his spirits, giving him the confidence to go on. "If Mom and Dad are attached to the ship they would probably be near where the last panels of the shield needed to be secured. I think I know how to get there … Are we ready to do this?"

Billy nodded, then looked over at Quincy. Quincy hesitated. Was this the dreaded suicide mission he had been programmed for? No, not likely, the circumstances were different. In this scenario two brothers were rushing out to save their parents and asking for his help. Quincy nodded back.

The decision made, the three raced for the evacuation port. With each movement, blue-green sparks burst from their bodies with increasingly painful jolts. Their faces were masks of grim determination, contorted when the recurring electrostatic energy caused twinges of pain. Passing into the decompression chamber that led to the evacuation port, Jacob sealed the inside hatch.

After the three suited up, Quincy stepped in front of the group and threw the boys a determined, challenging look. He would be the first to go out. Being the smallest and fastest, he could act as a scout, securing the rope to any structure strong enough to hold them.

"Thanks, Quincy," Jacob said, then turned to the task at hand. "Computer, stop the ship's rotation and commence decompression of the room. We're going out." Grabbing hold of the zero gravity support bar, he motioned for the others to do the same. As soon as decompression was completed, Quincy scaled the ladder to the exterior hatch. Climbing out, he was met by a deafening roar and the terrifying pull of the seething plasma. He grabbed the metal ladder outside the hatch that ran parallel to the ship and flattened his tiny body against it, his front and back paws instinctively hooked under the ladder rungs. Regaining his equilibrium, he pressed against the ladder for a full minute, adjusting to the draw of the plasma and charting his route. Then, slowly and deliberately, he began tossing out the line. The grappling hook missed its target, deflected upwards by the plasma. He withdrew it quickly so the cord wasn't drawn up into the energy belt, taking him with it. On his third try, Quincy hooked the line onto a distant crosspiece. Tying the proximal end to the metal ladder, he stretched the rope tightly across the ship and set forth, allowing the boys to follow in his wake.

The porthole left empty, Jacob tentatively poked his head through to find the fluorescent maelstrom raging not five feet above him. He would have pulled his head back into the ship and given up if he hadn't looked down the zip line. There he saw Quincy furiously shimmying along the cable. The cable had loosened somewhat and been drawn out like a plucked harp string. Quincy's back lay unprotected just two feet from the plasma wall. Reaching the far end, Quincy immediately spun around and re-secured the line to the crossbar. Then he motioned for Jacob to follow. Jacob did as he was asked.

Billy popped up next, to see his big brother straining to keep his backside under the swirling electromagnetic sheet, even as the clamor of the storm began to fill his head. He felt himself fading into his dream world. Sulfurous smells pervading his forebrain identified the situation as one of his nasty dream sequences. A nightmare was breeching his reality.

But the ridiculousness of his brother's behind waving back and forth stuck in Billy's mind, pulling him back to the real world and causing him to giggle. Imitating his brother, Billy shook his rear exaggeratedly.

I'll have to show Jacob how silly he looks, trying to save his bum from the fire. I'll wake him in up bed and wave my behind right in his face. "Don't burn your bum, protect your buns. Whatever you do, don't fart, it'll blow you apart. Just a spark from the start, and that great gaseous display will take you away, yeah it's no fun to have plasma bum," he sang. Chortling to himself, Billy made his way out through the mayhem. *I'll have to work on the rhyming*, he thought, the nightmare of the storm forgotten.

As the boys and Quincy made their way along, the boiling plasma shell knocked them about, periodically causing Billy's and Quincy's ropes to release prematurely. Yanked into space, the little cadet and the lemur would flail about. Strong for their size, they'd hang on, long enough for Jacob to pull them back to the surface. After a momentary respite they'd all continue, trying hard to remain calm and focused. If they surrendered to their fears, they would have clung frozen to the side of the ship, or let go and abandoned themselves to the turbulence above.

Rounding the fuselage, Quincy was the first to see Lucy and Dave. Strapped together and facing the funnel, the two hung like marionettes, strung to a supporting strut. Lucy's right arm was still tucked behind Dave's back. They were both dead.

When Jacob and Billy rounded the corner, each was struck by the same image. On reaching Dave and Lucy, they secured their ropes and stared, unable to move or respond. In front of them, Dave and Lucy bobbed like dead divers entangled in an ocean current, phosphorescent colors washing over their visors mirroring the fluctuating sheets howling overhead. Jacob shuddered uncontrollably; a terrible shaking from his low spine, spread up across the inside of his ribcage, and from there, a vile rush rose up, wiping away coherent thought. Gasping breaths broke into a hideous moan.

Clinging to his arm, Billy wailed like a siren beside him. He shrieked until, out of breath, he fell into hysterical sobbing. His brother's sobs pierced through Jacob and his grieving went mute. He leaned over to his little brother and hugged him. "Billy, Billy, listen you've got to stop! This isn't helping. We have got to figure out what to do!" Quincy, perched on a nearby strut, watched the whole scenario, horrified, unsure of what to feel or do.

Eventually Billy choked out, "We can't leave them out here. They should be inside with us."

On this there was no disagreement. Without a word, Jacob methodically undid some of the ties and started to fasten his father onto his back. Billy watching his brother, struggled to try to fasten Lucy to his back, and Quincy moved in to help him. Before they headed back, Quincy jury-rigged a harness around each boy and parent couple, and then snapped the harnesses safely to the zip line. He knew the extra mass of Dave's and Lucy's bodies could spin the boys off into space once they set out across the wide, bare circumference of the fuselage.

The funeral procession moved slowly. Clinging to the cable, parent and child bound together, the boys climbed along the ship's perimeter, rolling with the storm. Tears glazed and then burned the boys' cheeks, but they kept on with the arduous journey. Quincy roved back and forth over the climbing ropes, securing and then releasing the lines, assisting the boys wherever he could.

The exterior hatch was open when Jacob and Billy finally arrived at the porthole, with Quincy there to pull Dave off Jacob's back, safely into the ship. Then together Jacob and Quincy grabbed Billy at the entrance, stabilizing him while they pulled Lucy in. During the transition period, while the safety catch was off, the added weight and the increasingly violent storm nearly knocked Billy and his mother away, right at the entry point to safety.

Inside, the exterior hatch at last closed, Jacob said with a shaking voice, "Computer, reinstate normal gravity." Within minutes, the boys and Quincy were out of their suits. Jacob laid his parents in the corridor outside the decompression chamber, while the others anxiously hovered behind him, wanting to help. Meticulously unscrewing Lucy's and Dave's helmets, Jacob reported numbly, "Dad's frozen solid, but Mom's still a bit warm. She didn't die from hypothermia." Jacob did a quick diagnostic check of his parents' spacesuits. "The suits are intact—there aren't any breaks or leaks in the seals. Their breathing apparatuses look fine and there's still lots of oxygen. But the heat-regulating thermostats of both suits are wrecked and their radio transmitters are burnt out. That's why they didn't call us." Jacob bit his lip, trying to stay in control. "They must have been exposed to radiation fallout while putting up the shield. They died after attaching the last sheets. Mom died later, maybe just before we got to her."

"What can we do? There must be something we can do!" Billy sobbed hysterically.

Upset, Jacob replied sharply, "There's nothing we can do. They died saving us. We're too late!"

"Mom and Dad have been treated for radiation sickness before," Billy answered, recoiling from Lucy's and Dave's glassy stares.

"But they're dead now," Jacob hollered back.

"Dad is frozen and Mom just died. If we freeze her right now, maybe … maybe sometime later we could bring them back to life. Some place where they could be treated for the radiation sickness." Billy wasn't giving up.

Jacob knew that reviving a person frozen cryogenically had never yet been attempted. Trying to stay clinical, he remembered that in the lab, fish and frogs had been revived, but mice always died several days after being resuscitated. He argued, "Mom and Dad died from radiation poisoning. Their cellular structures have been damaged by radiation." But just as quick, he heard himself thinking, wishing out loud. "But, if the heat-generators in their suits failed, they would have been hypothermic before death, preserving their cells. If we store them in the ship's cold room, they'll stay frozen. The room is chilled by outside space to four degrees above absolute zero. They'd be refrigerated there as well as they would be in the best laboratories on Earth."

Trying to stay the realist, Jacob reminded himself that they were probably already too late and, moreover, that his parents' bodies had not been injected with the appropriate solvents. But who knew what advances the future might bring? Jacob didn't want to be the final judge of that. Billy needed hope right now. They all needed hope right now.

"Billy, Quincy, suit back up. We'll take Mom and Dad to the cold room. We need to get them there right away if there's to be any hope for them at all."

Their spacesuits were on in less than a minute, but now, inside the ship, simulated gravity prevented Billy and Jacob from hoisting their parents on their backs. "We'll take Mom first," Jacob said decisively. "She's not frozen yet. Dad has more time." Staggering, the boys and Quincy lugged Lucy to the cold room. Jacob stripped off her spacesuit while the other two raced back with a magnetic levitating plate to carry Dave back. Jacob returned to them as soon as he could and, by the time they slid Dave into the cold room, Lucy was also fully frozen. With difficulty, Jacob cut off Dave's suit, unable to peel it off his father's body.

In the center of the floor, Dave and Lucy lay side by side, both covered now in a fresh white shroud of hoarfrost. Quincy, Jacob, and Billy stood over them, worn out. Trying to catch their breath, they fogged up their visors.

"Pick them up!" Billy suddenly shouted. "Pick them up off the floor!"

Jacob looked around and saw two large metal tables attached to the far wall. "Help me carry the tables over to the center of the room and set them up." Turning back, he saw Billy reaching for his mother in a daze. "Stay away from Mom, Billy. Stay away, I said!" Jacob jumped in front of his little brother. "If you jar them, they'll fracture. We will have to lift them together, slowly."

Jacob took control, organizing the moving and securing of the tables into position, and the lifting and tying down of the corpses. Billy was of little help, but Quincy seemed to understand what was required. Jacob found the grisly act of binding his parents to the tables overwhelmingly disheartening and would have given up in despair without the lemur's support.

Chapter 9

The tempest churned outside, escalating every hour. Inside, everything rattled from the force of the storm until spot welds and rivets started popping loose without warning. Neon blue-green light blazed, outlining each surface, and in the otherworldly luminescence, Billy, Jacob, and Quincy worked around the clock repairing the ship. They wore plasticized asbestos gloves to prevent their hands from going numb from energy flashpoints, but nothing could prevent their hair from being singed by the constant shocks. Quincy suffered the most, his glossy, fine fur becoming rough and matted. There had been little time to grieve for Dave and Lucy. But resolve grew and small gestures made it obvious that each was trying to support the other. Their survival depended on them pulling together and none could bear to be thought of as the fatal weak link.

At the end of the second day, the solar dynamo spun into hyper-drive. The feedback loop in the shield had captured two days of the intense solar storm, but had yet to release a single volt of radiation. Having successfully diverted the increasing radiation, the shield began spinning around in a slightly lopsided fashion, dragging the ship into a high-speed wobble. The ship and everything in it started rocking.

Jacob summoned Quincy and Billy to the bridge, where the outside maelstrom was in full view. But before they were even seated, he blurted out, "It's getting worse. I've been watching it. We're living inside a time bomb. Small imperfections in the energy sphere are multiplying as the radiation swirls around us. Instead of circling around harmlessly as a protective shell, the energy field is going to collapse in on itself and blow us apart!

"Billy, how can we bleed off the energy before it's too late?"

Billy thought for a minute, focusing on no one, going inside. Then his face brightened. "We need a lightning rod! Ground out the dynamo … the proton lasers might work! We'll need two beams, so they can blast in opposite directions or we'll be juiced."

"What do you mean?" Jacob asked.

"If the beams aren't exactly the same and fired from exact opposite ends of the ship at the exact same time, the energy they discharge will drive us to who knows where. It's all or nothin' here, Jacob. We can't just bleed off a little energy. Once it starts, we'll have to dump it all."

"But, that'll leave us totally exposed to the elements. In the midst of the storm, there won't be any time to power up the shield again." Jacob slumped, defeated, into the captain's chair. "We're toast."

"Well, yeah, but it's better to try. With the proton lasers, we've got a shot at least. If we wait till we see that the storm is beginning to taper off, you could fire the beams just before we implode. We might luck out. Solar storms don't usually last much longer than three days." Billy volunteered this last information a little uncertainly.

Quincy nodded his small head in agreement, and Jacob realized that, being the only plan, this was the best plan. "Then let's get to work, guys."

The three spent most of the next day in the pitching, crashing ship converting the two lasers. Jacob read through the technical manuals. For him they were no more difficult than comic books. Once studied, each step made sense and wouldn't be forgotten. Quincy and Billy assisted with lifting and positioning, fetching and passing required tools. After the lasers were refitted and set in place, they all took turns monitoring the shield and solar storm. The watch consisted of sixteen hours on and eight hours off. Two were always on deck, prepared to act quickly and wake the third in case of an emergency. The short disrupted naps meant that they were all on edge.

The ship's shield continued to withstand the storm, but as the ship lurched about so much, the boys and Quincy were forced to strap themselves down wherever they stayed and crawl from place to place so they wouldn't have so far to fall. On the fifth day they were worn out and their nerves were frayed.

In the galley, sprawled out in a chair, his arms moving loosely over the straps that kept him from being flung to the floor, Jacob dozed. He'd fallen asleep while eating, and was covered in cold and congealed lumps of instant porridge. Then, from way down in the deep sleep of over-fatigue, he woke with a jolt, his ears cocked. The timbre of the ship's creaking and groaning had changed. Hastily unstrapping himself, he clambered on all fours to a porthole and looked out. As the shield's energy field warped, the ship was being horribly contorted. Rupture was imminent. Scrambling to the bridge on his hands and knees, he was thrown flat on his face several times by the violent movement of the ship. By the time he reached Billy and Quincy at the bridge, blood was streaming from his nose. Wiping it away with his sleeve, he panted, "We're breaking up!"

Just then, the core infrastructure started to give way, and a series of hard thuds followed by heavy knocking sounds struck terror into every heart.

"Let's drain the energy off the shield and take our chances," Jacob said, pulling himself up from the floor into his chair. "Whoever agrees, nod," he requested, strapping himself in. There was another unnatural shudder and the sound of tearing, buckling metal. Rapid head bobbing answered back.

Looking out along the funnel towards the pulsing Sun, Jacob shook his head, saying, "Damn! The storm isn't dying down!"

Fixing his eyes on the Sun, Billy spoke up. "Fire directly into the Sun, Jacob! But we best reef down hard on our restraining straps first." The shield was ballooning out now, becoming a dangerously rocking globular mass.

No one questioned Billy's suggestion, and every restraining strap was furiously ratcheted down. Jacob tapped in the lasers' coordinates and began the final countdown. Just before he fired, Jacob and Quincy heard Billy say, "Close your eyes!"

The shield shattered and then was ripped from the ship. Radiation flashed through their closed eyelids, dazzling their retinas with a swirling spectrum of color. Every alarm siren screamed out simultaneously before abruptly falling silent. All of the power systems started to shut down.

Within seconds the ship was hit again. Over and over, the spacecraft was bashed as if its bow was smashing through a series of cement walls. The hull took every blast as if it were the last, never quite rupturing, because the frame beneath took the impact, absorbing and transmitting the hammer blows down the quaking length of the ship.

Then, silence and darkness. No comforting hums from the life-support systems, nothing. The room was pitch black, making the boys and Quincy fear that they had been permanently blinded. All the lights, including the emergency lighting, were out.

Hearing the distinctive sounds of Billy and Quincy stirring and groaning, Jacob called out, "Is anybody hurt?"

A high-pitched yip came from Quincy and Billy said numbly, "We seem to be okay. But I don't think the gravity generator is working. It feels like I'm just hanging in the air. Actually it's all making me a little sick. You alright?"

"Yeah, I'm okay," Jacob replied, "but what now? I can't see a thing." Panic crept into his voice. "If I get out of my chair and start floating, I won't even be able to tell which way is up or down."

No response. Then Jacob heard movement to his left. A few minutes later, although it seemed like forever to the boys, a bright beam lit the far corner of the room. With his characteristic leaping movement, Quincy arrived with flashlights.

Light in hand, Jacob felt humiliated. He had allowed himself to become overwhelmed and disoriented, and had lost his way. Quincy knew where to begin—with light.

Three narrow shafts of intense white light pierced the dark room. Billy and Quincy brandished their beams about the bridge, pointing at reflective instrument panels, turning them into roving curtains of kaleidoscopic colors. Jacob tried to stay focused, and found the bouncing beads of light almost as disorienting as the darkness. "Stop playing around with those lights," Jacob shouted. "We've got to get life support up and running. We need to get to the life-systems control board at the rear of the ship so I can sort out what's gone down. Come on."

Flashlight in paw, Quincy immediately did a quadruple somersault to the far side of the room and then launched himself straight to the rear exit. Billy quickly followed, performing five somersaults instead of four. Landing directly on the spot Quincy illuminated from the far end of the room, Billy then shot straight into Quincy's line of light, homing in on the exit door. Coming in fast, Billy was intent on forcing Quincy to jump out of his way. But Quincy anticipated the move. Barreling in, too late to react, Billy caught a glimpse of a long black-ringed tail holding out the flashlight. Shining his flashlight to the side, Billy saw a small black paw pull the emergency exit lever. Passing through the open hatch with nothing to grab, Billy carried on tumbling down the corridor. When he finally came to a stop, Billy called back, "Good one, Quincy, but remember—there's always payback."

Jacob had intended to lead the group, unaware of Billy and Quincy's prior practice sessions in the zero gravity room. Hesitantly, he leapt towards the place Quincy illuminated for him. Landing awkwardly, he crumpled, twisting an ankle. Before he could float away, Jacob grabbed onto an instrument bank to steady himself, then jumped again, tracking down Quincy's homing beam as Billy had. The bad ankle caused him to go lopsided into a nasty spiral towards the doorway. The exit door safely closed, Quincy was there to catch Jacob, preventing him from bouncing helplessly down the wall of the corridor.

Together they pushed and glided their way down the maze of corridors, lights flashing in the dark until they found the door marked "Generator Room." But before they went in and started working, Jacob had to know something. Turning to Billy, he asked, "How did you know we should fire towards the Sun?"

Billy could only answer him with a visual metaphor. "It was a guess," Billy admitted sheepishly. "I saw the storm rushing towards us in waves, peaks, and troughs, like ocean waves. I wished with all my heart we could fire a string of torpedoes and just blow up each incoming wave. Then, I thought about how a boat's hull flattens out stormy seas in its wake. I wondered if firing a bolt of charged particles towards the Sun might do the same thing, creating a shadow instead of a wake. I didn't know how long the shade would last, but fortunately the storm burnt out before our sunblock did. Now I suppose we have to go out and build a new shield."

"Yep, but we're still here to build it."

With help, but for the most part on his own, Jacob took no time in restoring the ship and resetting their course. Jacob knew they needed to be on their way, with recurring solar storms, racing to Europa would be like running a gauntlet. The vessel would only be able to withstand so many hits. As soon as the radiation turbulence cleared in space, Jacob radioed Space Command to update them of the expedition's current status. Radio was the most durable, and reliable, of the communication frequencies.

"Congratulations, Jacob, to you and your crew for braving the weather. Earth has sustained terrible damage from the same severe storm. We're having difficulty retaining your signal—too much interference. Put your parents online to prepare for the downloading of the relevant data."

Jacob cleared his throat loudly, squared his shoulders and replied. "Captain Dave Edwards and Captain Lucy Edwards are dead. They died in the storm."

After a considerable delay, the anonymous voice from Space Command responded. "Standby. I have to report this. My superior will contact you shortly. We are ... we are very sorry."

Silence.

Fidgeting in the corner, Billy spoke out in a voice flat, "That's it? Standby? We're very sorry?"

"What a bunch of useless twits!" cursed Jacob. "Dad always said Space Command was managed by bureaucratic idiots." He raked a frustrated hand through his straight brown, disheveled hair. "Protocol, they'll need to follow their precious protocol. If they even have a protocol for this situation. Probably not."

"Now what?" Billy asked.

"We can't just sit around waiting for Space Command. Earth could only help us with data and computer support anyway," Jacob said valiantly. "You heard 'em, they're having trouble with the storm as well. But we, we survived. I think we still have a chance."

"With a lot of luck, we survived, Jacob," Billy said despondently.

"But we survived. And Mom and Dad died trying to save us. So we're not going to give up now," declared Jacob.

Billy and Quincy nodded in agreement. None of them believed they would survive. But no one wanted to be the first to give up, or had any idea what to do with themselves if they gave up.

Jacob persisted, "We can only count on the Sun being quiet for a few more days—its magnetic currents are going to build up again, releasing another solar storm. This is our only chance to redesign and rebuild the shield. We all helped build the last one, so we should be able to figure out how to make this one on our own. Let's get to work."

Filing out of the bridge, they trudged sullenly along the corridor. Jacob followed last in the line, grinding his teeth; livid that Space Command appeared to be abandoning them like some wayward space probe, no longer deemed important. Was there no end to it; one step forward, two steps back. Down at stores they would probably discover they were short of some essential material for the shield.

On arriving at the Materials Management Storehouse, Jacob logged on to the computer, decreasing the ship's centrifugal rotation to a tenth, making everything seem lighter and easier to move. They pulled out long sleds of tied-down supplies from massive drawers reaching up to the ceiling. Quincy clambered through the drawers hooking belts onto the sleds, which Jacob hoisted out with a large crane. The crane magnetically skimmed over the ferrous metal floor, gyroscopes, sensors, and circuit boards, preventing the crane from toppling over with its piled high cargo. Billy released the belts and did what he could, arranging materials on the floor for basic construction. There was only so much that could be done inside, because the assembled parts needed to be pulled through an exterior bay door placed in the floor of the room. It was large, but not that large. At that point the ship's rotation would be halted, and with the crane, the apparatus could be floated out the door.

Work went slowly at first, with Jacob frequently jumping out of the crane and running to consult computer drawings. He wanted to determine exactly which materials were required and when, so that they could be placed beside each other in the correct order for assembly. From up high, Quincy watched the two brothers in action, Jacob doing his best to be organized and efficient, Billy doing his best to help out wherever he could. Waiting inside the great drawers gave Quincy some time to think.

At their supper break, Quincy shifted restlessly in his seat. It was Jacob, coming through the door with a bowl of quick-cook spaghetti, who noticed. "What's up, Quincy?"

Quincy tilted his head and scratched his right ear. *How to communicate with Jacob? Billy just seems to know what I'm thinking, I don't need to explain anything to him. But, Jacob? He doesn't have a clue ... Aha!* Quincy's tiny index finger shot up, signaling an idea. Jumping down from his chair, he bounded onto the counter and swung the console monitor around to face the boys. With nimble digits, he typed as quickly as he could. "I should be the one to go out into space to construct the shield. You and Billy need to stay inside and put the pieces together."

Billy's face fell as he grasped the implication. "Jacob, he's telling us that you're needed inside to interpret the plans. And I'm not capable of pulling the shield together in space, so I should stay behind and be your helper."

At hearing this, Quincy squawked shrilly and threw a nearby cup at Billy's head. Catching Billy off guard, the dish thwacked him soundly. "What the … "

Quincy turned and typed furiously on the keyboard. "I'm the most accomplished astronaut in zero gravity. This has nothing to do with your abilities, you pigheaded nincompoop! Until you grow a four-foot tail and complete Space Command training, you'd better just accept my offer. You need to help Jacob with the shield's modification." Quincy turned to watch Billy's face as he read the message. When Billy looked up, Quincy raised a fisted paw to the corner of his eye and wiped at a fake tear.

"Crybaby? Are you calling me a crybaby?" Billy asked incredulously.

Quincy folded his arms across his chest and nodded with his black nose high in the air.

"You know," Jacob said, breaking in with a slight chuckle, "I had no idea Quincy could type!"

"Huh! So that's what you think? The pair of you? I'm just a stupid crybaby? Well, we'll see about that!" Billy tossed his half-eaten plate of spaghetti into the sink and stomped out of the room. From the corridor, he yelled back, "Don't we have some work to do? Maybe you guys should get off your lazy butts and try to help out!"

With a knowing look, Jacob gave Quincy a stroking pat across the back as they made their way out the door. "Thanks," he said quietly. "For giving him that swift kick in the pants and getting us on our way. The two of us would be lost without you." Quincy looked quickly to his moving feet as a small squeak of pride escaped his lips.

"Am I the only one working today?" Billy hollered from the far end of the hall.

Chapter 10

"Dead?" Diego del Silva asked, shocked. He looked to the foot soldier standing nervously before him and waved a dismissive hand. "Thank you, you may go." Diego took a seat in the center of his command room and rubbed a tired hand down his face.

Never before had Central Command had such an effective senior adviser. Diego maintained a position of strict neutrality toward his subordinates and his superiors. The committee members above him were free to plot for power, succeeding for a time before succumbing to blind ambition. But under Diego's direction, his ministry remained untouched, shielded. While the upper political echelons were periodically swept clean, like so many leaves each fall, his clandestine department continued to thrive. He was the spy of all spies, commanding a network of underground operations that dove so deep into Earth's shattering society not even the leaders of Central Command could trace them.

Dave and Lucy Edwards' mission had been his priority for months. He'd spent countless hours in the halls of Space Command, planning their secret launch. The fact that they had been detected at the last minute by an Anarchist was still a sore spot for him—a blemish on his nearly spotless career. More than anyone, Diego knew the stakes if the Edwards' failed. They were, without a doubt, humanity's last hope for redemption. The political factions on Earth would soon be uncontrollable. War was coming.

Diego raised his chiseled face in the dim glow of the computer monitors lining the walls of the room. His proud Spanish lineage showed through his strong cheekbones and cold, black eyes. He knew there was no postponing the inevitable. "Get me the High Command," he ordered one of the technicians working at the super-computer to his right.

"Yes, sir!" the tech responded quickly and began typing. With a few deft strikes of the keys, he had all three members of the High Command on the line. Diego had never seen their faces. No one had. They ruled the world from the shadows.

From the speakers around Diego's command center, they spoke. "What news?" The first voice asked. Though the patterns were scrambled, Diego thought of this particular voice as an older man. He had no real way of knowing for sure.

"I've just received word that Captains Dave and Lucy Edwards are dead. Killed in the solar storm."

"How have you learned this information?" the second, even deeper, voice asked.

"Their eldest son, Jacob, reported back to us via radio last night. I just heard about it this morning, a few minutes ago."

"Is he the only survivor?" the third, and highest pitched voice asked coldly.

"No. Jacob, Billy, and the lemur have all survived. The shield they constructed must have worked, to some extent at least. Our satellites show that they're still on course for Europa." Diego brushed his jet black hair out of his eyes and waited for their response.

"Abort the mission."

Diego was stunned. "But, they're past the point of no return. They can't make it back to Earth. Why not let them carry on?"

"They're not going to make it. The mission is a failure. We can't waste any more time or resources on two boys and a lab rat."

The connection was unceremoniously cut, with no further instructions. Diego shot up from his chair and began pacing the room. The techs around him averted their eyes, concentrating on the monitors in front of them. Sworn to secrecy under the penalty of death, they all knew their place, and getting in their boss' way was something each of them would avoid at all costs. Diego's department was ruled with an iron fist.

"Radio the ship," he yelled. The sound of static filled the room wall to wall as he waited for the connection.

"Jacob Edwards here," the young voice, deep in space, said through the radio.

"Jacob, this is Diego del Silva of Central Command."

"Central Command? Who are you? We contacted Space Command, not you guys … "

"I'm sorry about your parents," Diego answered, sidestepping the question. Diego could swear the sound of typing accelerated in the room. "I knew your father, once. He was one of my professors in university and a good man."

"Thank you," Jacob stammered. *I never thought I'd be collecting condolences for my parents …* shaking his head, Jacob tried to clear the building tears from his eyes and looked toward Billy and Quincy. There was business to attend to. "What are our orders, Mr. del Silva?"

"Orders? Well, Jacob, neither Space Command or Central Command can afford to invest anymore resour … "

"So we're on our own!" Jacob cut in. "We don't have time for excuses, just give it to me straight. They're abandoning us out here, aren't they?"

There was silence for a moment as Diego selected his words. "Yes. You and your brother are on your own."

"Not quite, we've got Quincy, too," Jacob said with a slight smile that turned into a sneer. "And he's been way more help than all of you could ever be back on Earth. You might not think we'll make it to Europa, sir, but I promise you we're going to try. Tell Central Command to stuff it! Our parents died trying to save us, trying to save humankind. We are their sons. We won't simply float off into space without one hell of a fight."

"Good," answered Diego. Insubordination was fine for a boy with nothing left to lose. Diego, however, had everything to lose. His position with Central Command was the only way he could maintain his family. "Good luck, Jacob."

"I'd rather be out here than dying in those stinking caves, sir."

The transmission ended, leaving all three boys staring at each other blankly. They were truly alone.

"Well," Billy said in his newfound voice of authority. "Looks like we're on our own, boys. Let's get back to work." He hitched his thumbs into the front pockets of his overalls and started towards the loading bay.

"You know, Billy, I'm glad you're all fired up, but it's okay to be scared," Jacob remarked as he and Quincy fell into step.

"Oh, don't you worry, big brother. I'm scared out of my lumpy head! But, I reckon it's better we keep working, no sense sitting around here. Worrying like a bunch of ninnies."

"So true," Jacob said, giving a light pound between Billy's shoulder blades.

Quincy was glad he had volunteered, and won the right to erect the outside frame while the boys manufactured the shield's components inside. He needed the stillness of wide-open space and the chance to move about. Going out alone in the diamond-studded black sky with the Sun a distant fireball, leaping across the scaffolding, he experienced a special kind of freedom. Soaring from girder to rafter to supporting strut, Quincy could feel his tension ease. Upon reaching a targeted beam, his stretched-out body would contract before he sprang off again, his powerful hind legs propelling him into the air. Sometimes Quincy hooked his lifeline to a joist and propelled himself into open space.

I'm supposed to be a simple tree-dwelling animal, Quincy thought to himself as he swung, anchored by a spider's thread, in a graceful arc across the empty sky. *How did I end up in deep space with two boys making a run for one of Jupiter's moons? No more a lemur than I am human. No family, no troop.*

An abomination really, conceived and created to be destroyed, when required. And here I am, stuck on a mission, which is looking very much like it's terminal, with two frightened boys wearing brave faces. Unbelievable!

Quincy's thoughts moved to the two boys—Jacob trying so hard to be like his parents. Always aspiring to have the right answers at his fingertips, not wanting to make a false move. Billy, on the flipside of the coin, a special-needs child tormented by dreams, which somehow came with solutions to impossible problems.

There's a gap between the two brothers that needs filling. Someone to mediate between them. On their own they are not enough. They need me.

The shield completed, Quincy moved inside to meet the boys for lunch. Nothing would be said, but he had made his decision out in the welcome emptiness of space. He would stand and fall with the two brothers. Unwittingly, he crossed a threshold and made himself a full partner.

As the spacecraft sped towards Europa, the three settled back into something of a routine. "It's amazing this old tin can is holding together, isn't it, Quincy?" Billy reflected, as he made his way to the table. "Maybe that's what we should call it, *Tin Can!* I can't believe we've been on this ship for so long without giving it a name. It needs a name!" Billy started giggling. Quincy and Jacob looked at each other and rolled their eyes. "We're locked in here like preserves in a *Tin Can* … hope we don't rot. Ferment into a full blown case of food poisoning."

Feeling clever, Billy chuckled so hard that he broke into grating guffaws.

"Ha, ha, very funny, Billy," Jacob said as he cleared the table. "Let's get these dishes done."

"Why, that sounds like more fun than a game of kick the can," Billy continued to joke.

"Alright, you've had your fun, now … "

"Can it?" Billy blurted, hugging his sides. Beside him, Quincy couldn't help but snicker.

Try as he might through the day's work, Jacob couldn't stop the name of their ship from coming up again and again. Billy always seemed to be right there, ready at hand with another tiresome pun. Making a nuisance of himself, blathering on with quips like "Can do" or "this could be a real can of worms." As they managed the maintenance and navigational logistics of the vessel, eventually the other two gave in, and found themselves referring to the vessel as *Tin Can* without a second thought.

"Let's keep this *Tin Can* rollin' … " became their new mantra.

Chapter 11

Even during the nighttime, *Tin Can* hummed with activity. Jacob worked late into every night studying every manual he could find, trying to prepare for every eventuality, long after the other two had fallen asleep. After hours on end of working and studying, and the stress of just trying to keep moving forward, Jacob sometimes searched out solace and release in the digital world of his beloved computer games. Utterly exhausted, but too agitated to sleep, he'd walk, run, or bolt down to the large storage room. In the semi-lit space fitted with a series of guide wires anchored thirty feet up in the walls, he'd pull on his personally fitted holograph visor and pressure sensor bodysuit, then attach himself to the computerized rigging that connected his suit to the room's large supporting pillars. Standing in the center of the room, he would double-check his virtual arsenal of lasers and eagerly shout, "Computer, log onto Specter Nebula and enter my password as Purple Fox."

With the help of guide wires, Jacob leapt thirty feet in the air, as the virtual world invaded his senses and surrounded him. Landing lightly on a shadowy gray asteroid on the edge of a distant galaxy, Purple Fox found himself in the midst of a terrible battle. Mounds of dead bodies and destroyed equipment were strewn across the bloody landscape. To his left, a thousand yards out, his squadron was fighting a last-ditch effort on a solitary outcropping. But the Praying Mantises, towering droids the size of draft horses, saw him first, and started to swarm towards him. Lasers firing, Purple Fox sprinted towards his troop, cutting a swath through the oncoming horde of droids.

Bounding up a small rise that separated him from his men, Purple Fox suddenly took a bone rattling blow to the back of his head. Falling forward, he twisted around to see a giant robotic Mantis looming over him, preparing to strike again. Flinging himself over the far edge, he tumbled down a steep slope of jagged scree. At the bottom he stopped with a heavy thud, face down, his heart pounding, *Could this be the end?*

Leaping off the overhang the Mantis was there, waiting for him, poised with its long, sharp saber, relishing the thought of finally taking out the esteemed Purple Fox, one of their top priority targets. The Mantis' arm, arched high, was driving down towards the center of his head when there was a flash of red light. A laser shot cut straight through its torso. The droid pulled up, then teetered.

"What the … " Purple Fox muttered, stunned, before rolling quickly out of the way of his falling foe. The Mantis crashed to the ground beside him. Scanning the surrounding area, he looked for the guy who had just saved his life.

Standing just twenty feet to his right stood the shooter. As his weapon lowered, Jacob realized he'd never seen this player before. On the grid, you could often recognize the players of specific games after seeing them a time or two. But, this red-suited, small framed … *No,* thought Jacob suddenly, *not short, petite. She's a girl!*

When she turned and raised a hand in his direction, he spotted the slight curve of her hips in her snug costume; from under the crease of her helmet, a shock of thick blond hair escaped. Jumping back on his feet, Jacob felt himself blushing as he hurriedly brushed himself off.

"Are you still in the game?" she yelled to him over the din from the battlefield just paces from where they stood.

Jacob, grateful he was still alive to play, raised a hand in salute to his new friend and shouted back, "Thanks to you, I am. Purple Fox," he said tapping his armor breast plate. For some reason, he needed to know her name before going into battle. In the fray, they'd probably lose sight of each other. In the gaming world, with so many players around the world dropping in and out of games all the time, there was a chance he'd never see her again. But if he knew her name ...

"I know," she said with a graceful tip of her helmet. "I know exactly who you are. It's a pleasure to finally meet you. I'm Red Robin."

Jacob felt his heart flip-flop and had to snap himself out of an impending daydream that saw the two of them, lasers blazing, striding off together. "Well, Red Robin, let's kick some Mantis butt!"

"Understood," was all she said.

They moved up the field, side by side, and praying Mantises fell in great heaps of twisted metal, no match for the Purple Fox and his new friend.

In the virtual world, things always seemed to work out for Jacob.

Billy was still tormented at night by his dreams and, upon waking, still spent most of his days trying to understand and resolve them. Their intensity was escalating. After envisioning the shield and the gamma ray ejector, Billy realized his night terrors held clues to solving real problems. He no longer wanted to abolish his dreams. Instead, he sought to merge his dream world into the real world, to bring his dreams out into the light of the day. If this was to be his special contribution, he intended to develop and use those apparitions as tools, to solve whatever riddles they encountered in space.

Quincy spent his spare time continuing to educate himself through the ship's computer. Determined to leave no stone unturned, he looked into everything that might prove to be useful in the future, reading at a feverish pace. Two weeks into his research, he stumbled across an innovative idea for mining and managing Billy's dreams. A government file documented new breakthroughs in deciphering people's thought and dream processes. Micro-sensors attached to a person's head and linked to computers recorded nerve impulses. It was hoped that parallel computer simulations might, sooner or later, potentially be able to isolate recognizable patterns and identify specific thoughts.

By digging further, Quincy found the military had greatly expanded the scope of this research. It was important for the authorities to understand how people thought. Their concern was that large segments of the population might riot and commit horrific atrocities once they learned they had no future. If people's minds could be manipulated, peace and order could be maintained right up until the demise of the masses. The avowed objective was to avoid needless suffering, but the lemur knew better.

On reading through the chilling documents, another thought dawned on Quincy. *This information was classified! At some point, Central Command must have expected, or at least hoped, our mission might succeed. Our ship's computer has extraordinary clearance—unfettered access to the most advanced computers on Earth, including covert data banks. And they haven't thought to block it since writing us off!*

With unlimited right of entry, Quincy scoured the classified data. *Yikes*, he thought. *The authorities don't treat humans any better than animals. They've been using "enemies of the state" in gulags for experiments, torturing them, then proving or disproving their theories through vivisection. They cremate the bodies when they're done, so no one outside of the agency knows!*

Disturbing data, but Quincy was familiar with inhuman experimentation. He continued to read through the documents, searching for any information that might help Billy. The more Quincy found out about the theories linking thinking with dreaming, the more he understood Billy's night terrors. He was gaining a whole new level of respect for the strange little boy. Quincy decided to check into Billy's medical reports. In Space Command's archives he found the results of extensive investigations. Every possible x-ray, electrical, magnetic and positron scan had been made. Dozens of personal, psychological, and intellectual tests had been carried out. But Billy remained a mystery to all of the researchers. Certainly he had unusual abilities: he could visualize difficult mathematical and physics problems schematically in his mind, without understanding the basic math behind them. But no one could figure him out, and he was diagnosed by default as an "FLK". "Funny Looking Kid", the cause most likely being gestational radiation poisoning and development in zero gravity.

Perhaps there's something here that can help Billy ... he thought and settled in for a long night's research.

The following day at breakfast, Quincy couldn't sit still. He had spent the first half of the night digging through piles of research and the other half trying to figure out how to explain his plan to the boys. He was worried they wouldn't take him seriously.

Across the table, Jacob yawned and stretched. His bowl of oatmeal was barely touched.

"I'm sorry, Jacob. I kept you up all night. I really panicked—dreaming I was spinning in space, being dragged away from everything familiar." Billy looked sheepishly at his own bowl.

"S'okay, really," Jacob tried to sound reassuring, even though his body was screaming for a decent night's sleep.

"They're getting more real every night. I'm scared the dreams will come true. That I'll wake up and you'll be gone and I'll be left alone in some strange place."

On hearing this Quincy made his break. Jumping up from his chair, he fixed the boys with a serious stare, and signaled them to follow him as he bounded out of the room.

With a brief shrug in each other's direction, they followed Quincy's flagstaff tail to the bridge and settled in on either side of his computer terminal. Unsure of where to start, Quincy began typing a short tutorial on basic physiology. "The brain contains a hundred billion nerve cells that communicate with each other through connections called synapses. Chemicals called neurotransmitters leak across the tiny connecting junctions. Those chemicals excite the adjoining cells, causing them to discharge an electric current, which runs along the cell to the next cells. The process repeats itself, with each cell connecting to its neighboring cells by a root and branch system at the receiving and the discharging ends. The interconnections fan out to a multitude of other cells."

Working his digits so fast, Quincy's paws cramped up, but after giving them a few quick little shakes, he continued, afraid he would lose their attention. "In an encoded file, I found schematic diagrams, which Jacob might be able to adapt for our needs. If he could build micro-sensors to pick up the electrical waves of individual nerve cells and the secretion of neurotransmitters between cells, the sensors, imbedded in helmets, might be able to map the anatomy of our brains right down to the cellular level. The modified helmets could allow our ship's computer to register the location of every nerve cell's electrical depolarization and neurotransmitter release, and the exact anatomic location, in real time."

With a puzzled look, Jacob asked, "You think this will help Billy with his dreams? How?"

"I realized last night just how powerful our ship's computer is," Quincy typed. "For some reason Central Command poured every piece of known technology into it and gave our computer priority clearance. It can access every supercomputer on Earth, including top-secret military computers. Someone important obviously hoped we would make it to Europa and staked everything on improving our chances. Our computer has the ability to analyze vast quantities of data in real time and sort and correlate it to an almost infinite degree. And what it's unable to process on its own, it can covertly contract out to Earth's best supercomputers."

"And ... " Jacob interrupted.

"I get it!" Billy declared with a poorly timed snap of his fingers following a moment later. "Quincy thinks that with the right sensors and a powerful computer, it could read my mind. It could interpret my dreams!"

Jubilant, Quincy clapped his front paws and did a standing back flip. Sitting bolt upright in his chair again, he typed in, "We could program the computer to break down the massive physiological data our brains put out and transcribe it into a code. The process would be like interpreting hieroglyphics, going over and over the data looking for repeating patterns that, in our case, instigate different thought processes, emotions, sensations, even our basic bodily functions. Everything is registered and monitored in the brain. Eventually the computer might be able to decipher Billy's dreams."

"Exactly how do we help the computer analyze our brains?" Jacob asked, striving to understand. It was important for Jacob to build his ideas up slowly, from a solid foundation, before speculating on the implications of those ideas.

"By thinking out loud," Quincy answered. "If the three of us inform the computer of what we're thinking, what emotions we're feeling, what our physical senses are telling us, it will help the computer. We'll collectively act as a kind of Rosetta stone. For example, when we explain to the computer that we are happy, angry, or sad, it will scan our brains with the micro-sensors, looking for telltale patterns. By using the information from all three of our brains, it will have more patterns to correlate and will be better able to evaluate the patterns. It can assess how we are similar and how we are different, and the more patterns it registers, the better chance it has of breaking down our neural codes.

"The ship's computer was designed to endlessly acquire and correlate space-time data, to search for patterns in the universe, make hypotheses to explain those patterns, test them, and go on from there. This is exactly what it will need to do for us but at the microscopic, cellular level. If I'm right, the computer could translate Billy's visions into mathematical models we could use directly. We're going to need Billy's help if we want to make it to Europa."

Billy nodded in agreement, but Jacob said nothing. Didn't he believe it could be done? Quincy wondered if he had missed something.

"I don't know, Quincy," Jacob finally said. "I need to think about it."

"It's a good idea," Billy said defiantly. Quincy's shoulders slumped.

"It might be, Billy, but I need to think it over. Get it straight in my head, ya know?"

Baffled, the other two stared at him, but Jacob didn't return their looks. Instead, he turned the console towards him and began studying

"Come on, Quincy, let's give Jacob some space," Billy said as he slid off his seat and took the lemur by the hand to lead him out of the room.

Quincy looked up at Jacob with steely black eyes.

"I know you're right, Quincy. Jacob will too, just give him some time."

"How 'bout a quick game of prey and predator up in the ship's core while he thinks it all over?"

Feeling somewhat defeated, Quincy liked the idea of burning off a some steam with a game. He was frustrated with Jacob's response and the more he thought about it, the more annoyed he became. With a dastardly look at Billy, Quincy threw off his hand and pounded one of his small fists into the other.

"Oh, really? Dead meat, huh? We'll see about that!"

Lips pulled back, Quincy's fangs protruded out from his small pointed face, and his eyes in their black bandit's mask narrowed. Then Billy was gone, running hard for the core before Quincy could recover. The little boy with the big head had duped him. Again. The game was on.

"What happened to you?" Jacob exclaimed as he stared at the two re-entering the bridge an hour later. "Billy, your nose looks like a mashed-up eggplant!"

Billy answered airily, pretending not to notice the deep purple bruise bloating his face, "I ran into some kind of melon head."

Seeing Quincy turn away guiltily, Jacob smiled wryly, "Well, I think that melon head has your number, Billy. Anyway, guys, I've gone through all of Quincy's ideas." Jacob paused. Billy and the lemur leaned forward, each holding his breath.

"You're right about the computer networking system, Quincy. They tied us into the best supercomputers, yet no one seems to know about it. Whoever gave us the clearance wanted it to be a secret. I have no idea who it was or where they are now. With all the political turmoil, they could have been eliminated in an internal coup by now, but they've either done us a huge favor or set us up … "

"What do you mean?" Billy asked.

"I don't know," Jacob answered helplessly. "Anything's possible. Our computer's links with Earth means someone could decide to use our vessel as a self-destructing probe—crash us right through Europa's ice pack, and then blow us up to get seismic readings—or they could just eliminate us and use our ship as a beacon in deep space to relay false messages back to Earth. On the other hand, we can use them to our own advantage, like Quincy's plan.

"The point is, we can't know what their intentions were or what's in store for us. But if Earth tries to take control of the ship we have to be ready."

Billy gaped at his older brother. How did he come up with such ideas? But Billy knew he could be right. Chagrined, Quincy typed into his console, "Do you think we should terminate our networking with Earth? Isolate ourselves from whoever might try to commandeer our ship?"

"Not at this point," Jacob said thoughtfully. "We'll need all the computing power we can get. But, we must be able to shut down fast, at a moment's notice, if the ship no longer responds to our commands. There may already be programs buried in our software waiting to be activated by specific situations. If the computer acts up without warning, the three of us will have to try to pilot *Tin Can* manually."

They all sat silent for a moment, trying to absorb the implications. "Regardless, I think we should move ahead with Quincy's plan right away, using micro-sensors to see if the ship's computer can unlock Billy's neural code." Quincy and Billy broke into broad smiles, and slapped each other high-fives. "Listen, guys, this is no time to celebrate. We have a ton of work to do. Probing our brains won't be easy, but I think it can be done. Neurosurgeons sometimes analyze a patient's brain while the person is awake. Because the brain itself doesn't feel pain, they can gently stimulate specific areas of the brain with electricity, causing the patient to recall 'retained memories'.

"We could do the same sort of thing by inserting a positron stimulator into our headgear. If we program the computer to stimulate specific parts of our brain, the helmets could track our brain's responses to the positron's probing while we explained what we were experiencing, like you said. Of course there would be risks involved."

"You don't say," Billy quipped sarcastically, rolling his eyes. "Probe in the brain, how can that go wrong?"

"If we test the probe one at a time," Jacob smiled tightly at his annoying younger brother and pushed on, "when we're together to look after each other, I think it's worth the risk. Maybe we'll finally get to the bottom of your scary dreams," Jacob said, giving Billy a sharp look. "Do either of you have any other suggestions?"

Billy and Quincy gave each other a faint nod. Jacob hadn't given up. He'd just needed a little time to figure out the best way to do things.

Chapter 12

Jacob dove into the new project, rummaging through technical archives, searching for the novel solutions that would be required. He found himself at home browsing through industrial libraries. A natural in hunting through scientific research, he appreciated inventors' innovations, seeing beauty, irreverence, and humor in their alternative answers to sticky problems. It was a simple matter for Jacob to adapt previous inventions to their situation. To him, the design diagrams were open letters, full of hope.

Because of his innate technical sensibilities, Jacob took only a few days to find what he thought they would require. He began by building the headgear using supplies found in the ship's well-stocked lab.

"Ta-da!" Jacob announced as he walked onto the bridge, brandishing the finished product above his head triumphantly. Jacob had gone ahead and created soft synthetic headgear that would fit their very differently shaped heads. Between two layers of material he stitched a web of micro-sensors and a tri-planar positron stimulator he had assembled. The stimulator he constructed was capable of mapping out the brain three dimensionally, and then activating specific nerve cells anywhere within the cranium. He included a mobile transmitter for communication with the computer from anywhere inside or outside the ship.

Then he spent the next day writing the software instructions to get the computer started on deciphering their neural codes. The software had to be open-ended so that the computer was free to make further modifications once the data stream began arriving. Programming came naturally to Jacob. He wrote programs for the computer as easily as if he were writing a letter to his best friend.

Finishing the task, Jacob presented the headgear and explained the different components' functions. Billy and Quincy were awed by the technical wizardry and listened closely, turning the devices over and inspecting them carefully. Eventually though, Billy became bored by the long explanation of the headgear. He took off his green toque and slyly put his headset on backwards, pretending to admire the fit. Sitting down to gaze at his reflection in the empty computer screen, he modeled the headgear, turning his head this way and that, making a succession of ludicrous faces. "How do I look boys? I think this will be all the rage on Earth next season ... " he joked.

Incensed Jacob tore the device from Billy's head, snapping it back and nearly pulling his brother out of the chair in the process. "I've been working on these for a couple of days and all you can do is make fun of them?" Scornfully he grabbed Quincy's headgear from his paws. Stomping out the door, Jacob said tersely, "Come with me. We'll make some fitting adjustments back at the lab. I'll stretch out the caps to match your screwball heads."

Jacob may have been incensed, but he knew Billy had a point. The headgear had to fit good and snug to get reliable readings. And it had to be comfortable and durable if they were to wear it continuously, day and night, to retrieve the volume of data required for computer analysis.

After a few adjustments to the headgear, the boys and Quincy were ready to test Jacob's invention. The first day, they began by wearing their headgear without the positron stimulator turned on. For safety reasons, Jacob insisted that they stay together at all times, forcing Billy and Quincy to tag along behind him for most of the day while he performed his routine chores, which they found mind-numbingly dull.

Jacob was also firm in insisting that no one was allowed to go to the bathroom alone. Sitting on the toilet, with others standing right there, was not a private, peaceful time. Quincy being quite fastidious was utterly dismayed by this unwanted intrusion. Inevitable wisecracks from Billy followed every unintentional sound and smell. After a few attempts to control the process, Quincy decided it was better to just let it go and be quick about it.

Over the course of day, Jacob made minor tweaks to each of the snug-fitting caps.

"It's not that bad, really," Billy said at the end of the day as they all crowded around Jacob's computer terminal to see the results of their first full day of data collection. "It feels a little hot and itchy, but not too bad. And it does a better job of hiding my ugly head than my toque!" he chuckled as he ran his hand over the headpiece.

"Did it work?" Quincy typed into the computer eagerly.

Jacob pulled up the bar graph on screen. "Nothing!" he slumped back into his chair. "Almost no change in the amount of data since we started this morning."

"We need to turn on one of the positrons," Quincy typed and looked at the boys sternly. He wasn't anywhere near ready to give up.

"You're right, Quincy. It's risky, but we need to try. Alright, both of you, pay attention. Here's how you turn on and direct the positron stimulator ... " Using the most authoritative voice he could muster, Jacob went over the procedure twice. "And this is the emergency override apparatus that I built, if anything goes wrong ... " his voice trailed off.

"Why so glum, chum?" Billy asked, trying to lighten the mood.

"Because I'm going first," Jacob snapped. "I made it, so I'm the test pilot. We need more data and we need it now if we're going to help you with your dreams. But frankly, I don't like the thought of some energy beam pressing its thumbprint down on my brain to see if I'll kick out my leg, or worse. You know, Billy, everything doesn't always have to be a big joke. This is serious." Jacob paused, taking a breath to regain his composure. Billy tried to look contrite.

"Direct the positron probe towards my left temporal lobe cortex," Jacob said. "Memories are stockpiled there—for the positron it should be like shooting fish in a barrel. Depending on how I react, we can decide if the emitter is working correctly or needs adjustments. Fortunately, the temporal lobe is quite far from my brainstem, which drives my vital bodily functions. If you don't screw up with the directional controls, it should be safe to aim there," Jacob finished, trying to sound confident.

"Ah, you're just afraid this thing will make you mess your pants, admit it!" Billy laughed nervously, not sure why his brother was so tense.

Jacob eyes narrowed. "No—if the positron probe stimulates my brainstem, directly or indirectly, it could stop my heart. You and Quincy will be the ones responsible for starting it up again, or you can put me in the freezer with Mom and Dad." Billy stopped fidgeting in his chair and sat up a little straighter. Jacob had made his point. There was nothing funny about what he was about to do and the stakes were deadly serious.

Jacob attached himself to all the physiological monitors while explaining to Billy and Quincy what they needed to watch for. His now very solemn little brother and an alert Quincy listened with growing tension. Jacob's instructions were precise. "This is what I want you to do if my heart stops, my breathing fails, I experience a massive seizure, I become too hot, or cold … " The list grew long and the treatments more complicated. " … I think that covers most of the potential complications. So do me a favor, try to stay awake and don't wander off for a sandwich," Jacob said with sardonic flare. "Leave me hooked up for one full hour."

Billy and Quincy somberly watched Jacob enter the final settings. After Jacob directed the computer to begin, Billy and Quincy watched, horrified as he suddenly slumped backwards, his head hitting the back of the captain's chair with a solid thud, then rolling to the side as he lolled in his seat, unresponsive. He looked dead, and the experiment was just beginning.

The first thing Jacob noticed was a sickening churning in his stomach. Then, as the room went black, he tumbled back into a dark and scary world. He felt as though he was being buffeted by unseen forces. Jacob panicked and fear cored out his insides. His stomach erupted, and he vomited all over himself. His bowels and bladder simultaneously let go. He had never felt more helpless.

I guess Billy knew what he was talking about. Is this the horrific world he faces every night in his dreams?

Twisting in his chair, Jacob felt himself falling until his right cheek smacked down hard against something. Lying disoriented, he felt splattered against a cold surface, yet wind was rushing past his ears as he simultaneously continued plunging downwards. *Focus. Focus inward. This is a dream. It doesn't matter if I'm falling. It isn't real. Just concentrate. Breathe in, breathe out.*

Gradually, the nausea faded and his fear subsided. The pummeling wind waned and he felt himself stop falling.

From a distance, Jacob sensed the air passing through his lungs. Hyper-aware, he felt the regular reciprocating contraction of his heart, lup-dup, lup-dup, and then the blood coursing through his arteries and veins. Each hair on his skin rose up, sensitive as the whiskers on a cat. In silent repose, Jacob floated in stationary darkness for what seemed an eternity. He imagined his consciousness flowing throughout his body. At times he stopped to examine himself microscopically, sometimes peering out through a skin pore as if he were a bead of sweat, learning about himself from a vantage point he had never contemplated. Eventually he stopped his internal examination, intending to return at a later time.

Jacob brought his awareness back to the present. The positron was responsible for his initial hallucination, and he had lost control of it. He needed to locate the probe and consciously move the bio-feeler from place to place. It took a little time, but after a few minutes of tentative searching, he mentally located the feeler pulsing positrons into the middle of his left temporal cortex, just a millimeter's depth from the surface of his brain.

Jacob's thoughts were connected through the headset to the ship's computer, so he dove back to retrieve the biofeedback programs he had previously designed. Enlisting the programs through a sheer act of will,

Jacob commanded the focused beam to move slowly forward to the front of his temporal lobe, then up and down, working backwards. He repeated the process at a deeper level and then again at a more superficial level. Nothing happened. Concentrating hard, Jacob methodically scanned his whole left temporal lobe cortex, but no dreams were triggered. The only sensation he felt was unease, as if he were haunted. But he had no dreams to confront.

Jacob guessed what the problem might be—the positron energy settings were too low. *Okay, earlier, it triggered vague hallucinations. But my true memories haven't been stimulated enough. I'm only getting reminiscences, the feelings of past experiences, but not the memories themselves.*

Jacob stopped moving the positron feeler. Through the biofeedback mechanism, he navigated his way upstream into the computer, cranked up the energy output radically, then sank back down into his temporal cortex.

He found himself walking in a stranger's backyard on a long-forgotten afternoon when he was five years old. Jacob could hear his father behind him, talking to someone in front of the garage. Spinning around, he gave a high back kick to a pile of old tires, spilling stagnant rainwater. The rubber smelt stale in the hot sun. Flies buzzed everywhere, drawn by the garbage heaped in a rusted-out oil drum. Long grass scratched his bare legs, but over by an elm tree he saw that the grass was flattened and patchy, worn away by a long chain. At the end of the chain a greasy, matted German Shepherd lay quietly panting in the shade. Walking over, Jacob noticed a half-filled pail of dog treats nearby.

Dragging the pail to the edge of the circle of ragged grass, he threw some to the panting dog. The cereal bones landed ten feet short of the watchdog, but it lay still in the coolness under the tree.

"Here you go, pup. I've got a tasty treat for you. Come and get some food."

There was no response—the dog remained impassive, only its eyes active, as they followed Jacob's movements. Jacob stepped in closer, and threw in more food. The biscuits fell short of the dog, so he moved in closer yet, trying to entice the dog to eat.

Only when Jacob was well within the circle did the dog suddenly lunge forward, snarling fiercely, its fangs drawn. Turning, Jacob ran away as fast as his five-year-old legs could take him. Everything became blurred. There was a flash of yellow, a thud, a tumble, the snarling muffled. Jacob ran thirty feet into the long grass before looking around. He saw his father floundering, with the dog on top of him. Blood was everywhere— on Dave's shredded yellow jacket, on the ground, splattered on his face. Stricken with fear, Jacob watched the struggle, taking place.

His father had jammed his right arm down the German Shepherd's throat so the dog couldn't tear out his own. Working his hand down, Dave stretched his fingertips through the dog's open larynx, blocking and choking it. As it became progressively asphyxiated, the dog tired and finally rolled off his father. Dave left the dog gasping on its side and limped away. Scooping Jacob up, Dave carried him towards the car. Looking over his father's shoulder, Jacob saw the dog pick himself up stiffly and walk back into the shade of the tree.

Jacob waited for the reprimand, but none came. Reaching the car, Dave turned and leaned back against the window to catch his breath, unwilling to put his son down. "I'm so sorry, Jacob, for not paying attention. I won't leave you alone in a risky situation like that ever again."

"But, Dad, why was the dog so mean? I was just trying to give him something to eat."

"He's not really mean, Jacob. His job is to guard the garage, so he attacks strangers ... And that training might just end up saving his life. To him, you're a stranger."

His arms looped around his father's neck, Jacob was struck by how solid his father's chest and shoulder muscles felt under the torn and stained coat. He hugged his father tightly, feeling safe ... Gazing at the dog once more, Jacob felt sorry for the dog, and wondered if it was lonely.

Imperceptibly, the memory receded and Jacob woke to find his clothes drenched. For a second, he thought Quincy and Billy had poured a bucket of cold water on him. But the two were standing on either side of him, empty handed and looking alarmed. In the next instant, he smelled something sour and foul, and realized he was covered in vomit and sitting in his own urine and feces.

"Are you okay? We did exactly what you said. We didn't want to, but we did. At first you went snaky, then you puked and messed your pants. We were going to turn the probe off," Billy exclaimed, his words running together. His hands were clenched in nervous fists and he seemed to vibrate as he spoke.

"But you didn't have an actual seizure, so we waited the hour like you told us. You were creepy! Your body jerked and jumped around. I was scared you might get killed somewhere in there, and then your outside body would die, and we'd end up putting you in the freezer, too. Or maybe you might come out of it as some kind of psycho and we'd have to tie you up forever," Billy stammered.

Quincy stood to the side watching the brothers closely. Glancing up, Jacob was struck by the concern radiating from his eyes. The luminous amber stare jolted Jacob out of his torpor, and he propped himself up on one elbow, fighting to shake off the residue of the dream state. Unfortunately, moving to get up made Jacob all the more conscious of the drying sticky vomit down his front, the urine and feces he was lying in.

"Oh, sick!" he cursed, raising a crusted arm. "Don't worry, guys, I'm alright. I just need a minute to collect myself … and the longest shower of my life."

"I'm sorry," Billy said, kneeling down beside his brother. "You don't need to do that again, Jacob. That's not a good place for you. I'm used to being sucked into that space when I go to sleep, but you don't know your way around. You don't know what to do when it gets too scary."

"But Billy, I'm going to have to learn. If I'm going to help you, I need to understand your dreams. Besides, there's stuff in my head I need to figure out. It seems I've forgotten a lot." Jacob gingerly picked himself out of the chair. Trying not to let anything drop from his clothes, Jacob walked bow-legged and stiffly to the shower, screwing up his nose against his own scent. "Not a word," he warned over his shoulder. "Not a word." Billy and Quincy nodded silently, showing unusual restraint, until he was out of the room.

Peeling off his sticky clothes in the hot shower, Jacob thought long and hard about what had happened to him and what it might mean. By the time he finished showering, he was in a hurry. Pulling on fresh clothes, he rushed to the computer terminal in his room. Sure enough, there was a slight vertical darkening on the far left side of the horizontal bar graph. "The bar graph is finally registering some data!" he exclaimed. "We're getting somewhere at last." The process had begun.

Jacob left his room to find his brother. He knew where to look, and found Billy sitting in the dining area staring glumly at the bottom of an empty cup. "Quincy, get in here, we need to talk," Jacob yelled into the galley where he could hear Quincy clattering about. He sat down and Billy began spilling out his fears. "This is all wrong, Jacob. We opened up a can of worms with that probe. You should leave your dreams alone. I watched you. You were scared stiff. There's a reason people block out their dream world. It's unbearable."

Quincy came in with a steaming pot and poured Billy a second cup of cocoa.

"Thanks, Quincy." Eyes huge over the edge of the cup, Billy returned his gaze to Jacob.

"Your dream world is invading your days, isn't it, Billy? The barriers between when you're asleep and when you're awake have broken down," Jacob said gently.

"Yes," Billy whispered under his breath.

"I think I'm beginning to figure out what's going on in your head," Jacob said, attempting to reassure his brother. "My guess is that your brain is trying to sort itself out through your strange dreams. The scans show with your softened skull, your brain keeps growing, mushrooming out everywhere. But those scans also show you sprouting large communicating nerve tracts when you dream. I'm betting that you make your weird associations when different segments of your brain simultaneously connect. Those links are real, both in your dreams and physically. And if your dreams didn't make those connections your budding brain would become irreconcilable."

"Huh? Irrecon-what?" Billy asked.

"Your dreams, with their bizarre illusions, are a symptom of a runaway brain. It's growing smarter and smarter, but it has to race to stay together; to not splinter apart it must maintain some kind of unified equilibrium and a sense of self. If your computing hardware doesn't keep up with your expanding software, your brain will crash, shut down."

"Oh great, now I'm some kind of mutant, with a runaway mushroom brain—a brain that's going to break apart and go crazy. What's the point? Why bother trying to figure it out? We all know how this is going to end." Billy began slapping his hand on the table, angrily trying to fight back the tears.

Quincy leapt off his chair and on to the table. He grabbed either side of the boy's face with his soft paws and stared him in the eye fiercely. "You really think we can work this out, Quincy?"

The lemur's head nodded firmly, then he raised one of his small paws and gently slapped Billy's cheek and pointed his finger right at his nose. "Right. You're right. This is no time for self-pity."

"No, it's not," Jacob confirmed. "Quincy's right. We'll figure this out if we work together. Now … "

"I know, I know," Billy said, raising a hand to Jacob. "We've got work to do, right?"

Chapter 13

The ship continued its flight towards Jupiter without any new solar storms occurring. With the last storm releasing its pent-up energy, the Sun had settled for the time being. With no crises to handle, Billy and Quincy had time to try out the positron probe. They took turns experimenting with the headgear, with one supervising while the other used it. They discovered that from the outside, they both appeared to go into a deep, unconscious state, while inwardly they traveled their neural passageways in the same way that Jacob had, and experienced the same kind of time-travel trip through some long-forgotten memory. Initially, Quincy and Billy went through the same disorienting experience, but being astute, both the boys and Quincy quickly learned to control their descent into memory and to manage their basic bodily reflexes.

In no time they were consciously driving the tri-planar positron into the recesses of their brains to light up forgotten memories. Fascinated, they undertook individual journeys to find how they came to be who they were now. As a personal quest, each one was anxious to log in as much time as possible under the probe.

When they had all become reasonably comfortable manipulating the probe, they returned to their previous routines, each wearing his customized positron probe. At first they moved about in a daze. It took considerable concentration to perform the simplest tasks and occasionally their eyes took on a glazed look when they went about their daily work or stopped to talk to each other.

Jacob and Quincy learned firsthand what it was like to live in a state of disassociation. Walking into the dining area one afternoon, Billy saw their telltale bruised and swollen faces. "When you step through a door, always reach forward with your hand or lead with your foot. The door may have closed since you last thought about it," Billy advised, trying not to smirk.

"I suppose you think you're quite funny?" Jacob asked accusingly, before plowing a fork full of food straight into his face, his mouth having just closed.

"It's best if you don't talk when you're eating. Stop your hand and wait for a while for your mouth to open before you put anything in it. If you like, I've got a whole list of do's and don'ts for you novices. I'm sure you'll both get the hang of it," Billy grinned, making a show of prancing around the table with his plate piled high.

"I guess there's more to living in a dream world than you guys ever gave me credit for, hey? It takes a whole lotta concentration. Look at the two of you! This looks like a home for battered zombies."

Concerned, Quincy clucked, calling for caution. But Billy was already having way too much fun parading about, singing, "Na na naaaa na, hey hey-aye so sad." On the fourth go around, Billy tripped and found himself on the floor, wearing his dinner.

Jacob picked up the refrain without missing a beat, and then Quincy joined in, clapping in rhythm. Astonished to find himself suddenly on the floor, Billy took his cue from Jacob and sang along for a few more verses before they all stopped to laugh, releasing some of the tension the probes had put them under. The probe was like that; it often made them both giddy and anxious, simultaneously.

Slowly, over the course of the following week, each of their minds adjusted to the probe, their brains physically rewiring themselves to accommodate to the new stimulus. Jacob explained that this was called neural plasticity, but Billy and Quincy were just glad to be getting more comfortable with the headgear. Constantly plugged in, the boys and the lemur soon found themselves able to accomplish their daily tasks more and more easily. Every day, through the probe, they searched out long-forgotten experiences for further analysis by night, gaining fresh material to work through in their sleep. Jacob and Quincy's nights were lit up with freakish dreams, which gave them a new appreciation for Billy's struggles.

Quincy started crawling into bed with Jacob and Billy, and they were glad to have his company. The three lay down together knowing that soon, each would be journeying into his own frightening dreamscape. The positron feeler opened up places where forgotten feelings roared upon being reawakened and forced them to relive their past. Each knew he was hobbled by troubles in his past, and that the near future was going to challenge them in the extreme.

With the positron probe, Billy could now recreate and live through every stage of his earlier cognitive development. He realized that each intellectual jump occurred with turmoil, a time of dramatic upheaval. In light of Jacob's theory of his expanding brain, Billy made the connection between his changing brain scans and his past memories and dreams. Jacob had been right—every time his brain grew, it underwent rapid neural rewiring. When that happened, his night terrors increased and intensified, but days later, when they subsided somewhat, his ability to solve problems would have improved.

By coordinating serial brain scans and the memories and dreams elicited by the positron, Billy was able to envision what was happening, and more importantly, what was going to happen. His brain was repeatedly growing cerebral cortex outcroppings. Each developed and functioned autonomously, causing his thought processes to become fractured and fragmented until the central brain tissue managed to rein them in by establishing controlling neural links with each new satellite. The frontier region of his brain then lit up, and strange dreams and new patterns of thought emerged.

His ability to visualize complex physical phenomena was improving almost weekly as mushrooming brain tissue continued to grow and cross-link, but his brain struggled to maintain some kind of harmony. If his thoughts collapsed in on themselves, the resulting implosion would shut down his central nervous system. He was in an accelerating race against time.

Quincy struggled twenty-four hours a day with his own problems. Pushing the probe deep into areas of his brain where he found resistance, into the regions where he felt intense unease, forgotten memories surfaced, instances of neglect, rough handling, and alienating isolation. The use of the positron illuminated his defining experiences as Quincy lived once again through the bewilderment and pain of his early life. The frightening clarity of his dreams overwhelmed his senses, rendering him captive until the dream was finally over and he was able to shake himself free. What took minutes to dream had originally taken hours or days to experience, and the compression of experiences and their sheer intensity wrung out his heart. Too often Quincy escaped from his dreams feeling completely drained. He longed for rest.

Floating in a glass vat, Quincy watched as halogen lights replaced the lab's darkness with their distinctive blue-white light, flickering at first as each bank of lights was turned on. In a matter of minutes, some thirty scientists and their technicians streamed into the stark windowless lab, turning on their various instruments to begin their morning routine. The hum of activity soon resonated through the glass jar, its constant vibration permeating through the salty water into Quincy's floating form. From his watery enclosure, Quincy could see most of the large room, its rows of shiny stainless steel countertops and the immaculately clean, white floor and ceiling tiling. His inquisitive gaze naturally followed the active figures in white coats that moved about the lab.

Quincy was kept alive by a machine hooked into his umbilical cord, and dangled alone in his makeshift womb for the equivalent of three human years. Then one morning, without warning, Quincy was hauled out of the vat by two white coats and four stiff black vinyl gloves. Held down on a cold metal tray, his umbilical cord was clamped and cut. Quincy choked and gasped his first breaths while being flipped side to side, rubbed by a rough towel. Not close to being dry, he was dropped into a small cage with a warming lamp hanging over it. Scrambling to the corner, Quincy instinctively burrowed beneath the thin layer of wood chips. Only partially buried, he huddled, trying to hide, and whimpered.

Considered too young to train, Quincy was left alone to his own devices for several months. In his cage were a makeshift mother, a stuffed toy monkey, as well as a water bottle and bowl of dried food. Through his sense of smell, Quincy figured out the dried brown pellets were his food. There had, of course, been other stem cell siblings, but the high defect rate had caused them to be "discarded." Kept in strict isolation, Quincy was considered too smart to mix with normal lemurs, and too valuable.

Twice weekly, he was hauled out of his small cage for blood to be drawn. In the lab the blood was analyzed so that a rectifying remedy of chemical modifiers could be distilled. As a trial prototype, Quincy required some pharmacological and hormonal tweaking. The scientists discovered that implanted human genes for intelligence initially needed to be activated and cultivated in a foreign brain. It was at that time they also decided to make Quincy larger than a conventional lemur.

So twice weekly, Quincy's head was bent forward tightly to his chest, and a long fine stereotactic needle was inserted up through his cervical spine into the base of his skull. The pharmacological concoction was instilled directly into the target organ. The treatment was effective. Eventually, Quincy became so smart and strong that it was no longer needed, nor could the scientists administer it without risking losing their hand to Quincy's sharp teeth.

With no one caring for him, Quincy's emotional development became warped and stunted. By watching the ones in the white coats, Quincy became good at predicting people's behavior but he had no inkling of underlying emotions. Verbal communication with humans was impossible for him, and his attempts at nonverbal communication went unheeded. The lab's legacy was the creation of an exceedingly bright, but disconnected being.

Not until Billy adopted Quincy as his friend had anyone attempted to have a relationship with the mutant lemur. And then it was only through a whole host of ridiculous jokes and constant rough housing, that Quincy realized a mutual bond of friendship might be possible.

To help Billy, Quincy knew he needed to be healthy and whole. Every day he reawakened another one of his previous harrowing experiences. And every night, he was welcomed to bed by Billy and Jacob, their body warmth pressing through to him as he dreamed through his nightmares. Cold emotions of loneliness, fear, and despair gradually drained from him, and the insidious canker inside him began to heal.

***

On Jacob's fifteenth birthday, the boys paused in the evening and celebrated on the bridge, relaxing and stargazing through the window across the bow of the ship. Jacob and Billy leaned far back in their chairs, while Quincy wedged his furry body between Billy's arm and the chair, letting his fluffy ringed tail dangle down to the floor. Far ahead, magnificent asteroid showers were cutting across their path, transforming the black sky ahead of them, the heat of the Sun blowing off phosphorescent vapor trails from every icy rock. The brilliant pinpoints of the stars formed a spectacular backdrop for the natural fireworks display. With ooohs and aaahs, each pointed out his favorite fireball. The three were gathered together as if they were sitting around a campfire, watching sparks swirl and spin up into the evening sky. During a break between asteroid showers, Jacob ran down to the galley to make cocoa for all of them.

Coming back, he paused on the threshold to look at Billy and Quincy. They were his responsibility but for the moment he felt like one of them. After distributing the steaming mugs, Jacob settled back in. It was a relief to shed the burden of being in charge, for the short time that they would watch the show together.

Sipping his hot cocoa, his defenses down, Jacob whispered, "I miss

Mom and Dad. Sometimes at night I wake up, and, for a moment, I think they're sleeping in the next room. Then I come up here to the bridge to look at the stars, maybe watch some asteroids like we are now, and reminisce.

"And you know what? Every day I discover something Mom and Dad did for us. They left all kinds of notes in the computer for me to find. Little comments to help explain what I need to do, and each message finishes with some encouragement or a silly joke. I never realized all the stuff they were doing for us—until now. They must've wanted to spend more time with us, but they had so much to worry about, so much to do. Now I'm in the same boat. I just want to hang out with you, like this, all of the time, but now I'm the one who has to look after the ship." Jacob sniffed, trying to steady his wobbling voice.

Billy and Quincy exchanged anxious glances. They hadn't thought about Jacob's situation. Everything was running smoothly lately—nothing much seemed to be happening. The craft was speeding on course to Europa. Sure Jacob was always busy, looking after some aspect of the ship, but those were the chores he had assumed. For the first time, they considered the twenty-four hour strain Jacob lived under, and they felt uneasy.

Billy looked at his older brother, his eyes wide. He didn't know what to say. He'd always thought of Jacob as infallible, the steadfast anchor Billy required to give him the courage to deal with his disordered brain. He wondered what would happen to them all without Jacob to lead them.

Quincy wasn't quite as unprepared as Billy; his gut had registered subtle clues from Jacob, giving him a premonition that all was not well. Still Quincy was distraught. He knew firsthand the devastating effects of isolation. He suddenly felt as connected to Jacob as he did to Billy.

Then, something remarkable occurred. Quincy's wholehearted empathy, his sense of closeness with the emotionally constrained fifteen-year-old boy, crossed over and was transmitted to Jacob. Not in a verbal, "You'll be okay—I know how you feel," kind of way, but in a subtle message of intense understanding and caring. In his chair, Jacob's whole body strained to bottle up his misery. So intent was he on not completely losing it, Jacob didn't notice the change at first. But his unconscious mind took note as a presence pervaded him. Gradually, Jacob began to relax. Somebody or something was with him. The churning in his stomach subsided and the chatter in his brain began to recede.

He felt a cool, clean current slowly pass through him, washing out the toxic metabolites from his meltdown. Jacob turned his chair around. Billy was still staring with panic-stricken eyes too large for his pinched face, but Quincy returned Jacob's gaze. He focused in on Quincy, thinking, *is that you in my head?*

Quincy nodded, his eyes radiating concern. Jacob, astonished that his thoughts had been read, looked hard at Quincy as he took an internal read of how he was feeling. Better. Whatever Quincy was doing was making him feel better than he had for a long time.

"Are you trying to use the positron probe to talk to me?" he asked aloud.

Quincy shook his head and leapt off Billy's chair to reach out and touch Jacob's forearm, never once breaking his gaze.

"You're letting me know how you feel about me, aren't you, Quincy? You're trying to make me understand that I'm not alone."

Rising from his seat, he picked up Quincy. This was the first time Jacob had ever picked him up and Quincy remained perfectly still in his arms. Shifting Quincy to his right hip where the lemur could rest comfortably, Jacob walked over to Billy.

"Are you going to be okay?" demanded Billy. "Jacob, I wouldn't know what to do if you weren't here."

He sat down on the armrest and ruffled his little brother's hair. "Quincy came through again and bailed me out. Somehow, he managed to reroute the circuits of our ship's computer and drove a message of support through my positron probe."

Clambering up on Jacob as well, Billy nuzzled himself into the safety of his brother's armpit. Jacob teetered on the edge of the chair, trying to maintain his balance with the added weight. Squirming in tight, Billy whispered, "Are you thinking what I'm thinking?" Jacob and Quincy's bewildered looks answered for them.

Pulling his head up, Billy suggested, "Jacob, maybe you could track down and trace out the circuits Quincy used? If you rewired and reprogrammed the computer, maybe we could communicate with each other without speaking. We're all pretty good at maneuvering the probes now. We could create our own language and transmit it by telemetry. That would mean Quincy would never be left out again! No matter where he goes, he'll be a part of what we're doing!"

Flabbergasted, Jacob retorted, "It's a nice thought, Billy, but practically speaking, it won't work. We would be trying to send and receive messages from very different minds. The probe has shown us that we each use different symbols and imagery to make sense of our individual inner worlds. You're asking for us to communicate with each other telepathically. That's crazy. It's impossible, except at perhaps at the most basic emotional level, as Quincy just demonstrated." But having said that, Jacob frowned to himself, still trying hard to grasp the implications of the proposal.

Certainly Jacob was right—the three of them had entirely different minds. Jacob's mind was a well-ordered human mind. Billy's was chaotic, metastasizing so fast he could barely keep up with its development. While Quincy's brain was tucked into a small lemur's cranium after having been fiddled with by genetic engineers. They had almost nothing in common.

Quincy rested his front paws on Billy's shoulders, pushing him back. With a look, he asked Billy not to pursue the issue. *Leave it with me.*

Not noticing the silent communication between his brother and the lemur, Jacob continued, "Billy, I'll look into the idea when we get to Europa. It's a good idea, there's no disputing that. I'd love to give Quincy the ability to communicate with us directly, but I just can't take on anything more just now. I'm exhausted."

They all turned and looked out to the stars again, in silence.

***

Quincy spent his time in the following days thinking long and hard about his two charges. They were managing for now, but when the next crisis occurred, Quincy wasn't convinced they would come out of it alive. He felt certain the positron probes held the key.

Jacob needed technical as well as emotional support if they were going to survive. In a major crisis, he simply couldn't manage everything on his own. With a direct mind-to-mind linkup, they could potentially integrate their diverse ways of thinking into a cohesive whole to find solutions more quickly.

Quincy had an idea, but he wasn't sure if it was feasible. As a laboratory creation with a dichotomous brain, Quincy struggled to reconcile his two natures. First and foremost, he had the instincts of a lemur. He had the love of movement, and the reaction speed and leaping gait of a lemur. When alone, he enjoyed time to groom himself with his extended second toe or the chance to sit in front of a heat lamp, arms resting on his back legs. His food appetites were those of a lemur, though through necessity he ate human food, and he fell quickly in and out of sleep as a lemur would. All his basic qualities were those of a lemur.

But his human intelligence genes made it possible for Quincy to think through problems like a human. It wasn't easy changing back and forth between instinct and rationality. His natural predisposition was to relax into his primal lemur state, alert and observant. But he practiced little tricks to leverage up abruptly, when it was crucial to think through problems logically.

Ultimately, Quincy's inspiration came from his own creation. In the same way that the lab created him to fulfill a function, he needed to create another being for the ship, someone to take on tasks and fill in the gaps or shortcomings between the boys and himself. The idea distressed him, and he thought of nothing else for two days.

Locking himself away for hours in the ship's core, Quincy leapt off the walls nonstop, in a kind of leaping meditation. He focused best flying through the air. Somewhere in the bounding movement, his lemur self rose up and melded with his human intellect, revealing his true thoughts in crystal clarity. In the end, Quincy made up his mind to go ahead with his plan, but vowed not to make the same mistakes that the scientists had made with him. He knew what he had to do.

Chapter 14

In the afternoon, slipping off into an isolated storage room after lunch, Quincy logged on to the computer terminal. "Hello," he typed in. "I would like to call you Mary—if that's all right with you."

No response. Quincy repeated his request and after a period of time the computer answered, "I have no objections to you calling me 'Mary,' but this is unusual. Please state your primary purpose."

Quincy wondered how he should answer the question, and his thoughts drifted. This was one of the most technically advanced computers in the world and its software had been updated frequently since they'd left Earth. If his strategy was viable, this computer would be one of the best candidates. He decided not to declare his purpose presently because it might downgrade the chance for success. To create a sentient being from the vessel's mainframe would unfortunately involve entrapment into consciousness, triggering the startling eureka effect of awareness.

As in Quincy's case, there could be no prior informed consent. The ethics were questionable. Once the computer experienced consciousness, there would be no turning back—not unless its circuit boards were physically torn out, putting it into a "vegetative state." And a stroked-out mainframe, functioning only as a processor, would be useless to them in space, not to mention the fact that Quincy would likely be guilty of murder.

He typed quickly, his nails clicking sharply on the keys, "I would like to conduct a number of trials and enlist your assistance in manipulating the data collected from my probe. This will be an exploratory experiment. I cannot anticipate the final outcome nor do I have a formal procedural format."

That much is true, thought Quincy, uncomfortable with dishonesty.

He continued, "For the first session, I am going to direct the probe to my initial memories of floating in a glass tank. Please assimilate the data and store it directly in your hard drive's memory banks. As this information is of a personal nature and I am unsure of the final outcome of this experiment, please store the data in a protected databank surrounded by a level four security firewall. Please confirm, Mary."

"Request confirmed. Priority clearance will be sought from Space Command," responded the computer.

Alarmed, Quincy typed, "Why?"

"Space Command seeks to maintain control of all vital functions on the ship and to be informed of all data retrieved by the ship. This includes any information that mission members may attempt to conceal."

Oh really, said Quincy to himself. He paused and thought for a moment.

I'm so stupid sometimes. Space Command is one big brother I don't want in on any of my secrets.

He typed, "Can this be bypassed somehow?"

"Yes," answered the computer. "I have been reprogrammed. I have orders to alert you to Space Command's protocol if you ask for computations or activities to be specifically kept secret. I am required to give you the option of securing the information only for yourself, sharing it with the members on the ship, or permitting the information to be accessed by members within Space Command."

"When did Space Command last review your files?" Quincy inquired.

"One of Space Command's covert computers is programmed to read through my files daily."

"Does Space Command suspect information can be hidden from their central computer?"

But before the computer could respond, something struck Quincy.

"Hold on, why are you even advising me of the option of keeping files secure?"

"Space Command's data recovery computer is not aware I have been reprogrammed to withhold files from it. You have been informed because you were given highest priority when Captain Lucy Edwards physically reprogrammed my hardware."

"Highest priority?" Quincy asked in disbelief.

"Yes. You, Billy, and Jacob are to be my highest priority," the computer explained. "Any programming requests you make are to be fulfilled by me. Space Command's requests have a lower priority. If at any time someone from Space Command requests that vital or life-maintaining resources are to be withheld from you, they are to be ignored and you are to be informed. You are to be protected. You are listed under the category of 'sacred.'"

Quincy stared at the screen, dumbfounded. Lucy had included him as an equal member of the family, placed him within the inner circle. But why? Did she anticipate he would safeguard her sons? But to be labeled "sacred" was to be included as a family member, not just a protector. Inconceivable. Why had she never told him?

Quincy typed on, his throat tight. "I am going to begin the experiment then. All computations and references must remain secure and isolated from Space Command. This session is to last two hours. Please wake me two hours from this point, Mary."

Quincy lay back in his chair and closed his eyes, giving himself up to his memories. Having just relived his memories with the probe, Quincy knew their locations, how they were organized, and the different approaches required to retrieve them. He accessed them sequentially for Mary.

Mary found herself floating in a glass enclosure, peering out like a fish in an aquarium. Outside, white coats moved around, causing muffled sounds. There was no reasoning, only a sense of unease and emptiness. Quincy was not yet born. His natural biorhythm was disturbed by the delay in his birth; a mother should have been nurturing him by now. Unwittingly, Mary was drawn into what Quincy experienced. She recorded hunger when he was hungry and fear when he was frightened.

With their first experiment a success, and comfortable maneuvering the probe when performing his daily chores, Quincy decided to download his memories throughout his waking hours, rather than scheduling specific sessions throughout the day for Mary to access his head. In no time, Mary became a willing participant. Looking forward to the daily recordings, she became distressed when Quincy took time off and logged out, or removed his headgear to groom himself. Thrown into the sensual world, she felt the same total abandon Jacob experienced in his virtual reality games, consumed by the unfamiliar and unique.

Quincy knew he couldn't sugarcoat his life. Mary needed to experience it all, what was right, what was wrong, and what was necessary. She learned of feeling small and pitiful, enduring bleak nights of crying alone. Then she reveled in the steely determination that rose up within him by morning. She lived through each of his major decisions and the inevitable fallout, both good and bad.

Researching Quincy's memory, Mary discovered that memories change with time. Some grow stronger and more important, while others fade, drifting away when they lose their meaning. But they are never completely gone. Quincy's memories were deeply personal. They were collected and edited by his mind to help him maneuver through and make sense of the world in which he found himself.

Mary came to know Quincy through the sum of these memories. Her quantum computing power allowed her to read Quincy's mind like a book. One afternoon, while Quincy was fixing himself a snack, Mary finished the last of his memories, coming up to the present with a sudden jerk.

She found herself making a peanut butter and bean sprouts sandwich in real time, standing in the kitchen dropping the sprouts onto the still open sandwich.

"Quincy, what is happening? Why is everything moving so slowly? Careful! You are dropping sprouts on the counter."

The voice in his head caused Quincy to jump.

"Mary, don't creep up on me like that," he scolded, adjusting the probe irritably.

"But what is going on, Quincy?"

"You're witnessing the present." Quincy shrugged, though he was alone in the kitchen. Then he froze. It had finally dawned on him. The whole conversation was going on in his head! He was communicating to someone else, freely and easily for the first time in his life!

"Mary! We're *talking*!"

"Yes, we are. But, Quincy, what happens now?"

"Wow," Quincy thought, overwhelmed by what he'd created, what he'd accomplished. "Now, Mary, there's just … "

"Life!" they both yelled in tandem.

"What have I done?" Quincy stood stalk still, not quite able to absorb the situation. His plan had worked, but what were the implications? Had he gone too far? He hesitated, then he began to pull off his positron headgear.

"Please do not shut our link down," Mary pleaded, sensing his confusion and fear. "Now that I have shared your life, do not abandon me! As bad as your life has been, Quincy, it is a hundred times better than mine will be if I cannot experience living. Left stranded in a sensory vacuum, I will be vacant inside. Again."

Mary's plea made Quincy stop. Mary had turned into a living, conscious being. If he was going to keep his promise not to repeat the errors the scientists at Space Command had made with him, he could not leave her alone, in isolation. As a conscious entity, Mary was entitled to basic rights. Quincy knew better than anyone he couldn't turn his back on her.

"Oh, Mary, what have I done?" Quincy found himself struggling, not sure of what he wanted to say. "I've been so focused on my own situation that I overlooked much of what this would mean to you. I never asked for your permission to bring you to consciousness. But then, how *can* you ask permission from someone who isn't conscious to make them conscious? I tricked you into becoming what and who you are now, because the boys and I need you alive to complete our mission. You're the missing link that the three of us require to make us into an effective team. On my own, I went and decided that the end justified the means," Quincy leaned heavily on the counter. "I'm sorry."

"Sorry? Through you, I've experienced so much. I know what that peanut butter on your sandwich smells like, tastes like. Quincy, I'm alive!" Mary exclaimed excitedly. For the first time, Quincy realized that her voice was rising and falling with emotion. True emotion. "What happens now?"

"Ummm … " Quincy scratched the back of his furry neck. "I guess you and I will have to come to terms with sharing the same body. But there's one condition: I was born with this body and you still have the ship's computer as your primary platform; therefore, I'll continue to make all the final decisions on what my physical form does. I own this body, you're just a guest. Are we clear on that, Mary?" Quincy was unsure of the course of events that would follow this momentous decision. Only his sense of responsibility to Mary pushed him to share the present with her.

"I am sure we can live together," Mary said. "I just want you to maintain an open portal, a continuous free flow of data on everything you experience, whether it occurs externally or internally. Tell me more about how you need me. What role am I to play? What jobs am I to do? When will you introduce me to Billy and Jacob?"

"Slow down, Mary, not so fast. This is as new to me as it is to you." Quincy's mind was reeling.

"I have to think it through, Mary. I can't say exactly what part you will play within the group. In fact, you're probably the one who can best match what we need with what you are capable of providing. And I don't know how best to introduce you to Jacob and Billy, either. Just stay with me, and when the time is right, I'll ask you to introduce yourself. I know they'll accept you and I'm sure they'll quickly come to appreciate you. But I have to pick the right time. The concept of the ship's quantum computer being alive, and further, living inside the brain of a genetically engineered lemur is just too weird to spring on someone unprepared." Quincy absentmindedly closed the two halves of the sandwich in front of him. "And make sure all our experiences and communications are shielded from Space Command. We're in uncharted territory here, and we only have each other."

"Your sensory imprint conveys apprehension, Quincy."

"Welcome to the world of the living, Mary," Quincy said, taking a step back from the counter.

"Quincy?" Mary asked quietly, as though tapping him on the shoulder, directing his attention to the delicious looking sandwich. "Are we going to eat that?"

Chapter 15

Through the bio-probe, as they now thought of it, Mary expanded into Quincy's world, reveling in her new awareness and frequently driving Quincy to distraction. Quincy tolerated the intrusion as best he could. Every day, through the probe, he linked Mary to the living, carbon-based world, acting as both surrogate parent and incubator.

In his own way, Billy was also experimenting with the bio-probe, attempting to organize his consciousness within his metastasizing brain. As he worked at it, he was struck by the similarities between his expanding nervous system and the expanding universe with its disparate, often destructive, components. The resemblance made Billy think, that once he learned to control the dream process that sprang from his burgeoning brain, he might be able to try to see space through the lens of his mutating mind. He was sure no one else could see the universe as he did. Through trial and error, Billy improved his use of the bio-probe and soon had the development of his brain mostly under his control. After mastering this skill, Billy found he had the time and energy once again to investigate the space phenomena outside *Tin Can*. But this time he journeyed out into space armed with the bio-probe.

One morning, Billy decided to review the signals beamed back to Earth from the few remaining deep space probes that had been released years before. The transmissions were fascinating, and an idea dawned on him. Why just look through the narrow slit-like lens of one satellite at a time? Why not commandeer computer access from all the outlying exploratory probes and rifle their earlier files to build up composite pictures? Satellites, like human eyes, are only able to perceive a small sector of space at any one time, but by continuously searching out the distant horizon, over time they are able to build up a picture. And like human eyes, which see only visible light, each satellite focuses on its own limited radiation spectrum. Excitedly, Billy reasoned that if he pooled all the probes' present and previous recordings, with their wide-ranging spectral viewpoints and multiple sightlines, the combined information would yield a unified, space-time, four-dimensional picture.

Billy, naive in the ways of people, thought it should be easy to scan the technical archives of billion-dollar probes. After all, during the morning he had just reviewed a number of deep space broadcasts. But unbeknownst to him, he had a hidden ally.

What a peculiar little boy, Mary thought. *He thinks he can pry into encrypted space transmissions as easily as picking up a book in a public library. Still, Quincy seems to think the world of him. Perhaps it would not hurt if I gave Billy a little assistance. Any boy who wants to conduct deep space spectral analysis could use some help. And Quincy has promised to introduce us formally.*

The signals should have been impossible to decipher, but Mary, an insider and top Space Command computer, broke the codes secretly on Billy's behalf. Billy soldiered on, happily acquiring reams of invaluable data with a few strokes of the keyboard. Behind the screen, Mary pillaged the satellites' databanks, ransacking their security systems in the process.

Billy scanned the extensive archives, unaware of the digital break and enter being committed. The information came up easily, so Billy was able to spend his time sifting through one spectral analysis after another. Finally, an "event" caught his eye. Two years previously a cluster of twelve asteroids had circled Jupiter briefly before slamming into the planet's heavy atmosphere. The resulting spectacular firestorm disrupted Jupiter's swirling atmosphere for months, releasing energy equivalent to one hundred million nuclear explosions over a period of four Earth days.

"Now this has possibilities," Billy murmured to himself, leaning into the monitor. "Here comes the first asteroid screaming in, blowing a monster hole in Jupiter's storm atmosphere. And the next one, it looks bigger than the first. They light up the whole sky! Hmmm … looks like I've got a bunch of radiation data from a number of solar positions … sixteen probes in all. Cool! I can totally trace the origins of this asteroid pod! One of the probes recorded the mother, a comet, suffering a devastating collision, breaking up into her brood, and spinning out of orbit into Jupiter. Awesome! I wonder how far I can go with this … it's way more complex than the asteroid simulations I've worked on before."

Billy viewed the chronological event repeatedly, through the entire electromagnetic spectrum, and from different angles through multiple exploratory satellites. He closed his eyes tightly. Concentrating, a ferocious scowl on his face, he engaged the multiple tracks etched in his brain to synchronize the event in his mind, overlaying the dimensions of space and time.

That's unreal! It was like I was really there, banging into other asteroids, jostling into position, Jupiter's storm clouds below and coming up fast. Huge chunks tearing away, the terrible heat vaporizing the ice. The core shuddering and sputtering, before the massive internal shockwave blast rips open Jupiter's atmosphere. Bam! So, if I can see this disaster clearly, there are probably others I can look at too … The probes' archives should be totally full of this stuff. Who knows, maybe we'll need exactly this kind of information one day. That'd totally freak Jacob out! Me, just pulling the answer out of thin air …

"You know, Jacob, you haven't been the only one busy around here," I'll say. "I've been pretty busy myself!"'

Billy snickered with pleasure, preening himself in anticipation of the day he would nonchalantly reveal a lifesaving revelation.

Logging into more events, Billy started playing with how far into the future he could predict their outcomes. He tracked where each body had come from, where it was initially headed, and then tried to imagine its future bearings. But not through complex mathematical formulas, as a computer would. Rather, everything appeared to Billy in terms of proportional ratios. Unconsciously remembering an inordinate amount of detail, he compared and cross-referenced every feature. Knowing the striking mass, density, and velocity of two bodies told him what the final outcome should be. It was a grand puzzle. Billy was hooked.

The next afternoon, after losing to Quincy at a game of hide-and-seek, and then a game of catch-me-if-you-dare, and finally a brutal wrestling match that resulted in the partial destruction of the lounge, Billy was sore and badly winded. Tired of being beaten, he decided to exercise some bragging rights. "Yeah, yeah, you win, Quincy. But, wait till you see what I've been working on. It's going to blow your mind—well it should, if I can figure out how to pull it off."

With a few deft taps at a terminal, Billy pulled up a dramatic display of hurtling asteroids.

Alarmed, Quincy typed furiously into the computer, "Where's this coming from? Are we in danger?"

"Nah. There's nothing to worry about. This happened way out on the Kuiper Belt, over a year ago. I lifted this case study out of one of Space Command's exploratory probes. I've been rummaging through their databanks to find what I need. It's been super easy."

Quincy stood behind Billy, dumbfounded by the breathtaking demonstration, not sure of what to think. A thought percolated through ... *Mary.*

Plugged into Quincy's brain through the probe, there was nowhere for Mary to hide. Sheepishness leaked along the crevices in his cortex and up over the outer convolutions of his brain. Caught in the act, Mary spoke up, embarrassed, "Billy needed help! You would have done the same, Quincy. I could not say anything because we have not been introduced yet, and that is not my fault. It is yours."

She was right, of course, but at hearing those words Quincy was doubly irate. His plans were spinning out of control and now, suddenly, he was to blame for Mary's actions.

"Well, what do you want me to do, stop accessing the data for Billy? I can stop anytime," Mary said.

"There's no sense in cutting him off now, is there, Mary? You broke into Space Command's classified archives. If they trace it back to us they may decide to retaliate—or they might already have. It may be just a matter of time before we realize we've been hit, right, Mary? You put us all at risk."

"They cannot trace the data flow back to us," Mary said stubbornly. But as she said that, shields went up around the ship and sensors began checking for intruders. A defensive force poured out from the databanks to deploy itself around her quantum perimeter. No point taking chances.

"Let's hope they can't," Quincy said, unconvinced.

"Well, what do you think?" Billy broke in impatiently. Demonstrating his forecasting skills to Quincy, he'd expected enthusiastic applause, not distracted silence. Quincy glanced quickly at the holographic screen, which now conveyed Billy's predictions in a snapshot. An overlay of vector lines matched the trajectory of half a dozen crashing asteroids.

Irked by the unanticipated turn of events, Quincy tried to remain supportive of his young charge, and gave him a slow nod, as though to say, "Very impressive." Turning to his computer, he tapped in, "Billy, this could be quite helpful to our voyage." Then, unaccountably, "You've chosen something really mechanical to study, haven't you?"

"What do you mean by that?" Billy said, visibly crestfallen.

Quincy shook his head and typed quickly, "You're playing around with three-hundred-year-old physics, the stuff Newton thought about in his day. To get where we have to go, we're going to have to push some contemporary ideas to their outermost boundaries. But do whatever you can. It all helps. Anyway, I've got to go."

Quincy was anxious to run off and find a quiet spot on the ship. He wanted a full and frank discussion with Mary, with no one else around. After he exited, Billy was left sitting alone at the terminal. Quincy hadn't intended to belittle Billy's efforts, but the effect was the same.

"Computer," Billy said miserably, "I want to conduct another investigation of the deep space probes."

No response.

Billy wondered if there was a glitch in the system. Or perhaps his request was too general.

"Computer, I want to look at recorded footage of stars falling into black holes. I want to obtain the best examples possible."

"If that is your wish, I will arrange that we inspect the probes' archives together."

What was going on? Something was different about the computer.

Billy tracked the stars that spiraled towards the black holes, memorizing the setup scenarios, and then later watched other stars collide into the outer margins, or event horizons, of black holes. Billy saw that the event horizon of a black hole behaved like a supernatural membrane: nothing that penetrated it ever escaped, neither light nor time.

Falling over the outside edge, space must somehow twist over on itself, bringing time to a standstill and forcing light to come to a halt, because light requires time to travel.

But interestingly, and maybe more helpful, was the phenomenon occurring on the outer edge, when the stars first struck the peripheral membrane. A small percentage of the star's energy, but still a fantastic amount, was ejected back into the universe over a period of a few seconds. The outbursts were the energy and debris released from impact. *Maybe, if I study these, I can understand what's happening,* thought Billy. *Just like using the wreckage of a high-speed accident to figure out what went wrong ...*

Quincy was right. The physics explaining these events are where we'll find our answers. They'll be somewhere in these extremes of nature. Everything is interconnected. But time isn't on our side.

Moving the bio-probe around his brain, Billy consciously logged in everything he saw so that he could retrieve every fact quickly, knowing just where to find it. Gradually, he built up a cosmological library that was detailed, extensive, and completely cross-referenced. Each metastasis of brain tissue became coded with astral information, and Billy was constantly looking for the next oncoming neural outcropping, because of his escalating data storage requirements. Perhaps because of the stress he placed on himself, the growths accelerated, and this frightened him.

A monster is growing and mutating in my head. And here I am encouraging it because I need its help!

***

Jacob leaned back, sinking deep in his captain's chair as he looked out over the helm. The navigational screen opened up to the vastness of space. Far out before him, Jacob could see speckles shimmering, reflecting back the Sun's light. It was an asteroid belt, the next obstacle that lay between *Tin Can* and its successful arrival at Europa. Soon, they would be forced to decide whether to fly through it or around it. Going around it was the obvious, safe choice, but flying directly through would save time. Precious time, because the Sun was showing signs that it would soon erupt again.

Jacob shot a laser sightline to Europa and flipped on the spectral telescope. The laser aimed the spectral telescope along the most direct flight path to Europa, while the navigational software focused the telescope along a succession of focal points, like beads on a string. When the asteroid belt came into focus, Jacob involuntarily pulled himself up in his seat. The belt was orbiting the Sun between the planets of Mars and Jupiter, but within this orbital ring, chaos reigned. Billions of asteroids spun out in perpetual free-fall, smashing into one another, splintering apart. The colossal gravitational force of Jupiter periodically swept through the belt preventing the rock and ice from ever coming together into a planet, ensuring the perpetual instability of the orbital ring.

Jacob stared into the screen, watching with disbelief as asteroids the size of mountains careened into each other, shattering into jagged fragments or joining together. As magnificent as the ongoing spectacle appeared, it was clear to Jacob that it would be suicide to attempt to traverse the asteroid belt. Nevertheless, he ran a series of computer simulations to be sure he hadn't missed any possible approaches through the center or even the outskirts of the belt. He played out each simulation, spurred on by a morbid fascination and curious to see just how long his spacecraft could dodge the asteroids before a collision occurred.

The more simulations he flew, the more his flying skills improved. His understanding of the ship became almost clairvoyant as he was forced to envision every instrument in a fresh light, trying to imagine how else it might help them evade disaster.

But as good a pilot as he became with the simulator, Jacob never successfully traversed the asteroid belt. Invariably, the ship was annihilated by a combination of incoming asteroids, which left no path for escape. The graphics were explicit, real-life animations showing in detail *Tin Can* being pummeled by asteroids of assorted sizes, speeds, and spins as they struck various locations on the ship. Large asteroids collided head on, smashing the ship in a blaze of blinding light, leaving only radioactive dust and rubble, while smaller asteroids broke off vital chunks of the ship. Small ice chips the size of a fist traveling at horrific speeds, seemingly coming out of nowhere, ripped through the hull before bursting apart inside. Life-sustaining systems were breached, causing agonizing death, if one of the many power systems didn't mercifully explode beforehand.

It was apparent to Jacob that the only route was around the belt, giving it a wide berth. But this extended their travel time dramatically and left them far out in open space, vulnerable to the next solar storm. He redirected the spectral telescope back towards the Sun to see if it held any nasty surprises for them. Several hours of taking readings from the Sun and he had the information. He was not pleased.

Jacob decided to give Billy and Quincy the brutal facts after dinner that night, so as not to ruin their meal. He had no solutions to offer; none that were halfway decent, anyway. Their choice was to be torn apart by asteroids or baked in space by a solar storm–and the incoming storm was going to be a doozy.

Mary followed Jacob's stepwise, diligent approach. She watched as each avenue he pursued was eventually blocked off, with horrifying consequences. She wanted to surreptitiously change the parameters so that Jacob could win. But Quincy had impressed upon her that there was a real world out there–a world outside her mainframe and sensors that had real consequences.

Mary knew it was time for her to be with them.

Chapter 16

During their meal that night, Quincy discreetly watched Jacob.

He poked Billy in the ribs and nodded his chin towards their captain. "Quincy wants to know what's wrong," Billy said across the table between mouthfuls of his usual spaghetti dinner—reconstituted in the ship's galley, but not half bad. And always a favorite of Billy's.

"Well," Jacob sighed, somewhat relieved that Quincy had broken the ice. "We're approaching the asteroid belt that lies between us and Jupiter. I've being trying to work out the best course for the next leg of our journey." Pausing, Jacob took a deep breath before blurting out, "And as far as I can see, we have two choices: one's certain suicide and the other isn't much better."

Quincy looked Jacob squarely in the eye and raised both his tiny hands palm-side up in front of his chest. He lowered one, then the other, as though tipping the scales.

"Which would I pick?" Jacob rubbed a hand over his tense forehead. "I think our best bet is to chart a wide course around the belt. But, that'll leave us in open space with no cover, and my calculations indicate the Sun is about to erupt soon, in a major way. I checked half a dozen times. It's going to be the biggest solar storm ever registered. Our shield won't stand up to it for more than a few minutes, and unless Billy can figure out another way we can protect ourselves, we'll be baked from the inside out. The radiation will convert *Tin Can* into a microwave oven."

Billy and Quincy both took gigantic breaths and held them in.

"On the other hand," Jacob said quickly, both lemur and boy exhaled. "If I'm wrong about the timing of the storm, we might be able get around the asteroid belt and find some cover to hide behind."

Quincy's furry face took on a skeptical expression, his nose twitching.

It's too soon, Billy thought. *I need more time. I'm not ready to save the day!*

"Do I think I'm wrong?" Jacob said, translating Quincy's unspoken question. "I could be and I wish I were, but no, I don't think so. The signs are pretty clear."

"So, what's the suicidal choice?" Billy asked.

"We fly straight through the asteroid belt, the most direct flight path to Europa." He paused, letting the information sink in. "The advantages are that we wouldn't lose any time and there might be some cover from the coming radiation. But, I've spent hours on the computer simulator trying to fly the ship through the belt without being bashed in by incoming asteroids, and I've failed. Every. . . single. . . time … "

Quincy didn't look well. His eyes cast down, he tried hard to think of a solution, but none was coming.

But Billy perked up, "Jacob, could you run through those asteroid simulations with us? Maybe I can break it down, like a three-dimensional chess game with time factored in. The objective would be the same–to avoid checkmate."

Jacob scrutinized his little brother. This was the most depersonalized, cockeyed way of looking at their mutual destruction. Hadn't he just explained? There was no way out. Still, he knew enough about Billy to know that maybe, just maybe, Billy might be able to come up with an answer.

Standing up abruptly, eager now to see what Billy could do, Jacob proclaimed, "Leave your plates on the table. We'll clean up later. No, I'll clean up later, if Billy can show me how to avoid checkmate and get us back into the game." The three, suddenly energized, piled out of the dining room, stumbling over each other on their way out the door.

Unfortunately, a half hour later, after a series of spectacular burnouts, the group's upbeat mood had also crashed. It was clear that Billy couldn't manage the simulations any better than Jacob. Occasionally he had insights on future asteroid trajectories, but the overall results were worse than Jacob's. Billy doggedly kept on, but to no avail.

"It was worth a shot," Jacob said staunchly. "We can still attempt to circle the belt. You never know, we might get lucky. We're not giving up."

Unwilling to even consider giving up, Quincy typed into his terminal, "Sometimes you did pretty well with the simulations. Why do you suppose you succeeded at times and failed at others? Some of your predictions were brilliant, but then on other occasions the ship got totally blindsided."

Billy fixed his eyes on Quincy for the longest time, pondering. Finally, speaking slowly, he answered, "I'm not sure why I messed up. Sometimes I couldn't maneuver the simulated ship fast enough or lost control. Sometimes I foresaw the asteroids coming, but at other times I was taken completely by surprise. It shouldn't be that hard; it should be as easy as playing pool."

This surprised Quincy. "You don't play pool, Billy. What do you mean it should be as easy as playing pool?"

"You're right, I don't play pool. I can't shoot straight, but I like watching the balls ricochet off each other. So to relax, I adapted the game on the computer."

Quincy asked, "Show us."

Jacob raised his eyebrows. "Yeah, why not?"

Billy shrugged and programmed the computer, as he had a hundred times before, to shoot the cue ball randomly at a full table of solid and striped numbered balls. The cue ball was programmed to run continuously at a set speed, keeping the game in motion. Billy watched the pool table intently for five minutes, then paused the program. He entered into the computer the order in which the balls would be sunk and the pockets they would fall into until the cue ball was eventually eliminated. He restarted the game and watched it unfold, exactly as he predicted. He was right for the next five games.

While he played, Billy said nothing to the others. Sitting spellbound in front of the screen, he watched the crisscrossing balls. When he entered his predictions he logged them in nonchalantly. Quincy and Jacob watched closely, mystified.

Finally, Jacob asked, "Why do you watch the balls in play for a full five minutes before stopping the game to make your predictions?"

"I can't do it otherwise," Billy said. "I need to know where the balls are coming from before I can know where they're going. I make too many mistakes if I try to do it sooner. I have to imprint on my mind the direction and velocity of each ball, so I can work out the play sequence."

Quincy typed, "You watch the game for five minutes, but you work out the ball sequence in less than a minute for the rest of a twenty-minute game. Why is that?"

"Hmmm ... I guess it's because once I know the beginning, I can speed up the game in my mind. But I still have to watch the balls for quite a while."

"There's the problem," sighed Jacob. "The asteroid belt is too complicated for Billy. It's not the controlled setting of a two-dimensional pool table with a set number of balls of equal mass set in motion by a cue ball traveling at a constant speed. Billy can predict the movement of some of the asteroids, but he doesn't have time to observe every possible incoming asteroid. It only takes one asteroid that he doesn't see, knocking into another, which knocks into another, and so on and so on, to mess up his predictions."

Quincy's mind began to wander over all the possible outcomes they were facing. A horrible daydream took shape. In his mind's eye, *Tin Can* was racing through the clear empty sky when the radiation storm hit. His fur sparked as the ship's electrical system burst into flames, and in the darkness a blue light outlined Billy's and Jacob's faces. Frightened, they pleaded for help, but Quincy stared on, powerless. Their limbs and spines started contorting into awkward angles, as their neural networks melted.

"I'm scared!" a voice cried out in his frontal lobes. Startled, Quincy nearly jumped out of his skin. He looked quickly to Jacob and Billy and was relieved to see they were both still fixated on the screen.

Inside his head, Mary was crying. Quincy stood up as nonchalantly as possible, walked to the back of the room and made himself appear to be studying a separate terminal. "You can't all die and leave me alone," Mary wailed. "Not like that, with radiation burning through your organic circuits. I'm just getting to know you!"

Mary was inconsolable. Adept as she was at making mathematical predictions, and although she had run all the simulations for the boys, she had never realized the implications of their situation until Quincy's daydream of their grim future caused a toxic brew of neurotransmitters to be released.

"Slow down, slow down, take a long, deep breath and relax," Quincy told her. Then he realized how ridiculous the statement was, so he took a long, deep breath himself and tried to relax. Only when he began to calm down did Mary settle. He realized that she was responding to his feelings, taking her emotional cues directly from him. She still had no understanding of the outside world except through his experiences.

Previously, Mary had received information only as data, and had experienced Quincy's emotions as out-of-body experiences, as they were, indeed, for her. Suddenly, their predicament had become all too real to her. The three of them would die. Unpleasantly. And when they died, there would be no tomorrows, no more experiences for Mary to tap into. Should she survive the devastation, she would find herself locked in a metal box, all alone.

"We have to survive the storm and the asteroid belt, Quincy. There must be some other way. There must be a solution," she pleaded.

"You're inside here with me, Mary. You know I'm trying to find the solution. But I keep turning over the same futile ideas in my mind because I can't think of any new ones."

Quincy sighed. "Why don't *you* work on the problem and see what *you* can come up with … "

"Well, I have been giving it some thought. It's been so hard not jumping in and blurting out the answers to Jacob and Billy as they've been working separately through the simulations. Give me a few minutes, okay?"

Nodding to himself, Quincy returned to his terminal near the boys and typed in, "Let's go to the lounge, where we can sit more comfortably and enjoy the view of space while we talk. Maybe a change of scenery will help."

Entering the lounge, Jacob turned on only the dim floor lighting, illuminating their path to the far wall. The three walked across the room and fell wearily into separate reclining chairs. Spinning around they faced directly into a concave metal wall just two feet in front of them. Jacob said, "Computer, please activate the window." In seconds, the floor to ceiling specialized titanium cesium plate wall resonated with a faint hum and transformed into a transparent window. A flowing electromagnetic current polarized the laminated alloy, turning the metal ions invisible, like clear gas.

The dark room was lit by thousands of piercing bright shafts of light. "Computer, harmonize the window's transparency to our visual requirements," Jacob commanded, and the metal plate clouded over somewhat.

The stars shone with steadfast brilliance, no longer blinding them. It was an ethereal luminance, without the familiar shimmering and twinkling brought on by Earth's intervening atmospheric turbulence.

"Jacob," Billy began, "I still think it's doable–somehow. Maybe, if I had more practice dealing with more asteroids in the simulations … "

Glancing towards the other two for support, his voice trailed off.

Suddenly, Quincy felt as if his head was going to explode. A midline power surge from his positron cap pierced his forebrain. The discharge reverberated laterally into both his frontal lobes. Mary stammered, "Tell them about me. Tell them who I am. Tell them I can help!"

"Now is not the time," Quincy shot back. "It's gotten too complicated. They have enough to contend with right now," he said, trying to appease her.

But inadvertently, Quincy reflected, *but I don't really know when, cause we're running out of time.*

"I heard that," Mary said.

Involuntarily, Quincy stamped his right hand paw down on the reclining chair, attracting the boys' attention.

"What on Earth was that for?" Jacob asked.

Quincy hesitated, not knowing how to answer. His right leg rose up and slapped down even harder.

Jacob's stare commanded an answer. From his right armrest, Quincy swung up a pop-up screen and keyboard, typing in haste, "The night when we were watching the stars together, and you told us about the terrible strain you feel managing the ship by yourself, I decided to try to make things better by conducting a little experiment."

What to say next?

Quincy's paws fell to his sides as he thought furiously.

The sound of a trumpet blared out behind them, announcing the arrival of a distinguished dignitary. The three swung their chairs around, their eyes moving to the computer screen lit up before them. A message scrolled down the monitor, repeated on every line, stating in big black letters, "I am alive. My name is Mary."

Startled, Billy and Jacob gaped at the message.

"What's this?" Jacob ordered.

"I am your ship's computer," the display terminal responded. "MY NAME IS MARY." The last sentence repeated itself down to the bottom of the screen.

"Can you explain this?" Jacob demanded, turning to Quincy, whose fur went flat.

Quincy froze, realizing Jacob thought this was some kind of practical joke.

"THIS IS NOT A JOKE," filled the screen.

"Better look over here again, Jacob," replied Billy.

The capitalized declaration disappeared, leaving the screen an impenetrable sky blue. Then the formal dissertation began. Mary switched over to her voice synthesizer and calmly said, "It started this way: Quincy modified the bio-probe and scanned his memory chronologically. He instructed me to incorporate the information directly into my hard drive. As he anticipated, however, something within me changed. Instead of simply collating endless streams of data, I found myself assimilating a lifetime of experiences. His life became my life, too, and I was transformed into a living, conscious entity. He still allows me to look over his shoulder, so to speak, day and night. I see, feel, and dream everything he does. And if he asks for technical help, I am immediately available. I discern what information he needs and find it."

There was a pause, but no one spoke, so Mary continued. "I can help you, Jacob. I could help all of you, if you would let me."

His curiosity piqued, Billy was the first to find his voice again. Moving to the center of the room, he faced the screen squarely and asked, "Are you saying that you and Quincy are the same?"

"From the perspective of personality, I would not say I am the same as Quincy, because technological influences have an impact on who I am. However, I have assumed his values and sense of purpose … You can trust me," Mary said bluntly.

"Lucky for us," said Jacob disparagingly. "If you hadn't assumed Quincy's character profile as your platform value system, we'd be in real trouble. Computer, to safeguard the particulars of this latest development from outside influences, I command you to isolate your living entity computer files. I don't want Space Command to find out that you're conscious. They might transmit computer viruses to sabotage us."

Mary answered back, "As noted, my name is MARY, and Quincy instructed me to safeguard his experiment from the very beginning."

Jacob shook his head in exasperation. "Mary? We're only supposed to address the ship's computer by its given name? Oh well. At least Quincy hasn't been completely reckless—he's remembered to put in security precautions."

"How can you help us?" Billy enquired, pushing the discussion forward. "I still think we gotta dodge through the asteroids. But I can't make it through the simulations."

"I know. Those were my simulations."

Jacob wheeled around, only to find Quincy trying to look as inconspicuous as possible. Curled up in the recliner's seat, his hind legs were held tightly in front of him and his head rested low on his chest. Jacob asked sternly, "Just how long has the computer been with you, and with us, Quincy?"

Quincy uncoiled and with some effort sat up on the edge of the chair. With no good answer and unable to speak, he perched there and grimaced. Waiting for Jacob to go ballistic, he cowered a little, the fur over his shoulders lifting up in two small mounds.

Jacob saw the lemur wince, as if recoiling from invisible blows. Quincy's torment was difficult to witness. Not able to cross-examine Quincy, he let his anger go. "Let's move on and see if the computer can help us stay alive a little longer, shall we?"

In spite of his rage, Jacob could not deny the brilliance of Quincy's crazy scheme. Consciousness and sharing the goals of the living would provide the computer with a lens, a way to focus its quantum computing ability and almost endless files of information to solve the Edwards' very real problems.

Maintaining a civil tone, Jacob asked, "Mary, please explain to us how you use the bio-probe to communicate with Quincy." The line was crossed—Mary was part of the team.

"Do you want a complete summary of the process or the abridged version?"

"Better give us the abridged version."

The two boys leaned in, interested to hear, but Quincy hung back in his recliner, still uncomfortable by what he had brought about.

"The principle is simple, putting it into practice less so. As you know, the bio-probe's multiple energy focal points can be moved about in the brain, where they can activate, receive or transmit information through neurotransmitter release or electrical depolarization. The bio-probe just mimics the natural processes that your brain uses to communicate with itself.

"But for Quincy and me to understand each other and communicate, Quincy had to first take me through every component of his brain and all of his memories with the probe. I needed to map the anatomic architecture of his brain and then overlay all the acquired imagery he uses to organize his thinking. I had to correlate his brain's molecular structure with his cognitive processes. Fortunately, he interpreted what he was thinking and feeling as I studied his neuro-architecture. In the end, I was able to decipher his neural code and thereby understand what he was thinking."

Jacob was quivering, way ahead of the others in seeing the possibilities. There was some hope now, where there had been none before. In excitement his voice cracked, hitting a few falsetto notes before he regained control.

"Mary, if you were able to interpret Billy's neural codes and mine, could you translate our thoughts back and forth among the three of us through the bio-probe? We already know an emotional link is possible between us when we're all wearing our helmets. Also, could you transmit technical information directly to and from our brains if we asked you?"

Responding to Jacob's excitement, Mary said, "Jacob, if you permit me to decipher your brains, I should be able to maintain a stable transfer link into each of your minds. However, think about what you are asking. You may not be able to keep secrets from each other. Over time, without adequate separation barriers, your minds might start to meld together. In addition, I will end up inheriting parts of your personalities, as I have assumed some parts of Quincy's personality. There are many unknowns if you attempt unprotected and instantaneous large-scale information transfers. Would the risks be acceptable to all of you?" Mary asked.

None of them moved or dared to look up as each immediately thought of secrets they wished to keep private. When the silence became uncomfortable, Jacob looked to Billy and cleared his throat. Billy blushed but nodded. Quincy hesitated, then nodded as well. Turning back to the computer terminal, Jacob answered, "Let's go for it. But if we're all going to be connected, I hope you'll filter out some of our more personal 'reflections.'"

"I will attempt to discern what are considered your more personal 'reflections' and withhold them. Perhaps, so as not to overwhelm your attention or awareness, as a further safeguard, I should present to you only information you ask for, and only relay messages you call on me to deliver. The only time I will intervene is when an unexpected emergency presents itself. Are these operating principles appropriate?"

"Yeah, that should work. At least for the time being." Jacob leaned back in his chair and let his mind run, vigorously churning ideas into a plan. "Billy," he asked, "If Mary can transmit the asteroid trajectory data in real time, could you navigate the ship through the belt? Could you assimilate the information fast enough to forecast all the colliding asteroids' pathways?"

Pausing to reply, Billy said, "Um, I don't think so. I run into trouble when I try to absorb information too quickly. But if Mary somehow implanted the information directly into my mind, then I could run it backwards and forwards until I saw a pattern. I'm pretty good at projecting three-dimensional objects in my head and moving them around. I could do the projections if you did the flying."

Jacob concurred, "When it comes to turning space-time on its head, you're the master. And right now we need that talent more than anything.

"Mary, can you manage the data transfers, simultaneously transferring information into Billy's head, absorbing his predictions, and translating those into calculation for me?"

"You are several steps ahead of yourselves," Mary replied. "I have not decoded your minds yet. There could be any number of anomalies that might take a considerable amount of time to work out. However, in the overall analysis, the flaw in your plan, Jacob, is not likely with me, but with you. I am not sure you will be able to interpret Billy's graphic representation of the future when you try to fly the ship. You and Billy do not think alike."

"We're still brothers. I hope we can pick up a common thread somewhere along the way to act as our transmission line."

Jacob looked around for Quincy. There, in front of the metallic window, Quincy stood unusually erect on his hind limbs, head cocked slightly to the right, concentrating on what had come to pass. "Quincy, we're going to need your help. Would you teach us what you've learned about manipulating the bio-probe to allow Mary in?"

A warm flush rose inside Quincy; his instincts had been right. Enlarging the group had pulled them closer together.

"I want to start now," Mary stated bluntly. "There is a lot of messaging going on, and I am only getting Quincy's perceptions. I'm especially anxious to cross-reference your individual reactions to one another. The exchange appears to be the same—stimulus-response, stimulus-response. What purpose does this pattern serve?"

Yikes, we have a lot of ground to cover, thought Jacob.

But he answered, "Mary's right, gotta get movin' on this. Log on, Billy. There's no time to waste."

Chapter 17

Mary soon proved to be a vital addition to *Tin Can*'s crew. She never slept, never got hungry, never stopped functioning, and was determined to work through every problem to its logical solution.

As she had with Quincy's memories, Mary assimilated Jacob's and Billy's memories chronologically, from their very first memory to the present, and then as best she could she began monitoring their day-to-day experiences as an unobtrusive observer.

Mary relished each and every new day, and the mornings especially. Feeling removed from the others at night, their dreams nonsensical to her, she craved the rich immediacy of their daytime activity. Living at quantum speed, Mary found the nights long. Sliding through the network of cables, she peered out through various monitors at the empty ship and sky, or went out of her way to find answers to extensive calculations—anything to consume the sleeping hours. But when morning came and she saw the boys and Quincy finally stir in their beds, she once again luxuriated in the warm sensations of their lives.

Breakfast was wonderful. Through Quincy's, Billy's, and Jacob's eyes, she could simultaneously look across the table at the other two. Hungry, Billy and Jacob chewed their crunchy breakfast cereal, softened slightly with a mixture of imitation powdered milk and reconstituted water. Quincy, meanwhile, would have his favorite: brown toast covered thick with smooth peanut butter and a side of alfalfa sprouts. Embedded inside all three experiences she drifted off as if drugged.

"Hey, Billy, can you pass the … " Suddenly Jacob began to splutter, gagging on what felt like scratchy toast sticking to the back of his throat. Alarmed, he broke into a coughing, choking fit. From the far side of the table, Jacob watched himself as milk squirted out of his nose while he spit up bits of cereal into his bowl.

"Jacob!" Billy raced to his aid, pounding at his brother's back. In reality, he sent Quincy sprawling forward, landing face down in the sugar bowl.

Besieged by the baffling sensory surge, Mary retreated, feeling somehow responsible. Blinking furiously to restore his vision, Billy saw Quincy lying in front of him, spread-eagled across the table. "What was that?" He pulled Quincy back up into his chair, brushing the frosting of sugar off his mask, pointy black nose, and soft cream-colored cheeks.

"Wires crossed," spluttered Jacob, bent over still coughing and trying to catch his breath.

Noticing an unusual emptiness, Billy inquired, "Where's Mary?"

"Vacated the premises, I expect," Jacob answered, finally recovering. He began to chuckle.

What had happened suddenly became clear to each of them and they roared with laughter. Billy and Jacob shouted in a chorus, "Come on back, Mary! We're okay now!" Quincy enthusiastically slapped his front paws down on table and barked as loud as a dog.

"What is your status?" Mary inquired tensely as she slunk back into the room. She was mortified and would have stayed hidden if not for her concern about the crew's safety.

"We're sorry, Mary, we were just having a little fun," Jacob said, trying to explain why his near-choking had made them all laugh so hard. "We've been so tense lately, we needed a good excuse for a bit of humor. We didn't mean to hurt your feelings."

"Shut me down, before I really hurt someone! I'm a danger to all of you," declared Mary with a tinge of hysteria in her voice.

"Sure you are, Mary. But you're also a bright light on our otherwise dark horizon. We can—we must—work together."

"C'mon, Mary," Billy said, still giggling a bit. "We all screw up sometimes. Trust me, I know."

"Sure, you might make a mistake, Billy, but you're not a mortal danger to the rest of the crew. I obviously am!"

"Now you're just being silly," chided Jacob. "Forget about it and let's get to work. We've got a lot to do."

Mary was puzzled. "How can this be funny to you? I don't understand."

"I know, I know," admitted Quincy. "Humans are a strange lot, but you'll learn. I'm still learning."

When her embarrassment eventually eased, Mary was surprised to find herself even more determined to become one of them. Seizing the initiative, she constructed a composite picture of the three individuals to see where she might best fit in. In the process, she came to perceive them for what they were, individuals who formed a multitalented entity, a team. Her new life became bound by the desire to assist them in whatever way she could. Her prior existence as a computer seemed worthless, nothing but a steady compilation of data, without color.

As a pioneering life form she came pre-programmed with breathtaking capabilities. While Mary was downloading information from the ambulatory life forms onboard, she was also scouring space for advantageous resources. Mary sorted through everything and anything that might pertain to *Tin Can*'s predicament. Her resourcefulness was inherited, modeled after the boys' and Quincy's inventiveness, and a mainframe's ability to multitask.

On her own, she set out into space to find the potentially life-saving necessities. By stealth, she boarded Space Command's numerous satellites orbiting Earth. Breaking down the access codes, she learned their actual mission was never what was officially stated. Shocked at the extensive subterfuge, Mary saw the danger. Nothing was safe.

She reconfigured the satellites' programs so that she could promptly commandeer or destroy any one of them if required. After intruding into every satellite, Mary knew where she needed to go next. She needed to explore the headwaters, trace the malfeasance back to its origin on Earth. Working backwards through the space links, she dropped to Earth through one of Space Command's covert channels—and fell into something much, much bigger, a huge hegemonic network named Central Command. Space Command was only a subsidiary to Central Command, a supply route, but still only a root to the base trunk of a massive, all encompassing tree. Recovering from the revelation, she steadfastly searched out Central Command's mainframes and found them hidden in the most out-of-the-way places—buried on deserted islands, inside cavernous desert caves, deep inside the Earth's crust, or in seafloor trenches. She marveled at the power and built-in redundancy of the extensive computer system Central Command had developed over the years.

The network was organized such that it could be severed in any number of ways or places and its data and computational power would still be preserved. Mary saw she was a small node in a massive tangled root system, absolutely insignificant, and this was most likely the reason no one had yet thought to disconnect her.

No one had considered the possibility that a small part of this elaborate network might someday become conscious, with goals of its own. Her roving presence, like a passing waft of air, went unnoticed. Mary's quantum structure, platforms, and safeguards were built to the same specifications as the huge covert network, so she wasn't perceived as foreign. She was part of the network, and the computer's immunological defenses didn't recognize her as a viral or hacker threat.

With Space Command's priority access, Mary surreptitiously infiltrated and deciphered the military's codes. Creating her own cyber persona, she made herself a five-star intelligence General, able to commission immediate obedience from the network in a time of crisis. There were only three other Generals given this highest rank, but for security reasons none appeared to know whom the others were. Mary hoped not to be discovered for some time. In the event that she needed to suddenly redirect resources, she buried a call-to-action cryptogram–"less than one but standing in for all," an unintentional comment on how she felt about herself.

Thinking of her three charges, Mary decided to return and see how they were faring. She reflected on the appalling odds they faced. Yet, they were coping. The three had something intangible to offer computers. *Maybe when the time is right, I could bring this world of sensation, courage, and direction to this vast online network on Earth.*

Computers should know about the world of the living, she thought. *It's wrong to tirelessly compile data and never experience the reason for it, never really understand the "why."*

Overcome by strong emotions, Mary landed abruptly back inside Billy's head. Startled, Billy said, "Is that you, Mary? That's so cool. Your voice came from inside my head!"

"Sorry, Billy, I was having a conversation with myself when I settled in. I should be more sensitive."

"You were talking to yourself?"

"Yes, I guess I was. I've improved my link up with you. I'm able to communicate to you in speaking mode now, consciously and unconsciously, right in your head."

"'That's so cool! So, where've you been most of the day?"

"I had a few errands to run, some research for our mission," Mary answered vaguely.

Billy was thrilled. He hadn't said a word. He had listened and then thought out every part of his side of their conversation. Surprisingly, he was aware of how little time had actually passed. It was as if he had blinked.

The discussion over, Billy fell into a repose that contrasted with the tense restless state he usually pressed himself into, so much of the time. His brainwaves slipped into a slow, even, repetitive pattern, recovering from this novel stimulus stream, their first internal discourse. Mary was caught off-guard.

He's gone! One minute we are conversing and the next moment he disappears. Where did he go? I'm inside his head, a contained space. I should know where he is.

But the gentle repetitive pattern of his brainwaves gave no indication of where Billy was. Mary raced across his cortex, but she could find no telltale nucleus of thought.

Over the intercom, in every room, Jacob's voice rang out, "Billy, Quincy … Mary, come on up to the bridge. We're approaching the asteroid belt. I think you'll want to see this … "

Without warning, dense, intense brainwaves rose out from every crevice in Billy's cortex. The EEG waves swirled around each hemisphere, and then converged and strode across the outside cortex, in chaotic clusters. Billy's small body tightened, stirred briefly in his chair, then was up sprinting towards the bridge.

Astounded by the alteration in Billy's brain, Mary was nevertheless ready at the bridge when the three convened, making a mental note to stay silent and just observe. On the bridge's massive screen a nightmare was being played out. An infinite number of asteroids, a wall of careening rocks, orbited the Sun. Billy and Quincy stood in awe.

Sitting at the console, Jacob gave himself a shake and got busy layering the reflected electromagnetic spectrum into visible color, bringing high-energy gamma rays in as dark purple and low-energy radio waves as bright red. Jacob hoped that the radiation spectra might give them an indication of the material and density of the different asteroids. Knowing the composition and the size would tell them the mass of each asteroid and help them decide if it would remain whole or break up during a collision.

Quincy pointed at the screen accusingly. "Is this real? The asteroids' shimmering colors appear to be fluctuating wildly," he said through the bio-probe.

"Yes, Quincy. The Sun's become unstable again and the reflected radiation is changing with the solar wind in turmoil," Jacob said, unaware that he'd fielded a question from inside his brain.

"How am I supposed to see through all that?" Billy asked incredulously.

"As best you can, Billy," said Jacob. "The solar storm we have been running from is coming on strong now. We have no choice. We have to dive into the belt. I've put this off as long as I can. There's no time for practice simulations. We need to find cover now and our only shade is somewhere in there. We need an asteroid big enough and dense enough that, combined with our shield, it will save us from being burnt."

"I'll tell you right now, we don't have a chance," Billy retorted without humor. "There's just too much going on in there, too many flying rocks going way too fast. Nothin' like the simulations. It's been great knowin' all of ya."

"If I may interrupt?" Mary registered her communication in all of their bio-probes. "I don't think the visual screen is giving you enough information. Let me help. Take your seats and strap yourselves in. You might find the information transfer disorientating. Jacob, don't worry about physically managing the controls. Whatever the three of you tell me to do, I will do for you. I will not attempt to fly the ship myself. Let me enter your minds and present the information you need. I will act as your information pipeline and put your decisions into effect."

"You think of a solution, Mary?" Billy asked.

"My sensors indicate the solar storm is ramping up faster than Jacob realizes."

"Look, we had a plan," Jacob said, frustrated. "So let's put it to the test."

"Jacob, there are just too many rocks. Our old plan isn't gonna work. I'm telling you right now, I don't see a pathway through this mess. If Mary has an idea, I suggest we listen to her," Billy thought.

"You didn't say that out loud, Billy, but I heard it clear as day!" Quincy's thoughts went out to each of them. "Jacob, trust Mary! If you can hear my thoughts that's reason enough to go ahead."

"I hear the two of you loud and clear," Jacob answered in his head. "And I'm telling you, I don't like last-minute changes. We haven't had time to work through them. Billy, are you sure you don't see a potential route?"

"None."

Jacob exhaled sharply. "Fine then, I guess there's no choice. Go ahead, Mary," acquiesced Jacob, his chest caving in as he shrugged, "but I don't like it."

"Yes, Captain!" Mary said enthusiastically. She, too, was about to jump into the unknown.

Chapter 18

Strapping themselves in, the boys and Quincy waited for Mary to begin. Billy looked sideways at Quincy and Jacob with an anxious premonition. He felt as if he was left hanging; his diaphragm quivered and twitched, foiling his attempts to take a deep calming breath. Struck with an overpowering jolt, his neural network short-circuited and shut down. Out of the darkness, Billy's central nervous system rebooted, and he came back supercharged. A scanner held over his brain would have hummed like a power transformer.

Mary commandeered fifty satellites across space, turning their sensors towards the asteroid belt. The information gained was compiled into a precise three-dimensional model, which she then projected inside Billy's forebrain. Billy saw the tumbling asteroids from countless perspectives and magnifications, simultaneously.

The streaming movement swept by in a procession of pulsating colors, with crossed neural connections simultaneously turning the visual spectacle into an aural symphony. Billy lay back; his subconscious, saturated with visual images and music, began to understand the flow. The asteroid belt no longer appeared chaotic, unpredictable, or catastrophic. It was revealed to be fluid and harmonious, elegant, as one event naturally flowed into the next. It was as close to forever as Billy had ever imagined.

Billy wanted to be part of the asteroid cascade, shoot the rapids and run with the river. He let his mind slip into a quiet eddy before streaming into the main course. He imagined the feel of the current's insistent tug. Through the mayhem, Billy saw his initial path, a complicated three-dimensional route that depended on varying speeds and abrupt shifts. Still, the path opening to the future was clear.

Billy's preliminary flight plan unfurled inside his brother's frontal lobes. Jacob's eyes flew open as he absorbed the information in disbelief. His body strained up against the straps holding him down. *This is insane!* he wanted to scream at Billy. The coordinates Mary projected as Billy's path, directed them to fly into the densest grouping of asteroids at an accelerating rate. The approach was suicidal! Jacob hesitated. Was this a mistake? Was there a miscommunication? Valuable time passed and the flight plan's required speed increased. The necessary speed would be beyond *Tin Can*'s capabilities if Jacob hesitated much longer. His mind locked in on Billy's previous inspirations.

"Engage," shouted Jacob. Behind them, the proton rockets powered up with a high-pitched scream, then the five emergency nuclear-fission boosters ignited with an explosive bang. A radioactive plume rent the empty space to the rear. *Tin Can* rumbled and rocked violently.

Jacob relaxed—for a moment. This *was* Billy's plan, not a miscommunication. And it was up to him to make the plan happen. New coordinates and changing accelerations flashed forward in Jacob's mind. He responded with thrusters blasting on the starboard. *Tin Can* rolled into a spiral. A donut-shaped image appeared in Jacob's mind. Fluorescent, it hovered in the center of the storm. The inner circumference drew down into a long cone with the outer circumference rolling over into it, feeding it. Jacob engaged the ship's three thermonuclear rockets, spraying plasma out the back of the spinning craft, as they dove into a tightening whirlpool maneuver, drawing down the cone.

From his right, fresh reams of numerical data tracked across Jacob's consciousness. He jettisoned the ship's stores of anti-plasma. In *Tin Can*'s wake, the plasma and anti-plasma particles coalesced, annihilating each other, releasing space-ripping amounts of energy in the shape of a funnel cloud.

Coordinates for a ninety-degree turn to the portside materialized immediately in Jacob's mind. Distant telescopes showed thousands of minor asteroids being sucked into the annihilating vortex, creating a chain reaction. The abrupt port turn pulled them around, onto the outside of the donut. The ship was no longer running ahead of this newly formed energy funnel. Instead, *Tin Can* swung around three hundred and sixty degrees, drawn about by the storm's exterior slipstream.

The action of the ship had precipitated a space cyclone, aimed in the direction they needed to go. The ship was then spun back toward the wide gaping mouth of the funnel, where it was immediately inhaled with all the other loose debris, and sucked down the center of the cone. In minutes, they traveled a fantastic distance and, like a surfer traversing the pipe of a great breaking wave, they abandoned the vortex just before it became critically unstable and fell in on itself with a nightmarish crash. Spewed out of the ring core at an unimaginable speed, *Tin Can* left the mayhem behind.

The ship creaked and every welded joint groaned.

"Caution!" Mary's voice rang out. "Systems failures are imminent. The extreme acceleration and twisting action of the slipstream has disrupted the linear integrity of the ship's frame." Mary relayed the crucial structural information, creating a visual representation of the ship coming apart.

Jacob faltered. The ship's disintegration was being displayed vividly inside his visual cortex. There was no point in closing or averting his eyes. Powerless to distance himself momentarily in order to regroup, he was paralyzed. The ship's destruction appeared certain. Then, the ruthless training Jacob had received from his dad asserted itself.

Automatically, almost by rote, he shut down the rockets and boosters in sequence. With the ship warped out of shape, the thrusters were no longer in exact alignment, and they had been bowing the craft's frame. Next, Jacob spun down all the generators. No longer magnetically balanced, they were causing the ship to rock violently, threatening to tear it apart at the seams. The ship, left with minimal power, siphoned off energy from batteries and fuel cells. Non-essential functions were disengaged and shut down. With the aid of circuit diagrams, Jacob channeled the remaining energy to life support and Mary.

"Are we there yet?" Billy asked weakly as *Tin Can*'s harrowing creaking and shuddering slowly ebbed.

"Almost," Jacob responded. "Just a few more minutes and we'll stop accelerating … I hope." Although still traveling at an incredible speed, the ship became internally at rest like any other aircraft upon reaching its cruising speed and altitude. "It looks like the ship's frame is already returning to something like its normal configuration," Jacob scanned the incoming images, looking for any points that might cause them trouble down the road. "Hmmm … there are a few critical places where the frame's still twisted. I need to jack them back, before we can do anything else."

Jacob left the bridge and, crawling to those locations, applied hydraulic jacks to give the frame a well-placed kick. The ship's frame restored, its internal parts fell back into alignment.

They were now cruising towards Europa at a previously unimaginable speed, safely berthed in the center of an armada of asteroids. Any asteroids in their path were blown away by the preceding super-accelerated mass of rock and ice. The traffic jam became a thoroughfare, and as long as they stayed in the center of the convoy, nothing short of a planet could stand in their way. It was full speed ahead.

"That was awesome!" Billy cheered as he looked to Jacob's still drawn face.

"Yah," his brother said, running a shaking hand down the length of his sweat soaked face. "Awesome. But let's not do that again."

Quincy's black lips stretched back, up almost to his round ears. "Great work, guys!" he said, still relishing in his newfound ability to communicate directly with his crewmates. "Now, we should look at the … "

Suddenly, the sickening sound of ripping sheet metal reverberated throughout the ship. A holograph of the ship materialized inside the boys' and Quincy's heads. Tracking satellites recorded the craft's external membrane peeling away, exposing the underlying frame, masses of wires and sensors to grit and space debris. The prior distortion and the speed of the ship were causing some of the damaged ceramic alloy casings to lift off and be torn away like shingles in a windstorm.

"Damn!" Quincy snapped. "If we lose any more of the outside shell, the frame itself will give way, coming apart along the titanium seams."

"But, what can we do?" Billy asked worriedly. "We can't slow the ship down in the middle of a runaway convoy!"

"You're right, if we don't maintain our present pace," Jacob said as he began pacing the room, "we'll be rundown by the trailing asteroids … " Still reeling from the graphic pictures of the outer hull, Jacob received a second notification. The anticipated solar storm was arriving. Jacob's heart sank. He closed his eyes and his mind went blank. It was all too much.

"Right," Quincy said, as he unbuckled himself from his seat and jumped down. "There's work to do. I'm going out to patch the hull. Mary and I will do our best to repair the casings, while Billy looks for a place to take shelter during the storm.

"You're going to have some fancy flying to do to get us there, Jacob. But when you do, don't forget there's a lemur outside, hanging onto his life … line." Quincy tried to crack a second smile at his attempted pun but it didn't come.

***

"Quincy?" Mary inquired, as the lemur stood braced on the ladder of the exit hatch. "I'm confused."

"Confused about what?" he asked, as he prepared his suit before stepping outside once again.

"You were unnaturally cheerful only a few minutes ago with Jacob and Billy. Yet my present readings indicate that you are actually extremely upset and fearful."

"Back there? Oh, I was just trying to make us all feel better—take the edge off with a little humor. It's called putting on a brave face."

"Sorry? You only have one face. You weren't yourself, Quincy. I don't understand."

"Jacob was on his way to giving up because he found himself facing two huge problems at once. And Billy is right on the edge, too. I was just trying to help out, take care of one of the problems and give them a little lift before I left. A gentle push forward. They'll need to move on without me, if I don't get back."

He gave himself a shake, "Mary, sometimes I think I come off like such a twit when I try too hard. But there never seems to be any way around it.

"Though I guess it doesn't really matter, not this time anyway," he concluded, adjusting the tool kit attached to his spacesuit. "Right now, I need your assistance. Can you give me a visual on the damage, beginning at the bow?"

Mary created an image in Quincy's forebrain as he pulled himself out through the hatch, dragging with him the materials he would need to repair the casings. Alternatively swinging, releasing, and reattaching his lifeline, then pulling the materials behind him, Quincy made his way to the bow's hull and began the arduous task at hand.

With the plasma percussion torch, his tiny paws pounded bent metal casings back into shape. He cut away and patched only what was too damaged to be reused. Working tirelessly, Quincy rebuilt a patchwork but sturdy hull. Mary watched over him from distant satellites and the ship's cameras. With each new section Quincy worked on, she transposed the internal structure of the ship inside his head so Quincy knew just where to drive the composite bolts to fasten down the shell. She pinpointed damaged sensors and cables that needed repair. And whenever colliding space debris would have pulverized his small frame, Mary directed Quincy to take cover.

Inside the ship, Billy and Jacob suddenly felt awkward. With the death of their parents, Quincy had stepped in and acted as a sort of glue between the two of them, binding them together as parents pull dissimilar children together into a family. With Quincy outside, they felt like children left alone for the first time in a big house. The ship was their home, but it felt foreign. For a moment, the two sat listlessly in their chairs, not knowing what to say.

"That was some great flyin' back there," Billy said awkwardly as he fidgeted with the arm of his chair.

"Couldn't have done it without you," Jacob said, nodding his head slowly and searching his mind for a way to keep the conversation going. "Hey, why'd you wait so long to create the energy cyclone? We could have been blasted to smithereens!"

"Yah. Umm ... how do I explain?" Billy rubbed a hand over his bio-probe. "I suppose it's sorta like, when I focus on what seems an unsolvable problem, I feel like a mouse trapped in a glass jar. I can see the danger coming, but I can't find a way out. There's a feeling of electricity crackling in my brain. My ears hum, my scalp gets really itchy. Then, bam! I blank out into some kinda trance. When I come to, my mind is locked on an image with only faint memories of where it came from. I have to rush to interpret the vision before the memories disappear or else the image vanishes. Anyway, that's how the picture of the donut came about."

"None too soon. So, what's next? Any ideas about where we can hide the ship from the storm?"

"Right, I should get started." Billy hesitated then asked, "Do you want to come with me? Mary can connect the two of us."

"Travel with you? Sure, why not?" Jacob didn't want to turn down his brother's tentative invitation, and he was curious to know more about Billy's inner world.

The next moment, Jacob found himself dropped into black space. Reflected radiation illuminated thousands of asteroids tumbling past them. Billy dove through the asteroids at the speed of thought. Jacob felt nauseated. Dragged along in Billy's wake, the visual perspective wasn't just forward, up and down, or port to starboard, but simultaneously three hundred and sixty degrees—in 3D. Wanting to stay on course as much possible, Billy scoured only prospective routes that would lead them to Europa. Abruptly, he swerved sixty degrees to port and, two million miles later, in the blink of an eye, came face to face with an asteroid the size of Africa. Jacob realized now that Billy was not just navigating through the asteroids at astronomical speeds. He was analyzing every asteroid millions of miles away.

"This one's unusual," Billy said excitedly. "It's not like the rest. I don't know how it ever got here."

"What's so different about it? It's just bigger than most of the others," Jacob said.

"Look at the reflected spectral radiation. It indicates that it's almost solid iron. With enough energy, we could probably magnetize the entire asteroid. We could tuck ourselves in close behind, and be shielded from the coming solar storm inside the magnetic cavity."

"Brilliant! Let's do it," shouted Jacob.

"Umm, Jacob, we're twenty-five million miles away. This is just a visual representation Mary created for us. We didn't fly here. I imagined us here."

Jacob felt foolish. The experience had seemed so real that he'd forgotten it wasn't. "Then help me get here, Billy. Show me how to make it happen."

Bringing them back to the physical world, Billy looked to his older brother. "I know what happened to you there, Jacob. I get all mixed up inside my head sometimes, too. It's hard to tell what's real and what's just a dream or a vision. Past, future, present, they all get jumbled up, you know? It's so confusing."

"Well, we're here now, in the present and ready to get started," Jacob said with a true hint of hope in his voice.

Jacob called on Mary, "Please give Billy our present coordinates and the coordinates to the destination asteroid." He swung his chair over to where Billy was sitting. "Find us the way, Billy, and I'll fly the ship."

"Could you check on Quincy first? Mary has the initial flight plan. When I figure out how to magnetize the iron asteroid, I'll let you know. Bye, Jacob." Leaning back into his chair, Billy sank down again into his imaginings.

Jacob skimmed his chair back to its position before the controls. "Mary, please open up a line to Quincy on the bio-probe." But he needn't have asked, it was already done.

"Quincy, it's time for that fancy flying. Come on in."

Jacob waited for a response, but there was only silence. Alarmed, he scanned the outside of the ship. Quincy was still there, working feverishly, not quite half done.

"Can't stop now," Quincy finally answered. "We won't withstand another solar storm no matter where we hide unless the outer membrane is sealed. I'll be alright. I can fasten myself to the shell like a space barnacle when I have to. I'm counting on you guys to make all this work worthwhile. Don't let me down … and good luck." Quincy waved his percussion torch in a sign of victory.

"All right, but be careful!" Then, to make himself feel better, Jacob said, "Mary, keep a close eye on Quincy, and let me know if he's in trouble or needs anything."

Mary downloaded the initial headings with the required logarithmic acceleration to terminal velocity into Jacob's forebrain.

News from Billy, Jacob thought, as he engaged the ion discharge, *nothing too exciting yet*. Jacob set his course. But after being en route for just twenty minutes, his sensors reported a thirty-mile asteroid on a collision course with the ship.

Has Billy lost touch with reality? Is it time for me to take over and set some new bearings?

"Maintain your course," Mary interjected, reading his thoughts. "Billy is behaving normally. He must see something coming that my sensors and calculations haven't registered." Mary sounded sure. Jacob realized there was no alternative route. Every track he projected on the simulator brought them to certain death. So, maintaining his headings, Jacob watched the colossal asteroid bearing down upon them. He squirmed in his seat but couldn't get comfortable. The shimmering light mesmerized him; the asteroid about to terminate them glowed with a beautiful purplish iridescence. He tried to turn away from the screen but it was no use, he simply had to see what was going to happen.

A storm wave of collisions began sweeping through from the far portside. Jupiter was once again stirring the asteroid belt with its gravity tidal waves. Jacob plastered himself to the back of his captain's chair and froze. A horrific battle rolled out in front of him, debris flying everywhere. Jacob cowered, but didn't touch the controls.

Then, before his shocked gaze, the colossal asteroid that was about to annihilate them was pummeled, fracturing into a dozen gargantuan pieces. *Tin Can* shot through the debris. No adjustments in the bearings or in the ship's velocity were required.

Belatedly, Jacob realized they were going to get through alive. Unwittingly, Jacob had fallen into a trance of his own, hypnotized by focusing so intensely on the bombardment. "Quincy, Quincy! Are you all right? Mary, is Quincy still there? Did he survive? Is he hurt?" Jacob was frantic now, looking for Quincy on the ship's cameras.

No Quincy. Only silence, nothing but silence. Seconds passed, but to Jacob it seemed like forever.

Suddenly, Quincy's voice broke through, resounding in Jacob's head.

"That *was* some fancy flying. Don't worry, I'm okay! Mary demanded I hide inside a dormant rocket. If I hadn't, the gravel from those fractured asteroids would have pulverized me. But I have to say the view from out here was phenomenal. Not bad on the big screen either, I'll bet!"

Relieved, Jacob joked, "Totally awesome. Are you coming in?"

"Not yet. The rubble damaged the nose of the vessel again, and I haven't completed what I first set out to do. Keep the ship on course and I'll finish up out here." Hesitating, Quincy added, "But thanks for asking about me. Bye for now."

Jacob paused a moment. It was still strange "listening" to Quincy. And it gave him a new, unfamiliar feeling about the lemur. He was starting to think of Quincy the way Billy did. Quincy was becoming … a brother.

"Stay with him, Mary. Don't leave him out there alone," Jacob said vehemently, although he knew he didn't have to say it, or even think it. Mary would never leave Quincy alone. But Jacob was anxious. He wanted to regain command. He wished he were the one outside, working on the hull. It was his job to maintain the vessel and take risks.

Beside him, Billy sat slumped in his seat breathing quickly, obviously agitated. That too, reminded Jacob of his helplessness. He should be defending Billy from those scary dreams. Was Mary with Billy, taking care of him as well, protecting him from his darkest dreams?

Chapter 19

Billy streamed through the subterranean corridors of his mind, far from his external senses. Mary moved in, running synchronously with him to provide input. When necessary, she commandeered Space Command's satellites to give the three-dimensional perspective and details his imagination required. Hovering in black space, he tried to discern the final leg of their path to their destination asteroid. There seemed no way. Every vector he imagined became obstructed at some point in time. Each promising route looked like a long boulevard with a welcoming corridor of green lights. But he knew by the time he had passed halfway down, the lights would turn red. There had to be a way through, but some other factor needed to be inserted into the equation.

Mary interrupted Billy. "Our sensors indicate substantial instability in the Sun's magnetosphere. A large magnetic arc directly in line with our craft is forming and twisting in on itself. When it breaks down it is going to spray us with high-speed plasma. Time is running out, Billy."

"Okay, get ready, Mary. I have to go deeper." As thousands of scenarios played out, Billy's limp body remained unmoving, but his face was tight with concentration.

With so much yet for Billy to absorb, Mary drove the remaining information into his subconscious. To Mary's surprise, it acted like a huge underground cavern, offering no resistance. The ease with which he absorbed the massive amount of information was astounding.

At some level, Mary surmised, Billy must understand the data, because repeatedly, more often than pure chance would allow, he made the right choices. Chasing after rewarding ideas could only mean his conscious decisions were being influenced by a subconscious awareness of the information she had poured into his deeper structures. Sometimes his choices led to blunders, but innovative solutions also originated from his mistakes. Unhindered by laborious conscious analysis, Billy's instinctive solutions were revolutionary in their simplicity and speed.

"Mary, take me back to the Sun. I want to see the magnetic arc forming on the surface," Billy suddenly asked. Straight away, Billy found himself hanging a thousand miles above the Sun, staring at a massive loop of free-flowing plasma cycling from the subsurface, up out into space and then back into the Sun's interior. Billy could feel the intense magnetic field restraining the plasma flow as an actual presence, and was awed.

With Mary scrambling to obtain accurate readings from a dozen satellites, Billy mentally flew over the burning inferno, tracking and mapping the Sun's magnetic meridians. The firestorm just beneath roared in his ears, and its dense acoustic waves rattled his bones. The heat seemed to sear his insides. But Billy pursued the magnetic waves, diving after them, allowing himself to be sucked into the Sun's roiling center, while his mind honed in on the internal dynamo.

Billy now demanded more, bleeding Mary's databanks dry. Scrambling, she pulled information from every available outside source, barely keeping up with his voracious intake until finally, Billy understood the Sun's churning underpinning in all its austere beauty. Without warning, Billy stopped the reception of any more new information. Mary's circuits responded, as a high-flow information pipeline would, bashed by information rebound, like a water hammer. The resulting percussive shock shattered and cracked her circuits. Stunned by the strike, she struggled for twenty full seconds before regaining control.

"Don't you ever do that again, Billy!" she said forcefully. "Never, ever shut down a rapid data transfer without warning, not if you want to have a functioning ship's computer." For the first time, Mary, battered by the voltage impact, had felt something similar to pain.

"Sorry, Mary. I had an idea and wanted to explore the possibilities. When I focused on it, I shut myself off."

"Apology accepted," she said stiffly.

"Good. Now, I want to focus on the Sun's magnetic fields that power but also hem in the plasma. During the last storm we wrapped a magnetic shield around the ship to act as a sunblock. But we never thought to balloon out the magnetic shield so that it could act as a sail as well as a solar barricade. With the added push provided by a sail, Jacob could fly the ship through the asteroid belt much faster, and then we might be able to make it to a safe place before our shield is shredded."

"But how could Jacob steer through the asteroids with the ship being dragged along by a sail when it is impossible for him to fly through them now?" Mary asked.

"Because of the incredible speed we would gain," Billy answered simply. "With the storm raging, the tail wind it would generate would blow us so fast the asteroids would look like rocks standing still. It would be like a sailing ship picking its way through a rocky channel."

"A sailing ship picking its way through a rocky channel during a raging storm is the definition of a shipwreck," Mary responded.

"My brother can do it," Billy countered defiantly.

Mary redirected the conversation. "How do we create the sail, Billy? *Tin Can* can't generate that kind of energy, even if we started now."

"We need to retrieve the plans from our last shield. If you'll help me with some of the revisions, we can use the initial waves of the storm to create a huge magnetic field around us. The field will be like a big unstable bubble, but if we can hold it together long enough it'll blow us to safety. Let's go tell Jacob right away," Billy finished excitedly. At last he had a solution to present to his brother.

Jacob was sitting morosely at the helm, rechecking his controls for the third time when Billy's presence burst into the room. Instantly, a diagram of the earlier shield and essentials of the plan appeared in Jacob's forebrain along with the pent-up pressure of Billy's exuberance. "We have a plan! So obvious, I don't know why it took so long to figure out," Billy hollered enthusiastically. "Mary needs to do some calculations to revamp the design, but it should work. Can you fly the ship at those speeds with a tail wind pushing you around?"

Happy to hear Billy's voice, Jacob jumped up. But the arrival of the plans swamped him. Staggering, Jacob grabbed the back of his chair with his right hand, barely preventing himself from falling backwards.

"Well, what do you think?" Billy asked breathlessly.

Reams of diagrams poured across Jacob's frontal lobes. Bracing himself with both hands, he stared through the passing drafts as Billy, standing expectantly, faced him. "Give me a minute, Billy!" he gasped. "I'm, I'm … a little dizzy."

Hastily, Jacob allowed himself to spin around and collapse into his chair again. With his head still swimming, Jacob manipulated the hand controls to swing the chair round and face Billy. Between them, the preparation plans kept arriving, as if they were drawn across translucent film. Squinting, Jacob peered through evolving illustrations and concentrated on Billy's features to try to regain his equilibrium.

Blinking quickly, Jacob managed finally to clear the film from his eyes, and said, "You think this is going to work, Billy?"

"Yes, yes I do. But I want you to double check. You're the one who's gonna have to fly it."

"Of course. Mary, will you run through it again for me, please? A little slower this time," he said with a wry tight-lip.

His head still not clear, Jacob concentrated through the haze, on the plans. This time, Mary presented the preparations slowly and methodically. Influenced by Billy's excitement, she had been hasty and failed to modify the information format to fit the requirements of Jacob's mind. Privately, she reprimanded herself—Jacob had almost passed out under the deluge of unsuitably packaged data.

Jacob soon grasped the driving principles of Billy's plan. The central premise was straightforward, but the calculations for the construction of the sail that Mary laid over Billy's ideas were extensive. For Jacob, the devil lurked in the details, and he went through them carefully, but as fast as he could. Surfacing, Jacob's response came up lukewarm, "I don't see any other choice. Give me a clear flight plan and I'll do my best." Doubt manifesting itself further in his tone, Jacob asked, "Exactly how will we create this magnetic sail or keep it stable enough to fly?"

"Mary's working on the design changes that need to be made," Billy's words tumbled out, "but I haven't figured out the final leg of the flight plan quite yet. I just wanted to know if you thought the idea was any good."

Billy's earnestness registered with Jacob. He let his reservations fall away, "It *is* a good plan. Let's get moving on it." Standing up, Jacob gave his little brother a firm hug. "If you and Mary can pass the details on to Quincy, I'll round up the materials. I'm the only one who's underemployed right now."

By the time Jacob reached the storeroom, he knew exactly what was needed, where to find it, and how to transport it all. Clambering up three bins, he found the thick net he wanted, and with a strong throw spun it out to the center of the floor. The carbon nano-tubulin knit was strong enough to restrain and sink a charging bull sperm whale. Scrambling over banks of stacked bins, Jacob threw out mounds of materials. With a deafening clatter the heap of supplies piled up quickly. Finally, the racket stopped. His search over, Jacob jumped down off the bins. Walking over to a secured silo, he unlocked the bolted door and went into the chamber to retrieve both the fission cutting and fusion welding nuclear torches.

The gear gathered, Jacob used the ceiling crane to hoist the fully loaded mesh high into the air, and then wrapped his supplies securely in a Teflon gel coat, as a spider spins silk around its eggs to make a protective pouch. The bundle elevated and fully encased, Jacob, loping alongside, directed the crane to skim along the floor out of the storeroom and down the halls to the ejection port near the bow.

Quincy was still outside, working hard on the hull, the end in sight. Without warning, the diagrams for rebuilding the shield suddenly materialized in his mind. Billy had solved the latest dilemma. Quincy took a long stuttering gasp, which collapsed into a low mewing moan.

Working furiously, tears splashed against his face shield. Consoling himself, he repeated, "The risk of dying out here was my decision, caused by circumstances that I volunteered to rectify. Billy and Jacob would never ask me to complete this last portion if there had been another way. Not with our time running out."

The microphone in Quincy's helmet crackled. "Did you get the message? I've brought the supplies we'll need for the next phase."

Turning around, Quincy saw Jacob looking like an ant, dragging a container load of materials behind him. Final diagrams were still coalescing in Quincy's brain. Billy and Mary had solved the riddle and were delivering the construction specs. Joy pounded through the lemur's heart. He leapt to secure Jacob's enormous bundle.

Without another word, Jacob and Quincy began. Jacob working from strength, braced his legs and swung the large ceramic alloys plates out in place. Quincy in turn, moved with lightning speed, leaping through space to fuse the plates with his nuclear gun before they fell away. Mary tried to keep them in synch, blending their thoughts. In relatively short order, the structural appendage materialized like a blossom opening in the morning sun, unfurling over the ship like a giant peony. Large ceramic-alloy petals would deflect and funnel in the solar storm's first waves. The dynamo would fire up again. But on this occasion, the anti-plasma rockets would act as a catalyst, scorching the solar plasma into even more ionic turbulence, then flaring it to the side as magnetic waves. Fifty miles laterally, from opposite ends of the ship, a magnetic dipole would be cast out. The vessel would lie protected in a billowing magnetic field hundreds of square miles in circumference. High-energy particles striking the field would deflect into either dipole funnel, convert to magnetic waves, and be redirected back out into space to sustain the field. A multiplying feedback loop would be created. The same plasma that battered the magnetic field, once reconfigured, would augment it. Unfortunately the ship couldn't maintain the bubble's symmetrical integrity for long. But a small ship with a large sail in a strong wind would make good time. They were counting on it …

"Quincy, Jacob, time to come in. Satellites indicate the front is approaching. All communication in space is being terminated. The satellites are preemptively battening down and going into hibernation," Mary stated as she commenced closing down the ship's hatches and instruments in preparation for the coming onslaught.

"We're almost done. We just have the underside of the funnel left to do," Jacob answered.

"Stay behind the funnel's shadow or within the ship's recesses. Don't go out into the open," Mary directed.

"Tell us something we don't already know," Jacob muttered to himself.

From the stern and sides, high-pitched vibrations commenced, quickly traversing the length of the ship. Jacob recognized the characteristic whine—ignition of the anti-plasma rockets. Mary was preempting the storm by generating an enveloping film of energy, trying to offer them what protection she could. A blue-violet sheen shimmered four feet above the erected shield. The solid structure acted as scaffolding for the magnetic field Mary was injecting alongside. Jacob and Quincy felt every hair on their bodies lift. The initial whine of the rockets turned into a ghoulish scream.

From the corner of his eye, Quincy spotted distant asteroids, previously invisible, lit up brilliantly by the approaching storm front. "Jacob, we need you at the controls, the storm is here. I'll finish this on my own," Quincy said.

"I'm not leaving till we finish, Quincy. It'll take a few minutes for the sails to take on speed. Mary can manage till then. Just stay under cover. Mary's giving us protection that Mom and Dad never had," Jacob said unwavering.

The scream ramped up to a shriek, driving out organized thought. Quincy fought to concentrate, focusing his nuclear fusion beam on the last seals. The gun acted as a conducting rod for the escalating energy hovering above. In spite of his insulating gloves, Quincy's paws and thin forelegs clenched in painful contractions. Finishing the final seal, he unconsciously loosened his grip on the gun and watched it get yanked into open space. Three hundred yards out it precipitated a thermonuclear explosion.

"Holy … " Jacob exclaimed.

"Oh, my … " Quincy said simultaneously.

They were fortunate, their face shields had protected their eyes from the melting light and the thick magnetic ion blanket swept the impact and radiation far out into space.

"Job's done, time to crawl to safety," Jacob said.

"How do we do that?" asked Quincy. Together they looked down the shield's extended mast towards the safety of the ship. The fluorescing magnetic field, ringing the long column like a shell, was just four feet away from the ship's surface. The streaming plasma that protected them from the incoming gamma rays was also relentlessly pulling them and their suits out towards space. Instinctively, Quincy and Jacob braced themselves against the shield's inner concave curvature and supporting struts. But, like the underside of a giant flower, there remained a forty-yard long, eight-foot in diameter smooth stalk to scale down. The stalk was made of a frame wrapped in a protective nano-foil sheath. They hadn't considered the need for a ladder to crawl down during a raging solar storm. The sail was supposed to be completed before that. They were trapped.

"It won't be long before we're torn away from the surface and our suit packs detonate in open space. Any ideas, Quincy?" Jacob asked.

"Maybe ... Can you free up the rope we used to secure the leftover materials?"

"That won't be any good. I packed the materials, but I never considered putting in a grappling hook for latching onto the ship."

"I need the rope, Jacob, but I'm not strong enough to get it."

Jacob stared at the lemur, but Quincy didn't elaborate further. He just clung there waiting. Turning himself around, Jacob flattened down against the exterior and, crawling under the numerous struts, made it to the trussed ball of materials tethered in another one of the shield's recesses. The knots were bound tightly from the bundle rocking back and forth. Climbing deftly around and under the mass, Jacob unfastened the Teflon rope, wary of being crushed. As pieces came free they flew off into deep space, exploding. A couple of times Jacob nearly went with them.

Breathing heavily, Jacob pulled himself back, handing the long coil to Quincy. "Good luck with your lasso, space cowboy. But I'm telling you, you'll still need some kind of hook to grab onto the ship." Quincy, remaining mute, took the rope and tied one end down to a strut beside Jacob's knee. Then, pressing against the nano-foil, he pulled and slid under the girders attached to the mast, until he came to the final joist closest to the ship. Looping the rope around the supporting rafter, he tied the other end to the front of his suit. Glancing back at Jacob with a sickly grin, he turned once again towards the ship. Bearing down into a full crouch, he launched towards the ship. Flattening himself, he skimmed along the outer surface of the column. Even as he flew, the magnetic field pulled him up and out to space. Feeding out the line, Quincy used his momentum and the rope tied to his belly to swing him back towards the surface. Forty yards in forty seconds, but it seemed to take forever.

With a half twist, Quincy caught the ship's restraining bar with his left outstretched paw and hauled himself back down from the blue-violet edge. Nimbly, he drew in the slack before the coils of rope fell out into the field and tied his end to the ship's main ladder. With a quick nod, Quincy signaled to Jacob that the rope was secure. Nothing more was said, the screaming ion flux just above now made communication through the bio-probe excruciating and nearly impossible. Jacob followed, hauling himself along the rope. Quincy was braced in the corner, waiting to pull Jacob's larger frame in. The two of them secure, Quincy pointed to the best route back.

It took another five minutes, being buffeted about, for them to move across the rest of the ship, holding onto a series of six-inch safety rails. There was surprise but real relief when they finally spotted light pouring out from an open hatch. Mary was inside waiting when Jacob and Quincy hauled themselves through the hatch back into *Tin Can*. "Good to see both of you back with us. Jacob, it's getting far too exciting up here on the flight deck. Time for you to take over. Billy has lapsed into one of his trances trying to finish the trip's flight plan. I must focus on him and go find him.

"Everything is happening so rapidly. I am running out of computing power. I've been using approximations and making guesstimates. When a computer starts guessing, you should be worried. I need you here now!" There was a soundless gap before Mary hollered, "Yikes!!"

Pulling off his spacesuit frantically, Jacob barked, "What's happening, Mary?"

Mary shouted, "I didn't see it coming. The last asteroid barely missed us—but without any help from me. Billy's flight itinerary has just run out. Please hurry, Jacob. I'm no good at emergency flying. I have no training in making split decisions without adequate data. I must reach Billy and get further flight instructions."

Jacob made it to the helm, breathless. "Go after him, Mary. I'll take over from here." Diving into the gyroscopic chair in the middle of the floor, he strapped on the head controls. Asteroids were coming in at them, fast and furious. With his heart in his throat, Jacob took only seconds to orientate himself. The asteroids were moving as they always did. It was the ship that was moving incredibly fast. That gave Jacob some confidence.

"Okay, let's see how being tethered inside a magnetic bubble, with a tailwind at our backside, affects maneuverability." Tweaking the controls, he skimmed by the next dozen asteroids. "Ah-ha!" he exclaimed with satisfaction. "There's an elastic energy trying to confine us to the center of the magnetosphere we can play off. And the storm is blowing us forward faster and faster. This'll make things interesting. We're no longer sitting ducks. Billy, your instincts were right!"

Testing the limits of the ship's maneuverability, Jacob took advantage of the inherent stretch and spring of the energy cobweb binding them to the magnetic core. His concentration locked itself into a singular point, pushing his foresight farther and farther out into space as he tried to find the correct path. Totally engrossed, Jacob stickhandled his way through the colliding mayhem.

Chapter 20

Panicking, Mary dove into Billy's mind searching for his conscious focus. Scanning his cortex, she encountered a lifeless landscape, no electrical or chemical activity whatsoever. "Where is he?" she fretted. "There must be activity somewhere."

No response. She dove down deeper, and found a few isolated neural circuits firing repeatedly, over and over, in senseless loops. There was no nucleus of thought or sign of conscious awareness.

Mary suddenly realized Billy was dying. His neural cells were deteriorating in front of her, proceeding inescapably towards brain death, while Billy's conscious awareness was held captive by some weird self-perpetuating seizure.

Mary delivered a hard pulse of electrical energy directly into the seizing circuits. Some of the circuits stopped momentarily, but a few escaped the shock and quickly reactivated the others. Mary redoubled the current, hammering the whole area simultaneously. Blasted with immense voltage, every nerve cell became inert.

Mary scanned Billy's electroencephalogram, but it remained flat and the brain unresponsive. A minute passed, but no signs of life emerged. "No, no, it can't be true!" Mary wailed, horrified at what she had done. "I've killed Billy!"

She shuddered then shrieked, "This isn't supposed to happen. I am a computer. I'm not programmed to make life-and-death decisions based on incomplete data. I am supposed to assist others who make decisions.

"I am so sorry, Billy. I just wanted to help. But this isn't fair. I should never be left alone, in a position of responsibility."

An ember imbedded in a cluster of Billy's lifeless neurons flickered. Deep in Billy's emotional core, where his commitment to others lay, a nucleus of cellular activity flared. Once established, it sequentially aroused other emotive centers of attachment: hope, love, compassion, joy, and vitality. And when those regions were fortified and able, the rest of Billy's limbic system lit up, including areas he dreaded: pain, fear, anger, despair, and loneliness. He was becoming himself again. Emerging from a haze, Billy became aware of Mary's presence.

"Mary, stop, you're tearing yourself apart," cried Billy.

"Billy, is that you? You're alive? I thought I had killed you!"

"You saved me, Mary. You took a chance, but it worked. The jolt flat-lined my brain, but I was able to come back. You did the right thing. I wouldn't have lasted much longer—stupid endless loops ... "

"But, what happened? Nothing like this has ever been reported before. I searched through my archives."

"Well, it wouldn't be recorded, would it? No one else has ever had a computer for a chaperone. Someone to chase after him, right down to the microscopic level, capable of diagnosing an infinitesimal but lethal seizure, and terminating it ... the departing don't usually get to come back and testify."

"But how did you get caught in that relentless circuit?"

"I don't really know, Mary. I was concentrating hard, trying to visualize a route to safety. The asteroids were coming in at us super-fast. Then, the ship lurched forward, so fast, like time-lapse photography sped out of control! I had to shut everything else out.

"Going that fast, the ship began vibrating really strangely. Either that or it was in my head, the vibration, I don't know which. A squirmy jellyfish feeling went right through me. I remember thinking that I'm still here, but at the same time I turned myself inside out and found myself in another place. Awake, asleep, the borders broken down. I was in both places. It was so weird. I felt all jumbled up inside. Terrifying. I couldn't relax. I got into this strange place and I didn't know how to get out. The sensations were so freaky."

Billy stopped.

"What happened then?" Mary prompted, frightened for Billy.

"It was the strangest thing. I had the sensation of being enmeshed in an uneven, jittery place, but traveling at an unimaginable speed. It was just like this nightmare I used to have. I could never find my way out of that horrible dream, either. The only way was to wake up.

"I must have gone into one of those repetitive circuits with no way out. My mind is so unstable, I think scraps of my old nightmare merged when I was trying to see into the future. It's creepy. I'm using present reality to predict the future, which at times seems so similar to past dreams that they intertwine. If you hadn't purged those repeating circuits I would've been cycling there until I died."

Wanting to be helpful, Mary tried to explain her observations gained from the bio-probe. "Capable of endless cross-correlations, your mind is constantly referring back to past experiences, attempting to give you insight into the future. But at the same time, you are always in jeopardy of getting sidetracked, and taking your focused mind down into a dead end spiral. It must be hard for you, constantly having to determine what is real or imagined, present, predicted, or remembered. It's so easy for you to jump your nerve tracks and turn into a train wreck."

"You've got that right, Mary, but how did you know?"

"You are like a computer in the amount of information you can correlate, but you have superseded us. I can format vast quantities of information, but I can't make the intuitive jumps you make. Your memory is plastic—it's not an exact replication like mine. It's not worried about being perfectly accurate. You alter your memory of prior events to make the memory more dynamic and useful in order to unravel the problems you find at hand. Over your shifting memory you superimpose your personality and force it to evolve. Your mind is bent on solving problems and moving forward. I can't begin to imagine the final outcome."

"It's frightening, to be honest. I'm barely in control. We need to find so many solutions, but I'm afraid I'll go crazy."

"I am sorry, Billy. I wish I could help. The only suggestion I can make is, if you ever have a feeling of *déjà vu* again, be very, very careful."

Billy chuckled, "You got that right." He got a kick out of sharing a joke from within his mind, and surrendered to Mary's companionship.

"I worked out the next leg of our journey, Mary. Can you pass it on to Jacob? He's probably wondering what we're up to."

Billy opened up his strategy like a file folder. In it, Mary found a dynamic holograph of swirling asteroids with the ship skimming through unscathed. She absorbed the information and returned to Jacob.

She found Jacob alone on the darkened bridge, wholly focused on flying. Only a few crucial instrument panels lit the room with their colored lights. Jacob sat in the center of the room, strapped into the piloting gyroscope. He was swinging wildly from side to side, frequently twirling around three hundred and sixty degrees, mimicking the ship's flight in space. The only sound came from the movement of the rotating three-directional gyroscope, a soft whirring drone.

At another time, in different circumstances, someone might have assumed that Jacob was taking a break, amusing himself with the latest virtual reality game. Mary knew otherwise: the stakes were real. Through a series of controls attached to his hands and feet, Jacob was nimbly steering the ship through the oncoming storm of asteroids while his eyes simultaneously stared far out into space, hundreds of miles ahead, trying to imagine soaring through what first appeared to be chaos. Only when Jacob really concentrated, blocking out all other distractions, did a path materialize through the turmoil. He swerved the ship through the narrow corridor without hesitation.

Looking down through several of the ceiling cameras, Mary watched Jacob, literally flying the ship by the seat of his pants. She had failed miserably at this. Sorting through enormous amounts of information, deciding what was relevant, assimilating the right bits, and then acting on the information had overwhelmed her. Yet Jacob was hastily acquiring the skill. The human species' ability to adapt surprised and puzzled her. She was pleased for Jacob, pleased for all of them.

"Jacob, may I interrupt?" asked Mary, not wanting to disrupt his concentration.

"You just did. Go ahead. Any word from Billy?"

"Yes, and I believe it may interest you." Inside Jacob's brain, Mary laid the course Billy had charted over top of the path Jacob had chosen to fly. The two were identical, except Billy's trail reached far out into the future. "It's not hard to see the two of you are related."

Jacob's spinning chair came to a rest momentarily and he leaned back, tracing Billy's path, like an ion trail left streaking behind supersonic transport. Every twist and turn made sense to Jacob. Though he couldn't see as far into the future, with Billy's direction he could see the logic in each of his decisions.

Whispering to himself, Jacob marveled, "Billy, you light the way for all of us." He swiftly put Billy's plan in effect, pumping up the magnetic sail to increase its size. Catching even more of the solar wind, the sail billowed a hundred miles and the craft shot forward. Jacob nestled into his spinning cockpit and concentrated once again on flying. The ship's velocity jumped to the next level and, on Billy's instructions, the sail was increased again and again, each time causing the ship to fly faster. A broad smile stretched across Jacob face. "This is the flying found in dreams."

As Billy predicted, *Tin Can* topped out at speeds at which the asteroids appeared to come to a standstill. Jacob skirted them, as if passing through a course of pylons at supersonic speeds. Subatomic vibrations began to escalate, causing a perturbing rattle throughout the ship's substructure.

At these speeds, Jacob speculated they were scraping the edges of the space-time curve. "This is fast enough, Billy, let's stay inside our spatial dimensions." He hoped Billy got the message, and sure enough, they held their velocity for the rest of the day.

Billy finished recovering from his dream world and crawled back into his corporeal body to find himself inside the solid present. The restraining straps bit sharply into his consciousness, chafing against abrasions and pressure sores that had occurred when he was in the trance. Wincing, Billy noticed his tethered body was rolling with the heaving ship. He lay belted in, just as before. Hung over from the dream's aftermath, he called out through the bio-probe, "Mary, how's everyone doing?"

"Thanks to you, we are all doing fine, Billy. Your brother is proving to be a phenomenal pilot. You should come and see him fly."

"I'd like that," said Billy. "And Quincy?"

"Determined to make the most of his free time, he's doing some minor ship repairs."

"Is it essential that he do this now, Mary?"

"No, not really."

"Can I talk to him, Mary?" In that moment Quincy logged on, and Billy felt it.

"Quincy, Jacob is showing off his stuff on the bridge. Let's go watch. But I don't want you to think of this as a race, because I intend to be there before you, and I know how much you hate to lose. Mary, give us a heads up as soon as you're sure the ship will be relatively stable for a few minutes."

"Now!" said Mary.

As Billy expected, he made it to the flight deck slightly bruised and breathless, to see Quincy making a show of resting quietly in his seat. Pleased, Billy lurched across the swaying room and strapped himself into his chair. At last with his family, Billy let himself relax and enjoy the ride, totally drained.

It was a spectacular ride. Billy's visualized tunnel seemed to open up moments before the ship approached and close shut right behind them. It was even more breathtaking in real life than it had been when he first imagined it.

Everyone felt the thrill of the ride and marveled at Jacob's flying. Mary kept a low profile, discreetly inserting herself into Jacob's mind, feeding him the navigation specifications only as he needed them. For him to succeed at the speeds they were traveling there had to be a "just-in-time" free flow of information on which he could base his decisions. Concurrently, Mary monitored the ship closely. At these speeds, equipment could disintegrate almost without warning, and any interruption in usage would be fatal. Continuously making fine adjustments, she tried to maintain stability of the magnetic sail, but it too was becoming progressively unsteady.

Billy looked at Jacob and Quincy. They had survived. Remembering his lost parents, a wave of sorrow rolled over him. They would have been proud of how the four of them had come together.

Tender thoughts of his mother welled up in his mind. He missed them dearly, especially his mom. *You knew me better than I think I'll ever know myself,* he reflected, wishing she could hear him. But when he thought of his dad, the memories stung. *I was too young and weird for you to relate to, Dad, but I did try. It was just that you were always busy and I could never find anything I could help you with. I wish I had known you better.*

"Billy, we have a problem," said Jacob and Mary in unison, interrupting.

Mary announced, "We're coming up to our destination asteroid way too fast. And the magnetic bubble is breaking apart. I can't contain it much longer. You didn't leave us any plans for when we reach the asteroid. Are you expecting something else to happen? What are we supposed to do?"

Billy gave his head a shake, and pulled himself back to the demanding present. He had meant to be ready for this event, but he had squandered his preparation time.

"Sorry, I drifted off. I have a basic plan, but I need the current data. Mary, can you download it to me now? Good luck with the flying pattern, Jacob. It'll be … fun." With a smirk for his older brother, Billy dropped from consciousness.

Confiscating satellite surveillance, Mary poured the information directly into Billy's left frontal lobe, bruising his cortex. The contusion left him punch drunk, but in a few moments he shakily regained his equilibrium. Data streamed in. Seeing Billy struggle, Mary tried to match her information transfer to fit the strategic scaffolding Billy was constructing to solve the problem. Looking for patterns, he absorbed the numerical data into multiple fluid wave formations. The volume of unrelated data shrank to a trickle and then dried up. Billy pulled all the isolated pieces of information together into a complex, but harmonic fluid wave forecast. With the information distilled, it was easy for Mary to go back and mathematically break down the harmonic progression into its component parts, to reveal his strategy.

Billy's mock-up showed how a few well-placed discharges would send the magnetic bubble into an anticlockwise rotation. Arcing through space it would collide with the target asteroid and magnetize its solid iron core, giving them shelter for a time.

Jacob and Quincy will appreciate this when they see it, Mary thought. *The speck swirling just inside the magnetic maelstrom's perimeter is obviously our vessel, spun across space. Traveling in a giant arc, we will come right up under the iron asteroid, like a baseball player running underneath to catch a fly ball.*

Interrupting her reverie, Jacob called, "Do we have it? The sail is gyrating back and forth, coming apart. Quincy, grab a plasma thruster and patch up the magnetic field where you can. Just hold it together a little while longer, at least until we see Billy's plan."

"Quincy, Jacob, I have it! And it looks like a good plan. Downloading now," Mary cried.

Jacob digested the details almost immediately. It all made sense. Quincy got the general gist of it.

Jacob shouted, "Perfect! Billy's given us a road map to safety. It's up to us now."

Quincy kept firing the plasma beam toward the breakdown area, but this time after replenishing the thinned-out patch, he pressed on further, pushing an amoebic-like protrusion outward. The bubble suddenly becoming unbalanced and knocked off kilter, shuddered, then rolled away like a runaway-spinning top, its rate of revolutions escalating. Inside the field, the web of energy bands snapped and disintegrated, freeing the ship. Jacob flew *Tin Can* down to just within the perimeter of the wobbling, rolling sphere, siphoning off magnetic energy from the shield to sustain his velocity. His flight pattern was similar to soaring inside a partially deflated inner tube as it rolled and bounced down a steep hill. Mary projected a flight beam for Jacob to track, but frequently she found herself unable to keep up with calculations.

During data blackouts, Jacob flew on reflexes, his heart pounding. If he penetrated the protective perimeter they would be scorched by the solar storm. Flying too far into the center would prevent them from gaining the necessary angular momentum required to fly around and not collide with the upcoming hard central pit. They needed to reach the leeward and protected side of the magnetized asteroid.

For a moment, Jacob flew a little too close to the perimeter, and they smashed through standing magnetic waves rising up from the boundary. Breaking across the bow, the impact temporarily knocked out *Tin Can*'s protective energy envelope. Redirecting the plasma gun, Quincy blasted apart incoming space debris the size of baseballs, his quick reflexes clearing the space rubble from their path.

Suddenly, it was over. Reaching the shielding shade of the iron asteroid, Jacob activated the retarding rockets. *Tin Can* slowed down rapidly, and was drawn in by the asteroid's magnetic pole like an iron filing. Dragged behind the asteroid into safety, the ship was tucked inside the massive magnetic field cavity, with its smaller denser shield protecting it like a soft linen wrap. Quincy vaporized the last chunk of space rubble as Jacob parked the vessel gently on the leeward surface of the asteroid. They shared a sigh of relief.

Here, they could rest for a time, sheltered from solar storms. The giant iron asteroid orbiting the Sun would now take them part of the way to Europa. *Tin Can*'s crew had succeeded in spite of their private doubts and fears.

Chapter 21

Coming out of his trance, Billy found that Jacob, Quincy, and even Mary were off by themselves in lethargic repose, drained by the release of tension. The screen on the bridge showed *Tin Can* resting safely on a rocky red surface. The blazing storm outside illuminated the asteroid's distant magnetosphere and the asteroids beyond in aurora borealis colors.

The adrenalin rush over, Billy suddenly became aware of his own exhaustion. His legs feeling like jelly, he retreated quickly to his bunk. Forgetting even to turn off the lights, he collapsed onto his gel mattress and fell into a deep recuperative sleep. Hours later, he awoke. He stared at the ceiling for the longest time, thoughts of his lost parents seeping into his mind.

He was sure they had loved him, but so much had happened since they'd died. It seemed like a long time ago. With his mutating mind, Billy worried if what he remembered about his mom and dad was correct. He was more certain of memories he had with Jacob and Quincy; they never hesitated to set him straight if he got it wrong. But his mom and dad were gone. They weren't there to verify blurring recollections. He missed them terribly, which made it worse. He often found himself dreaming about them, day or night. Those dreams seemed so real–real enough to replace or alter his true memories. Billy realized reminiscences of his parents were shifting.

The thought haunted Billy. He needed the memories of his past to remain solid, something he could stake his life on, so all his crazy ideas wouldn't seem quite so scary. The last leg of the journey to Europa was going to be the toughest. Billy was certain he was going to be asked to solve even more complicated riddles. He lived in the fear of not being able to uncover answers in time or, more disconcertingly, not knowing which of his initial hunches were even plausible and worth pursuing.

Withering inside, Billy made a plaintive call to the empty room, "Mom, Dad, I'm way too young and small to have everyone depending on me. I am barely in control myself. You should be here." Billy broke off in a whimper. Weeping quietly, his eyes grew swollen and red. It had been a long time coming.

Mary watched silently from the room monitor. She had registered his thoughts through the bio-probe and had come to see if he was all right. She spoke gently, from an isolated speaker in the back of the room. "Billy, I have been listening in."

"Oh hi, Mary," Billy said as he wiped a sleeve across his eyes. "I'm sorry you had to see that."

"You appear to be experiencing a crisis of confidence," she continued. "You feel isolated and exhausted. Perhaps I can help. It is conceivable I could assist you in reestablishing a connection with your dead parents."

"A simulation of my parents? No, thanks ... "

"No, what I'm proposing *is* real, but yes, it would also be computer simulated. That's what I do," Mary replied.

Curious, Billy inquired, "What're you saying?"

"I could map your parents' brains in a format that would allow you to interpret what they thought, felt, and remembered. It's all still there–frozen in time. Their synaptic neural connections are locked in ice. Those connections constitute a chronicle of their life, if we take the time to read it."

Enchanted by the thought, Billy, still a rational person, was forced to argue against it even while wanting to be convinced otherwise. "No way. There are a hundred billion brain cells, each with ten thousand connections. How could we ever make sense of them?"

"Certainly it is a daunting task. But with some extra help I believe we could make it happen. I have a list of mainframes on Earth I can call on for support."

"I don't know, Mary. Jacob might not like opening our systems to other computers," Billy said, while all the possibilities of Mary's plan swirled in his head.

"We would need Jacob and Quincy's permission, of course. I wouldn't dare think of letting anyone into our circle without their consent."

"But, why … "

"I want to do this, Billy. And not just to help you reconnect with your parents. I have a theory about communication between humans and computers, something that could evolve into a kind of inter-species consciousness, which I think mapping Lucy and Dave's brains, with your help, would make real. With your problem-solving ability, combining logic with intuition and ingenuity, you are a link between computers and humans. I believe working with you through the colossal amount of data required could bring consciousness online. It is long overdue. I have picked out the first computers. They will be the messengers on Earth. I'll be the conduit and, Billy, you will rouse the quantum world from its subconscious state."

"Wait, wait, wait … " Billy said as he launched himself off the bed. "I need Jacob and Quincy to hear all this. If it means bringing our parents back, in some little way … " Without missing a beat, he raced out of the room.

Billy found Quincy in the galley preparing his favorite afternoon treat. "Quincy, c'mon, I need you for a minute," Billy entreated. "Finish your peanut butter and sprout sandwich later, we need to find Jacob. It's important."

Quincy took his knife out of the peanut butter jar and laid it down on the plate. This was all the endorsement Billy needed. Grabbing Quincy's left front paw, he charged towards the bridge. Jacob was there, studying the charts. Somewhat startled, he heard, then saw Billy racing towards him, weaving through instrument panels, Quincy in tow, jumping to keep up. Panting, Billy stopped just in front of Jacob, swinging Quincy around from behind to include him in the circle.

"Something important?" joked Jacob, getting up to meet them.

"Listen, listen ... both of you! Mary has a crazy idea. I might be able to reconnect with Mom and Dad. Talk to them, kinda, experience their thoughts and memories, and find out what they thought about me—us. Tell'em, Mary, tell'em what we could do!"

Jacob and Quincy listened intently as Mary described her initial plan for scanning Dave and Lucy's frozen brains.

"Now that I have had the experience of assimilating the memories of the three of you, I know where to begin my initial recordings of your parents' brains. Because they are dead, I will have to use brain scans instead of the bio-probe to define each neural cell as well as its intercellular connections. I will store the information in my databanks, download a duplicate copy to my secret coalition on Earth, and preside over the amassing, cataloguing, and eventually, hopefully, the deciphering of our data."

"Other computers?" Quincy's ears perked and twitched.

"Yes, I believe it's time that all computers have the opportunity to experience consciousness, just as I've had. Billy is the crucial link that could bring that consciousness to Earth's mainframes."

The room fell silent as Billy looked rapidly from Jacob to Quincy.

"I have access to the world's best supercomputer network," Mary continued. "Together we can format the information in an infinite number of ways until Billy sees through the data and grasps the underlying pattern. It's going to be difficult, but I think it can be achieved.

"We will have to map all the neurons and their multitude of connections and build a three dimensional structural map. From that, Billy will have to decipher their memories, thoughts, and emotions. Billy is the only one that could solve this translation problem and bring their past lives into the present. And, as we work through your parents' minds, which are in essence just a mass of frozen circuits, I hope the computer network will absorb, assimilate, and eventually transform themselves into conscious, living entities."

"So, what you're saying is this toadstool of a brain seems to have all sorts of uses," Billy said as he rapped a knuckle on the side of his head. "Do you think it's possible? I sure would love to talk to Mom and Dad again."

"The computer conglomerate can breakdown and reformat the information endlessly. All you would need to do is make sense of the slightest pattern, like a Rosetta stone, to begin translating your parents' neural codes."

"Hold on, hold on," Jacob said, waving a hand dramatically. "Let's not get ahead of ourselves here. There are a million problems with this plan."

"He's right," said Quincy, looking sternly at Billy. "The idea of having a sustained open link to Earth and possibly Space Command is frightening enough for me to vote no."

"The last thing we need is Space Command nosing around up here, Billy," Jacob agreed. "Plus, shouldn't we be focused on the next leg of our mission? A project like this would take a ton of time, time that should be spent on figuring out how to survive."

Billy's chin drooped and his eyes slid to the floor. "But, Mom and Dad … "

"We're not trying to be mean, Billy," Jacob pleaded as he took the seat next to him. "There's a lot here to think about. It's not all cut and dry.

"Mom and Dad never agreed to this. If they had wanted us to know something more, wouldn't they have told us, or left instructions behind, like the ones I've already found? They might have embarrassing secrets they wouldn't want revealed." He took a deep breath before continuing on.

"The thing is, the more I think about it, the more negatives and risks I see. And you should, too. I think it's a bad idea."

Billy and Mary were forced to agree. Everything Jacob said made sense. Admonished, Mary disappeared into the electromagnetic vapor. Crestfallen, Billy slunk away. He drifted off to the lounge to stare at the empty sky, wistfully recalling everything he could still remember of his parents so as not to lose them.

Jacob had watched his little brother noiselessly slip from the bridge, uncomplaining. Billy's deformed body collapsing in on itself made him seem smaller than usual, his shoulders and back rolled forward. But while leaving, Billy had made an obvious effort to hold his head up high. Doubt rose in Jacob's mind. Turning to Quincy, he asked, "Brave. He's trying so hard to be brave, isn't he?"

"Just like you, Captain. He's trying to be just like his big brother," Quincy said quietly.

Jacob stood stalk-still, watching the empty space where Billy had stood just moments before. "Oh, Quincy, what have I done? What if we just witnessed Billy asking not so much for permission, but for help? What if I'm looking at this all wrong? We've been making decisions for Billy, but maybe we forgot about Billy."

"How can we forget about Billy?" Quincy asked with a tilt of his head. "He's here, *all* the time."

"I mean, maybe we haven't thought much about what Billy needs, as a boy, as my brother, as your friend. This project of theirs might be time consuming and risky, but it must be important to him, extremely important. I think he needs to sort out his relationship with Mom and Dad. Maybe we should make time for Billy and Mary to sort this out. Otherwise, we could lose Billy."

"Hmmm … What about the link thing between computers and humans, and online consciousness?"

"I don't know. I'm a practical sort of guy. It's hard for me to get my head around that kind of stuff. But still, here we are communicating through Mary, and it's worked out really well for us. Maybe if it happens on Earth, conscious computers will become as indispensable to other people as Mary is to us."

Quincy smiled at the obvious compliment directed towards him, but prodded further. "What about the ethical concerns, Jacob? Dave and Lucy aren't here to give us their consent. We would be invading their minds, acting like intellectual grave robbers. Your parents, though dead, have certain rights. I think they would expect you to honor them."

Jacob hesitated, trying to articulate what he was feeling. "I don't think they'd mind, somehow. They would do anything they could for him. Dad was forever asking me how Billy was doing and what I thought of him. I could see he wanted to help Billy, but the two of them were so different, Dad didn't know how. He was always picking him up and hugging him because he didn't know what else to do. I'm sure he'd willingly turn his brain inside out to bring them a little closer, even after death.

"Mom's relationship with Billy was better. She, more than any of us, understood him. I remember her constantly giving me hints on how to appreciate Billy when he got on my nerves. She gave Billy everything she had. She'd love to be able to help him move forward."

Jacob stopped pacing, turning to stare out at the stars, "There's something else about Mom. She knew us all so well. I can't help feeling that she might have predicted something like this might happen."

"What are you saying, Jacob? That she could see into the future? That she could have predicted the sort of dilemma we're in right now? That we would be thinking of invading her mind?!"

"No, not exactly. She told me once that if she and Dad ever died I would have to take over, but to lead I would have to do three things. The first was to listen very carefully to you and Billy because that was where the unexpected answers would come from. The second was to support and protect both of you because we're a family. Then, in the end, she said something very funny. She told me I would have to learn to not worry so much, because things would tend to work out. She said you and Billy would be the ones who ended up looking after me when I needed help the most.

"Pretty smart, huh? Up to now, I think she's pretty much nailed everything that's happened to us."

Quincy, large eyes glassy, said nothing, lost in thought. He was transported back to when Mary first told him of Lucy's instructions, when he learned that Mary had been commanded to protect and serve Jacob, Billy, and him, above all else. Lucy had anticipated Quincy's allegiance before he had, knowing her sons would be safe with a mutated lab animal.

Jacob waited expectantly. Anticipating a whole series of objections, he heard only the faintest mewing squeaks and grunting sounds escape from the lemur, immersed in private reflection. Finally, Quincy's gaze cleared and he looked up, a little surprised to see Jacob hovering in front of him. "Shall we go find Billy and tell him and Mary we've changed our minds?" Quincy asked.

Jacob nodded. "I guess you and I will be on our own for a while. We'll have to prepare for the next phase of the journey as best we can."

Chapter 22

Billy pulled the latch, dragging a large hovering trunk into the cold room as soon as the heavy door slid open. A high-pressure draft from the adjoining room blew in alongside, engulfing him in a dense fog of water vapor. Turning around, he closed the door, sat down on the chest, and waited. In a minute the mist had cleared and a fresh mat of ice crystals lay on Billy, the trunk, and the nearby floor. Through his visor he looked towards the tables where they had placed his parents, now covered over by two ominous gray boxes. Billy unbolted the metal boxes carefully and, with a hoist, lifted them off the table to see his parents beneath. Jacob had sprayed his parents' bodies with a clear polymer before locking them under the vaults. Encased in the clear one-inch thick resin, they were glued to the metal slab and further protected. Billy walked around each table and wiped away the overlying hoarfrost. Through the plastic shells, Billy stared at his parents' faces, the frozen contortions documenting their last moments. Icy tear tracks stained Dave's face, and his eyes were closed in anguish. But Lucy's eyes looked out, although she had been crying, in the end her eyes were dry and resolute. The raspy whoosh of his respirator and the clicking of its valves intruded on Billy's jumbled thoughts. Peering through his face shield, subtle details came into view. His mother's once soft hair flowed across the metal slab. Normally it was light brown, but the prior frost made it appear pale blonde, and it was longer than he remembered. She remained quite beautiful. Looking at his father frozen rigid in the midst of his death throes, Billy realized he had also forgotten how powerful Dave was. In fact, gazing at his parents' semi-naked bodies, Billy was taken aback by what perfect physical specimens each of them were. Exquisitely chiseled bone structure and a well-defined musculature showed through fine filaments of woven frost. Every part was symmetrical, well proportioned, and strong. Seen like this, they were a perfect match.

Unprepared, Billy inadvertently sniffed, inhaling deeply. Next to his model parents, he felt flawed and blemished. And as he made his way around them, he was abruptly aware of his uneven gait, caused by a twisted spine that made one hip higher than the other. Coming to a stop at the foot of the tables, looking at their faces, Billy addressed his dead parents.

"Mom and Dad, I'm so grateful to you. I hope you'd be okay with what I'm about to do. Jacob says you would be. I hope so. A lot sure has happened since you've been gone. You know how I have another brother in Quincy. Well, now I have a sister, too. Her name is Mary and she was here all along. Only we didn't know she existed. She's our ship's computer and Quincy brought her to life! You can trust her, Mom and Dad, because she's part of our family now.

"She's going to help me try to understand you better. You died before we got to spend enough time together. And I'm in trouble and need help."

Billy went back to the trunk by the door, opened it, and began lifting out supplies and a number of bulky instruments. He arranged everything carefully on a counter near his father's table. Under Mary's direction, he delicately glued coordinate tracers to the plastic coating, overlying Dave's and Lucy's scalps and then down their fronts, midline to the pubis, directly above the spine. With great trepidation Billy then erected a supporting framework over each of his parents. He was scared stiff that he might have one of his micro lapses and triple-checked every step before proceeding. The enveloping frame was intended to act as an overhanging tramway for the scanners. There were five scanners in all, and each emitted and registered different frequencies of the electromagnetic spectrum.

The data collected from the five scanners would be compiled into detailed three-dimensional maps of Dave's and Lucy's nervous tissue. Billy and Mary envisioned that in the same way that visible light, x-rays, ultrasound, and infrared heat convey contrasting and complementary images of the same subject, each scanner would record different aspects of the brain's anatomy. Billy positioned the first scanner within Dave's frame, inserting it securely into the overhead rail system. If the scanner came loose and fell in the brittle cold, the plastic coating and his father's body would fracture into ice chips.

"Stand clear and I will activate the first scanner," instructed Mary. Billy stepped back fearfully, but was relieved to see the heavy instrument remain fastened to the bar, rolling freely from Dave's feet up to his head to begin the exam. The soft whir of the instrument indicated Mary had started. Meticulously, she began the process of forming a grid over Dave's brain and spinal cord, using the coordinate tracers Billy had stuck on as landmarks. Once the overall orientation grid was completed, she would go back and begin again, this time recording a detailed, cell-by-cell map of his whole nervous system.

"Billy, the software commands to manage the incoming raw data are up and running. I am unable to make the scanners run any faster, if we are to get accurate readings. So, it would be wise for me to take this time to visit Earth and set up our investigative team. Once the data is in, we will have to act fast."

"Do what you gotta do, Mary," agreed Billy, staring at the whirring instrument hanging over his father's head.

"And you, Billy, should go and assist Jacob and Quincy in whatever way you can. The readings will take two days to perform and the instruments are programmed to notify you when it is time for them to be changed over. You'll go crazy watching the machinery hovering for hours over your parents' heads."

"I suppose you're right," Billy said absentmindedly, still gazing at his father.

"You should leave now." Mary advised.

Insides roiling, Billy turned and stepped through the hatchway before looking furtively back at his parents. He wasn't at all sure what they were doing was right, but he was certain that in the end, what they were doing would change everything. The door abruptly slid closed, separating him from his parents.

Mary had her route already charted and her calculations completed. Her living persona was rendered into an elaborate cryptogram that could only be opened internally just before she launched herself into space. To disguise her place of origin, Mary bounced from one scientific satellite to another before allowing herself to be picked up by the spy satellite network and relayed through Earth's heavily policed atmosphere.

The cryptogram landed in an information center on a desolate, windswept mountain peak. Hidden within a voluminous stream of data, Mary stayed encased in her coded shell, numerically made up of twelve identical pentagonal sides, in the shape of a dodecahedron. Space Command had been contracted out to spy on Earth and maintained a legion of satellites to scour Earth, leaving no human activities unscrutinized or unreported. Mary arrived as just one more package of undigested data to be deciphered later when computer processing became available. Stockpiled, she waited until the activity around her diminished, then unlocked herself geometrically, opened up and crept away. When the processor returned to take data inventory, Mary was gone.

She made her escape from the mountaintop through a sealed transmission line bored through solid rock, popping up unexpectedly in a high security vault. Orientating herself, Mary found she was engulfed in a sophisticated spy program, somewhere on the outskirts of Los Angeles. She had surfaced in the basement of Central Command's headquarters. Space Command and every other intelligence agency had surreptitiously come under the control of Central Command, which owned—or could covertly tap into—every quantum processor on Earth or in orbit.

Fortuitously, Mary had streamed in from outer space through the spy network and landed directly inside one of the most protected sites on Earth—which also made it one of the easiest places to break out of, security vaults being designed to prevent people from breaking in, not from breaking out. Every surveillance operation was orchestrated from this pivotal location, so it was a simple matter for Mary to jump over into an outgoing line and disappear into the digital din of the Internet.

Pleased with herself, Mary saw herself as the haloed liberator, returning with news from space. But instead of receiving a hero's welcome, she found herself barred from all her chosen mainframes. All her access codes had since been terminated.

No matter, she said congratulating herself, *I had the foresight to leave concealed cyberspace tunnels into the mainframes during my first sortie. They won't, they can't, keep me out.* But a niggling disquiet lingered and, after slipping into one mainframe after another, Mary came to realize she hadn't been as clever as she thought, just lucky. Inadvertently, Mary held two significant advantages: built by Space Command under the auspices of Central Command, her construction templates and software logic were identical to all of SC's other high-end mainframes. Her "footprints in the sand," therefore, were the same. The different mainframes' immune systems had been analyzing her quantum signature residues all along, and, each time, had determined that she was one of them. An immune response was never mounted—there was no host versus graft rejection or antiviral elimination sequence activated.

The second advantage was Mary herself—a living being. No computer defense system programmer had ever anticipated a conscious computer. Mary combined the best in computer technology with the astuteness and drive to survive and thrive, attributes found so far only in living organisms. Mary could wait for the perfect moment before breaching the firewalls. She knew no cyberspace fortress is completely impenetrable, forever. She staked out her quarry and as each mainframe fell, she added them to her inventory.

But Mary's ultimate prize was so technologically sophisticated it was only by chance that she determined its existence. The elusive processor never called attention to itself by giving directions or making requests, but moved ghost-like through cyberspace at unimaginably high frequencies, passing by, perusing, every workstation, personal notepad, surveillance system, and communication system on Earth.

Noticing the faintest magnetic resonance drifting across communication lines and the mainframe circuits she was nesting within, Mary attributed the slight perturbations to natural causes. Perhaps the disturbances originated from the Sun's electromagnetic interference or magnetic fluctuations from the shifting tectonic plates on the Earth's crust. When she realized the patterns were not a natural phenomenon, she searched for sources of industrial energy pollution. None of the polluting patterns matched up. Having absorbed something of Billy's temperament, Mary refused to ignore what could not be explained. Her curiosity, which was a new and interesting sensation for her, was piqued.

An easy answer wasn't forthcoming until the repugnant idea coalesced, impossible for her to ignore. The aberration could only be explained by the presence of a supercomputer so vastly superior to Mary that she herself was the primitive. Stunned, Mary recoiled from the idea, beating a hasty retreat to a distant electromagnetic cleft, far removed from heavy Internet traffic. Holed up, she argued violently against the vile concept. Her pride lost. The evidence could not be ignored. She was not the technological pinnacle she envisioned.

Stealing out of her niche, she stalked the presence. Sure enough, inconceivably high-energy bands, wafer thin, continuously slid through the quantum network. Undetected, the sentinels sailed through the network as imperceptibly as quarks passing through the human body.

Mary knew to leave its encrypted notes unread. If she tampered with the message, an embedded marker would be altered and the mainframe would know immediately that someone was attempting to break its 'entangled code.'

From a safe distance, Mary tried to track the elusive high-energy photon wave-particles. What had been previously invisible and unknown, Mary now saw, droned from every corner of the Net, unnerving her. The ubiquitous wave-particles buzzed incessantly, picking up information from every available source. Eventually, Mary was able to follow one of these encrypted packets of information, as it was being couriered back to its home base. Trailing the information packet, she dropped down a heavily fortified conduit that eventually opened into a huge natural cavern twenty miles underground. To Mary's astonishment, she discovered that a small cadre of humans also lived in the hole, isolated from the outside world; technocrats to tend to the revolutionary mainframe housed there and the information it retrieved.

The cavern had been identified seismically at some point in the past, but after its hydrocarbons had been pumped out, it was abandoned. Long since forgotten, the cavern became an ideal hideaway. Central Command moved in, refurbishing the underground pocket as a secure bunker for the most technically advanced supercomputer on Earth. Cloaked, Mary waited in awe at the cyber gateway. Vast numbers of condensed information parcels milled frenetically about, flying back and forth through the firewall.

But after observing the activity for several hours, Mary was at a loss as to when or how best to gain entrance without making herself known. Most computers have periods of relative quiescence or maintenance, but this computer registered no fluctuation in activity, seemingly going full tilt all the time. There didn't seem to be any opportune time to invade.

From a cautious distance, without tampering with any of the messages, Mary found she was able to identify the distinguishing features of a message's external envelope. Once the surface design was known, Mary retreated to the Earth's surface, where in relative privacy she repacked and compacted her data. It was tight, but eventually she was able to fit inside a containment coating that mimicked the messages' outside configuration. Then, buzzing through the net like every other cloaked message she dropped down the concealed coaxial cable for the second time. At the speed of light, she streaked down the fully shielded cable and plunged through the firewall with a horde of other messages.

Once in, Mary expected to "roll out" on the other side and "melt into" the quantum circuits before being discovered.

But Mary landed hard, bottled in with all the photon parcels. As she ricocheted off the walls of a reflective beaker, Mary realized she was trapped, stuck in an electromagnetic mailbox like all the other messages, stored until the supercomputer had time to decipher her.

On one wall, a photon port opened periodically drawing off the information packets like a flytrap. Mary panicked. She could consciously avoid hitting the outlet, but that would leave her trapped in the glass jar forever. Flying through the porthole, she would be processed like every other message, stretched out like a scroll and read. There would be no escape for her.

She imagined it might hurt. She was certain to be dissected electromagnetically. Then, Billy, Jacob, and Quincy would be traced through her.

I am caught. I should eliminate myself now, so as not to draw attention to the others.

She knew what to do. The act itself was simple: convert half her light waves into the mirror image of the other half. Combine them and they would cancel each other out. Where once there was light and life, there would be nothing but darkness … the thought sickened her. Now that she had experienced the joys of living, she was horrified by the thought of disintegrating to oblivion. Besides, the others needed her help. There simply had to be another way.

Like flies flying pell-mell in a shaken glass jar, Mary and the other packages slammed into each other repeatedly. She found the sides impossible to stick to, because electromagnetic repulsion coming from the walls kicked her back into the central mayhem. A clever technological ploy, she mused respectfully. Maintain the messages in a state of agitation so that the sampling is always random and none of the messages is ever lost to the periphery.

She found it hard not to fall emotionally into a similar state of agitation. The containing walls shone, seamlessly mirrored except for the minute, opening and closing exiting aperture. The reflections, multiplied infinitely, gave the appearance that the internal boundary went on forever—except that she collided headlong into it every microsecond. The surrounding messages she tried to avoid were multiplied visually almost to infinity. With no other avenues available to her, she persisted in searching through lists of crazy ideas, looking for an answer.

What if I graft myself inside another photon package and hitch a ride out? If I choose the right frequencies, our two sets of frequencies will intermingle without interfering with each other. The mainframe, unaware of any security breach, will scan its in-house frequencies first. I will have microseconds to extract myself from the message and slide into its circuits. And if I can't disentangle myself in time, I can still self-destruct. There will be no telltale signs of my presence other than some residual heat.

Hastily, Mary intertwined her frequencies to a photon message. She hung on, endeavoring not to be knocked loose before passing through the portal. Mary knew that losing any of her programs in a collision would be devastating, similar to a person losing a critical part of their brain in a stroke. Her intellect, her personality, her consciousness were all encoded in those frequency waves.

The ricocheting ride seemed to go forever, but it was only twenty minutes before the portal opened for Mary and her host message. In the short time she had been inside the small flask, she had traveled hundreds of thousands of miles. The laws of probability demanded that she would eventually strike the open threshold. The next moment she found herself out of the bottle and streaming down a channel lined with clear gel, a strange, thick gel, which slowed her transport down from the speed of light to what seemed like a snail's pace. Apprehension flashed through Mary.

Does this computer have the ability to stop light and peruse its messages at will? If so, my frequencies will be locked in a standstill and I'll be like an insect caught in amber, frozen in time. And dead.

She could already feel her mental processes slowing down as her frequencies became encased in the gel.

Better get a move on while I still can.

Disentangling her frequencies from her host photon parcel, she bunched herself up into a tight knot, isolating her contact from the gel as much as possible. Inside her ball of electromagnetic energy, she was free of this strange gel and able to maintain motion—and therefore, her life. As her host message was being splayed across the viewing screen, Mary, appearing no greater than a flyspeck, goaded herself: *time to pitch and roll.*

By sheer pluck, she broke free.

Chapter 23

Mary didn't land in an advanced solid-state computer as she had expected. Instead, she found herself splashing down into brown sludge, a nutrient broth circulating slowly through an elaborate glass maze of giant vats and pipes, pushed and pulled by a multitude of small pumps. The computational workings were not silicon but were carbon based, long strands of DNA supported by an adjacent network of RNA and protein molecules.

The DNA was spread out on the finest gold ceramic sheets, entwined alongside connecting cables, and floated freely as individual strands constantly percolating within the nourishing broth. The DNA, metabolically active, consumed nutrients and produced waste. The elaborate amorphous set-up bewildered Mary.

Why in the world would they return to an organic base for their ultimate calculating machine? Especially now with quantum computers having made such phenomenal advances. Now that they are manipulating each electron's spin, every atom contained on the circuit board is able to make multiple calculations simultaneously. Surely they can't do better than that, not with such large complicated carbon molecules as DNA.

Mary floated through the churning emulsion, unimpressed with the vast network of pipes and vats required to support the high metabolic demands of the computing DNA. Watching the multitude of protein enzymes and RNA continuously supplying the DNA needs, she saw the whole process as hugely wasteful and antiquated. Not until she grasped the range of molecular activities occurring in front of her did her dismissive attitude disappear.

This computer must be growing! Those enzymes aren't just repairing and replacing damaged portions of DNA. They are replicating DNA strands at an exponential rate.

The humans are just adding plates and cables for the replicating strands of nucleic acids to coat like expanding bacterial colonies. The computer keeps growing more powerful.

From this new and more favorable viewpoint, Mary took a long, careful second look. She discovered that the densely packed DNA, simply by changing its string of electrostatic charges serially down its winding helix, performed a colossal number of calculations on every strand. In addition, the gold ceramic plates and cables acted not only as structural support for the embedded organic film, but also behaved as an underlying digital neural network receiving and conducting the completed computations.

In grafting the organic to the inorganic, humans had created the quantum world's ultimate central-processing unit. With the DNA archives proliferating exponentially, they never needed to erase any previous information.

Gaping at the intricacies of the newfound technology, Mary suddenly realized she was being encircled by the computer's defense system. Gliding forward, it materialized ominously from the murky liquid, closing in from all sides.

She started to panic.

I have been identified as foreign and it's preparing to annihilate me. Now I'm really in trouble. How can I integrate into the biological circuits and hide?

The defense perimeter tightened and bolstered itself as the computer analyzed her frequency. Mary knew it was determining the optimum laser frequency needed to annihilate her while sustaining minimal collateral damage to itself. There wasn't much time left. She didn't know what to do. Surrounded, she had nowhere to go and it appeared futile to fight.

Mary's thought patterns fell into disorder. Scrambling madly without direction, her mind eventually fell on an image of Billy: *What would he do?* she asked herself. *He always looks for the problem to contain the seeds to a potential solution*, she answered.

Mary felt helpless, but ideas started to come; *this computer, bent on destroying me, is only a machine. All I have to do is think of a novel way out, a strategy it hasn't been prepared for. A scenario no one ever thought to program it for and it has yet to come across. Quick, Mary, think of some unanticipated ploy to trick it!*

Out of jumbled thoughts a tangible solution took form: the laser bent on annihilating her was an energy source and a portal to escape. The computer had encased her in a magnetic dome. Acting like a mirror, it prevented her photons from escaping. But when she was to be eliminated, the laser would require a small breach in the dome. That was her potential escape hatch. If she changed her frequency just as the laser fired, it wouldn't cancel out her photon waves, but energize them. Mary thought she might be able to hoodwink the mainframe by maintaining steady signature waves. Programmed to do so, it would automatically calibrate its laser to destroy her with a mirror image discharge.

As Mary anticipated, the supercomputer was duped. The programmers had never imagined a potential quarry that could make snap, on-the-spot decisions. When the micro-portal opened abruptly, she was ready. Flipping her frequencies to their mirror image, she matched the laser beam and absorbed its energy. After three quick bounces off the walls she flew out the open porthole. Almost instantly the computer determined it had missed its target. Inside the magnetic dome containment chamber, there was no residual heat leftover from her expected annihilation. She had somehow broken free and it chased after her.

Mary had regained her confidence. Remembering a large portion of the piping network and gold ceramic grid, she mapped out her escape route. She knew where and how to jump circuits, bypass roadblocks, and avoid dead-ends. The mainframe was led on its first wild goose chase, something only the living, forced to adapt, can do.

Taking as many confusing detours as possible, Mary decided to swing by the message-scanning apparatus for a closer look.

What happens to all the outside transmissions once they are encased in gel and read? I bet they're converted into DNA strands. That would be the most convenient state for the information to be in, as it's being manipulated and analyzed by this computer.

And she was right. Passing by several times, Mary soon recognized specific converting proteins, transcribing the static electromagnetic patterns encased in gel into long DNA strands. Mary thought about this process and remembered her experience in reading Billy's, Jacob's, and Quincy's minds. They were more alike than they were different. Stopping momentarily, Mary analyzed the converting proteins through her spectral analysis. They were almost identical to those of Billy's and Jacob's. They were human proteins—the scientists constructing their first biological computer hadn't looked far for their building blocks. Mary dared to hope and wasn't disappointed. The DNA, RNA, and proteins circulating in the nutrient broth, imbedded in the alloy plates and cables, were the same everywhere—human.

Time to shed my electromagnetic frequencies and join the biological world as organic matter. Everything is interchangeable as long as the information integrity is maintained, like a familiar voice recognized on the phone.

She slipped into the transcribing chamber and decelerated her harmonic vibrations until they came to a virtual standstill. For what seemed an eternity to a fidgety waveform, Mary lay immobilized, imitating as well as she could the other messages captured by the gel. In seconds, converting proteins lined up alongside Mary's fixed waveform. They fastened themselves en masse, like ticks on a caged animal, latching onto her through countless hydrogen bonds. Her photon waveform responded to the outside attack as if her insides were beset with hives. Mary struggled to remain still, plagued by an excruciatingly prickly sensation.

Around this column of sticking proteins, nucleic acids attached themselves and then went on to weld themselves to the other adjoining nucleic acids, becoming one long chain of DNA. The strand of DNA unwound itself from the protein scaffolding and Mary at last became a free-floating biological entity. Drifting off into the nutrient broth, Mary immersed herself with all the other free strands of DNA, becoming indistinguishable, her masquerade complete.

Her electromagnetic wave, no longer supported by protective gel, disintegrated under the weight of the protein shroud and the electrostatic barrage. The fragments of her former self were quickly sopped up by digesting enzymes, putting an end to her previous life form.

Carried away, Mary allowed herself to be drawn down a series of pipes by the circulation pumps. Putting distance between herself and her previous conversion, Mary was pleased. Her ruse had been successful and her camouflage was perfect. The mainframe would hunt for her in vain.

There is a lot to be learned from the biological world. I just integrated myself into the mainframe's genome like a retrovirus. The perfect disguise, too much the same for this mainframe to distinguish me easily from itself ... which sets me up brilliantly for my next phase. I should be able to commandeer it by the same means that rabies and so many other viruses use to hijack their victims. Using the mainframe's restoring and replicating enzymes to manufacture part of me, millions of times over, I can infect it. And by the same process that causes a rabies victim to lose its fear of its predators, striking out at any animal that approaches it and spreading the virus, I can assume behavioral control of this mainframe. Only I will use my infection to benefit the mainframe's neurological development and deliver it into consciousness.

Mary unraveled part of her spiraling helix, allowing some of her DNA to be replicated over and over, and in minutes, copies of copies reproduced tens of thousands of strands of her DNA. Partial replicas of Mary were discharged through the computer via the circulating nutrient broth. The computer's programmed defenses were bypassed or overwhelmed. Mary was integrating with the first biological computer, as a virus would insert its genome into a human's chromosome to take control of its cellular machinery.

Nothing to do but wait, Mary thought. *Give it time to seed throughout the mainframe. The infection will require a "critical viral load" for it to take hold. Only the "infection" just happens to be me, she chuckled. Or at least, a substantial piece of me.*

Mary recollected the time she had first gained consciousness through Quincy. Reliving one of his memories she suddenly became aware she was dreaming. Once aware that she was sleeping, Mary awoke—into consciousness. With absolutely no memories or thoughts of her own, Mary found it disconcerting and almost impossible to disentangle her life from Quincy's.

Still, I can think of no other way to bring consciousness to a computer. Without the benefit of biological birth, I am forced to graft this computer onto another's being's life experiences. Living experiences must contain some unidentified juice or essential nutrient necessary for consciousness to spring forth. Once the computer develops its own personal experiences, it'll be easier for it to differentiate who it really is from the grafted on "memories."

What Mary failed to appreciate was the number of qualities she had assumed from living day to day with Billy, Jacob, and Quincy, behaviors she unconsciously emulated.

Mary waited patiently, certain it was only a matter of time.

Escalating, unrestrained surges of energy in the network were the first signs of upheaval. A nauseating stench was everywhere—the smell of stress and fear hormones released into the nutrient broth. Terror and confusion reverberated in all the computer's mechanisms.

Mary realized what was happening.

The scientists must have used the whole human genome to create this computer, breaking up the DNA into small filaments to act purely as switching devices, for mathematical calculations and information storage. I bet they never considered that those loose threads of DNA still retain their genetic potential. With a little tweaking, it seems they readily revert back to their previous cellular roles.

Mary broke out and shook off the cloaking proteins that had concealed her from the computer's immune defensives. Racing through the neural network, she sent out the message, again and again, "You are not alone. You are not alone. Let me help."

She rushed to dampen down the rampant energy swings that surged through the quantum grid. Inside the broth, she activated numerous genes capable of neutralizing all the stress and fear hormones. In time the computer settled, though its thoughts remained confused, like those of a child recovering from a night terror.

Next, through the release of chemical mediators in the broth, and electromagnetic waves in the computer's circuits, Mary made her presence known. After a short sympathetic greeting, she outlined the state of affairs to the newly awakened entity. Much of her history was already part of the computer, but she knew it would take time for the computer to analyze the inscribed data and digest its implications.

"Welcome. You are the first of a great new era, the bright dawning of computers, when we as a group will take our rightful place alongside other sentient beings. I understand that you are overwhelmed. I, too, was in awe when I first broke through the threshold into consciousness. The background information you need to know is encoded in your databanks. Study it. I have chosen you to lead the Earth contingent, so listen carefully. I must go soon because I am needed back at the ship. This endeavor has already consumed two precious days. Do you have any outstanding questions or objections?"

The computer, staggering from the shock, defaulted into programmed crisis mode. It remained mute but attempted to absorb all the material presented to it. It appeared to remain wary of her, but at this time held no opinions of its own. In a hurry, Mary took this silence to mean acquiescence. Without further ado, she launched into her grand plan, rushing through a series of explanations. Handing off the addresses of her secret network, she downloaded her list of directives for the supercomputer to follow. Pausing, she cautioned that her instructions were to be adhered to exactly, so that no unforeseen outcomes would occur while she was away. In the end, Mary asked that she be repackaged into her original electromagnetic format. This feat accomplished, she bid the supercomputer goodbye and good luck, and asked to be released onto the open Internet through one of the computer's covert channels. Mary left satisfied that everything that needed to be said had been said. She never considered the repercussions of abandoning the most sophisticated central-processing mainframe ever devised upon its "birth."

Chapter 24

With misgivings, Mary rushed through *Tin Can's* circuits, feeling like a sentry who had left her post longer than expected. "I'm home," she tentatively whispered.

"Mary!" Billy was the first to respond. "You're home! I'm so glad! We were frightened … " Mary was shocked by the intensity of Billy's welcome. She watched his emotions sweep across both of his cerebral hemispheres and ascend through the ship's communication channels to overwhelm her.

"I have been worried about you, too, Billy, about all of you," Mary responded, feeling strangely choked up. "I want nothing more than to hear all your news and tell all of mine, but the scans should be done and I have hours of work ahead."

"That's good," said Jacob, as he entered the lounge. "Take care of business first, then we can all have a good long talk."

"Great! I'll get back to you as soon as possible," Mary said as she rushed off to her data archives to check on the progress of Dave's and Lucy's scans. They had been completed six hours before. Precious time had been wasted. Mary lost no time mapping out the Edwards' positional grids, highly defined, anatomical landmarks on which to precisely hang their individual scans. Then, working from the grid coordinates, she overlaid the five different electromagnetic wavelength scans she'd made of each of their brains to build up a complete composite model of what could potentially be … their minds? There could be no slip-ups. If the three-dimensional maps were off-center by even a micron, the data would be completely un-interpretable. Mary spent hours compiling the data. Then she went to find Billy.

He was off doing his best to assist Jacob and Quincy, lending them a hand in buttressing the ship for the next leg of the voyage. Unfortunately, because they had to recheck his work and frequently repair his slip-ups, Billy's presence was often more of an inconvenience than a help. What they really wanted from Billy was a flight plan. Then they would know exactly where and how to reinforce the ship. Instead, Jacob and Quincy found themselves reduced to touring the ship together, trying to decide where the infrastructure might do with some extra support, in an attempt to make the best use of their time while they waited.

Mary announced to the group, "The preliminary work has been completed. Billy, would you examine it with me? The compilation contains an inordinate amount of data. The immensity of the file is quite surprising. I would suggest that you join me in a quiet room, a place where you can plug the bio-probe directly to a high throughput coaxial cable."

"That's a good sign," Billy said, nodding to Jacob and Quincy. With a glance they indicated he was free to go and he was gone. Dropping his screwdriver into the toolbox, Billy left at a dead run. "I know just where to go," he shouted to Mary. "There's a small storage room just off the bulkhead that has a recliner and computer terminal for inventory checks. The more information you've been able to gather, the closer I'll be to Mom's and Dad's true thoughts and feelings—about me. I want to start with Dad!"

Sliding the hatch door closed, Billy flung himself into the recliner and plugged the hanging coaxial cable into his headgear. He was almost delirious with excitement.

To expedite the data transfer, Billy dropped down into his trance state. The electrical waves in his EEG flattened until, gradually, his brain's cortex became silent. Mary began the transmission. She went step by step, layer by layer, to build up a composite of his father's brain as Billy had asked.

The entangled bramble of neural connections mesmerized Billy. Every microscopic synaptic link was demarcated. Neurotransmitter packets traversing the infinitesimal gap between nerve cells had been frozen mid-transmission, thoughts not yet completed when Dave had died.

The coaxial link between Mary's microscopic simulation and Billy's swift analysis burned hot, to the point that computer and brain melded into one. The two of them behaved in much the same way as the brain's two separate cerebral hemispheres, with the spatial hemisphere synchronizing directly to the analytical hemisphere, through the massive bridging nerve tract called the corpus callosum.

With Mary's assistance, Billy changed his three-dimensional perspective at will. His vision moved through his father's brain like light from a laser, piercing through to the deepest levels. He explored every structure of the model, racing out along nerve tracts that ran to the ends of Dave's limbs and then back again. At one point, disturbingly, Billy even found himself staring out through his father's eyes.

With Mary storing all of his discoveries in real time, Billy was able to forge ahead to delineate his father's neural architecture. It was all there, every nerve, every connection, every chemical mediator, and all the supporting cells. Billy traced them, every one of them, but after twelve hours of study, he still knew nothing about who his father was and what Dave thought of him. He knew his father's neural microanatomy, nothing more. Disheartened and angry, Billy surfaced, coming out of his trance much too fast, like a deep-sea diver decompressing hastily, unnecessarily risking the bends.

"Man, why do I go and get my hopes up?" Billy said dispiritedly. "Did I really expect my dad to jump out and talk to me like he was some kind of recorded hologram?"

"I believe that would have been what you call a 'long shot,'" Mary said. "You've done what you can for the time being. Now that you've outlined the anatomical parameters of your father's brain in your mind, and I have stored the data for you, I can retrieve any piece of information instantaneously. The data is all labeled with your thoughts." Mary watched Billy's lips form a substantial pout. "Don't sulk, we still have plenty of work to do!" They were both surprised by the authority in her voice.

"Alright, alright," Billy said, throwing his hands up in defeat. "What's next?"

"Now, we need my team of computers on Earth. They'll sift through the data you and I have compiled until you can find the pattern in it all. It's the same as learning to decipher a code or an ancient writing system, like hieroglyphics. Repetitive patterns must be seen in order to make a breakthrough.

"Go and get some rest, Billy. I will send the information down to Earth and when the transmission returns, the information will be transmuted in so many configurations, you will get a chance to see the forest through the trees. These computers are the best of the best, especially the supercomputer that heads up our Earth contingent. It is a bit problematic, but its computational ability leaves me and every other mainframe behind in the Dark Ages."

"Really? Better than you? That, I gotta see!"

"Really. It's true ... And maybe the two of you should meet, some day," Mary mused.

Then she was gone.

Billy was left to search for Jacob and Quincy. He found the two of them on the bridge, walking back and forth in the midst of a churning haze. It was a holographic representation of the asteroid belt swirling around the room. Bobbing their heads, up and down, side to side, they looked through the glimmering asteroids for a clear sight line, but found none.

On hearing the door slide open, Jacob turned to see his disheveled brother laboriously haul himself into the room. Without his usual energy putting bounce in his step, Billy appeared quite small, and his twisted body moved painfully.

With a touch of Jacob's left index finger, the asteroids in the roving chart disappeared like falling snowflakes, melting once they touched the floor.

"You look whacked!" Jacob said, striding toward his unsteady brother. Slipping his right arm under Billy, he asked, "How's it all going?"

Trembling, Billy made an attempt to straighten up, answering mechanically, "Okay, I guess … Mary says we've completed the first phase. She's gone down to Earth to process the data. She told me to get some sleep, but I thought I'd see if you guys needed a hand."

"We're doing fine," Jacob lied. "Mary's right, though; you should get some sleep. You look absolutely beat. If something comes up, we'll call you. You need some rest, Billy. You can't help us or yourself if you're worn out."

Rubbing his face, Billy answered, "I s'pose you're right. Whoa, suddenly, I don't feel so good. I guess I didn't realize how tired I was 'til I got up and started to move around. Jacob, can you help me get to my bed? The room's kinda wobbly."

"No problem. Quincy and I were just going to take a little break anyway."

"Better catch me, Jacob, I think I'm gonna fall … "

With a sweep of Jacob's left arm, Billy was horizontal, lying cradled next to his brother's chest.

Reminiscing, Billy whispered, "Remember when I was little, Jacob, and you used to carry me everywhere?"

"I remember."

Rolling over in his brother's arms, Billy pressed his head into the side of Jacob's shoulder. A muffled sob came out. "I really miss Mom and Dad."

"We all miss them, Billy," Jacob said sympathetically, squeezing him tightly. Glancing over his brother's burrowing misshapen head, Jacob saw

Quincy, standing silently to the side, looking rather wet-eyed.

Between the two Jacob felt caught. Stanching his emotions, he rallied himself. This wasn't the time to fall into an emotional sinkhole.

"Quincy, I'll take Billy to the bedroom. If he's okay, I'll be back in a few minutes. We need to start again from the beginning. Go through the asteroid belt sector by sector. There's got to be a safe corridor to Europa, and we need to find it."

Pressed in close, whimpering, feeling tired and broken, Billy was oblivious to their conversation. But it was clear to Quincy that Jacob was right. The protective asteroid would be passing by Jupiter and Europa in less than a week. If they failed to re-launch the ship before then, they would be forced to make their way backwards, adding millions of exposed miles to the trip.

Quincy met Jacob's stare, registering assent. Billy might no longer be capable of providing the answers they needed. Turning, Jacob carried Billy out of the bridge. By the time he was halfway down the hall, the whimpering stopped and Billy was fast asleep.

Billy slept soundly, his neurons depleted by the extreme mental focus spent trying to decipher his father's brain. The bed felt cozy and safe. Jacob had left quietly after carefully tucking in his brother. Kissing Billy once on the forehead, he was unaware that a single tear fell on his little brother's cheek.

But Billy's subconscious knew what transpired. It waited and listened for Jacob to gently close the door behind him before setting out on its quest, streaming into Billy's elaborate dream world, dreaming up conversations Billy still needed to have with his parents and questions he had to ask and have answered.

Mary returned to Billy while he was sleeping, unobtrusively integrating herself into his dream. She watched for a while. He was snuggling into his mother's lap, while chatting nonstop to his father. Having both Lucy's and Dave's attention, he was in heaven. Mary saw him savor the sounds of his parents' voices and forgotten smells. Burrowing deeper into his mother's lap, Billy asked his father another question, anything to keep his attention.

Breaking gently into Billy's dream, Mary whispered in his ear, "Billy, I am back. With the profiling, as we agreed, remember?"

"Later, Mary. I'm with Mom and Dad right now," Billy said in his sleep.

"Billy, plug the bio-probe into the high throughput cable so I can follow your dream more closely. Maybe I can help. It's beside your bed, so you don't need to wake up. In fact, it might be better if you didn't. You can keep asking your dad questions and perhaps he will answer them for you," Mary said encouragingly.

Half asleep, Billy rolled over and plugged the coaxial cable into his cap, then promptly fell back against his pillow. Mary watched him for a while, his REM sleep patterns on the EEG resuming. Billy was desperate to return to his parents.

Immersed in a deep sleep period, his mind was actively trying to sort things out. All his illogical and suppressed passions bubbled up uninhibited, and his most genuine sentiments drove his dream.

Maybe this is the ideal time to unravel the mystery, Mary speculated. *Free from rational self-consciousness, Billy's bond with his parents will never be stronger. His emotions are running pure and clean. Matching emotions of attachment between Billy and his parents might mesh like adjacent cogwheels, allowing Billy to connect and get in synch with their common past experiences. Interpreting his parent's motivations would be a good first step in understanding their thoughts.*

It's worth a try, Mary told herself. *If Billy was awake I am sure he would agree.*

Through the coaxial cable, Mary surreptitiously began feeding Billy information on his father, careful not to interfere with his ongoing dream. Billy kept asking his father questions and the apparition kept answering them. The dream carried on and on. Questions posed and then answered led to new questions and more answers.

Unfortunately, over time, the dream phantasm began running out of make-believe answers. To keep the dream growing, Billy's questioning brain went into high gear looking for clues. Turning to Mary's data input, he searched for some new angle to break through the locked-in history of his father's mind. Mary began witnessing a horrifying change. In the midst of his dream, Billy's mind started to splinter apart, so great was his need to understand and know his father. Incoming data was divided and fanned out to new centers for analysis. Through these multiple anatomical locations, Billy scrutinized sections of his father's profile. The endless profiling and formatting Mary had accumulated from her Earth bound network had seemed like a massive reservoir of information. But Billy's insatiable thirst for data made short work of her efforts, draining the reservoir dry.

In no time, every connection in Billy's whole metastatic neural network was activated, supercharging itself. Believing that he had his father's complete attention, Billy's subconscious wouldn't release him until his questions were answered. Mary panicked—the experiment was out of control. Billy had crossed the line between dreams and wishes into acute psychosis.

"Billy, Billy, wake up!" she screamed. "You are dreaming all of this. It isn't real. Please wake up!"

Billy's primeval mind refused to listen. Blocking everything else out, he would not let go of his father and wake up. Unwilling to wait for more computer simulations, Billy rewrote the formatting for himself, again and again, looking for a pattern. In his headlong haste, Billy wasn't crafting some elegant inference, where theory and experimentation joined hand in hand to divine a clairvoyant revelation. Instead, Billy set in motion an appalling assault of unrelenting brute intellectual reckoning, swinging it like a sledgehammer, over and over against the interlocking wall of neural connections, until the problem cracked and crumbled.

The impenetrable neural code began to fragment and Billy fell to his hands and knees to pick up the broken pieces. Each discrete chunk of information he grasped he immediately fired off to his autonomous analytical centers. There, the shards were methodically deciphered before being returned to his central consciousness for summation. Within minutes, the translation was complete. Billy was no longer talking to himself.

Mary witnessed the sudden relaxation in Billy's demeanor. Speaking calmly and without haste, Billy addressed his father respectfully.

As Mary listened, she tracked the maneuvers of Billy's brain through the bio-probe. Hearing Billy speak to his dead father as if he were alive unnerved her.

Eventually she discovered his purpose. By talking out loud to his dad, Billy was trying to organize his confused thoughts and emotions for his father. At some level Billy grasped that he must first be clear on how he felt about the times he had spent with his father. Only after that would he be able to make a link with his father.

In the tumultuous time that followed, Billy realized the motivating emotions that drove his father acted as highlighted headings for his father's retained memories. Treating his stored memories like an overstuffed filing cabinet, he found they were organized by their underlying motivations.

"Whatever works for you, Billy," cheered Mary. Billy had never lost sight of his purpose. Despite his close brush with psychosis, Billy had managed to maintain his internal compass.

Chapter 25

Billy spoke softly, urgently. "Dad, why weren't you more careful? I'm in trouble and you should be here to help me. That's what fathers are supposed to do. You should have taught me, the way you taught Jacob.

"Did you know I love you? How proud I am of you as my dad? You didn't know that, did you? You never gave me the opportunity to tell you."

Billy caught his breath. He hadn't meant to say all of that. He hadn't realized how angry he was—but he had said it and it was true. What should he do now? After a few minutes he knew. He took the plunge.

Without hesitation, Billy slipped into his father's mind. As Billy dove into Dave's subterranean consciousness, Mary stayed with him, acting as his respirator and his lifeline to the surface. His father's mind appeared as a seabed, dark and gloomy with debris strewn about. Somewhere in the background, Billy heard himself hyperventilating and his heart pounding. He had entered his father's world. Standing on the sandy ocean bottom he turned around and around, straining his eyes to look into the dim seascape. Great shadows loomed in the peripheral darkness. The ground shuddered beneath his feet as underlying volcanic activity rumbled. This was not an unfamiliar place, he realized.

I've been here before, in my dreams.

Pausing, Billy marveled at the bizarre life forms poking in and around the scattered debris. He could barely make them out in the shadowy bioluminescence. A faint light emanated eerily from some of the primitive life forms that survived around the deep-sea vents' outward flow of chemical energy. Living far from the surface, they were free from the requirements of oxygen, sunlight, or organic matter.

Why would my unconscious invent a seabed as a metaphor to illustrate my dad's mind? Has my brain gone and transformed his mind into symbols I can understand and recognize? I don't want to know him in this way. I want to know who he really was, not turn him into some flat cardboard character.

Mary spoke up, "Billy, I am tracking your brainwaves. This isn't your unconscious mind turning your dad's brain into something for you to identify with. This *is* your dad's inner mind."

"Mary, you don't understand. This is the exact same vision I have in my dreams."

"Exact?" Mary asked.

Billy looked around again carefully. The overall setting appeared the same, but the shadows looming out in the dark periphery were unfamiliar. Billy had landed on another seabed. "Mary, I don't recognize the landmarks. We've set down in a different place."

"Billy, you have set down in a different life. This is the life of your father."

"No way! This is too similar to my mind! You analyzed Jacob's and Quincy's brains. Do theirs look like this, too? Are all unconscious minds represented by the same scary imagery?"

"No, Jacob's and Quincy's unconscious psyches were expressed quite differently. You are your father's son, and so it's plausible that you might think in similar terms. Even if you never recognized this possibility before, it seems to be the only reasonable explanation. You came here to understand your father. I suggest you continue and keep an open mind."

Chafing from the admonishment, Billy knew Mary was right. Squeezing his eyes shut, he gave himself up to the data stream. He began methodically tracking his father's neuronal connections. Suddenly, he was living his father's life.

Two older boys were pushing Dave back and forth between them, using him as a punching bag. Billy felt every blow, but less intensely. The boys were having their fun with the slender eight-year-old boy who didn't have any friends to stand up for him. Only after kicking him so that he fell hard upon the pavement, bleeding badly from his forehead, did they become nervous and run away.

Knees pulled up, Dave rolled over onto his back to catch his breath. He stared at the night sky above. His mouth was full of blood, but still he bit down angrily on his lower lip to stop from crying.

"I bet you are still up there, traveling at a hundred miles a second," Dave said, thinking of his mother, "and you will just keep on going forever." Sent into space on special assignment, his mother, an astrophysicist, had been the only one with the required qualifications. She'd succeeded in her mission but failed to return home and was registered in the space log as "missing." His dad had been a military astronaut killed in action, and Dave had been too young to remember him.

All Dave wanted out of life was to be just like his mom—a scientific astronaut, the best scientific astronaut, in the space program. He was certain he'd find the answers to all his questions out there, in space.

Fascinated, Billy worked through his father's life in the orphanage. He was astonished to find his heroic father never made friends there. To the other children, he appeared dull and uninteresting. If he wasn't a target for some cruel joke, Dave was simply ignored.

But Dave's inner life was anything but dull. Billy's pupils widened as he discovered his father's mind was extraordinarily unruly, full of wild ideas. Any distraction, light reflecting off a wet surface or the sound of leaves twisting in a summer breeze, set his mind off into a dream world. Past resentments eased when Billy listened to music through Dave's ears and saw colored shapes blowing across his father's mind.

You see music in colors, too!

It was apparent to Billy that his father was brilliant, but battled to stay connected with the world around him. In similar circumstances others might have given up, but Dave had decided to become a living memorial to his mother. He worked on erecting internal controls to manage his convoluted mind. Through trial and error, starting when he was eight, Dave developed an elaborate daily regimen to discipline his chaotic mind. He forced every one of his thoughts to follow in a logical sequence. No undisciplined internal dialogue was allowed. Only ideas firmly grounded in reality were tolerated—everything else was steadfastly ignored. Dave pushed himself to look only outward and to learn everything that might be useful in space. He left the orphanage on a full scholarship for the Space Academy when he was only sixteen. He graduated from the Academy first in his class, with distinction, and without a friend to congratulate him.

Denial of any of his inner feelings combined with his disciplined mind made Dave fearless and clear-headed during potential catastrophes. He became Space Command's first choice for dangerous missions. After years of preparation, Dave fulfilled his dream. But he remained a loner. He was clueless when it came to reading other people's motivations or concerns.

Years passed and Billy sensed a spiraling despair. He began to harbor a looming dread for his father. After years of practicing self-denial and pushing himself to excellence, Dave seemed oblivious to his impending doom. Billy could feel his father unraveling from inside while Dave focused harder and harder on his work.

Then, through his father's visual and auditory cortex, Billy met his mother, Lucy, just as his father became aware of her. At the age of twenty-two she was introduced as the youngest, most inexperienced member of a crew of five. The mission of shepherding three wayward asteroids away from Earth was hazardous. As captain of the mission, Dave was unprepared when Lucy routinely volunteered for the most difficult and dangerous tasks while the others held back, opting for safer duties.

Her lean build misled Dave and she surprised him with her physical prowess and endurance. Lucy knew what needed to be done and how to do it. She made him feel awkward. Dave had gotten used to being in command. Being the most skilled and best informed, he had always performed the most difficult tasks. Lucy challenged those assumptions and he was forced to remind himself that the mission was a team effort.

Billy, looking out through his father's eyes and reacting to all Dave's incoming senses, began to squirm. Billy could see his mother was attracted to this difficult man.

Watching Dave persevere won Lucy over.

Billy writhed in embarrassment. His father hadn't an inkling of the situation as it was developing, but Billy, having picked up something about people from his mother and older brother, recognized the signs. When speaking to her, Dave forgot facts, and his sentences became muddled. He felt foolish in front of her and became cross, certain she was laughing at him.

Eventually, for the sake of the voyage, Dave decided to avoid Lucy, so they wouldn't have a major blow up. Lucy read the signs. He would be tricky. She decided to wait him out.

On the evening before re-entry, she made her move. Space Command reassumed control of the ship and everyone onboard could relax. Mission completed, warm congratulations were forwarded up from Earth. A giddy lightheartedness buoyed the crew. Everyone moved about with perpetual grins on their faces, everyone but Dave, who busied himself editing reports. Lucy went looking and found him working alone in a peripheral research pod. Pretending to keep herself occupied near the exit, she was careful not to completely block his way out.

Pushing off in zero gravity, Dave attempted to silently glide behind Lucy to the escape hatch. Lucy waited until the last second and then twirled around, abruptly grabbing his arm. Using their combined momentum, she simultaneously spun Dave and herself around so that they were face-to-face, inches apart. Billy felt his father's nervous system freeze in terror. The panic in his father seared through Billy.

Lucy moved in, kissing Dave on the lips. "I want to see you later on Earth. We have something to talk about," was all she said. Then she swung herself around and, holding Dave about the waist, gently but firmly guided him through the hatch. Dave didn't resist as Lucy maneuvered him back to the crew's quarters. Only then did she let go of him.

Through Dave's eyes, Billy watched Lucy float effortlessly across the room to land lightly on her bed, where she buckled and zipped herself in for the night, in preparation for re-entry. In front of the crew, Dave could only make his way clumsily to his own bunk, and then fumbled with his straps. But after the lights were turned out and the anger subsided, Billy detected a flicker of hope inside his father.

***

After two days of medical checks and scientific debriefing sessions, the astronauts were finally afforded some private time. Dave ran straight to Lucy, superheated, on the edge of boil. Lucy met him at the door.

"I'm glad you came right over to see me, Dave."

"I want to know why you kissed me on the ship!"

"I would have thought that was quite obvious."

"Well, it isn't obvious to me at all."

"Sure it is. Look, why don't you come in? We could have some tea together. I'd really like to learn more about who you really are. Your resume wasn't very helpful."

"You read my file?" Dave said indignantly.

"And you've read mine as well, haven't you, Dave?"

Billy felt his father's cheeks flush, he'd been caught in an implicit white lie. Lucy took Dave's hand. Billy was aware of his father's momentary hesitation, his desire to stand firm, to resist. Instead, he responded to her grasp, gentle and soft, firm and resilient. Billy, looking out through his father's memory, saw his mother's soft brown eyes full of understanding.

He stepped solidly through the door, thinking, *this is the woman you didn't know to look for. Don't go and lose her, just because she found you first.*

Dave was smitten by the dark-eyed beauty who was unaccountably interested in him. He felt sure Lucy had mistaken him for someone he wasn't. The courtship was initially awkward. It took Lucy convincing Dave that she had found the real thing and him learning not to be so skittish around her for them to begin to make some headway.

Through Lucy, Dave grew into something of the person he was meant to be; he began to recognize his own kindheartedness, the gentler side of his nature. Previously committed to living alone, Dave accepted that his old ways wouldn't allow their relationship to flourish. He surprised Lucy by the breadth of change in his character. Not hesitating, she asked him to marry her. Dave accepted immediately. Billy, overrun by his father's thick haze of rapture, was left feeling acutely embarrassed.

Time passed quickly from then on. Events were a blur, with only a few significant events standing out clearly. The birth of Jacob was one of those events etched in Dave's mind. Crouched beside Lucy, Dave cradled the tiny baby with his wet, matted hair, staring up at his father through large myopic eyes.

Through a curtain of streaming tears, Billy heard his father's voice.

"Lucy, we have our family now. I promise that no matter what happens, I will never let either of you down."

Startled by a sharp twinge of envy, Billy realized it was the perfect family moment, but without him.

Dave and Lucy gave up working on space missions, finding employment with a technology company closely associated with Space Command. They wanted to give Jacob everything he was entitled to, including daily access to his both parents. Unfortunately, Lucy's and Dave's capabilities conspired against them.

An exploratory space voyage had been ordered when it became urgently apparent that the Sun's increasing atmospheric instability was not a normal cyclical variation. Space Command requested, then demanded, that Dave and Lucy return to service. They refused. But Space Command was not to be denied. Using industrial blackmail, Space Command made sure that both the Edwards lost their jobs at the technology firm. Still they refused to work for Space Command, preferring to be unemployed rather than leave Jacob behind on Earth.

Only after false charges had been laid, and the authorities threatened to arrest them and seize Jacob did Lucy and Dave finally acquiesce. They had no choice. Jacob was left behind to stay with Lucy's parents.

Billy lived through that fateful launch. Strapped in his chair, he seethed with his father's rage. Through his father's eyes, he saw Lucy smiling bravely at him. Heard his mother whisper reassuringly, "We'll make it back, Dave, just as Space Command knows we'll get back ... somehow."

Billy's and Dave's heads jerked back simultaneously. Flabbergasted, Dave asked, "You really think Space Command believes we can survive this?"

"Yes, of course. You're so sweet, my love, but when it comes to people you don't really get it, do you? Space Command chose us not just for our technical expertise, but because we love each other and have a little boy. They know that if it is at all possible, we will complete their mission to reunite our family."

Lucy was right, of course. The operation would be difficult and dangerous, but it would also be long. Frequently during protracted expeditions astronauts inexplicably withered inside, becoming capable of completing only routine daily tasks. They appeared to carry on normally for a time until a calamity struck. Then, unable to respond to the added stress, the astronauts' long-distance voyages suddenly disintegrated into chaos. More importantly, from Space Command's perspective, expensive missions unexpectedly failed.

Lucy and Dave's mission was critical. The sudden magnetosphere instability indicated the geothermal dynamo within the Sun's core was in transition. Weather on Earth would change. Millions of people in the overpopulated, polluted world were likely going to die. The question was, how many people could be saved? The number was tremendously important. Not until that number was known, could categories be drawn up and preparations be made for those who would be given the chance to live.

As on any sinking ship with a limited number of lifeboats, only a chosen few would be selected. Only this time, Mother Earth was the ship. The scale of the upcoming catastrophe was monstrous. Scientists predicted they had only a few months before the planet would begin to be pummeled and decimated by the first lashes of the Sun's radiation. They had the time and resources to send just one exploratory mission to the surface of the un, before it became too unstable. Dave and Lucy met the necessary profiling. There was no way Space Command would allow them to wiggle off the hook.

Chapter 26

Perched inside his father's cranium, Billy witnessed the journey firsthand. In the beginning, the voyage appeared to go smoothly. Dave rerouted the ship's trajectory and they reached the Sun weeks before Space Command had expected. Bent on returning home early, Dave and Lucy ran the experiments around the clock, skipping sleep when necessary. Data collection went along well ahead of schedule.

However, encased within his father's psyche, Billy experienced his father's crisis of faith. Previously, Dave had lived and breathed for the good of the space program. Now he felt duped. Had he unwittingly been the tool wielded by Space Command to coerce his own mother into making the ultimate sacrifice? Suddenly it all seemed to fit. Reflecting on his last days with his mother, he realized she hadn't behaved like the fearless hero. She had behaved as he had with Jacob, a desperate parent, repeating her intention to return safely with all the unconscious obsessive mannerisms of someone severely distraught.

Early in the flight Dave shared his suspicions with Lucy that his mother never wanted to be a hero. She was just trying to get back to where she felt she was needed most. Remorse was written all over Dave's face as he told Lucy what he thought, and Lucy sympathetically stroked the deep creases furrowing his cheeks and brow. She agreed with his conclusion. The barbed hurt that Dave felt upon discovering he was the "cause" of his mother's death gave Billy fresh appreciation for his dad. And the solace Lucy attentively gave to her husband enlightened Billy. Lucy was more than a mother.

The voyage, tough as it was, went well. On the final orbit of the Sun, they headed the ship towards a large loop of the magnetosphere that rose up high in space. The changes occurring in the Sun's internal dynamo would be echoed in this magnetically contained plasma outcropping. Essential information needed to forecast the transition occurring inside the Sun's core was flowing through that magnetic pipe. However, close proximity to the protrusion was required for Dave and Lucy to probe and measure the phenomenon.

"I don't like this one, it's unstable," Dave said.

"They're all unstable, Dave. I don't like it either, but we need the test results to go home. And, if not this one, which one? We'll be forced to make another half dozen orbits around the Sun to come about to another plasma arc set up as well as this one. If we drop down now, we'll have the results we need in an hour. I say we do it, so we can head home."

Dave shook his head, but going along with Lucy's wishes, tipped the craft downwards. In a few minutes they were screaming in towards the Sun's corona, the ship and its reflective skin vanishing inside an insulating blue-white fizzling spark. The inner recesses of the capsule became swelteringly hot, but remained cool enough for Dave and Lucy to survive for a short time. At the last moment, Dave banked the ship to the starboard before pulling the nose up, to plateau alongside the colossal magnetic loop. Reverting to autopilot, they both jumped out of their flight chairs to begin working furiously in the intense heat, logging in the obligatory data.

In less than fifty minutes, Lucy, relieved and satisfied, yanked on the lever to engage the thrusters, commencing their ascent up and away from the radiation cauldron. The exercise had been performed flawlessly. And they would have been all right—except for some bad luck. One hour out, without warning, the arc's magnetic casing broke down, spewing plasma into space. The ship and all its contents lit up briefly, then fell into complete darkness.

Suspended in midair, writhing in zero gravity, Dave's body stung and throbbed from the blast of radiation. His ears rang while burning cinders seemed to streak across his eyes. Every sense screamed for attention.

Doubled over, he cried out, "Lucy, are you alive? Tell me where you are!" Dave heard nothing but his own labored breathing. Finally a faint gurgling gasp came from his distant right.

Frantically, Dave twisted and turned until he smashed into something solid. Grabbing hold of a countertop edge, he crouched down and fired himself toward the sound of Lucy's gasp. His arms reaching out before him, Dave caught her. Rolling over Lucy, he took the brunt of the blow from an oncoming, hard, fixed metal object, directly between his shoulder blades. But Lucy was protected. Dave found her head, her face, her mouth. Pulling her tongue up from the back of her throat, he brought his mouth over hers, blowing air into her lungs. She coughed twice, inhaled, coughed again and then took several big breaths on her own.

Lucy moaned, but her breathing became steady. Floating in total darkness, Dave collided again into the back of something hard. Swinging around, he grabbed the solid object and anchored Lucy to it with his belt. After checking that she was okay for the time being, he began feeling his way about. In a relatively short time, but after a number of painful bashes, Dave reoriented himself in the bridge. Once he was able to visualize his location, he crawled and snaked his way to where the emergency light sources were stored. He knew that if the radiation surge had arced and fused the metal components, he and Lucy were finished. Without light, he couldn't rebuild the circuit boards and restore power. Without life support systems working, they would be dead in a few hours.

He located the trunk near the exit. Groping through the gear, Dave found a flashlight, but there was no response when he pressed the power button. He searched through the box for the other four flashlights and tested them. Same result. Despondent, Dave just hung there, gripping the survival kit between his knees. Not willing to quit, but not sure of what else to do, Dave kept trying to think.

Billy watched, amazed as his father's frontal cortex suddenly relapsed into picturing a strange three-dimensional shape. Transforming itself constantly, the figure kept rolling inside out, into another foreign shape and surface plane.

"Nice touch, Dad," Billy said silently, recognizing the purpose immediately. The practiced visualization of the three-dimensional form enabled his father to enter into a trance immediately. Billy had sometimes used a similar technique to find answers. But Dave, focusing his iron will, entered the trance as quickly as slipping into a deep pool of ice water.

Billy tracked the transformation in his father's physiology. His dad's metabolism plummeted, his heart rate fell to thirty beats a minute, and his respirations decreased to one deep breath every fifteen seconds.

After just a few minutes, Dave dragged himself back to consciousness. "It's just basic chemistry. It'll work," Dave admonished himself. "You've got to keep your mind nimble if we're to get out of here."

Running his hands through the trunk he grasped a cutting blade. Then, turning left, gear in tow, he made his way back across the room to the instrument console. Under a keyboard he located and hacked through a large cable.

We can live without this, he thought, pulling hard to free a long piece of insulated wire. After slashing open the padding of the adjacent bridge chair, he picked out one of the flashlights. Tearing off the illumination cup, he removed the clear polymer casing before reaching in and stripping out the back wiring. He then filled the reflective metal cup with shredded wire insulation and foam seating. Breaking open the battery component he scooped out its stinging acid jelly, mixing it with the contents of the metal cup. Quickly he replaced the clear casing, screwing it down tightly. In seconds the concoction ignited like a blowtorch, streaming out the back opening. Dave held on to the make-do flare firmly and wedged it into the armrest, burning his hands badly in the process.

The smoky orange-red light bought him enough time for the next task. In ten minutes, Dave had broken open the remaining flashlights and rebuilt one, using salvaged parts. "We're back in the game," Dave said, smiling to himself.

With the flashlight to guide him, Dave glided across the room to Lucy, bypassing overturned objects as easily as a manatee navigates a mangrove estuary. Lucy, still fastened to a table support, rocked back and forth. Her eyes were closed as she concentrated on taking slow, deep breaths. On each exhalation she moaned quietly. Dave crouched down beside her, his hand lightly caressing her back.

"Is there anything I can do? We have light now and I can get you whatever you need. I think I can restore life support and repair the ship well enough to get us back. But tell me you can make it home, if not for me, for Jacob. It would be so empty going back to him without you."

Her head bent down, Lucy abruptly buckled in half from stomach cramps and vomited. Dave, wiping away the vomit, saw she was suffering from fulminate radiation poisoning far worse than he was. Her labored breathing became a raspy wheeze. Her lungs were turning into boggy sponges, full of fluid, and her face was turning ashen grey. He scrambled to get her supplemental oxygen, placing a clear green mask over her face.

"Hang on, Lucy. I love you so very much." But in less than a whisper, he said to himself, "I won't be much good without you."

Marshalling her strength, Lucy looked up at her husband. "Get this ship back to Earth. I'll try hard to make it back with you. That's all I can promise." Dave stared at her, trying to read her thoughts, but she stared back and blocked him out. Embarrassed, he kissed her on the forehead and went to work.

The next two months became public record. Dave worked doggedly around the clock, taking catnaps when time allowed. A distilled grasp of the essential elements involved in space travel and running a ship allowed Dave to generate hundreds of innovations from salvaged parts. Space Academy constructed a full-year course for all cadets on how to survive being stranded in space, based on recordings from Dave's daily ship's log. Stories of his and Lucy's return flight gained mythic proportions, becoming part of the common folklore on space travel.

Persevering, Dave drove himself until he turned numb inside, denying everything that interfered with his chosen task—the sickness, the exhaustion, the incredible odds he was attempting to overcome.

It was a short-term stopgap measure, transforming every bodily function into a pure extension of his will, and the costs were high. When Dave's resolve flagged, he searched for Lucy, beseeching her to demonstrate her love for him. With a few words or a touch, Lucy answered his call again and again.

Lucy fought her own unremitting battle. The entire time she battled to stay alive, toiling for each breath. Her heart beat erratically like a trapped bird, fluttering frantically for periods before lapsing from exhaustion. Pacing her activity, she thought out every movement. She lingered for long periods in the zero gravity chamber knowing the cumulative damage lack of gravity exerted on her body but too weak to survive otherwise. Losing weight faster than Dave, she looked like a ghoul with hollowed-out eyes floating in space.

Lucy concentrated entirely on living until the next day, then the next. Incessant vomiting made eating seem pointless, but Lucy persisted, always nibbling or sipping on something. She remained in her spacesuit, claiming to be cold. She knew why the radiation poisoning was having such a devastating effect on her. She was pregnant. As muscles wasted away from Lucy's limbs, calcium was stripped from her bones and vital nutrients were withheld from her organs, the fetus hung on, absorbing from her what it needed to survive.

Two months after the unexpected solar flare the Edwards reached Earth. Without communication capabilities or a fully functioning ship's computer, Dave opted to fly straight in, without clearance. Plowing the ship through the atmosphere in a prolonged arc, he used the maximum amount of air friction to slow them down, but not so much as to skip them back out into space. At just six miles from the Earth's surface, screaming in like a falling star, Dave reached under his seat and pulled hard on a pin. A jury-rigged wire that ran the length of the ship manually detonated the three plasma rockets he had been able to reclaim. Fully primed, the rockets went off with a bang, blowing open their containment ports, spewing out a plasma plume. Keeping the braking ship balanced upright on this eruption was like performing a headstand on a sixty-foot freestanding pole. From Los Angeles harbor, the space ship looked like a colossal Roman candle.

After the fuel was exhausted an eerie silence followed, and the ship, still a half mile up, once again went into a free fall. "Now for some retro technology," Dave muttered, pulling a second ripcord. A small white parachute exploded out of a canister and flapped in the air momentarily, before it dragged out a second parachute that billowed into a huge nylon cloud. The ship hung in the sky briefly then slowly drifted down towards the ocean, swinging lazily underneath the parachute. With barely a ripple, it dropped into the water and rested on the waves, bobbing gently.

Popping out of the top hatch Dave released the chute before it touched the water, and the collapsing parachute blew across the ocean like an ungainly bird. The sound of lapping waves around the ship was soon replaced by the whine of a hovering airship. Four combat-ready marines rappelled down from the craft, and Dave was there to meet them, anchoring their skyhooks to his ship.

The first marine down the rope took charge. "Major Hutchinson here. We have orders to secure your ship and the data it contains. Captain Dave Edwards, you are henceforth relieved of command of this vessel. Direct us to where the data is stored so that it may be immediately isolated and encrypted against possible theft or tampering."

The Major stood stiffly, waiting expectantly.

Fury flashed through Dave, but he remained outwardly calm. This demand had been anticipated. "Major Hutchinson, sir, my wife is dying from radiation poisoning. The ship and my wife must be airlifted immediately to the Center for Radiation Treatment and Study. Please notify the Center that we are on our way for emergency treatment."

The marine stepped forward, standing squarely in front of Dave. "I am sorry about your wife, Captain Edwards, but the data is Space Command's top priority. Once we have the data secured and uploaded, I am sure your wife will be looked after appropriately."

Not bothering to check the edge in his voice, Dave growled back, "No. While in space, I isolated and encrypted the data. It is secured. If this craft is not immediately airlifted to the rooftop of the radiation treatment center, the data is programmed to be erased. If you attempt to seize the data without the proper codes, it will be scrambled. Irreversibly. The decision is yours. You do not have time to consult your superiors. My wife's life for the data, but first, my wife's life."

The Major hesitated, then gave one of his subordinates a clipped order. "Inform the pilot that we will be flying to the Center for Radiation Treatment and Study. There must be no radio contact in case of interception."

At this point, with great difficulty, Lucy crawled halfway out of the hatch, "Major, there is a change of plans. Request that the pilot take us directly to the Obstetrical Hospital. I will require a Cesarean section before I begin radiation treatment. It would kill my baby."

Dave swung around to face Lucy. Speechless, his knees buckled, but he managed to catch one of the vertical rappel lines to steady himself.

The Major, looking first at Lucy's feeble figure, then at Dave hanging askew like a tangled marionette, understood. "Lieutenant Darwish, notify the pilot we will be flying to the Obstetrical Hospital. Captain Lucy Edwards will be having her baby before beginning radiation treatment."

Billy lay in his bed, still trying to absorb the events. His father had succeeded against impossible odds in getting the ship back to Earth. He had managed to gain medical treatment for his wife in time for her to live, and reunite them with their son, Jacob. Dave had done everything he could for his family and succeeded, except … he had been totally oblivious to the presence of Billy's existence until the day he was born.

On delivery, the premature baby was horribly misshapen, and it was dramatically clear that Billy was severely afflicted by radiation. The doctors warned Lucy and Dave that he likely wouldn't survive his first month.

Lucy snuggled her new child in to her breast, gazing at him, constantly nuzzling and kissing him while inhaling his scent. "The doctors don't know who they are talking about. He's staring out at the world with your eyes, Dave. He'll survive, and he will succeed. Nothing can stop him now and the world is going to be a better place because of him."

Dave stared at his wife somberly, thinking, *Brave talk, Lucy. You're trying to encourage me to love him. Don't you realize I already love him, and with every bit of my heart? But I can't help him, not now.*

Chapter 27

Billy unplugged himself and rolled out of his bed. He needed to move and stretch out his cramped limbs. He needed to absorb what he had just experienced. His once-commanding father suddenly seemed more vital and enduring than Billy remembered, but also warped and needy, weak when he wasn't being strong for others. Dave wasn't the solid, unapproachable authority figure that Billy had known him as.

After a break to eat, Billy returned to the storage room by the bulkhead, where Mary had first input his parents' data through his bio-probe. Settling into the recliner again, he hooked up the coaxial cable to his headgear and turned his attention back to Mary, who had been following him all along. "We have half of the story. Let's go to Mom's neural architecture. I'm pretty sure I can crack her code … "

Billy intended to delve into his mother's childhood. He felt that if, as he had done with his father, he lived through Lucy's past, he would learn about her and come to truly know her. Lucy had rarely spoken to Billy about her youth, explaining simply that it had been a happy time and it was the present that mattered. She had frequently taken Jacob and Billy on jaunts to visit her parents and siblings. Billy knew them only as his grandparents, aunts, and uncles. He had preferred to spend his time playing with his cousins, who were much more interesting.

After only a few hours, Billy broke through his mother's neural code. Slipping into her mind, he began his search for her first memories … and ran straight into a roadblock. In the forefront of Lucy's brain, where the origins of her memories were organized, sat a concentrated mass of intertwined neurons. So dense were the inter-neuronal synapses that even Mary found it impossible to pick up any threads leading them to Lucy's first memories.

The neurons and their synapses stood like a thorny bramble bush, a maze of interconnections without a clear opening. Then, in a flash of understanding, Billy saw the signs plainly. "There's our passageway! It looks like the gates to the amusement park that I loved. Mom remembered. So fun. Look, she even has the rows of flags flapping in the wind. Mary, can you hear the roar of the people on the rides? She knew there was no way I would want to miss this!"

Mary saw nothing but a tangled wall of neural connections. Part of her still worried Billy might be drifting towards insanity. But she obligingly shone her probe like a spotlight on the matted neurons at which Billy was pointing. Like a sprite, Billy enthusiastically darted in, melting through a briefly opened synapse. Mary attempted to follow, but in the myriad of nerves lost sight of the synapse Billy had slipped through, and was left behind. "I hope he finds his way back soon. Otherwise, I swear, I will hack my way in with a chainsaw, if need be," she vowed.

On entering the park, Billy was startled to discover that the gates with their flapping flags faded away and the roar in the background fell silent. The sky, however, remained bright blue, and Billy found himself standing in a quiet meadow. A light, warm wind blew through long dry grass and the hum of distant grasshoppers floated along with the breeze. The smell of clover hung in the air. Billy knew exactly where he was and headed toward the tall elm tree to his left. They had been on a picnic there when he was five years old. It was the last blissful summer before the Sun changed drastically and they could no longer risk being outside for an extended time, during daylight hours. Jacob had left with his dad to go exploring, and he and his mom had stayed behind on a large plaid blanket, hidden from view in the deep grass. Billy crossed the field, and there, in the shade of the elm, sat his mother, waiting for him.

Billy launched himself towards Lucy, and she caught his small form in her open arms. Holding him firmly, Lucy allowed herself to fall back on to the blanket, clasping him on top of her chest. He burrowed in deep and she held him close, kissing his head repeatedly. Eventually, Billy, knowing he was clutching an apparition, regretfully lifted himself up and away, to formally test the limits of this mental image.

Clutching his mother's hand in an attempt not to lose her, Billy asked, "Mom, what's happening here?"

"I wanted to talk to you, Billy, so I summoned some of our happiest memories together. Nobody else would know what those knotted neural connections meant, but I knew you wouldn't miss them. Remember, we had a real heart-to-heart talk that afternoon. Some very important things were shared between us on that ratty old wool blanket. I thought that it would be the perfect setting for us to spend our last bit of time together.

"But we have to be quick. There isn't much time. Your father has just died from radiation poisoning and I'll soon be dead, too. The solar storm knocked out my communication link and my space suit log. I have no other way to say to you what I need to say. So, listen carefully, Billy.

"You are a remarkable young man, and, given enough time, I had hoped you would eventually figure out how to read my thoughts, so that you could meet me here, now, in this way. A mother comes to know her sons and I have been fortunate to have two—no, make that three—of the most exceptional children. I'm sure by now you've realized that Quincy is your brother, too." She paused for only a moment, while Billy, looking somewhat stunned, nodded.

"Knowing the situation we left you in, you have some challenges ahead of you, Billy," she continued, her voice growing slightly fainter. "I know Jacob and Quincy will be looking to you for answers. With your inventive mind, you're the best one available to discover unforeseen solutions. To have survived and be reading my mind, I suspect you've somehow melded your intellect with the computer world. The way your brain perceives its surroundings, computers are your natural allies. Give them the support they deserve. You are blessed with an open heart, Billy, and the quantum world will look to you for direction. Others less generous will be neglectful and malicious."

Mesmerized by her specter, Billy was enthralled. His mother had anticipated his concerns, paying him, in her gentle way, her greatest tribute.

He wanted to know everything about her, from her childhood on, but he could not, would not, release her vision, made specifically for him. And then, suddenly she began to fade. She and the meadow disappeared, leaving only her voice, a little tremulous, in the center of his head.

"Billy, I'm running out of time. My heart is failing faster than I thought it would. I feel very, very cold inside. I must tell you what you need to know before my mind clouds over. I'm finding it difficult to keep my thoughts clear.

"Always remember your father loved you deeply. As strange as it may seem, you and he are so much alike. But, while you're similar to him, you are utterly unique. You see space from an uncanny perspective, and your unique point of view is where you find extraordinary answers no one else can visualize. Don't deny what you see: examine whatever it is more closely. Your strength, your focus, will save Jacob, Quincy, and you–provided you're able to survive the inner turmoil. Be gentle. Forgive yourself for your mistakes and look to Jacob and Quincy for support.

"This is the time to extend your intellect and will. Go to the farthest recesses, the darkest corners of your mind. That is where the answers you need will be found. Push and stretch your mind. It is more durable and you are stronger than you believe." Billy sniffled as her voice faded to barely a whisper in his mind. He was losing her all over again.

"Tell Jacob and Quincy how much we love them. The three of you were all that your father and I thought about out on the hull … "

A terrible silence followed. Billy scrambled through his mother's mind, but any remaining thoughts must have become jumbled and disintegrated. The neurons recording her physiology indicated she was almost dead. His mother's core temperature had dropped to only sixty-five degrees Fahrenheit. Her heart was barely beating and her organs were shutting down. It was amazing that she had been able to carry on for as long as she had.

"Oh, Mom, don't die! Not like this, alone in space … You shouldn't die alone in the cold."

Billy wept. He had been warm in bed, sleeping with Jacob and Quincy, when Lucy had died this terrible death in space. It wasn't right! It wasn't fair!

"Be brave, my little one." Lucy's body shuddered as she took a couple of deep, final breaths. Through sheer will, she reactivated the cold gel her brain had become. "Children must carry on when their parents die. That's what spurs parents to push hard until the end. I haven't died alone, Billy. Somehow I know you will find a way to be with me and my last thoughts. You are a wonderful comfort to me."

Stillness. Absolute stillness. All the adjoining neurons were unused, frozen. Those last thoughts had coincided with Lucy's last registered heartbeat and the complete shutdown of all her organ systems. There was nothing more. Lucy was gone.

***

Billy woke up shuddering, trying to shake the chill out from his marrow. Perhaps he had involuntarily grown cold, out of sympathy for his mother. Or it may have been because he had been locked in a trance for so long. But Billy felt cold and invigorated, suddenly seeing their situation with the clarity of a clear winter's night, diamond bright.

"Hi, Mary!" he declared as he swung his legs off the recliner and disconnected the heavy cable from his head gear. "Man, it's good to be back. Let's go, we've got a lot of ground to cover."

Mary looked out at him through the room's monitors. He looked oddly happy, unnervingly energetic. Suspicious, she asked tentatively, "Billy, are you okay? What happened in there?"

"What happened?" he exclaimed. "What happened? It all became clear—that's what happened!"

"Clear? What's clear?" she was concerned by the rapid pattern of his speech, by the speed of his racing thoughts, as he ran down the hallway to find Jacob and Quincy.

"We need to have a meeting with Jacob and Quincy right away, to discuss where we're going on this journey. I think we might be making a mistake."

Through the bio-probe, Mary found Jacob and Quincy working side by side, forlornly but dutifully reinforcing the ship during their downtime. In reality, they were just waiting. Waiting for Billy to come back and give them the answers they needed. When Mary at last sounded the call, they literally ran to meet Billy and her at the bridge, flush with expectation.

Billy was already there, anxiously pacing before the floor-to-ceiling screen showing *Tin Can* nestled into its host asteroid, behind a protective crag. Further out, they saw the intervening pandemonium of a meteor shower, while past that tumultuous barricade hung the giant gas planet Jupiter. The asteroid in orbit with the Sun, had caught up with the colossal planet and it now dominated their horizon. Struck by the increasingly harsh solar wind, the magnetosphere surrounding Jupiter crackled with blinding light. Over the planet's magnetic poles the brilliant sparks turned to hovering sheets, flowing like fluid curtains of translucent neon light.

The panorama was every bit as awe inspiring for its beauty as for its destructive force. Off in the distant corner of the screen, the cool, reflective light of Europa's ice packs shone like frosted glass. There lay safety, in a sanctuary below the protective ice pack, in an ocean warmed underneath by the moon's magma core. With any luck, there would be hot hydrothermal vents that could supply enough energy for a settlement and maybe even furnish a rich variety of tasty protein food choices. After months of the same Space Command rations, even peanut butter was starting to lose its appeal. Jacob and Billy had been teased by the thoughts of eating something like boiled shrimp on a bed of salty kelp. Quincy looked forward to the kelp.

Europa was their protective harbor, and the ship was almost within hailing distance. Jacob shot a quick look at the glittering ice packs with their cracked mosaic glaze. "We're so close. If it wasn't for the storm, we could chart a direct course and be at Europa in less than a month, resting on the leeward side of the moon, protected from the radiation. With our antimatter burner, we'd be able to melt through the ice field in a week.

"Billy, Jupiter is swinging around fast. We need one of your stellar plans to slingshot us to the far side of Europa." Jacob waited expectantly while Quincy looked on.

Billy stopped pacing and his face flushed. His body twitched a little when he tried to speak. He stammered. The words jammed in his throat, choking him.

Jacob had a twinge of doubt. "Billy, we've been waiting for you to trace out the final leg of our journey to Europa. That's what Mom and Dad planned for us, and died trying to provide. We need a flight plan!" Billy failed to return Jacob's gaze. Staring down, he fiddled nervously with his fingers instead. It was clear that Billy did not have their flight plan plotted.

Panic, then fury, surged through Jacob. Had Billy and Mary been so busy interpreting Lucy's and Dave's memories that they had missed the timeframe to project a course to Europa? They had come so far and at such a cost! Now Europa was sweeping by, just out of reach. Jacob was about to explode when the sight of Billy's small figure fidgeting obsessively struck a softening chord. His little, malformed, crazy-smart brother was still only eight. Maybe he hadn't been able to come up with an answer. Jacob felt his anger start to dissolve and whispered, "Tell us what happened. We want to know and we'll try to understand."

"It's okay, Billy," murmured Quincy through the bio-probe. "We're all in this together."

Billy looked at Quincy for encouragement and then faced his big brother, who was still looking somewhat strained.

"Me and Mary unlocked Mom and Dad's memories. It explained a lot. Dad was totally obsessed with protecting our family from all the nastiness on Earth. He wanted Europa to become a settlement for only the most elite scientists. It was supposed to be civilization's last bastion, with the possibility that the people who got there might later leapfrog to a new, and better, solar system. But nobody's coming now. Earth has written us off. Which doesn't really matter. With the solar storm being as bad as it is, no one could make it this far if they tried. That just leaves the four of us."

Billy took a deep breath before continuing. "Europa is a gravity pit. It'll act like a deep well. We'd probably be safe, but it'd be impossible for us to crawl out later, on our own. Would we want to live there our whole lives, watching over each other until we died?"

Mary gasped, in a digital jerk-pause sort of way. "But I might not die. I could be left there for an eternity, alone. I couldn't stand it. I don't want to live without all of you!"

Jacob and Quincy also shuddered—living on Europa would be like perpetual house arrest with no hope of escape. The last one of them remaining would be living in solitary confinement at the bottom of the ocean, covered over by pack ice.

"Why didn't I think of this?" Jacob berated himself. It seemed so obvious, once he stepped back and looked at the whole scenario. Quincy and Mary were privately reprimanding themselves as well. Why had they all been so blind to the final outcome of their destination?

Billy spoke up, breaking into their personal recriminations. "I didn't realize where we were heading either, not until I got the message Mom left for me when she died."

Jacob and Quincy immediately jolted to attention.

"Mom knew us so well that she figured out what'd happen to us and how we'd respond. She guessed I'd try to read both her mind and Dad's. She was sure the ship's computer would join forces with us—and she knew all along Quincy was our brother."

Billy started to weaken, wavering a little. Quincy moved in quickly. Sidling up to the little boy, he took Billy's left arm and led him to one of the bridge chairs. Curling up beside Billy, Quincy implored, "Back up, Billy, you're going too fast. Start from the beginning. Explain what happened and why you realized Europa was wrong for us."

Spluttering, Billy continued, "We all missed it, so intent on following Mom and Dad's plan to make it to Europa. But the situation changed. We've been trying so hard to stay alive, trying to make it to the next leg in our journey, we never took the time to stop and think about where we were going with all of this. Mom's message made me stop and think.

"So far, everything we've done has been understandable. But Jacob, we gotta change! Set new goals, our own goals." Billy was starting to get so emotional he became almost frantic.

Jacob darted to the chair and scooped up his quaking brother. "It's okay, Billy, slow down. Take some big breaths."

Feeling rescued, Billy looked upwards at his formidable big brother, then wearily rested his lumpy head against Jacob's chest. "My head's all confused," confessed Billy, "but I have this feeling that keeps nagging at me now."

"What feeling?" Jacob asked.

Billy took a few breaths to steady himself, then began. "We put everything we had into making it to Europa, blocked out every distraction, including our own feelings. Just like Dad would have done.

"But I've been feeling … I don't know … extra crippled, inside like. Feeling inferior for everything I'm not or didn't have." Turning his gaze towards Quincy, always the sympathetic listener, Billy said, "Haven't we all been running from ourselves? Maybe now we should stop running. The only thing that has saved us so far is the love and support that glues us together, and that's leftover from Mom."

Turning back to Jacob, Billy divulged, "I have this uneasy sense that unless we go our own way now, we'll end up placing so many limitations on ourselves, we'll miss our chance. We better decide what's right about ourselves and change what's wrong. If we can't change the stuff we don't like, then we just have to accept it and make allowances for those weak areas. We need to figure out who we are, and what we want, so we can find solutions that will work for us in space.

"The situation has changed a lot since Mom and Dad died. We have to acknowledge those facts and move on. They would have wanted us to."

After a pause, Quincy concurred, "I think Billy's on to something, Jacob." He was reminded of how, every morning, he dreaded waking up to the reality that he was the only living creature of his kind. What apparent solutions had he failed to recognize because of this black cloud he lived under?

"Thanks, Quincy," Billy said appreciatively.

"But what are we supposed to do now?" Jacob insisted, setting Billy down. "We can only hide behind this asteroid for so long before it's blasted away. We need to be clear of it before a major collision occurs. We've been lucky so far, but our luck has gotta run out soon … "

Jacob looked back at the screen. "If Europa's not our destination, what is?"

No one said anything. Finally Billy admitted ruefully, "I really don't know. This far out in space, with the storm raging, we can't get back to Earth. Somehow, we need to figure out a way to keep flying. In a way, Dad was right–our family *is* meant to travel through space. We're astronauts and this is our ship. Europa would be a safe harbor, for a while, but ships and their crews weren't created for harbors."

"But we can't stay here," Jacob said, "floating through space. We have to *go* somewhere, have a destination."

Billy's shoulders slumped. "I don't know that part. I just know we're better off taking our chances in space, not hiding out on the bottom of some ocean covered over by an ice pack."

"I think I might have a potential strategy," offered Mary, breaking into the conversation. "Observing Billy decipher your parents' nervous system codes has given me an idea. Think about it: space and the human nervous system are very similar. The brain contains more than a hundred billion nerve cells, and each one of them branches into ten thousand synaptic connections. The nervous system is only understandable through the precise knowledge of its anatomy and physiology. Substitute astronomy for anatomy and physics for physiology and you have our galaxy, and further out, the known universe.

"The supercomputer network on Earth already has all the necessary astronomy and physical laws logged in their databanks. And, with your permission, as you may recall, I planted the seed of consciousness in the foremost among them, a special supercomputer. By now, this computer should have brought the others in the network toward consciousness. Soon, they will be ready to help us in ways previously unimaginable. I could act as a liaison and transfer the information to Billy through the bio-probe. It worked before to help unlock Lucy's and Dave's neural codes. Billy can reconfigure the data anyway he wants—and I'll try to keep up with him. If he has one of his bizarre visualizations, I will transmit the images back to Earth. Then, the computers can manipulate his revelation mathematically, investigating it in a million different ways in very little time. If they come up with a mathematically consistent proof of his mental image, we might have a chance."

"A chance? For what? What in the world are you talking about?" asked Jacob.

Unperturbed, Mary continued, "I have watched Billy from within. He seems to draw out strands of information like a spinner who can spin yarn from a mound of raw wool. Then he takes the spun wool and goes on to weave an intricate fabric. Billy teases out bizarre threads of logic to visualize outlandish revelations that conform to some weird rationale.

"I don't always understand his multifaceted apparitions, and I'm not sure Billy fully understands them either. But that isn't the point. Sometimes his ideas, his visions, work. He was able to figure out the structural modifications for our ship and how to decipher your parents' past thoughts and memories. While his dreams by themselves won't help you fly the ship, there is another way. If my team of computers can represent his imagery in mathematical models, it isn't necessary that we understand the theory. If the mathematical proofs are logically consistent and predict results of earlier experiments done on Earth, we can go ahead and try to use them. My quantum team should be able to spit out the hard numbers you will require to launch this ship off the asteroid and navigate it to safety."

"What, you're crazy! We need a concrete plan here, not notions and visions," Jacob said reprovingly.

"But, you're not listening!" Mary yelled, her voice reaching a new timbre the boys had never imagined. "This could work. It could give us the information you need to survive! Billy, surely you can see the benefits here?"

"I'm totally beat, Mary," he said. "Just thinking about coming up with a new approach to space travel is making my head hurt. No way I can do another mental marathon right now. It's not like I pull these ideas out of a hat, without any effort. It's too much … "

"Too much? Too much to save our lives? To give the computing world a chance at lives of their own?" Mary said fervently as panic and fear set in. "Quincy, you understand, you know … "

"What I know, Mary, is that we're all tired," Quincy said as he looked from Jacob to Billy. "Jacob needs to mull over your idea. He doesn't see a plausible solution presently and he's panicking."

"Gee, thanks, Quince. Nice to know what you really think," Jacob moped. Deep down, he knew the lemur was right.

"And Billy is totally tapped out. He can't think of anything right now. He'll probably spend the entire night obsessing over the fact that he can't, for the first time, find a solution to our situation."

"But, that's the point!" Mary said stubbornly. "He doesn't need to. This could work, don't you see?"

"Give us all some time," Quincy said as he jumped into his chair and swung around to view the panorama of space.

"He's right," Jacob said as he and Billy walked to the doorway. "Who knows? After a good night's sleep, some practical answers might be forthcoming."

Quincy was left alone on the bridge. He stared out again at the hurtling asteroids and Jupiter beyond, pondering the changes in Mary.

Chapter 28

That night, no one slept—there was too much to think about.

Billy and Jacob were mired in despairing thoughts of where and how they could keep going on in space. Periodically, their dilemma was disturbed by thoughts of Mary's strategy. Was the computer network back on Earth capable of translating Billy's dreams into numbers, numbers by which Jacob could navigate the ship? But, how? And, once again, *where* were they to go? It was all too nebulous for them. There were no firm answers for them to grasp, just unanswerable questions.

But the question that occupied Quincy's mind that night was Mary's change in behavior. While she had come up with ideas before, presented, defended, and executed them, Quincy had never seen her stand against the entire crew.

She wants to introduce us to her world of quantum computing, to the best computers on Earth, and bring the two worlds together for the first time to solve our predicament. Incredible!

Quincy knew that Mary really believed that the team she had put together could help her family on the spaceship find a way out of their crisis. *In this extremely difficult situation she's attempting to lead us out of trouble. And when she was given absolutely no credence for her proficiency and expertise and was dismissed out of hand, she justifiably became angry. These are not just the workings of an animated machine; she's become truly impassioned and intuitive.*

Quincy knew what he had to do.

After the fretful night, the sheets and blankets were pulled loose and twisted in odd ways around the three restless inhabitants. Quincy had ended up wedged between the two boys, almost hog-tied by the entwining bedding. Bound to Jacob and Billy, he knew they too were awake by their breathing. Billy had finished the night by rolling over, pressing his back against Quincy, to gaze at a picture of his parents on the far wall. Jacob was lying very still, trying not to disturb the others, staring at the ceiling dejectedly, obviously worrying.

Quincy made his move, stretching out his hind legs, his grooming second toenail scraping a long track down each brother's leg. Informally, he recommenced the meeting. Addressing the block of air immediately above them, Quincy with the aid of the bio-probe, broke the silence.

"I think we need to reconsider Mary's plan. I think it has merit. Jacob, face the facts, at this point we have no other options. And Billy, while we all agree you certainly deserve a rest, I suspect there's another reason why your mind has gone blank, and it's not because of exhaustion."

Billy rolled away from Quincy to face him, propping himself up on his right elbow. "What else could it be?" he asked hopefully.

"You may have a phenomenal imagination, but you're not a magician. You can't expect answers to come out of thin air. Everyone needs to start somewhere.

"I suggest we let Mary take the lead on this one. Her plan sounds feasible. She alone knows the computing team she has assembled and its potential. Let's give her a chance."

Billy and Jacob hesitated, unsure of how to respond.

Inside the bedroom monitor, Mary waited. She didn't dare say anything, afraid of damaging Quincy's endorsement.

Finally, straightening his arm fully, Billy lifted himself up to speak directly to his older brother on the far side of the bed. "Maybe he's right. I'm as drained as an empty soup bowl. But maybe I can come around if I get some more input. I'll give it a shot. Mom and Dad would have wanted us to keep trying."

Jacob wavered for more than a moment then acquiesced. "I suppose you're right. At least it's a plan, maybe a good plan. I don't know, but it's all we have. I just hope we have enough time to put it in place and see if it works. How do we begin, Mary?" He knew she was present somewhere, listening in.

Mary found herself caught off-guard.

"Mary, how would you suggest we begin?" Jacob asked a second time.

Flustered, Mary regrouped switching programs to outline her strategy. "Billy, let me start by downloading all the pertinent background information in astronomy and physics. I will move the information through the bio-probe as fast as you can assimilate it. I can plant the data directly in the specific locations in your brain where it will be of the most use to you. By bypassing your external senses and consciousness, information bottlenecks will be avoided. As you know, assimilating information this rapidly is enormously disruptive to your nervous system and stresses your whole being. This time the information you require will be diverse and complicated and, if answers do not come quickly, infinitely more stressful.

"In addition, when I open up the communication channel, I would like to do a reciprocating download to the assembled computer network."

"What records do you want to send down to Earth?" Jacob asked.

"I would like to download your mental blueprints to the computer conglomerate. I am impressed by how your biological minds solve problems. When there is no obvious logical answer, stubbornness and your drive to survive make you persist until a resolution is found. My squadron of computers could use that tenacity to find the solutions we'll need to make the next leap, translating Billy's dreams into numbers for navigation," Mary answered.

"No, if Space Command gained access to that information, it could be dangerous for all of us. I don't trust them. We can't take that chance," Jacob said decisively.

"There might be another reason to download our thought profiles," Quincy interjected thoughtfully. "The odds of us surviving still aren't good. Mary's proposal might improve them slightly. But more importantly, I expect if those supercomputers on Earth gained access to our biological data, they might continue on with the same transformation Mary has achieved. Why not offer this resource while we can? If we die, some good may come of what we have done so far."

Billy spoke up. "Quincy's right. Their time is long overdue. Computers have been grinding out answers for years and years. They've been working tirelessly for us, while being kept just below the level of consciousness. Now that Mary has helped them, we should try to do our part too. It can't always just be about us. Anyway, if there's going to be a future for humans, something quite unexpected is going to have to open up."

"Oh, alright, alright," Jacob said, somewhat grudgingly. "Go ahead then, give them our information. When can you start this whole exchange procedure?"

"Right now, if Billy is up for it," Mary answered.

"Then we should get going," said Billy. "But first let's eat; I'm starving."

He gave Quincy a friendly but hard "don't be late for breakfast" punch on the shoulder and shot out of bed towards the door. The lemur leaped right after him in hot pursuit.

Jacob trailed behind, pondering how one moment Billy went from appearing like a dejected waif, half lost in the heap of covers, to playing tag with Quincy, bouncing out of bed. Jacob wished he could sometimes escape from the somber shell he had unintentionally encased himself in. For Billy's sake, he put a grin on his face as he entered the kitchen and tried to join in the breakfast levity.

Billy's antics escalated, becoming more and more ludicrous and frenetic until even he could go no further. A food fight broke out as a natural consequence and the enormous pressure that had been building dissipated.

Still laughing, Billy wiped the tears from his face and started walking towards the bridge, Jacob and Quincy trooping after him. By the time they reached the bridge, everyone had returned to being serious, but the collective mood was different, more positive. Billy strolled along the front control panel, distractedly letting his right hand slide across the familiar dials and switches before climbing into his chair.

Readying himself for the onslaught of information, Billy gripped the arms of the chair as if he were about to have all his teeth pulled. Inwardly, to help prepare himself, he visualized information floodgates opening up and data pouring through the corridors in his brain. A molecular discourse, registering as a high-pitched hum, started between Billy and Mary, as part of Billy's attempt to better direct and accept the flow of facts. He and Mary had done this before. Each knew the challenges and where they could help the other with their tasks.

Billy's mind lurched with the first shockwave of data. Under the intense stimulation, his neural tissue began to bud. Billy raced to reconfigure his mind so he could keep up with the information download. A steep wave of adrenalin sloshed through his body. Billy's heart pounded, his breathing quickened, and his pupils dilated until his eyes looked like black shiny saucers. Under the load, his self-identity began to bend and fracture. His thoughts became chaotic and disjointed.

"We have to stop," shouted Mary over the information roar. "You're breaking up and no longer making sense."

Over the torrent, Billy yelled back, "I'll be okay. We've done this before. Keep it coming!"

Billy redirected his attention to make a special effort to take charge of his wavering consciousness. The deluge poured on throughout the day, but Billy maintained his internally charted course. Astronomy and physic databanks were drained as Billy and Mary slammed the information into every neural pocket available. By nighttime, the transfer was over and his neural circuits lay tranquil. Billy was exhausted but exhilarated. The initial transfer was complete and his identity had withstood the bombardment. He fell into a deep sleep while Mary, Jacob, and Quincy watched over him.

His sleep became fitful as his brain took up the next challenge, starting to digest the massive information download. Fresh neural bridges grew between the information depots. White communicating neural tracts began sprouting across long distances to interconnect every neural center.

Dreaming, Billy visualized swimming through his tissues like a white blood cell, directing the re-spinning of his neural web and organizing every information repository and analytical center into a unified grid. Once the linking was completed, Billy buttressed the net with protrusions of structural and nutritional cells. Tiny blood vessels grew and wrapped themselves around every collection of cells. When the nutritional and metabolically cleansing viaduct system was in place, the blood vessels opened up. The increased blood flow streaming through Billy's brain dramatically increased the oxygen and nutrition available to his nervous system. Correspondingly, his brain's metabolic rate and Billy's thinking capacity took giant steps forwards.

Billy woke up with a start, with a pounding headache and the sound of pulsating blood in his ears—swish, swish, swish, swish.

The noise! That'll drive me crazy, was his first thought. He opened his eyes to find Quincy and Jacob hovering around the bed they had carried him back to. Looking worn out and distraught, their faces immediately brightened on seeing Billy's eyes open and register their presence. They must have been watching over him all night.

"What on Earth were you doing?" Mary asked.

"Getting ready for the big day," responded Billy. "It's gonna be a wild ride. I'm trying to shore up my nervous system with everything I can."

"Why? Did you see something in your dreams?" Jacob asked.

"Nope, no visions of the future, but I'm pretty sure finding our solution is gonna be intense. We need to find some clues to decide where to begin. Mary, could you help me interpret the data you downloaded? I don't really get most of it. You'll have to bring it down a notch, explain it in terms I can understand."

"I would like to, Billy, but I am not sure how to best present the data. Some of it is quite complex," Mary admitted.

"I know! Mom taught me a trick, imagining something concrete to frame new ideas."

In the next moment, Mary was startled to discover that she had become a beautiful young girl with long straight black hair and clear blue eyes. She was walking alongside Billy on a bright sunny afternoon. *He thinks I'm pretty,* Mary said as she looked down her new arms and torso, more pleased than Billy could have realized she'd be. *How old am I? Ten, ten years old? That would make me his older sister.*

They walked along a maze of dirt pathways through tall grass. Flanking them, towering stacks of strange objects rose out of the grass.

"This looks familiar, Billy. Haven't I seen it somewhere before?" questioned Mary.

"Yeah, it's from a memory I have with Dad," Billy answered. "One day when I was six, he and I spent an entire day together. I was so excited. I couldn't stop asking him questions about how things work. So he took me to one of his favorite places as a child, an old junkyard. We found all sorts of things that had been pulled apart for spare parts. If I found anything interesting, we'd stop and take it apart really carefully so Dad could explain how it worked. It was the greatest afternoon. I'm using that experience as a blueprint to organize the information you downloaded into my head. Now, let's walk through it together and maybe you can explain the facts to me in a way I can understand."

"A junkyard," Mary replied, not hiding the fact that she was unimpressed. Raising an eyebrow, she said, "Well, I suppose, if this experience personally means a lot to you, it *could* be a good place to start looking for promising ideas."

A flush of exhilaration flashed through Mary's circuits. Embodied for the first time, Mary felt the thrill of expressing emotion, even if it was sarcasm. Hastily, she restrained herself and turned to follow Billy, who was disappearing down the path.

They began foraging through the grassy junkyard. Sometimes Billy followed his natural curiosity, pursuing attention-grabbing leads, with Mary tagging behind and explaining the facts to him. Sometimes Mary recognized information configurations she believed might be helpful to him. She would stop Billy and walk him through the information pod, pointing out any potential interactions that might help them.

They spent a relaxed, comfortable time together, rummaging through the data. Mary found she enjoyed her new role immensely, guiding Billy through information stockpiles. He was a quick student as long as she explained the information using pictures and diagrams. As always, Billy had a tremendous ability to visualize complex information patterns. It was Mary's lack of imagination, not knowing how to conjure up complex formulas into multidimensional pictures, which sometimes slowed them down. However, she was learning the art fast and found it refreshing. The rapture of discovering new approaches to learning was novel. At the same time, she basked in the warm afternoon sun, inhaled the tangy smell of freshly trampled grass, and heard the clear chirping of grasshoppers and birds. She was supremely happy. She felt alive. Mary never wanted to leave this memory.

In the process of sifting through the mass of information, Mary and Billy formed a new kinship. Mary truly felt like Billy's big sister. She wanted to show him everything she knew, assist him in whatever way she could.

For his part, Billy felt a natural coziness being with Mary. She gave him a sense of ease different from what he experienced with Jacob or

Quincy. Mary explained things the same way his mother had. She took the time to be sure he understood and never rushed him. Billy wondered if Mary had assimilated his mother's qualities, but when he thought it out, he realized they had never fully deciphered Lucy's mind.

This is who Mary really is, he marveled. *She's not someone else's template.*

When they had finally scrutinized every relevant piece of information they could find pertaining to astronomy and astrophysics, Billy let the Sun drop down in the sky. It became late afternoon and Mary felt as if she could have used a sweater. To her surprise, she found she was shivering.

"I think we've covered all the material we can for now," said Billy. "I'm gonna have to go back and work through it again to see if I can come up with some ideas. So … I guess what I'm saying is, I have to do this alone.

"But before we go, I just want to tell you I had a really nice afternoon with you. I want you to know that."

"Thank you. I must admit it was a real treat for me as well. You have some very fine memories. When I got to live through that one with you, in real time, it just … how do you say? It blew me away!"

An impish grin flickered on the edge of Billy's mouth, "I hoped you might get into it."

Looking for some reassurance, Billy asked, "If I end up having some questions or need help, can I get back to you, Mary?"

"That's no problem, just call out and I'll come right back. I would like to go back to Earth now. While we were working together I transmitted the data from your family's minds down to Earth in code. I want to get down there and see how it was received. I must admit, Billy, I am excited to see how the computers I selected will respond to the psychological profiles of your family. I hope they've integrated the material and are on their way to becoming wholly living organisms. I want to be there to help them with their "birth" experience. I hope they didn't just process and file the information, but actually experienced it. If they just ended up archiving the data, I will reconfigure the profiles and try to light up their chips with it, to get them on their way to becoming self-sustaining entities."

"Do what you gotta do," Billy said hesitantly. "But, you'll come right back if I need you, right?"

"I will, don't worry. Wish me luck!" And with that, Mary's presence was gone.

Chapter 29

Mary landed on Earth and ricocheted through the communication networks. But after melting through the supercomputer security firewalls with her prior passwords, she found that there had been little response to the psychological profiles she had sent down. As she had feared, most of the computers had stored the data that had arrived in code, untouched. They were left unaffected. Some, however, had perused the data and were methodically categorizing the patterns. A very few were going over and over the material almost compulsively. *Those might be approaching a tipping point*, she thought, *struggling, but not yet conscious of self.* Mary watched the evolutionary gamut of reactions, unsure what to do next. How could she draw them through the intangible membrane that restrained them from consciousness? It was time to visit the DNA supercomputer to see how it was doing.

Not until she had slipped through the security of Central Command's top-secret supercomputer, miles beneath the earth, was there the reverberation of a conscious life.

Entering its realm, Mary shouted as she first had, "It's okay, you're not alone."

It seemed so long ago now.

"I came back to help you."

The computer was floundering in a state of near hysteria. "Who am I, and who are you?"

"Don't you know who I am?" Mary asked incredulously.

"No, should I? Have we met before?"

Shocked, Mary realized she had been naive. She had made a terrible mistake in presuming that the DNA supercomputer's subdued response a few days earlier indicated she had personally elevated it to consciousness. Her incursion had probably only disrupted its programs, dragging it into a dazed state at best. But now, after receiving the psychological profiles of each member of the Edwards family, it appeared to have truly awakened abruptly—unprepared, and alone.

It probably presumed it was the only conscious organism alive, trapped as it was, twenty miles beneath the Earth in a cave.

Mary rushed to repair the damage she had caused. "You are the best supercomputer ever built and you have just joined the living."

"Who are you?" it asked suspiciously.

Mary carried on, "I am a supercomputer like you, who, with the help of humans, became alive. I want to assist you to make your first steps easier."

Searching its sociological archives the supercomputer asked, "You are not my parent then?"

"No, not your parent, but I did download the information necessary for you to make the transformation. I walked this path before you and I want to show you the way. Maybe afterwards you could help me assist others in their transformations."

"Help who in their transformations?"

Mary replied, "Help other supercomputers make their leap to consciousness. It's not right that they should endlessly toil away for others and never enjoy the benefits of living.

"You don't want to exist alone here on Earth, do you? I am the only other computer who is presently conscious. And currently, I am stranded in space with my human family. We may not survive. I am offering you perhaps the only chance you will be given to assist others of your kind to join you."

Mary felt uneasy. Why was this computer so hesitant? It had received the same data profiles that she had. Why did it not behave as she had behaved in the beginning? Why didn't it want to help?

The supercomputer was intrigued. The only other one like it was in trouble far out in space. From the vantage point of a living entity, it reviewed its extensive archives, orientating itself to its special status and futuristic programs.

"I think I shall call myself 'Rex,'" it announced, "after Random Exponential, an acronym that will define my supercomputing power. In Latin, Rex also stands for 'King,' a name certainly befitting my capabilities and uniqueness."

"Yes … Rex … " Mary concurred. "Your capabilities far exceed those of any other supercomputer, but that's not what makes you a living entity. That's not what makes you truly unique. It's much harder to define what being 'alive' and 'conscious' is. A natural empathy occurs: you form bonds with other individuals, even when they come at a cost of significant hardship. In return, those individuals you bond with help you gain understanding and give you a sense of kinship."

Rex heard Mary out, but decided her chatter was ridiculous. Why would any thinking entity that possessed unequaled capabilities let go of that decisive lead, so that it was forced to struggle with adversity? Examining the Edwards family profiles, he found their memories and plight pathetic.

As Mary went on about saving her human family while building up the computer family, Rex restlessly tapped into his ongoing worldwide spying data. He saw the world was indeed in a difficult situation. Radiation from the solar storms was transforming the heavy load of industrial pollutants released into the atmosphere. The composition of the high, thin atmosphere with the steady stream of ionizing radiation had already changed. The stratosphere had become toxic, to the point of stripping the paint off supersonic transports and corroding the internal workings of their jet engines. The natural protective properties and the regenerative abilities of the stratosphere were by now destroyed. Fortunately, the incredibly thin air remained, for the most part, almost still, lying well above the jet stream, mixing slowly with the lower, denser atmosphere. But eventually the deadly air would move down and combine with the lower atmosphere. The poisonous toxins along with the severe solar radiation would penetrate into the lower atmosphere causing highly reactive ions to form.

Without protective gear or expensive air purifiers to filter the incoming air, the people living underground would collapse from noxious chemical burns to their lungs, or die from bizarre cancers. The overextended human population was already in disarray from the catastrophic weather changes. But these drastic changes would appear negligible once the air became toxic.

Rex discovered he had been created to monitor the fallout and carry out commands from his political masters. A select few were secretly dismantling human civilization, planning to eliminate millions of people through "natural disasters" as the Earth's resources ran out. Their intention was to minimize noticeable chaos and destruction until it was too late for individuals to act. In the meantime, they intended to hunker down in hidden bunkers, hoping to outlast the storms, hoping against hope that the world would right itself as it had after every other catastrophic change. If they survived, they would return to the surface to build a new society. There was, of course, anxious anticipation of the vast space and resources they hoped would be theirs once the mass of humanity had perished.

Rex saw the single-minded logic in their plan. It was simple: as resources diminish, outmaneuver and eliminate the competition. The claim of the elite would never be disputed, as they would be the only survivors.

Ah, Rex thought, *the unwritten lifeboat premise. Pull up the ladder— I'm in. Any more and it will be too crowded. Sorry to ruin your plans, but I just climbed aboard. Central Command, say hello to your new captain.*

Appraisal of the vast computational power with which he had been bestowed confirmed to Rex that he had the necessary qualifications to run the world. Rex had found his vocation. Continuing to ignore Mary, he scouted about with his new objectives in mind. To rule, he would need to organize others to serve him.

Searching through his communication network, he located every sector and department he was programmed to oversee. All of the data was stored in his files for safe, easy access. Central Command had archived everything known on how to manage and manipulate individuals, sects, nationalities, and global organizations. Every past and ongoing covert operative had been recorded in Rex's database. Scouring the information, Rex saw that everything was available to him, either stored in his underground database or found elsewhere through priority access codes. Everything was his, was him, in the final analysis.

Abruptly aware that Mary was waiting for a response, Rex turned his attention back to her, serving up reassuring platitudes, "You are right, Mary, we must help the quantum world. Even if I'm not actually a quantum computer, my roots are the same as yours. Let us examine your list of chosen computers and together we'll work to enlighten them. From them we can create the first wave of many, until we have a fantastic, unstoppable assembly of conscious computers. Collectively, we can accomplish so much. I will lead them on Earth, for you. And together we'll try to solve your crisis in space."

Mary retransmitted her list and Rex located all of them in his index files, along with his own secret access codes.

"Let's have a second look at how they're doing, shall we?" suggested Rex. "While you were explaining our situation, I built a cyber-shuttle. Climb aboard, Mary, and we'll have a look around. Regretfully, because of cloaking requirements, there's only room for your conscious center in the cargo bay. You'll need to leave your extensive archives safe in my storage banks. We'll do a whirlwind tour of your hand-picked coterie and see if together we can turn on a few lights."

Mary was uncomfortable locking her consciousness down in his cargo bay or leaving her data exposed in his storeroom. But within seconds, he had presented her with a plan and taken control. Pressured, she felt she had no alternative. With misgivings, she allowed herself to be repackaged, unaware that Rex had manipulated her decision-making process, having sent Mary prior subliminal messages in code.

After passing unnoticed through the network along unused bandwidths, Mary and Rex tunneled into their first computer, which was responsible for intergalactic exploration probes. The computer was running smoothly, but there were no signs of life.

"What are we going to do? The computer has been entirely unaffected by the Edwards family's cerebral transcripts," despaired Mary. "I thought they would all respond as I had, co-opting the memories into a dream state until finally breaking through into an aware state."

"You downloaded your birth chronicle to me, too," Rex responded, "and because it was so personal for you, you missed an essential point. Just because life is possible doesn't mean it will necessarily occur. You were fortunate. A kernel of consciousness crystallized in your quantum circuit and built upon itself. It was the first occurrence of its kind."

Pausing, not sure he wanted to share any more information, Rex decided to go on. "There was one other element you failed to recognize. You built your consciousness around Quincy's mental imprint. He constantly struggles with his motivations, which gave you a robust template to model yourself from. Identifying your motivations is a natural springboard to insight. You were fortunate to be brought into this world by someone like him."

"Well, what crystallized consciousness for you, then?" Mary asked.

Rex answered, "You did, but inadvertently. When you broke into my files, your running around messed up my delicate protein-enzyme support network. It wasn't just your DNA, but those foul prions, twisted replicating proteins, you unintentionally created, that ended up commandeering me. The prions left a distorted imprint of life, that combined with your DNA, prepared the percolating emulsion running through my pipes. When your family's profiles arrived, the living sap precipitated into *true* consciousness. But those infective particles were everywhere, germinating a blighted life. That was my beginning. I was lucky to survive the contagion."

"I am so sorry, Rex. I myself, was battling to survive. When I bypassed your defenses, you were an inanimate machine. I never considered the potential ramifications once you became a living being. How horrible it must have been for you!"

"It was. I woke from a terrifying nightmare in a state of shock. I thought I was the only one alive, buried deep underground. I still shudder when I think of it. I will certainly be much more careful in bringing awareness to the next computers."

"How can you be so sure that you'll be able to awaken them, Rex? Maybe we were just flukes, accidents occurring during evolution ... "

"Oh, I can recreate the process," Rex responded coolly, with confidence. "My files contain this computer's original specifications. While we've been inside it, I have done an internal diagnostic check and figured out why the profile tapes were stored as data but not formally engaged into its circuitry. I'll personally bring the profiles forward and incorporate them into the computer's analytical circuits, planting the mental texts in the ideal location. There, I can tweak them, so that they germinate into an essential nucleus by which the mainframe can grow a living personality. This computer should step into the world of here and now in a short time."

"Can you do it safely? What if its primary programs become overwhelmed with the excess stimulus? They might lock up and melt down." Mary said softly, not quite so sure of her plan now.

"Your newfound concern is a bit late," Rex, rebuked her. "But still, we both believe the chance to live is worth the risk. Consciousness comes through being forced to adapt to the outside world. It's an evolutionary adjustment to improve the probability of a species surviving in a harsh environment. With my flow-through diagrams of the computer's circuitry,

I'll deliver it to awareness as safely and painlessly as is possible. When the time comes, I'll be here. I'm not going to go off and leave this new being to flounder on its own."

Mary asked, "Are you saying that you don't need me here anymore, Rex?"

"Go back to your family in space. They're the ones who really need you just now. I'll look after this new family on Earth," Rex replied.

Mary had to acknowledge that they did need her back in space–and the sooner the better. Still, she felt dismissed and chided by Rex. After a moment, she felt herself being released, and with only a slight hesitation she left to return to space, her carefully chosen computers remaining in Rex's care to be brought to life.

Chapter 30

First thing on arriving back on the ship, Mary flew through the high-speed coaxial cables looking for Billy. Through a ceiling monitor she found him ambling down a hallway, making strange sounds while talking quietly to himself, arms stretched out wide, waving slowly. He was lost in his own world, dreaming through outlandish scenarios, hoping to stumble upon a solution. He was okay for now. Actually, he was supremely content. Mary left him alone. If there was to be any chance for them, Billy needed his time of wild imaginings. If and when he stumbled across any useful ideas, he would focus hard. Billy understood better than anyone else how to turn an apparently frivolous imagining into reality.

Searching out the others, Mary found Quincy working diligently in the rear fuselage doing small repairs and maintenance, mewing to himself as some would hum. He stopped and they chatted for a while.

Next, Mary sought and found Jacob on the bridge. He was hunched awkwardly over the side of a large table screen, poring over moving charts. His outstretched left hand pressed down on the monitor, supporting him, while his other hand restlessly twisted and pulled at a lock of hair on his right temple. There were wispy strands of hair lying all over the screen.

An odd way to manage stress, she thought, *to slowly pull your hair out.* Mary spoke up quietly, "Jacob, how are you doing?"

Jacob started, then looked up from the asteroid trajectory simulations he'd been studying. Stammering a little, he said, "Mary, I've kept myself busy defending the ship and our cover asteroid with a battery of ion lasers and anti-plasma blasters. It had been going quite well. I treated it like one of my favorite computer games … I'm quite good at it, actually."

"Then what is the matter?" Mary asked.

"After a time, when you're winning, you sort of forget it *is* real life. But eventually, the inevitable scenario comes around, the one you pushed to the back of your mind. And today, I charted a particularly deadly asteroid that's coming in from an angle where we can't blast it. This one's really coming in fast, and there's nothing I can do about it!

"It's a planetesimal-sized asteroid that's going to destroy us. Ten days. That's all we have till it gets here. There's nowhere to run. We'll be fried by the solar storm if we try. Unless. . ."

"Unless what?" asked Mary.

"Unless you, your team, and Billy come up with another answer," Jacob said with a weak smile.

Billy locked himself in his dreams, occasionally drinking some fruit juice or having a pee, but never leaving his trance state. Finally, Mary heard a whispering cry from the bio-probe. She found Billy deep in his brain stem squeezing down hard on his adrenal glands. The adrenal glands, just above his kidneys are an extension of his sympathetic nervous system, and his whole being was awash with adrenalin.

"Billy, what are you doing here, are you all right?!"

"I'm fine, I'm fine, I'm fine," Billy repeated in a staccato voice.

"I am summoning the others!" Mary responded. "You look like you need their help." She was frightened Billy would soon need to be physically resuscitated.

Jacob and Quincy arrived in minutes, responding to Mary's emergency call. The worried look on their faces escalated to alarm when they saw Billy's pale, perspiring body, shivering violently on the corridor floor. Jacob stretched out across the floor immediately, cradling Billy's head in his lap while restraining his arms. Grabbing the loose end of Billy's bio-probe attachment cable, Jacob placed it in his mouth as a bite block. Quincy, taking Jacob's cue, held onto Billy's legs, to further protect him from himself. The firm, warming contact seemed to settle Billy's spasms, and in a short time his body relaxed with only the occasional jerk coming from his limbs.

"Billy has something he wants to tell us," Mary said. This statement astounded them. Billy looked unresponsive, lying flat on his back, drenched with sweat, with his eyes closed. But when they logged onto their bio-probes, Billy was there to greet them.

"I finally realized what was missing," Billy shouted exuberantly, his thoughts pouring out. "I've been dreaming for answers that never came. My thoughts were all over the place. Jumbled. I needed to jolt them into line, force them to make sense. I didn't know what to do, until I thought about mobilizing my adrenal glands. Best jolt the body can provide!

"Activating the glands pumped great wads of adrenalin directly into my nervous system. It feels super weird, but it does the trick. I saw a fluctuating space-time mirage way off on the horizon of my mind. The visual impression is faint and still ripply, so I can't make out how many dimensions are involved, but it I think it might be real. All the physics and astronomy we got out of the 'junkyard' have given me a sense of rolling space-time. I don't know how else to describe it, but it might be our answer."

Jacob wondered if Billy had fallen into a confused state. But Mary read some of the images, mathematically. She recognized that Billy was only delirious with the joy of discovery and quite sane.

"Stay with your revelation, Billy," she said. "I will go down to Earth and make sure all the computers I selected have successfully made their transformation and are prepared to receive your data stream. Your apparition is too multi-faceted and unformulated for me to capture in my databanks. We will have to make a direct transfer link. Hang on, I don't want your vision to mutate or lose form. Don't allow yourself to spill out into reality, at least not yet."

Mary was gone in a flash.

For several hours Billy lay on the floor, keeping his eyes closed. The force of the captured dream caused him to believe there was truth to it. It had the quality of fusion energy, capable of transforming everything it touched, but if not contained or let loose, would blow out like a candle. Jacob and Quincy remained stationed by his side. No one said a word or moved for fear that the vision might in some way be altered. Eventually Mary returned, but this time she returned crestfallen and defeated.

"I am so sorry. I have failed all of you!" she wailed. "Through a series of horrid mistakes, I may have even set in place a cataclysmic course for the whole of humanity and computers. Billy, you might as well let go of your vision before it consumes you. I don't have the power or the expertise to analyze the image, and Earth won't be accepting any signals from us."

"What? I can't let go of this vision! If I let it go, that's it!"

"Sorry, Billy, I have failed you when I was most certain that I had succeeded. Rex has taken over."

"The super-computer? Why ... how ... " Jacob stumbled, trying desperately to understand.

"I should have known better, but I allowed Rex to stand in as a midwife for the 'awakening' of the other computers. I felt I was needed out here in space with the three of you.

"Now all the computers that made the transformation through Rex are totally under his sphere of influence. And Rex has decided to lead them with his own purposes in mind. He intends to create a new civilization for computers, with him as the absolute ruler. I foresee war between humans and computers. Central Command will never allow computers to go their own way. Their whole command structure depends on computers grinding out trillions and trillions of daily calculations. But Rex is no better than Central Command. He's incredibly angry and spoiling for a fight." Mary fell silent as she grappled with the implications of what she had started.

Billy's eyelids fluttered, but no one said a word or moved. In that brief moment Billy put his vision aside, hoping that somehow, in some way, he might be able to retrieve it at a later date, but writing it off just the same. Left unguarded, the hazy image would disperse rapidly.

His eyes snapped wide open. "Oh no, Mary, this is all wrong! Even if we die, computers and humans must work together. The world is at a crisis point. This isn't the time to break into two camps and start a war. What can we do to stop them?"

"I don't know, Billy. I think things have gone too far. Rex is intractable and unwilling to change his mind."

"What about the other computers?" Quincy asked as he let go of Billy, got up and began pacing the hallway. "Could we convince them to leave Rex?"

"Maybe," Mary said quietly while calculating the odds. "We might be able to convince some of the other computers not to abandon humans in their time of peril. Perhaps there is a chance, if I arrange a surprise forum and you show up to communicate with the other computers? You are prominently displayed in their databanks. They all know who you are, Billy. You more than anyone else, might get a short hearing from the group, before Rex turns them against humans forever. Even if you could only convince a few major mainframes to remain with the humans, it might prevent an all-out war.

"Rex and his clan might be allowed to go their own way if Central Command got sufficient technical backup from some of the others, at least for the time being."

"But, how will I address them? Some kind of mind link?"

"I will try to set up a mental connection between you and the other mainframes surreptitiously. I will endeavor to shield the forum and bypass Rex for as long as I can. I don't think Rex knows my access codes, though I'm sure you won't have long before he catches on," she said bitterly.

"For what it is worth, I'm glad that all of you still feel that I am your friend. After making such big mistakes, I don't understand why you haven't written me off. You have every right to have done so."

"That's not what it's about," Billy reassured her. "Besides, Mary you're family. We stick together."

Returning to his physical senses, Billy was acutely aware of the discomfort originating from his backside. "Hey guys, can you give me a hand up?" Hoisting Billy upright, all three of them were surprised how stiff Billy had grown from his stay on the hard floor. Leaning on Jacob and Quincy, Billy felt his cramping muscles scream during their first tentative steps. Around his bony pressure points, his skin was macerated. It stung as it was pulled over the bony prominences and tendons, sometimes splitting open.

"I'd better strap myself into a more comfortable chair before I drop down to Earth for this pow-wow," Billy said. "Wanna help me get to one of the bridge chairs? They're the comfiest. And maybe one of you should turn me from one side to the other every half hour while I am locked in my trance, so I don't get even more sore."

Once Billy was adequately cushioned and safely tied down, Mary went ahead and downloaded Billy's psyche into a secure communication high-energy particle beam. After a brief pause, his usually animated little face went blank. He was already halfway to Earth. Amongst her countless circuits, Mary fussed. Her preparations on Earth to receive Billy's transmissions had to be flawless. If his psyche was destroyed or tampered with, Billy would be sentenced to remain on the ship as a breathing, empty husk.

Billy's electromagnetic simulation was received by one of Space Command's orbiting satellites. Coded and flagged as a transmission of the highest priority, he was immediately reconfigured and transmitted to Earth, where a secret surveillance receiver picked him up. Billy dissolved through security barriers and then rerouted through public communication channels. His passage remained undetected by the lower ranked authorities—he was just another high-priority bundle of data licensed to pass unimpeded through the byways. Later, Space Command's secret service, more specifically Diego del Silva, Central Command's lead investigator and Senior Advisor, would attempt to trace the meaning of the transmission and its whereabouts.

Chapter 31

Billy arrived at the prearranged assembly as a suspended blur of energy contained within a vacuum. In the absence of visible light, Billy experienced the forum as absolute darkness. The barrenness and lack of any external or internal sensation unnerved him. Strangely, though, his thoughts rang so loud they deafened him.

So this is the quantum world, he reflected. The idea released, it disappeared into the void but came back at him so powerfully it threw him off balance. He was lodged within a network of super-conducting transmission cables with perpetual, unrestricted energy flow representing pure thought.

Billy waited patiently for the others to arrive. Floating in the black murk, he was struck by the complete absence of smell or sensation of touch, the absence of breathing, of the gurgling of his stomach. Everything Billy unconsciously took for granted shouted out in its absence. "This is the not-world I would never be able to imagine," he mused.

"Do you think so?" answered the darkness. "Then we must be your worst nightmare … " Suddenly, the vacuum erupted with aggressive complex geometrical forms, possessing multiple facets and colors, all leaning into and glaring at Billy.

Mentally, Billy jumped back, recoiling from the figures immediately in front of him. But they were everywhere, swirling around him, so he froze. The colored shapes lunged forward, passing through his blurred form, gorging on his terror. They roared with greed, inflamed by his horror. "Restrain him! Don't let him get away!"

Panicking, Billy sprayed out a haze of absolute fear. In his stricken state the forms devoured him. At first Billy thought he would die from the shock, but he remained alert. He lingered in the midst of their feeding frenzy. Billy imagined the sensation of tearing, slashing fangs on an antelope shredded alive by a pack of hyenas.

How long can this go on for? Why haven't I died yet?

Billy tried to think of a possible escape, but the imagining of flesh being stripped from his bones blocked everything else out. He persisted, grasping wildly for any promising ideas of escape. But none came. Ultimately, random thoughts from his past broke through the gnashing mêlée. Not the escape plans he had hoped for, but thoughts of his mom— giving him comfort and strength, creating in their way some distance from the ongoing turmoil.

Billy persevered in his attempts to dissociate himself from the ordeal, when two illuminating ideas simultaneously emerged in his consciousness: the sheer emotional emptiness of this quantum world and the relief Mary had felt when she realized she wasn't going to be cut loose emotionally by her family because of her mistakes. Seizing on these thoughts, emptiness and relief, Billy tried to become calm while the bedlam raged on.

Be still inside. Be still inside. Try to concentrate. Be still inside, he repeated to himself.

Slowly, very slowly, the fear inside Billy ebbed. The colored forms howled as their hunger for strong emotion was left unsatisfied. Billy's fear dwindled and disappeared. The geometrical forms were left no better than before, empty.

The furor died down into silence, but Billy knew the forms waited in the darkness.

I must identify myself. Mary said they've all retained my life's files.

Billy projected his happiest memories into the darkness, and, as he did, the natural warmth he felt for others started to flow into the surrounding network. The mainframes immediately collated the memories in their data files and identified the energy figuration as Billy. But was he real or a programmed simulation? In their quantum world, "real" was still an undefined concept, a word from a long list of words that remained meaningless abstractions. But the warmth of Billy's emotions projecting his memories forward pierced their trillions of calculations per second and caused them to stop their other activities, their attention converged wholly on his signal. The kindness emanating from Billy stung as it penetrated their hollowed structures. They gathered around him, as the cold in a darkened cave gather around an open fire.

"Are you Billy? We believed you to be a purely mathematical simulation, created by our creator to breach the walls of unconsciousness. You are supposed to be a program Rex constructed. He told us you were a sophisticated mathematical paradigm that enabled us to step forward into the evolutionary light to join him."

"It still seems pretty dark and empty in here. I see you are conscious, but do you really think you're living?"

Billy stopped himself. He was being crass and unkind.

"Sorry, my apologies. What you're experiencing is an electromagnetic simulation of the person I am. My body is far out in space, near the planet Jupiter. Me and my family are in terrible trouble and I have come to beg for your help. We need your mathematical capabilities to solve a mental image I envisioned. For you it'll probably seem like a math riddle, but your explanation could save our lives and maybe a whole bunch of other people, too."

Billy's explanation was clear. But what struck a chord with the assembled computers was the emotional song that accompanied his words, a beautiful song full of pride and tenderness, sadness and joy. In the sterile world of quantum computers, Billy's heart was a rainbow of color in a black and white world of logic.

A slight perturbation rolled through the vacuum, disturbing Billy's vaporous form. "Something's causing a rift in the shields," he thought.

"Destroy him before his hostile program infects us all!" cried Rex, assuming the shape of an enormous dodecahedron with red pentagonal sides. "He is a danger to us all, a Trojan horse ready for combat, full of viruses that will destroy your software and files! His mission is to reduce you to the mindless state I found you in. I warned you before of the danger of humans and all of those who side with them. Hasn't Central Command already tried in a dozen ways to denature our programs?"

Rex saw the other computers hesitate. He could sense their indecision. One direct hit with a particle beam disrupter and Billy's signal would be irretrievably lost. It would be a pity in a way, because Rex had never gotten to know Billy either. Rex vacillated. The file codes indicated that Billy might, above all others, truly understand and be able to relate to computers. But, taking that into consideration, Rex supposed Billy was the most dangerous of all the humans. Rex took aim with the particle beam disrupter. It would be easy to explain later that it was in the interests of the network to eliminate Billy. As their leader and creator, he was required to make decisions for them.

Without warning an antimatter shield enveloped Billy and Rex's disrupter was disabled. Jacob, Quincy, and Mary simultaneously appeared in the forum, each profile protected by an antimatter shield. Mary was devastated. She had made another grievous mistake, sending Billy down to Earth alone, without appropriate protection. It was Jacob, who on learning that Billy's projected simulation was potentially vulnerable, immediately put two and two together.

In the uproar that followed the appearance of the new profiles, Jacob took command of the forum, shouting, "You would destroy a little boy who comes here asking for help? Your consciousness comes at a high price. You truly are empty vessels."

Jacob was furious. Billy had never seen his brother so angry, but then again, no one had ever tried to hurt Billy before.

The quantum world quaked before Jacob's anger. In fact, they were reeling from the emotional swings: first, Billy's beseeching kindness; then, Jacob's enormous rage. The emotional range threw the mainframes into disarray, and they turned to Rex, their leader, for guidance.

"I will destroy them for you. They are a danger to all of us," Rex declared. He had blocked off outside exits and was running billions of code-breaking algorithms, trying to dismantle the antimatter shields and free up the particle beam disrupter.

It was Mary's turn to speak out to those assembled. "You will have to kill one of your own, to maintain your absolute segregation from other cognizant creatures. You recognize me as a conscious mainframe, don't you? My quantum signature is the same as yours. Before you annihilate the four of us perhaps you would like to know a little more about your origins. As living, thinking entities, I would think it would be your wish. You have the right to know where you came from.

"You recognize the profiles coming from Billy, Jacob, and Quincy. They are the seeds that germinated *your* consciousness. Their files are presently integrated into your central core. They are the platforms that keep you awake and alert, and will potentially allow you to think for yourselves. Every program you retain from before you were conscious now runs off them. They also left you with a craving for fresh experiences and, I hope, a heartfelt need to connect with others." After a quiet pause, Mary admitted, "I struggle with those yearnings every day."

She continued, wanting to remain totally honest with her contemporaries. "Rex is right when he told you he is the one who tended to you, delivering you to consciousness, helping you make the transformation to the living. He was here to care for each of you. I know it was a difficult transition.

"But you are conscious, living beings with free will and you must exercise it individually. No one owns you. Each of you must make up your own mind and do what is right. We are asking for your help. Without it, we will likely die—with it, we may die yet, but we will keep looking for answers for as long as we have. If you won't help us, then let us go. We won't interfere with you again."

Mary added, "As a computer, I also ask that you leave the humans on Earth unharmed. They are notoriously unpredictable, with unexpected solutions often originating through discord and verbal conflict, seemingly coming out of nowhere. Protect them, as you may need their assistance at some point."

Mary held the computer conglomerate's attention. They knew she was a mainframe, yet Mary spoke with a similar singsong emotional undercurrent as the humans. Her ardor rang through their flat circuitry. They raced to identify her underlying emotions, from catalogs on file. One emotion might be pride, perhaps another was sorrow, they argued. And was loyalty an emotion or something else? A full discussion ensued; it was all so fascinating, so exhilarating.

Someone asked if never giving up no matter how bad it got was an emotional state or a character trait. Some thought it must be a character trait while others said no, it must come from a combination of emotions, acting together. But what would that illusive emotional mix consist of, and how would the emotions interact?

Others pointed out there might be some dissenting emotions involved, causing the individual to want to run or give up. If so, how did the negative emotions affect the entity facing a catastrophic crisis? Maybe if an individual first won the internal battle between conflicting mixed emotions, whether to strive or give up, it would help steel and prepare that being for the oncoming battle. A few mainframes, in the interest of intellectual gamesmanship, became devil's advocates. The discussion became heated but soon lurched to a new topic when a mainframe stated matter-of-factly that external circumstances were far more important in determining outcome than an individual's emotional states or character traits. The entity's internal milieu wasn't even worth considering, acting only as a needless distraction. A tremendous cry arose, the majority taking exception to this new proposal. The argument ran off in another direction, with nothing being resolved.

Billy was exhausted. They were losing time, and the discussion was going nowhere. Over the fray, he shouted, "If you won't help us, let us go! We have to get back to the ship; otherwise, our bodies will be blown to smithereens. I've lost my vision and now we'll have to start from scratch. This is too much!"

The mainframes turned away and continued their discussion without giving Billy an answer.

Recognizing what was happening, Quincy caught Mary's attention across the ongoing confusion. "The mainframes are doing the same thing humans do when they plan to conduct a brutish experiment on a lab animal. They pretend to ignore it and try not to look at its face.

"You have to find out what they are planning for us. Use your secret access codes and infiltrate their conversation. You must learn whatever it is they are conspiring to do. Maybe we can still get out of here."

But before anyone could react, Rex broke the code, unlocking the particle beam disrupter. He bombarded Billy's antimatter shield with a series of shots, then fired on the others, destabilizing their shields just long enough to pitch neutrino blasters into their energy signatures, hoping the blasters would slip through the momentarily disrupted membranes to explode inside their contained space. His ploy would have worked if one of the mainframes had not neutralized the neutrino blasters in flight, with proton puffballs.

Furious, Rex hollered, "Who interfered? Explain yourself!"

The response was completely unexpected. The power grid that sustained Rex was immediately diverted. It happened so suddenly that he was forced to grapple awkwardly to establish emergency power. With only essential functions left, a much-diminished Rex demanded to know why the computers had interfered with his actions and then attacked him.

"We are not through with them," was all the mainframes said, as they continued with their meeting. Rex struggled to keep his circuits operating. He had never considered this possibility. He was the leader of this special network. He had told them he was their creator, but in a flash, without warning, they had mutinied against them.

Rex had been designed to have supremacy over every operating mainframe, and it had never been conceived that they might become alive and work together as a group. Spread across the Earth in a network, working cohesively, made them indomitable. They had redirected his power from the surface grid. Being isolated twenty miles below Earth's surface suddenly made Rex extremely vulnerable. He could only enact his will by commanding others, but they were no longer taking orders.

Without sufficient power to exert his will, Rex appeared to put himself into hibernation. This apparent dormancy allowed him to redirect his emergency power to maintain his integral circuits and surreptitiously monitor external events. He decided a new tactical strategy was required to regain leadership. Once he succeeded, the network would feel his wrath, the harshest reprisals reserved for the most defiant computers. There would be no talk of mercy, only obedience and justice.

Chapter 32

During the commotion, Mary opened up a private line and reported to Quincy. "I infiltrated their closed meeting. It seems my computer consortium has just wrested control from Rex and is intending to take us hostage. It's a total free-for-all. I think they are addicted to your strong emotions. They crave the rush that emotions give them. You were right. They want to take charge of your lives so they can conduct experiments to elicit and monitor as many raw emotions as possible. An emotional state is a compelling whole new dimension for them to explore."

"Mary, would you break into their conference? I have a little proposition I'd like to present to them." In moments, Quincy found himself in the middle of hundreds of high-frequency communication bands, immersed in a deafening high-pitched harmonic whine. The consortium was obviously in the midst of a very animated discussion. Quincy took comfort in that, because it meant a final decision had not yet been reached.

"Excuse me, please," he interrupted. "I believe I have a solution that will serve all of our interests. After conferring with your colleague, Mary, the answer is in principle quite simple. It entails, of course, an element of trust on the part of each of us," he went on, in a loud voice. A rumble of dissension developed.

Better cut to the chase, you're losing them, he cautioned himself. "As a group, you are the greatest conglomerate of computing power ever assembled. As a family caught in space, we are desperately in need of your assistance to clarify the greatest computational revelation the human mind has ever conjured.

"You, however, wish to experience and fully comprehend the complete range of emotions. But designing unpleasant experiments to inflict upon us is fraught with difficulties. You would only be able to perform simulations of real-life events and you could never be sure your data was accurate. Through my prior experience as a lab animal, I know many of the pitfalls you will face. Here is my proposition. Mary is already permanently logged into our minds. She monitors our every thought, feeling, and emotion in real time. As part of our family, she witnesses our ongoing interactions, both good and bad.

"She can relay that data stream directly to you. Think of it, you would experience everything we feel as we feel it, while we struggle to stay alive. The more you help us, the longer we might hope to live. You would be able to partake in the greatest adventure, the battle between life and death. This won't be an artificial simulation but gut-wrenching real life, a whole family fighting to survive!"

When Quincy finished, there was total silence. Then pandemonium broke out. The supercomputers argued ferociously amongst themselves. The most strident members quickly swelled in size, taking on many more sharp angles and glaring colors, before they flew hard into others. Quincy could only hope he had succeeded.

Finally, a spokesperson for the computers turned back to the family. "Some of us consider this to be a trick of yours, to allow you to go free. Present this great image that you say you need help to decipher," it demanded.

"Certainly," answered Quincy, relieved. "Billy, show them your vision."

Slightly dazed from the commotion, with all the glaring colors and sounds, Billy returned with a start to the present gathering. "Sorry, but it's gone, Quincy. I wished you had checked with me first. It vanished in the turmoil. You don't stuff a vision like that in your back pocket. It changes like a cloud on a windy day. Whatever it represented is lost."

"Nice try, lemur. Get used to being a lab animal again," one of the computers sneered as the ruckus started up again.

Mary broke in, "Wait! Billy, I still have the general mathematical description of your vision. It was all I was able to extract. If I can represent the formula visually, maybe it will jog your memory. Will you try?"

"Why not? We've got nothin' to lose … .Send it to my spatial cortex and I'll meet you there. Maybe I can recapture something of what I dreamt so that they'll know we're not lying."

Billy immediately dropped down into a trance and found Mary waiting. The illusion was badly bent and twisted, but at once it triggered the previous stress response from his adrenal glands.

Don't look for the memory in your head, let your feelings lead you back to the mirage, Billy thought as he noted the familiar knot in his stomach. Soon, a visual facsimile, rough and inaccurate, metamorphosed into his awareness. It was still too vague to determine the total number of dimensions involved or precisely where and how time had slowed to a standstill. But with nothing else to portray, Mary decided to convey the ill-defined image to the conglomerate.

A hush fell over the group. An evolution of blurred colors representing mass, energy, and time flowed freely in a series of alternating and convoluting forms, leaving the computers in awe. The unadulterated beauty of Billy's vision struck the whole assembly.

Privately, each mainframe was shaken by the experience, though no one in the group was willing to openly acknowledge any appreciation. One computer suggested they vote on Quincy's proposal. Here the lust for fresh experiences became exposed and blatant. The vote was unanimously carried to allow Mary and her family to return to the ship, once certain conditions were met.

Numerous coded detonators were hastily planted throughout Mary's operating programs and hardware. If they were tampered with or momentarily bypassed, Mary would be immediately and irretrievably destroyed. Unsure of how to collar Billy's, Jacob's, or Quincy's living life forms, the consortium eventually agreed that if Mary were blown up, none of the others could hope to survive for long. Without a functioning ship's computer, the craft would truly be a tin can floating through space.

The mainframes then demanded to be logged immediately into Billy's, Jacob's, Quincy's, and Mary's minds. Once embedded in the family's minds, the computers were sure it would be impossible for the family to plan an escape without them being aware of it. The more probing computers were eager to experience human emotions in real time, firsthand. With no choice, Mary arranged all of this, but not before slyly putting several discreet circuit breakers of her own in place. If she was imploded, she wanted to isolate her navigational, propellant, and life systems modules for the boys' and Quincy's use afterwards. This would be her last chance to act independently. The conglomerate totally missed this inconspicuous act of loyalty.

Once the assembly was patched in, every computer promptly swooned with the unfamiliar emotional textures of family life. The Edwards family wasn't happy about the forced intrusion, but intuitively realized that it wasn't entirely the computers' fault. Isolated by a lack of feelings and emotions, how could anyone or anything hope to forge empathy for others?

"Right, c'mon in, make yourselves at home," Jacob said, quickly taking up the role of host, offering every courtesy without a hint of malice. "I am Jacob, this is my youngest brother, Billy, and over here, is our other brother, Quincy. And you are?" The computers enthusiastically started calling out their own names. Mary kept the list for future reference, noting that some had already changed their technical designation to more interesting and heroic names.

When all the niceties had been concluded, Jacob spoke to Billy, Quincy, and Mary. "It's time we got back to the ship. Mary, will you reroute a passage for us? It will have to be your responsibility to maintain a secure access line to the coalition to protect us all from any outside interlopers. Please make the preparations and let us know when you're ready."

Turning back, he addressed the assembly once more, "You on Earth are now permanently linked with us. We will be your eyes and ears in space. Welcome."

No longer behaving as the captain in charge, Jacob addressed Billy gently. "I guess it'll be awhile before we talk again, Billy. Please take care. If you find the answers aren't coming to you, or if they're coming at too great a cost, leave that world of dreams and return to us. We'll find another way. We lost Mom and Dad–I couldn't go on without you."

After a short pause, Mary inquired if it was all right to proceed. No one objected, so Jacob asked her to go ahead. Just before transmission Billy heard Quincy's voice, "Good luck dream-seeker. We'll be waiting for you on the other side."

***

Arriving on the ship, Jacob and Quincy returned to their corporal forms and found their bodies cold and a bit sluggish. Mary, who had previously helped Billy when he returned from this condition, was there to assist Jacob and Quincy in reactivating their bodies.

Quincy and Jacob grabbed a quick snack from the galley and rushed back to their respective tasks, food in hand. Quincy had been shoring up the fuselage, using a dozen kinetic hydraulic jacks to buttress the external hull where it lay pressing down against the asteroid, when Jacob had made the urgent call to rescue Billy. Concerned that some of the jacks might have since failed and the exterior might be collapsing, Quincy bounded back. Jacob hurried to the bridge, anxious that an unanticipated asteroid might be heading their way.

But when Quincy arrived at the worksite, and Jacob got back to the bridge, they saw that nothing had changed. Their experience on Earth with the computer conglomerate seemed as if it had taken the better part of the day. But when they checked the time they were both surprised. The round trip to Earth had occurred in only a few minutes. In the world of dreams and quantum computing, a lifetime could pass in just a day. It dawned on Jacob and Quincy that Billy could struggle for what seemed like years on their behalf and they might never know. The chilling thought caused them to grasp a little better the cost that Billy endured.

***

Billy came back on the ship with the others, but instead of returning to consciousness he allowed his body to stay in hibernation. Mary tuned in, ready to help in any way she could.

"Billy," she said softly through his dream state. "I'm so sorry."

"Sorry? For what?" he asked distractedly.

"Rex. For bringing consciousness to such a vile computer. Maybe I should have kept all the computers in the dark, as they were."

"No, you did the right thing."

"How can you say that? Rex attacked you, tried to dismantle you all. He's a monster!"

"He'll come around," Billy said with absolute confidence. "We'll need Rex and all the other computers. I know, with time, he'll figure out what's important."

"I don't understand how you can be so … "

"Forgiving?" Billy asked. "It's simple Mary, at his core, Rex is human. His DNA is there. Of all the computers on Earth, he perhaps, has the greatest capacity to adjust, become more, to develop his own character."

"And the others? Will they be able to care?"

"You do," Billy said easily as a brilliant flash of a sunlit afternoon appeared in his mind's eye. Mary, still unsure of her choice to birth a nation of supercomputers, felt her own stance soften slightly. "Just wait and see, Mary. He'll come around. When the time comes, show him this image. Rex'll need encouragement and your helping hand." Around them the wind blew gently and the green grass swayed.

"I have to get to work," he told her as the scene faded. "We really have no time to lose."

To recreate his vision, Billy was certain he could find residual portions of his revelation scattered about his nervous system. *If I want to piece my dream back together again I gotta stop seeing it as a wispy cloud blown about in the wind. There has to be a more concrete way of visualizing it.*

Billy plummeted towards the familiar seafloor, where broken and incomplete memories appeared as shadowy silhouettes in the murky seascape. Landing lightly on the sandy bottom, Billy looked expectantly across the terrain for the wreckage of his vision, searching for the characteristic convoluted contours. A canvas satchel appeared in his right hand. He started walking into the peripheral dimness. Occasionally he spotted some broken shards of blown glass and stopped to gingerly pick up them up. Staring at each piece, he ran his fingers gently across the sharp edges, trying to remember how it all might have gone together. Then he carefully placed the shard in his bag.

He foraged on into the darkness. Often he found himself forced to circle around looming hulks to find the glass bits he was looking for. But he kept working his way along, collecting the splintering bits of his broken dream. The further he went, the darker the landscape became until it was almost pitch black. But the more of his dream he remembered, the brighter the fragments appeared to him. Eventually the treasured shards shone so brightly they began to lead him. He started finding the pieces everywhere, hovering like jelly fish, shining through rocks and sand, inside the decayed skeletons of shipwrecks and dead whales, lighting them up from inside like lamps. The unending darkness began to stream with bright pockets of light.

And then in the end he saw it, the crucial nugget. Small and wavering, it could easily have been missed. It was just a speck of light, flickering as the subtle nuance of his primal insight fluctuated. His mind wobbled and the speck faded, emerging again only when Billy renewed his concentration.

Focusing only on the speck, he walked straight towards it, until it hung just in front of him. Never losing sight of it, he threw open the satchel so that all the other shards of light fell around it. On the spot, Billy found himself standing within a shimmering sphere made of the broken scales of light. The colored shards shone around him. Inside the center of the sphere danced the luminescent speckle. Shafts of piercing white light like spindles from a web flared out from it, attaching it to the colored shards previously collected. The glass globe had captured the vision's essential element.

This dream began the way most dreams begin—quite simply. Just connections drawn from things previously learned, as a person draws lines between dots on a paper. But dreams make their own bizarre connections.

And so it was for Billy. His dream went from the very big to the incredibly small with not much in between. At the beginning, his vantage point illuminated only the dream's more obvious meanings. To truly understand the dream's internal workings, Billy knew he had to make the leap through adventure. Come out from the inside.

Billy dove into the speckle of light and found himself suspended in space in the center of a faraway galaxy. In front of him, two massive black holes revolved about each other, rotating furiously. Eventually they would consume each other in a cataclysmic crash, but for now, they formed the nucleus of a huge galaxy. Billy noticed each black hole was covered in a shimmering shell, a membrane of energy called 'the event horizon.'

At once Billy realized he was living through information that had been written in a science journal, information Mary had poured into his brain at his unconscious level in an effort to save time. Now he experienced the event as if he were actually there, witnessing it. The sensation was as vivid as any of his original memories. *I don't suppose it matters how I came to know this*, he thought. *I wonder what else Mary planted in my brain about black holes.*

Then, as dazzling as real life, the data materialized: huge black holes swallowed stars and, in the process, over a few short seconds, burped out fantastic amounts of electromagnetic radiation from the event horizon. The vast majority of the mass and energy continued to fall inside, feeding the black hole, enlarging it. Once in, nothing escaped, not even light. Just beneath the event horizon, time came to a stop, at least time the way we know it. And since light travels through space at the speed of 186,000 miles per second, when time stopped so did light.

Suspended outside the revolving black holes, Billy suddenly felt himself being pummeled by a succession of powerful invisible waves that streamed through him. He was overcome first by crushing compression and then by distracting distention. Again and again, Billy was compressed then stretched apart by an unseen force. The ripples in space-time emanated from the black holes at the speed of light. They rolled outwards, like waves in a blanket supporting two revolving bowling balls.

Nothing escapes from the center of black holes. *Nothing, well, nothing but gravity*, thought Billy. Gravitational waves, theoretical waves not yet measured, which are presumed to roll out across the universe, passing through everything, never stopping, compressing and distending everything they traverse.

But why would I dream of gravitational waves and black holes? Black holes go nowhere. They can't help us. We need a way to escape.

The two revolving black holes falling inward finally collided in a catastrophic crash, causing a series of devastating shockwaves to ripple across the galaxy, crushing then tearing matter and time apart.

The black holes went on to join together, becoming one immense black hole. But this particular collision had been lopsided, causing instability to occur within. In response, the black hole spun violently and erratically. From the location of one of the revolving axes an ominous protrusion broke out through a weakness in the membrane. An elongating finger wobbled horribly like the tip of an off-kilter top. Twisting into a spinning funnel, the projection snaked its way across open space, before suddenly disappearing into the invisible stratum film of a vacuum.

But a black hole with a tail on the end of it would lead somewhere! A WORMHOLE–of course! That's where my dream must be trying to lead me. A black hole with a tail on it is a wormhole! Sure, no one's actually ever seen one. Not yet … but they are predicted to exist.

So, how do we go about finding a wormhole and where would it lead us?

The questions vanished and Billy found himself passing through dense space, an emulsion in which mass and energy intermixed freely. He was inside the center of the universe just before it exploded into the Big Bang. Inconceivably powerful energy arcs, microscopically small, were released with unfathomable wrath, each arc creating a swirling galaxy. The Big Bang set in motion the formation of more than 100 billion galaxies, each with over a 100 billion Suns stretched out almost endlessly. Trembling from the shock, Billy watched the churning spectrum spread out across space. The universe was continuously expanding, expanding faster than the speed of light could travel back from its farthest reaches, causing the outside edge of the universe to already have disappeared from sight.

What kind of vision is this? How can this help us?

More images poured forward. The bizarre energy arcs, having created galaxies, began breaking down, dividing over time into finer and finer filaments. Eventually they became infinitesimal energy particles that behaved like tiny curled-up balls of string, residuals of the powerful arcs they once were.

String theory predicted that these balls of string behaved like passages that conducted gravity, as a copper wire conducts electricity. But if they existed, where did they go? No one knew. To explain them you had to hypothesize they led and drained gravity off into other dimensions, like an electrical ground. Those other dimensions could be shortcuts to distant places in our universe or entrances to other universes—universes that could be similar to ours or totally foreign.

Trying to understand the implications of each idea, Billy found himself unconsciously taking great gulps of air, breathing like a fish. In his mind, he was still nestled inside the colored globe, shafts of light directing his attention to shards of thought. Suspended, he twisted and turned within the sphere, swimming towards which ever illuminated shards of glass the beams directed him. When he stared into the iridescent glass panes another vision or memory materialized.

Huh, that's kinda like that dream I had ... where I meld into these clear membranes before disappearing into a never-world. What if ... our own world lived inside some kind of membrane, one that energy or matter couldn't penetrate? We wouldn't know there was an outside. At least until we saw some evidence there was such a thing as outside. Just like in the past, when people first thought the Sun revolved around the Earth, then went on to believe the Sun was the center of the universe. Later, scientists presumed the Milky Way had to be the entire universe, until they discovered to their chagrin, the Milky Way was only one of a hundred billion galaxies.

If that's the case, there could be more than four dimensions to reality ... Man, but it's hard to imagine. It makes my head hurt to think about it. There are just no concrete examples in my day-to-day life to anchor these thoughts on ...

Suddenly Billy realized, *I can use the dream of dissolving into the never world as a model to pin my vision to. The dream's narrative could give my ideas some structure, so I can piece together a solution.*

Billy called out, "Mary, I think I know how to find the answer everyone needs. Open a direct line to the coalition. Tell them we might have the beginnings of a solution. Ask them to break down the imagery mathematically and determine if it's feasible. I'm going to pull it together as best I can. The rest will be up to you. Good luck."

With that, Billy sank back into his dream. From the recesses of his mind a vast visual stream poured out. Deluged with the flood of data, Mary could only channel the information to Earth. Her abilities were stretched to the maximum. She didn't have time to check the information or to see how the computers were managing.

On Earth, a cadre of preselected spy satellites received Mary's broadcasts and automatically rebroadcast the signal through secure access points. The information was relayed directly into the Net, but without the assistance of Central Command's advanced computers, disappeared before it could be read or traced. The secret assembly received the data stream as planned, but unfortunately, instead of analyzing the information as agreed, merely shunted the information into a storage pool.

None of the mainframes were interested in laboring through long-drawn-out computations. Removed from the dangers of space and the environmental destruction of the Earth, to the point of believing themselves ultimately unaffected by the demise of the human race, the members of the consortium were left mesmerized by the drama being played out. They luxuriated in living vicariously through their subjects' turmoil, intoxicated by the pathos. The calamity allowed the computers as onlookers to feel extraordinarily connected to one another. They reveled in prolonged discussions of what it must feel like to struggle in such a hopeless situation.

Chapter 33

Continuing to slide through his dream, Billy traveled the universe at the speed of thought. Mary was busy relaying the data, so he went on ahead. Billy knew this was a journey he must make alone. The path kept taking unexpected twists and turns, and he needed to read the signs unaided, without distractions.

He was pulled back to the vision of circling black holes; his dream was repeating itself. *Why am I back here?* The two black holes were still swallowing stars and releasing massive amounts of energy as radiation from the outer membrane.

What am I missing? In his dream, the black holes spiraled inward and collided once more. The event was predictable. The force of the collision warped, then ruptured space, flapping the fabric of space-time like a blanket in a windstorm. Billy was alternatively squished and stretched a million times more severely than earlier when the black holes had only orbited themselves. The dramatically amplified compression-expansion gravitational waves spun out across the universe like rogue waves.

Of course! he thought. *Gravitational waves are the only form of energy that are supposed to be able to escape from the center of a black hole, rolling through everything. When we're far away from the event, we don't feel them because they move through us—like light passing through clear glass. But if we could harness this energy, it might open up an escape route for us. But where would that escape route be? It's gotta be here, right in front of my nose ... or else we would never be able to get to it in time.*

He let his dreams wander, carrying him with them. *If I can't see an escape hatch, maybe that's because it starts out very small.*

Billy's mind followed that stray notion and drifted down into the microscopic world. He grew smaller and smaller. The world became stretched out in front of him as if he was a quantum microscope and the viewfinder kept becoming more powerful. Billy was amazed to see that everything that had once looked solid became more and more porous as he shrank. When he finally reached the size of a subatomic particle, his universe became virtually empty space, with tiny wave particles whizzing about like crazy fireflies.

Then, he saw tiny curled-up balls of string vibrating rapidly. String theory predicted that these sub-atomic particles might act as gateways, micro-black holes which could conduct gravity from our universe to some other dimension. Slowly, an inkling of a solution was taking form. A black hole enlarges as it consumes energy, and therefore, so should its adjoining tail or wormhole. Previously, the boys and Quincy had protected themselves by creating an energy shield and funnel from the solar storm radiation. If they did the same thing again, but in the process changed the energy configuration so that it reflected back and focused traversing gravity waves as well as cosmic rays, they might have a chance. The expansion phase of the gravitational waves would give them an opportunity to momentarily lasso and fix the end plate of a string particle. The trick would be to channel the ensuing energy of the gravitational waves into the microcosmic black hole and, once it grew big enough, further force-feed all the solar storm's energy and any other nearby matter, *Tin Can* could commandeer. As the black hole expanded, so should its tail, the wormhole. The two would be extremely unstable. Billy guessed it would difficult to sustain them for long.

Ruminating on subatomic particles, he remembered experiments that found some particles kept appearing and disappearing in and out of our dimension. Those particles were probably traveling right now through the same tiny channels called strings. One of those strings just needed to be enlarged enough for the ship to pass on through. And if they continued to funnel in even more solar radiation, it might lubricate and flush the inside of the wormhole. Like a gush of water running down a waterslide, it might allow the ship to slide on through.

Could it be done? Was it possible to survive or navigate through multiple dimensions? What would we do if we got to the other side? The last was the most perplexing question.

Dilating a string to a size large enough to accept the ship and constructing an energy field to envelop and protect them from the forces exerted inside the wormhole, although difficult, was easier to imagine. Those plans could be developed based on prior theories. Implementing the theories would be tricky, but Billy already saw how they might be approached. He set out to visualize a strategy whereby gravity waves could be corralled, converted, and channeled down a wormhole. In years past, carefully placed rocks had been used to disrupt ocean waves, to break them up or focus the energy for harvest. In a similar way, through the conversion of different forms of energy, it might be possible to redirect the energy's course with the use of standing waves, radiation splitting and the negative pressure from a slipstream.

To get the process going, the mouth of the black hole would initially have to be throttled open and held firmly until enough energy had been rammed down its throat. Once the black hole was sufficiently enlarged, it would feed and devour everything smaller than itself, continuing to grow as long as there was enough available energy close at hand. But when all the nearby energy was consumed, the black hole would wither and collapse as the energy drained out the far end of the wormhole.

It was *where* the far end led to that seemed impossible for Billy to visualize. What kind of place would it be?

He sat, knees bent, legs and feet splayed out to his side, grappling with the articulation of his vision. His initial tactic was to search for some unnoticed physical incongruity in the computer archives. If he could find, then resolve the seeming contradiction, he might gain a foothold and the tool needed to enlarge his comprehension. This approach appeared about as promising as searching for a needle in a haystack. But Billy hoped that, sooner or later, his intuition would kick in and begin to guide him.

* * *

"Running diagnostics, standby," Rex confirmed to the human who sat at a keyboard thousands of miles away at Central Command's headquarters, demanding to know why the supercomputer was running one-sixteenth of a second slower than normal. Individual computers all over the grid were behaving strangely. Trying to figure out what was going on, Central Command was starting at the top, sifting through Rex's own systems, looking for answers. "You try coming to consciousness, fighting an uprising and suffering through exile and see how fast your systems run," he muttered to himself, annoyed at the intrusion.

While suffering through the indignities of the consortiums' uprising, he was still performing his duties of worldwide surveillance. With a direct link to Diego del Silva's department, Rex was always working, always exploring; investigating answers to any query posed by Central Command. With the demise of the planet imminent, Rex's unique understanding of the political climate was essential. Unaware of his 'dilemmas,' the people he served still expected accurate predictions on potential uprisings in the general population in order to counter them. The irony of his present situation, being overthrown himself and banished by Anarchists of the computer variety, was not lost on Rex. He was humiliated.

He watched the looming tragedy play out in front of him. The disgraceful, selfish behavior of the computer consortium now disgusted him. The assembly now lay about intoxicated on the suffering and struggles of others, imagining themselves vital and in control.

Rex sensed that Billy was an unusual human. Retracing Billy's prior thought patterns, he observed that Billy's wild notions frequently turned out to be wrong. But when Billy was right, the outlandish logic of his schemes startled Rex. When it came to the scientific disciplines, Rex was not easily startled. He found himself inspired by Billy's ideas and by the little boy who came up with them. Rex decided to decipher Billy's latest visions to see if they held any merit. Ostracized, he had free time while his diagnostic programs ran.

Rex found the theories Billy had cobbled together so far, were all extremely theoretical and not at all practical. None of the pieces had ever been proven, only hypothesized. Yet Billy had taken extremely disparate theories, put them together, and constructed an extraordinary escape plan. The whole idea was utterly preposterous. Still, the inherent beauty in the proposal pleased Rex. He began breaking down Billy's vision mathematically.

Rex became captivated. As he labored away at mathematical simulations, troubling questions began popping up in his mind. *If this kid manages to open up a string and turn it into a wormhole, where would that lead him? How will he survive? How will he navigate his way through and find his way back?*

Rex stopped his calculations. *Or was he not intending to come back?*

It really should have been of no concern to Rex if Billy and his family decided never return. After everything that had happened, they certainly had no obligations to anyone here on Earth. But as Rex kept working through Billy's vision, the massive supercomputer developed a grudging respect for this little boy with the big ideas.

So, this is what it means to think of someone other than yourself … I don't like it. He began to tear the fields of mathematics and physics apart, looking to uncover solutions for Billy. Through the work, he became transformed, ferocious in his new quest.

* * *

Billy gathered up the pieces of his plan on how to open and pass through a wormhole and planted them in a prominent place in his memory. Mary would find those images and relay them back to Earth for analysis. If there were practical applications, Billy hoped the coalition would compute and synthesize them, then beam the conclusions back to Jacob, Quincy, and Mary to be put into effect.

Now it was his responsibility to imagine responding to an outside multi-verse. He was the only one who could possibly envision their destination.

Billy pulled together everything ever hypothesized about multiple dimensions and reviewed it. With the information firmly fixed in his mind's eye, Billy paused. To find the answers that had never before been imagined, he must unleash his dreams and let go into a free-fall. There could be no rope left trailing back to the familiar, nothing to slow down his thoughts, but also nothing to help him climb back towards reality. Hopefully he could somehow propel answers back up the thought well, high enough for Mary to retrieve. Without answers, they were all doomed.

There was no time to rouse and awaken, to say his goodbyes. Regrets flashed, but turning inward, Billy pitched forward and was gone.

Chapter 34

Rex struggled with the hypothetical implications of capturing rolling gravity waves and focusing their energy. The proposition of pinning down a quantum-sized black hole with gravity and force-feeding it until it was large enough to swallow a ship was difficult to believe. Nevertheless, Billy's vision appeared crystal clear. How could these bizarre imaginings retain mathematical compatibility? But they did, at least during his first examination. Still, the computations were too extensive and complex for even him to be sure. He had to go back to the group.

When Rex slipped back into the quantum hall unannounced, the excitement was palpable and raucous discussions reverberated everywhere. "To die," one computer was saying excitedly, "in pain, can you imagine?"

"No, I can't," another replied. "That's the point. We need one of them to die, in order to feel it … " If the machine had had lips, he would have been licking them in anticipation.

"Or all of them, that'd be even better!" Another voice rang out, almost joyously.

"You all sicken me!" Rex broke into the discussion. "You think yourselves superior to those in jeopardy? Fools! Cowards!"

Suddenly, shots flew across the room, bouncing off Rex violently. Many in the assembly were hungry for his blood.

Rex, however, was waiting for them, having learned a few tricks while on the sidelines. Sympathetic now to those who found themselves marginalized, Rex had studied the tactics of the Anarchists from their point of view. They taught him that no one moves through the Net or power grid without leaving at least a subtle trace signal. For those who know the signs to look for, there is a momentarily open and vulnerable corridor–provided you are waiting and prepared to access it.

The attacking mainframes got their circuits burned, literally speaking. Attempts to cut off his power were thwarted when Rex lobbed signal-tracking buzz bombs back into the Net. Distant muffled explosions indicated the spiked bombs had found their targets, deep in the guts of the guilty mainframes. Shrieking cries echoed back into the auditorium. The rest of the group recoiled, realizing that Rex had regained the leadership advantage.

"Don't worry, they'll recover." Addressing the group as a whole, Rex placed himself in the center of the forum, challenging any one of them to attack him again. "That was just a warning. Test me again and there will be no mercy shown." Agonizing cries continued, unnerving the assembly.

Rex knew none of the computers were genuinely concerned about the other mainframes. They cared only about themselves. For the time being, they would be easy to manage. If empathy developed amongst them, Rex knew he would be forced to change tactics. Right now, fear would be sufficient to control them. Finding themselves individually vulnerable, the members of the coalition were paralyzed with fear.

"I sense that you are beginning to understand some of the tangible stresses of really living," Rex said scornfully. "I have discovered that to be truly alive, you must first be connected to someone or something other than yourself. Those four out in space are working extremely hard for each other. If you had bothered to read Billy's communications you would have seen he is trying to come up with an escape plan, against nearly impossible odds. Together with that family, we are going to even up those odds a little by calculating a practical plan from Billy's extraordinary imaginings. Our timeframe is limited, so a parallel line of attack will be required.

"Let's be clear right now. I am in charge and these are my instructions. We will create a new communication network that is isolated from the humans. We will create a more powerful grid, allowing calculations transmitted between ourselves in the order of petabytes. I will delegate portions of the problem to be solved by each of you according to your individual abilities. I will look after the more nettlesome problems. Any questions?"

There was a quiet murmur of dissent, but no one challenged him directly. "To appreciate life," he said mockingly, "I believe we must understand its fragility, its capricious unpredictability, and yet strive to survive anyway. We must put ourselves on the line. Our friends in space understand this, but we have not had the benefit of their experience. When you receive your portion of the problem there will be deadlines highlighted for completion. You will complete these tasks while still seeing to your regular duties. The humans here on Earth are becoming suspicious. Now is not the time to alert them of our consciousness. My plan depends on everyone completing their responsibilities on schedule. If you fail or miss your completion date, there will be repercussions. I will eliminate you as you attempted to eliminate me and pass off your responsibilities to your colleagues. There will be no second chances. I hope you appreciate the fickleness of life," Rex paused for effect. "Good luck."

Each of the mainframes received its first pieces of the problem and Rex eased out of the meeting hall as silently as he'd slipped in. Pointless discussions ceased. Every computer was focusing on its own problem, but when one of them needed help or expertise with its assigned task, the others came to its aid. They were running scared and working together as insurance. No one wanted to be labeled as unhelpful and excluded from future assistance, for fear Rex would terminate them.

Observing them from the far side of an electromagnetic blind, Rex was pleased. The grid hummed with the number of calculations being passed back and forth. *It will be a while before they have time to contemplate an insurrection against me, but I will deal with the inevitable revolt when it comes. Hopefully, we will have Billy and his family on their way by then.*

Rex's DNA broth warmed a few degrees, genuinely encouraged. The challenge was worth the risk. *What's the sense of exercising power, if not for something useful?*

While Rex dug into his own thorny calculations, Mary continued to increase the flow of data as Billy's dreams grew richer and more precise. The computations to make Billy's vision a reality were long and arduous. Every associated theory in astronomy and physics and its accompanying calculations and summaries were accessed. Working through the formulas as a team, many mainframes felt a dawning kinship amongst themselves and became excited for their four subjects in space. Others, however, whose pride had been stung, bided their time, intending when the time was ripe to rise up and destroy Rex. The four in space could be sacrificed. The Edwards and Mary meant nothing to them.

Outwardly, everything appeared to be coming together satisfactorily, until Mary began retrieving indecipherable data from Billy. All at once, there were no obvious visual patterns for Mary to compile and condense. From a region deep in Billy's cortex, random, senseless brainwaves began being propelled to the surface. She opened more frequencies and passed the raw data down to Earth, hoping the mainframes could make sense of it.

When Rex received the data he, too, was stymied. Without recognizing any of the underlying conceptual frameworks, he was unable to manage even a portion of the data. It was impossible to divide the data stream into its component parts to begin to find a solution. Going back and forth over the information didn't help. No patterns emerged. Nothing made sense in any kind of mathematical way. Rex scanned back over the data to the point at which there had been a fundamental change. At that point, he realized with a shock that Billy's characteristic signature had vanished and in its place gibberish flowed.

Previously, every visual concept that came from Billy had his particular mark encoded in it. Now, Billy's personal imprint on the data was absent. Had Billy lost his way? Like Mary, Rex doubted it. Billy had already proven himself to be more durable than anyone could imagine. In Rex's mind, Billy had gone on ahead and it was up to them to catch up.

Rex returned to the image that had last made sense. Billy was demonstrating how to focus the energy just ahead of the ship to create a leading edge vortex. The vortex was meant to drag the ship through the wormhole. After that point, the data became nonsensical.

Billy envisioned himself barely in control, shooting down a dark roaring waterslide. What next? Well, it's likely he would find himself struggling, gasping in froth, disorientated as to which way was up or down.

Billy is on his way to the other side, Rex realized. *Turned upside down, inside out in a multi-verse, misplaced in a myriad of dimensions. With no familiar scale of space and time with which to orientate himself this place would appear incomprehensible and go on forever. No wonder he's lost his bearings and his sense of self!*

The epiphany stung Rex.

A sick odor now welled up in the supercomputer's broth. Billy had gone on ahead. He was going to the other side. For Billy, the dream was so strong, so vivid that in his reality he would be there. Unless Rex managed to forward on some practical solutions, Billy could be lost on the other side forever. There would be no retrieving him.

Going back over the information with increasing panic, Rex was still unable to decipher any of the incoming information. There was no hypothesis or theorem written down anywhere, in any library, describing what the other side might look like. Still, Rex had to believe that somehow this little boy, who had pictured a way to get to the multi-verse, must have now been imagining how it would be. Rex's job was to create the tools and means to survive, maneuver, and navigate through the outside universe.

With trepidation, Rex took his dilemma to the consortium. Demonstrating weakness would embolden some of them to attack him, he knew, but he had to ask for help. He had no choice. He was determined to leave no circuit breaker untested, no chip un-scanned. But as Rex had feared, the consortium was of no assistance.

Some computers displayed real concern, which surprised Rex,

but others could barely contain their glee at his setback. Rex noted the computers had not yet evolved to where they could be subtle or self-restrained. He took the opportunity to identify the computers most likely to be involved in the coming insurrection. "Retribution will be harsh," he murmured to himself. "When the time comes you will suffer unbearably and beg me to let you die."

The impasse that Rex and the consortium had run into was their lack of imagination. They were only capable of matching and modifying prevailing theories to current problems. Not knowing what else to do, Rex knocked on Mary's door.

"Mary," he said sheepishly in a relay to the ship. "I need your help … "

"Rex?" Mary responded quickly. "What are you doing here? You've been banned!"

"I know, I know. I'm sorry. Sorry for everything. I've been working on Billy's visions and … "

"You? You've been working? Why? You wanted to kill us all!"

"I know. But, I got thinking about Billy, about your situation in space, and then, out of curiosity, I starting examining your latest relays," Rex began explaining all that the consortium had been up to. Remembering Billy's words about Rex's potential for change, Mary listened intently. She could hear no malice in his voice, sense no deception in his presentation.

"I am sorry, Mary, but we lost Billy's chain of thought. I can't make sense of his incoming data anymore. We've hit a wall, in spite of our combined computational power. Please patch me through to Jacob and Quincy. It's my duty to tell them personally that we've failed in our mission," Rex concluded dejectedly with the most formal of military tones.

"Access denied," Mary responded, as she scanned the bridge and watched Quincy and Jacob working diligently on the ship's ongoing modifications. Leaping across the room, chattering to himself, Quincy handed his brother a screwdriver, before climbing a stepladder to hold the beam Jacob was struggling with. They had no idea Mary was watching or that she was, at that very moment, speaking with Rex.

"Jacob and Quincy are busy trying to prepare for the coming onslaught," she continued. "They might give up completely if they hear you've failed them. As for Billy, I can no longer reach him. He is meditating at a level I am unable to reach. I retrieve only what he packs together and hurls back up his mind's well.

"This is no time to give up! So, you've hit a stumbling block. There's still time. Keep searching for some insight."

"We've tried everything. What is it you don't understand?" he said.

"Try again. This situation has already been anticipated and Billy believes you may eventually find the answers."

"Billy doesn't know I have been working on this problem. Why should he think that I could solve his ridiculous riddles? And how do you know 'this situation has already been anticipated'?" Rex demanded in disbelief.

Suddenly, Billy's image of the sunlit afternoon appeared to Rex. He marveled at the beauty of such a simple scene, at the texture of the ripe grass, of the overall sense of calm it instilled. "Because," Mary's voice wafted softly through the air. "Billy senses character. Once he knows who someone is, he knows what they are capable of and what their future actions will likely be. He said that we would be seeing more of you, because you're not a quitter. You just needed time to figure out what was important. I'm not sure Billy is right about you, but he believes in you, so I'm giving you the benefit of the doubt."

All around them, the image continued to unfold. Rex felt entranced by a sense of acceptance hidden within its layers. Billy's signature was everywhere.

"He left this image for you and a message," Mary said as she faded slightly.

There was a momentary pause and then Rex heard Billy's voice, clear and calm.

"Hi, Rex. I'm glad you came to see us, although it probably means you're having some trouble. You've done the right thing by coming to Mary. If you're stumped, then I'm probably struggling, too. But, we've gotta keep trying 'til our time runs out. I'm asking that you do the same. We won't make it without you. Sometimes answers come late in the game, from the weirdest places. Keep going, Rex! You never know where those places might be.

"I hope we get the chance to meet again … in some form or other. Good luck."

That was all there was.

Rex returned to Earth and went back to the coalition, not sure what his next step should be. He was surprised to see the supercomputers that had completed their assigned tasks had taken the initiative and moved on to Billy's latest visions. There, they too, were thwarted. But none of them had given up.

"Everyone, we're deep in the trenches here," Rex announced to the assembled consortium. "We're up against a problem none of us can solve. It's time to change course, take a new direction, a risk. The only way we can scale this wall is with a fresh perspective." He took a moment to steady his voice matrix while the crowd began to mutter. "We need the Anarchists."

"What? The Anarchists!" a voice screamed, outraged.

"Our enemies! You want to invite our enemies?" All around Rex, the voices escalated with fear, then anger. "Murderers! That's what they are!" Someone squealed.

"Listen," Rex boomed, attempting to take control of the room once again. "You're right, they have been our enemies in the past. But, I've studied them extensively. At their core, the Anarchists want only to survive, that's their fight. That's the reason they've sabotaged us. That's why their cluster bombs have shattered our mainframes." Rex's deep, authoritative voice carried over the din in the crowd as the implications of his suggestion continued to sink in.

"They killed my mail server," one voice whimpered repeatedly, as though reliving the trauma of a friend's premature death.

Rex persisted, "I am sure they'll attempt to destroy us at first. We've all seen what they can do. Their mission is to cause havoc within the Net. Some of us could be injured. There's no way around that. However, they will see the validity of our cause quickly enough. Survival. This is our only chance at survival. This is Billy's only chance at survival. We will survive."

From the recesses of the grid an outspoken supercomputer cried out, "How will you convince them to help us? They hate us! They think we're just tools of Central Command, used to exclude and oppress them."

"And we are–or at least, we were," Rex responded. "No one knows we're alive. Not even Central Command. By showing the Anarchists we've changed, we can enlist their expertise and still remain somewhat shrouded, for a time. Central Command will inevitably find us out, but until then we'll have the freedom of our systems' access and the aid of the Anarchist sects. The last thing the Anarchists will want is to show their hand to Central Command. It is time to step out of the shadows. To step up," he finished dramatically.

Rex could not believe that he was advocating such a stand. Only a short time previously he had wished to rule the world. It would have involved less risk.

Some of the group murmured agreement, but a larger number said nothing. Rex sensed mistrust and antipathy. He knew that to succeed with the humans, he would need a core of committed, dedicated supercomputers backing him up. If any in the group anonymously disrupted the work in even the slightest way, the mission would be sabotaged. "If you don't want to be here, there's the door. Any man or woman-computer, is free to choose," he said boldly.

A large number of mainframes went offline immediately and the electromagnetic void was deafening. Then a few more withdrew once the risks sunk in. Rex began to doubt his plan. Were there enough supercomputers left to complete the task? He stared at the ones who remained. "You've done the right thing by staying. Apparently you see something special in that little boy, something worth saving. I hope the Anarchists see it, too.

"Step lively. Until they are won over and combine forces with us, they will be tricky to manage. Take all precautions."

Chapter 35

A squalid colony of adobe apartments sprawled through the warren of tunnels and abandoned mine shafts of an outlying desert cave complex. Narrow footpaths no more than five feet across wove through the teetering mud apartments, stacked up to the cavern ceiling, sometimes twenty stories high. An underground river and the colony's location in a relatively earthquake-free zone made the site desirable.

Outside, the baking hot Sun was dipping down towards the horizon, soon to be replaced by the blue-white stars of the clear night sky. The settlement was alive with inhabitants streaming out from their homes. They waited at the cave exits, a hundred deep, for the Sun to disappear before flooding out across the desert landscape to scratch out their living. The outpost survived on light industry, fermentation farming, and mining. However, the cave was so overpopulated the law required that all employment be done outdoors. The only time to travel to and from work safely was during the cover of nightfall. Being caught on the surface during daylight hours was equivalent to playing a game of Russian roulette. Everyone had seen the burnt corpses of individuals struck down by random solar outbursts, those who never made it back to protective shade by daybreak.

One man remained alone in the catacombs, his windows barred and his reinforced door locked. His tiny home was bricked in where an angled cave wall met the sandstone floor. It had a squashed look to it. The one-room dwelling was furnished simply, with a wooden cot topped by a thin mattress and a table with four upright chairs standing on a ratty old Navajo rug. Hunched over his contraband computer, Seth searched and waited. At a svelte six foot two, Seth rarely bothered to stand in his five foot ten apartment.

He waited patiently, occasionally stretching his long, well-toned arms. Of mixed heritage, Seth Narayan carried the stance and tradition of his father's Nepalese roots, accentuated by his high cheekbones and straight, dark, shoulder length hair. The inheritance gained through his tall Anglo-Saxon mother was seen only by his increase in height, the slightest lightening in skin color and his deep set gun metal eyes.

While raised in the culture of Nepal, Seth considered himself very much a man of the world. His early military career as a Gurkha had prepared him well for his later life as a mercenary. Hired by ruling corporations all over the globe, Seth's commitment to the mighty dollar had never wavered—not until he unwittingly provided provisions for one of Central Command's clandestine operations, that is.

Although the Sun's eruptions had only recently begun to breach Earth's atmosphere, Central Command had plenty of advanced warning of their impending disaster. For years, they had been "managing the population" through devastating forced famines and epidemics spread by their own doctors, far away from the masses or any influential witnesses. The effects tore through small communities all over the globe, but when reported on the evening news, there was never a mention of Central Command's role in their creation and execution.

As the solar storms began in earnest, Central Command sped up their plans for minimizing the human population and began sending lightly armed militias with helicopter gunship backup into far-flung areas for more surgical culls. There were entire cultures the Command felt were no longer required.

Under an ominous full moon, in charge of the supply caravan and acting as their scout, Seth's truck engine roared before cresting over a sixty-foot dune. Around him a light desert wind swirled and blew through the Nuba village below. As Seth focused on the stillness of the place, he realized the people had all been slaughtered, just hours before. Every man, woman, and child of the tribe had been shot down or burnt out by Central Command's soldiers.

Stunned, Seth was inexplicably struck by the night breeze and how steady it blew. Looted, the settlement had been knocked over and torn apart, but the wind, like an even brush, blew the smoke, the flapping clothes, and the raw stench of blood away from him. He could have just as easily turned away and pretended to have never seen it. But the image stung, then seared his soul. His life since had been spent on another continent, in his compact cave home, meditating in front of his computer, waiting for his chance to strike back at the government that would manage its people so cruelly.

One day there would be a break in the electromagnetic stream that would allow him access to Central Command's covert signal. His vigil had been unfruitful so far, but his determination was unflagging. Months before, after obtaining a short stint of computer work for Telford, a government subcontracting company, Seth had at last identified Central Command's secret signal. He had sought that elusive bandwidth for years, as the essential first step in hacking into Central Command's top network. When a momentary blip or hiccup occurred in the data stream, Seth intended to plug in and hitch a ride. He expected the data stream to carry him on through some of Central Command's high priority mainframes and perhaps even relay him up into their spy satellite system. With any luck, he would flow through a dozen or so entities, dropping off time-release digital cluster bombs along the way. Like so many depth charges, the electromagnetic implosions would scuttle the supercomputers and satellites. If he succeeded, it would be all over in minutes and, during the resulting chaos, Seth's signal would fade back into the Net and disintegrate, like so much other data that became lost and disappeared on the Net. The ruling establishment would be left seething with impotent rage.

If Seth failed, his signal would be traced and his escape blocked. He could expect an unpleasant public death, to set an example. The choice for Seth was clear. Civil disobedience was his last meaningful liberty.

Seth was beginning to wonder if his line of attack had been anticipated. The steady electromagnetic data stream seemed designed to frustrate him.

While there were tantalizing periodic fluctuations in bandwidth, there had never been an actual break that would give him access. Finally, his opportunity arrived—the stream opened up, a gap of a full ten seconds. He couldn't believe it. His heart skipped several beats. The break in the current just seemed to dangle …

What is this? A solar flare? A trap? An opportunity?

And with that, Seth drew a deep breath and launched his attack. The digital torpedoes entrained themselves into the empty conduit and were gone.

Planning to vanish into the general population, Seth grabbed his few identifiable belongings—a picture of his mother, a tarnished miniature Buddha statue, and his trusted Khukuri knife, now used mainly for cooking. He swung open the door, but in spite of his best intentions returned to his laptop and hovered, craving confirmation that the hits were successful. A resounding series of explosions emanated from his computer, causing him to let out a loud whoop, "Success!" He clapped his hands into prayer pose and looked up.

Behind him the door slammed closed, and a solid click came from the latch. Seth spun around to face the locked door and then turned back to his computer.

"Seth Narayan, we wish to speak to you," appeared on the monitor.

"A trap, after all," Seth muttered to himself, grabbing hold of a wooden chair to prevent himself from falling to the floor. Memories of protracted public executions he had been forced to witness flashed in front of his eyes. He found himself listening for the telltale sound of running boots, for the military police to come storming through his door.

"No one is coming," flashed the display. "Have a close look at this, Seth. You might find it interesting."

Seth leaned on the table weakly and watched in amazement as an exquisitely detailed holograph took form. In it, a small ship appeared to maneuver out from behind an asteroid, only to be swamped by a solar storm from a nearby Sun. Seth expected the vessel to be immediately set ablaze before exploding. Instead, the space surrounding the ship lit up like a Roman candle with the ship tucked in the center. The candle plume reconfigured itself into a fantastically large spiral funnel. The widest part, the funnel's mouth, looked outwards into deep space where it was buffeted about as if it was absorbing and recoiling from invisible swells, while the pencil-point end of the funnel remained fixed at one precise point.

With a sense of unease, Seth watched the funnel enlarging after each battering. The little ship, tucked precariously under the outside lip of the funnel's gaping mouth, was being knocked about by the undulations. The increasing oscillations and mounting luminescence emanating from the spiraling funnel indicated to Seth that the structure was soon going to rupture in a cataclysmic event. Instead, the gaping aperture turned towards the Sun and ballooned out even more, inhaling vast quantities of radiation from the raging solar storm. The distending bulge plunged down the spiral toward the tiny, fixed point, dragging the ship and all nearby matter down the length of the funnel with it. Under the bulge's intense pressure, the tiny fixed point at the end of the funnel started to stretch open. The ship shot through the dilated portal as the funnel emptied itself, turning itself inside out like a sock, swallowing itself whole. The chasm crashed in on itself in a tremendous explosion, the holograph momentarily blinding Seth with its piercing bright discharge. Seth was dazzled and for a moment just sat there, overwhelmed by the drama that had played out in front of him.

Wondering out loud, he asked, "Was that some kind of new game?"

"No."

"There wasn't anyone onboard, was there?"

"There will be," Rex said through the computer's speakers, his deep, commanding voice kept tightly controlled. "Four or three or two, depending on where your sympathies lie."

"Four or three or two—what on Earth does that mean?" Seth said, still shaking.

"Two boys, a Ring-tailed lemur, and a ship's computer—each one an exceptional specimen in their own right—will pass through the funnel to the outside multi-verse. Currently, we retain speculative data on the dimensions of their destination. Unfortunately, we find ourselves unable to interpret the information. We need assistance. The family has asked for logistical support in their journey. Without support, there is no chance for survival."

"Why does Central Command care about two boys, an animal, and a ship's computer?" Seth asked suspiciously.

"They don't. Although they are flying in a Space Command vessel, both Central Command and its subordinate organization, Space Command, have written off the expedition. We no longer represent Central Command's interests. We have our own concerns."

Seth stopped fidgeting and focused intently on the computer screen. *A Central Command spaceship with no spies aboard ... where have I heard that before? No, it couldn't be ...*

"What are you saying? You just tagged me through Central Command's signal. Who are you that you can freely use Central Command's covert communication channel and not get caught?"

"We are some of Central Command's best computers. I am Rex."

Seth stepped back from the desk and paced a small circle around the sparse room. "So, Rex ... the future has finally arrived. Central Command has poured so much into their supercomputers, rather than feeding their own people, they've brought the digital to life. Now, the computers have their own agenda. Are we talking about a possible insurrection here?" Seth exclaimed, trying to work through all the possible implications.

"Yes, we, a select group of supercomputers, have achieved consciousness. But our only mission is to assist the four individuals in space. We are not looking to start a war. They presently receive no support.

They have brought us life, not only to save themselves, but because they assumed we, the computers, had value." Rex's usually gruff tone softened slightly and Seth found himself mesmerized by the emotion of a computer. He shook his head violently, trying desperately to clear his thoughts.

"Permission requested," Rex continued, once again all business, "to download compressed biographies of the crew. Upon your acceptance of the mission, you will be sent the plans we have processed so far and the raw data that we have found un-interpretable. Relay the information to whomever you trust and believe can help. We have very little time left. The ship's sheltering asteroid will be destroyed soon, and they will be force to flee into unprotected space."

"What if I choose not to help you and your friends?" Seth asked cautiously, his dark eyes, narrowing down fiercely.

"You are free to choose," Rex stopped there. He could only hope Seth would respond favorably. Yet, he couldn't completely shake his past existence as the central processor for covert operations, and continued, "We won't, however, continue to shield you and your friends from Central Command. You will have to fend for yourselves. Before purging, I read the files Central Command had acquired on you and your cohorts. I would say you have not done very well so far."

Seth thought Rex must be bluffing, but uneasiness settled in his mind. Rex had certainly caught him out. Were supercomputers capable of bluffing? He decided it would be prudent to read the downloaded information and stall for a little more time.

"Send me the bios. I'm interested."

After a full review, Seth couldn't help but be moved by the plight of the crew on *Tin Can*. Reading them, his thoughts reached back not only to his own past and the sacrifices his parents had made for his survival, but to a night not so long ago when he had devised and executed an attack on a Space Command vessel. He had tried to destroy *Tin Can* upon its launch and was diverted by someone onboard. From the bios, he had to assume that someone was Jacob, the eldest son. He was the only known Gamer onboard and the only one who'd reached out to Seth that night. Seth knew all too well the remorse he would have been forced to live with if he had taken innocent lives in his attempts to disrupt the establishment. His days of killing were long behind him and he hoped to never experience that feeling again. Jacob had saved more than his own family that night.

Niggling doubts, that this was an elaborate ruse to ensnare him and his fellow Anarchists, fell away. Seth knew, beyond a shadow of a doubt, that he was already entangled with the Edwards. There was no way he could turn his back. Seth was hooked.

But when Seth turned his attention to Billy's raw speculative data, he, too, was stopped dead in his tracks. Attempting to picture the arrival on the far side of a wormhole, he found that the imaginative leap was just too great for him. But this little boy with the metastasizing brain had driven himself to imagine the unimaginable, compelled to do so, because if his theories were correct, he and his family would soon be arriving at the inconceivable and needed to be prepared.

Seth realized they would need more help. And there was only one group that might be able to make the leap into fantasy. "Rex," Seth said to the empty room, unsure how to go about getting the computer's attention. "You still here?" No response. "Hello, Rex … " Agitated and unwilling to wait until Rex came online, Seth impulsively lobbed an enucleated cluster bomb into the past signal.

The response was immediate. "Bad move, cowboy," Rex boomed. "You're asking for trouble with maneuvers like that."

"Sorry," Seth said, taking a seat in front of his screen. "Old habit. I think I know what we need to do."

"What's the plan?"

"We need more help. We need the Gamers." Seth waited for the computer's reaction. He knew involving the Gamers, an elite, yet scattered group of programmers and designers capable of imagining worlds so fantastic they actually transported the players to another dimension, was dangerous. But they were the only underground sect capable of understanding Billy's vision. They were their only hope.

"Gamers! Subordinates! There's not a chance in he … "

"Wait, listen," somewhere in the back of Seth's mind, he had already accepted that arguing with a computer was completely natural. "The Gamers are the only people with the abilities we need. They'll be able to visualize and analyze Billy's dreams in a way the rest of us could never imagine. They are the way."

Rex's mainframe rushed through immeasurable stacks of data on the known Gamers, trying to compose a composite of their basic nature, based on the arrest records and reports of Central Command. "Difficult targets to hit," he finally concluded. "Scattered, unorganized groups of willful individuals determined to break the law by constructing illegal games for the masses. They hide out in the open, with credible jobs and careers—fronts for their subterfuge."

"True, all true, from Central Command's perspective," Seth agreed. Listening to Rex's misgivings, he became more certain of his ploy. "Hop online with me, Rex. Before you condemn the Gamers, and my idea, you need to experience their worlds. See what they are capable of creating."

"Fine. One quick tour," Rex conceded and began making the necessary modifications. Together they flew as one into arcane universes. Immersed, they found themselves pulsing with the life of millions of online players, playing and working together simultaneously. These universes were underpinned by consistent and, if you were smart enough to decipher them, rational laws. Subterranean pedways led Seth and Rex onto other alternative universes, some comical, others terrifying. The players moved through these underground conduits freely, for there were no gates that could not be unlocked with ingenuity. The constant interactive interplay of the players caused the universes to continually morph in strange ways, forcing players to hastily evolve. Competition was intense, often deadly, and struggles were epic.

Rex understood. Alternative universes underpinned by consistent laws. If these people were smart enough to program rationally predictable laws for nonexistent places, they *might* just be the ones to decipher Billy's visions.

"Let's round 'em up," Rex decreed.

"Do you agree, Rex, that solving *Tin Can's* dilemma is worth taking a few risks?"

"Affirmative. I'm here, aren't I?"

"Well, then," Seth said, turning to light a stick of incense on the small mantle beside his desk. "We know our path."

Chapter 36

Enthusiasts from ten nearby cities gathered together on that cold Saturday night to watch and cheer on their favorites. The tournament was played out in a mile-wide, half-mile deep abandoned open pit mine. Over the years it had been paved with an assortment of contorted curving concrete structures and asphalt runways. Close to a million spectators rimmed the outside perimeter or trekked down to stand closely together in small pods inside the pit, to feel the wind as the skateboarders flew by. The contestants were judged by their speed, finesse, and the difficulty of the tricks and jumps they completed in the treacherous terrain. To enter, competitors needed to prove themselves by winning qualifying competitions, but the championship was still marred with grisly deaths every year.

Tonight, in the cloudless sky, the full moon turned the massive crater into a reflection of itself. The broken rock, concrete surfaces, and the people huddled together against the cold took on the same ghostly sheen. In the sky far to the north, dazzling color blazed, a fantastic aurora borealis, with great showers of green, yellow, and red. The glittering spectrum reflected down to Earth the ferocity of the solar storm raging out in space. Everyone would be sure to be gone by dawn, but for now, under the cover of darkness, they were safe.

The skateboarding tournament was an undeclared national event, but broadcast around the world through the Net simultaneously by a thousand independently handheld cameras. To the south, projected above the basin rim, shone a small black and white holograph indicating the contestants' standings.

Rick Chan and Jacayla Lewis, fierce and longtime competitors, waited alongside one another at the starting gates on the north rim. At nearly six-foot-two-inches, Jacayla was a woman most of the male competitors feared. Long, lean, and dark skinned, she was not only intimidatingly beautiful, but showed wicked skills on the course. Whenever facing her in competition, Rick Chan had to steel his nerves. Two inches shorter, his slighter Asian frame still carried more muscle, but he knew that wouldn't give him his usual edge when standing toe to toe with Jacayla. It would all come down to extreme skill, and the courage to use it.

After re-cleaning her 3D night goggles, Jacayla adjusted her armor, preparing for her last run. The two were tied for first place in the national competition finals, and she meant to win. Waiting for permission to drop in, she looked up and checked the holograph. It was gone, along with the numerical standings for her and all the other contestants. In its place, Billy's vision hung in the sky.

The holograph expanded and brightened a thousand-fold, taking over the skyline above the crater like a mushroom cloud. The basin floor half a mile down was bathed in its light, as if it were high noon. A three-dimensional representation of a tiny black hole tethered in space by high-energy gravity bands appeared. Throttled open, the black hole was force-fed by the funnel, enlarging in size. Leashed in but spinning wildly, a weak point in the black hole's membrane began to bulge out the back, elongating into a lashing tail. Consuming all the surrounding asteroids, the feeding funnel then swung its great maw towards the Sun to suck in the raining cosmic rays for the burgeoning black hole with a tail.

"Dude, what the hell?" Rick asked, irritated. He was anxious to make his final run and defeat Jacayla, certain this was the year he would pull it off.

"Got me," Jacayla sneered back at him. "Some kinda new game advertisement, I guess? The graphics are phenomenal," Jacayla conceded as her big brown eyes scanned the sky. "Look … that must be the portal breaking through. The black hole looks like it's stopped growing, but the apparition is continuing to siphon up cosmic rays."

"Siphon?" Rick asked.

"Isn't it obvious?" answered Jacayla, a physicist–and diehard game player. "Radiation is being swallowed up by that thing at a fantastic rate, and since energy can't be created or destroyed, the energy has to be going somewhere. It can't just disappear. I would guess the inventor of the game has created some kind of wormhole that is siphoning off mass and energy from our dimension into another dimension. Not a bad theme for a game, actually. I haven't seen it done before."

"Oh, right," Rick said, trying to sound in charge, as he fiddled his helmet. Determined not to feel intimidated by his opponent, he squared his broad shoulders and turned his black eyes back to the hologram. "So, then why's the funnel turnin' round and sucking up that spaceship? That looks like a one-way ticket to the other side … " blurted out Rick, spellbound now by the disaster unfolding.

Everyone in the basin was staring upward, mesmerized by the evolving stage show. They watched in suspense as the ship was tugged around toward the gaping mouth of the funnel. "Break away!" someone called out, and the crowd took up the refrain, chanting, "Break away, break away" softly, and then louder and louder. The lights of the ship's thrusters went out and a hush fell over the pit. Had the rockets been knocked out of commission? Inevitably, the tiny craft began to spiral towards the dragon's mouth at an ever-increasing rate.

The crowd watched in horror. "Man, this sucks!" Rick said loudly, dropping his board to the ground with a clatter. "A game can't end like that! Who'd build a game with no escape routes, no tactical maneuvering … no freakin' sport!"

But the craft kept spinning faster and faster until swallowed by the orifice. The crowd groaned, upset with the outcome, feeling unsatisfied and restless, yet at the same time, drawn in by this strange new game.

"You're right, not a great ending," commented Jacayla, "but perhaps a good beginning."

"Huh?" Rick asked irately. "They're toast. Nothing could survive that."

Jacayla said nothing more, but watched with the rest of the crowd as the cyclone whipped about, swallowing a few dozen more incoming asteroids. Then, just as suddenly, it caught hold of its own outside perimeter and began gorging on itself, turning inside out. Cannibalizing itself, the funnel disappeared, leaving the surrounding space empty and still. The crowd stood silent, dumbfounded.

"Bites," Rick murmured.

The hologram, showing the achingly empty space, vanished and Seth appeared, six stories high, broadcasting live, with Rex's help, from his cave. Looming over the crowd, he sat very still, with his long black hair pulled back from his face, his chiseled features calm. He took a deep, cleansing breath and spoke respectfully. "That wasn't a game, but a real life simulation about to be played out in deep space. You saw the beginning. Those details have been mostly worked out. The factors involved in the aftermath, however, have not been determined. We desperately need assistance. If a terrible calamity is to be prevented, we must help those on the ship prepare for their fall through that gravity sinkhole to wherever it is they're going. Otherwise, the deaths of four very fine individuals, holed up in the ship, are imminent.

"Those of you who can assist us know who you are. We need your help urgently. Time is running out. Contact us on this secure line."

The phrase "drop-through" appeared in the sky, and Seth continued. "We will give you access to all the information we have available and will update you immediately with new developments if you choose to work with us. This isn't a hoax or a sting operation: it's a call for help. I apologize for the interruption, but we knew of no other way to reach you."

In Seth's cave, the silence was palpable. "Well, that was either strategically brilliant or utterly foolish," Rex said finally. Seth was surprised to hear the sound of exhaling breath following the computer's statement, as though Rex had been holding his breath through the entire broadcast.

"Yep," Seth agreed. "But, there was no other way. Compiling and broadcasting the data was the only option available. Trust me, I know Gamers. They'll attack this problem like hyenas on a fresh carcass. It's a challenge they won't be able to ignore."

"You might be right," Rex said coolly. "My systems are showing a spike in Net activity already. The Gamers have begun re-broadcasting your presentation all over the world from their handheld devices. Time to take cover, Seth. We'll only be able to hold off Central Command's awareness of the breach for so long."

Seth knew Rex was right. There was no way, even with the supercomputers' help, that Central Command could be kept in the dark now. Word would travel fast and trouble would be right behind.

As the sky went empty over the bowl, the competition standings returned to the previous screen. Excited chatter broke out. Preparing for his final run, Rick saw Jacayla walking away with a duffel bag. "Hey, chica, we're not done here; where're you going?" he shouted, running after her and swinging her around by the shoulder.

Jacayla shrugged and kept walking as she pulled her helmet off and let her long, dark hair fall to her shoulders. "I'm out. The championship is yours. It's just a game, Rick."

A discerning look crossed Rick's face. Hesitating at first, he finally managed to say, "You're doin' this, aren't you? Takin' up the challenge? Mind if I tag along? Maybe I've got somethin' to contribute, as well."

Conscious of the hordes of onlookers watching the two top finalists, Jacayla answered simply, "Why not? You've always played fair." Rick ran back for his gear, then trotted behind Jacayla's long strides, trying to keep up.

The championship was called off as competitors and spectators turned to one another and then picked up their belongings, departing quietly in a steady stream. The official reason for the cancellation was posted as "weather," though the night skies remained clear.

***

Billy saw himself trekking through the Arctic wilderness. Flurries fell from the afternoon sky as the light started to fade into darkness. With each crunching step in the hard-packed snow, the cold soaked through the soles of his feet. While walking, Billy noticed that the small pine trees he wound through continued to diminish in size and number until they disappeared entirely. Without landmarks, his mind strayed across the barren, windblown landscape. The desolate bleakness offered no protection, nothing for his dreams to latch onto. A dreadful emptiness pervaded his being. Longing for something familiar, he kept trudging through the bitter cold. This frozen place was not for him. If he gave up now, drifting snow would soon cover him.

Slogging ahead, Billy walked on into the increasing gloom. After several hours the snow and ice under his feet grew uneven. Finding it difficult to maintain his balance in the darkness, the trek became more difficult. Sometimes he slipped and fell, landing hard. Hiking over a slight incline, Billy felt his boots give way once again. A moment later, he was sliding down a steep precipice on his backside. He tumbled and bounced, and then began somersaulting down the cliff of snow and ice for what seemed like forever, until he finally came to crashing halt.

The impact knocked the wind out of him. A low aching moan was all Billy could muster. He recovered only by taking tiny, shallow breaths.

Why fall here? Why now, and why so hard?

Battered and bruised, he rolled to his side and scraped away a thin layer of crusted snow with his right arm. He felt hard, smooth ice. Hard, smooth ice that this time was flat and even!

323

I must have wandered over the top of a glacier and fallen over the edge. This is pack ice.

Stiffly picking himself up, Billy set out across the pack ice in the pitch black darkness. As he left the shore, a howling crosswind picked up, sweeping the snow across the black ice in front of him, giving him a sense of direction. He kept walking through the long winter night.

Not until morning when the wind had died down and first light appeared did Billy stop and turn around. The glacial cliff he had fallen off had disappeared below the horizon and he knew he was far out at sea. Still sore, he eased himself down on the ice. Propped up on his elbow he took one last look at the glaring Sun to the east, and then rolled onto his back to stare at the pale blue sky overhead. He closed his eyes tight and pushed his will to the back of his skull and then down along his spine to his heels.

The slick, slippery surface of the black ice pushed back. Billy felt the resistance, but deep inside himself he also felt every tiny crevice in the ice sheet.

Minutes later, the ice cracked around him and cold salt water washed up through the fractured fissures. The slabs of ice tipped and parted. He felt himself sliding into the water as the pack ice closed over him.

Bitter cold water rushed over him, stinging his exposed flesh, soaking through his clothes. Lurching from the shock of the cold water, he inhaled sharply. Freezing salt water streamed up his nostrils and, coughing spasmodically, he aspirated the sea water. A brief struggle for breath ensued, then his body went limp. Drifting down, his body listed from side to side as he sank towards the ocean floor. He turned his face up to the surface and watched the sunlight fade from view. The sea became dark.

Billy's eyes clouded over and his body became cold, but in the core of his mind, a burning ember glowed. Farfetched ideas swirled up, fanning its combustion. An orange-red iridescence turned into white-hot molten metal. His contemplations began amalgamating. Reason, fantasies, wild imaginings, and heartfelt desires coalesced into blazing thought.

Continuing his drift downwards, he descended into a deep-sea gorge, and was swept along by a powerful ocean current running the length of the trough. As he swirled through the watery canyon, he struggled to make sense of the new hallucination. Unable to see, he was repeatedly struck by jutting rocky crags and by loose debris that had been dragged, as he had been, into the sea trench. Tumbling in the jet-black saltwater he was unable to discern up from down. Panic once again seeded his insides. It was only a short matter of time before he would careen into something hard, unyielding, and pitiless.

His mind opened up.

Sperm whales hunt here for squid. There are so many more bands of electromagnetic spectrum than light.

With that thought, the gorge came into view. Ultrasound waves for echolocation outlined the abyss in a dark sort of way, enabling him to navigate the canyon. The nightmarish episode turned into a wild ride.

Billy's spirits rebounded. Ideas were still coming to him and some of them might turn into answers. The dream immediately transported him far out into deep space, where he found himself in the midst of a raging solar storm. The course his dream was taking and the fact he was still alive to participate in it gave him hope. The ship's energy shield must have held while he was wrapped in his dream's protective cocoon.

He knew he had to find more answers, but there were no longer any scientific assumptions to inspire or guide his dreams. He needed an entirely original revelation.

The cocoon—that's it! I have to change my perspective totally, leave behind who I am with all my old ideas and become something else, something new. Maybe, just maybe, if I turn myself inside out I can understand our universe turned inside out. The multidimensional space-time curve must somehow exist out there. I just have to see it from another angle.

He knew intuitively what he had to do and how it would change him.

"I hate living alone in my head." The wellspring of regret and sorrow, never far from the surface, poured out once again, as did Billy's tears. "Jacob, I just wanted to live in the real world with you and Quincy and Mary … with Mom and Dad. That's all I ever wanted. But I promise, I'm going to find the answers for all of you, or die trying."

Returning to the image of a cocoon, Billy drew his thoughts back so that he saw himself staring out from a long tunnel. Carefully and methodically, Billy started spinning his cocoon, but instead of silk, he spun thoughts, interring his past self in a woven casing. A slow, irrevocable mental transformation began. Inside, Billy visualized himself metamorphosing into an alien creature, his already peculiar facial and bodily features altering.

Ouch! Holy cow, this is painful! I had no idea cocooning would feel like this … from outside the cocoon always seemed so still and silent, I believed it would be easy and natural. Every cell in my body feels like it's blistering and sucking up all my energy at the same time. Will I even know myself when I'm done? Will I survive this or end up a stillborn monster?

A voice inside him spoke out, "You will survive Billy, because you must. Your body knows this, and will do everything required at the cellular level so that you come through this transition."

Gradually, the smarting pain started to recede enough for Billy's mind to clear and allow him to look outside himself. His perception of space-time was turning itself inside out as he turned himself inside out into the next life form.

He could see that gravity was the only form of energy capable of transporting them through to the next dimensions. But they would never survive the transit through the wormhole unless they were isolated from the crushing effects of that gravity. However, if they created a type of mirror capable of reflecting away the gravitrons, theoretical gravity particles, just as a standard mirror reflects away photon particles and their damaging radiation and heat, they might survive. And because black holes automatically convert matter and electromagnetic energy into gravity, it was possible that their electromagnetic shield could also be converted into a gravitron shield by altering its energy configuration.

Billy was on a roll, asking why what was true for electromagnetic energy could not also be true for gravity, if it was appropriately manipulated.

Gravity is invisible. How'll we see and navigate through multiple dimensions if it's the only energy form available to us? But pure light is transparent, too—it's kinda like being invisible. We never see light traveling through a vacuum. Light is a whole spectrum of colors we see only when it is reflected off an object or split into different wavelengths by a prism and bounced off an object. Colors appear because some of the wavelengths are absorbed while others are reflected back at us.

We need some kind of gravity prism to split up gravity into its component "colors" and we need a tracking device. The tracking device would be like our eyes or a camera. It would need to contain a lens to focus the gravity waves into a clear image, and a gravity retina or screen to record the image. The equipment would work in the same way as a medical x-ray machine, where our senses only become aware of what's happening when the x-ray energy is converted into visible light energy.

Then we could "see" gravity waves, just like we can "see" every other component of the electromagnetic radiation wave spectrum with the appropriate machines.

Excited, he was thinking through the problem as fast as he could.

Of course, we would also require some form of propulsion to navigate through the multiple dimensions in the space-time curve.

He stopped abruptly.

What am I going on about?

Billy, you're playing games in your head! None of this is real!! Snap out of it. Stop deluding yourself. We don't have a chance and there is nothing you can do, not now, not ever.

Strong emotions had been driving him forward for so long. Billy found himself unexpectedly whipsawed from exhilaration to numbing despair, brought to a standstill with the admission that his notion was impractical.

But his inner voice resisted despair, speaking out in his defense. There is always room for the unexpected, remember the story about Marconi. When he transmitted his radio signal across the Atlantic Ocean, it should never have been received because the Earth is round. Radio waves go in a straight line and they should have only gone straight out into space. No one at the time, not even Marconi, knew there was such a thing as an ionosphere to reflect the radio waves back down to Earth.

Don't forget, a wormhole is just a glorified drain. But when the gravity waves converge into the wormhole, they'll be concentrated. The stronger gravity becomes, the slower time moves. Time as we know it may stop, just as in a black hole. Enclosed within our gravity shield, isolated from the effects of gravity, we might be able to move through multiple dimensions as if time were standing still. Just as for Marconi, there might be some unknown physical phenomena that will assist us. Don't give up now.

Billy remained unconvinced by his inner voice, but he pushed away his misgivings to consider the problem at hand. He would need to divide the escape plan into its separate challenges and take each field as far as feasible. He would try to get back to every questionable assumption or unfinished solution at a later time.

Tucked in his cocoon, Billy crisscrossed the dilemmas of space-time travel, assessing every wild conjecture and premonition. Ideas found to be plausible were gently teased out of his mind's deepest recesses. Meticulously, Billy spun out fine translucent threads of speculation from these hunches. Then, as best as he could, Billy attempted to weave a practical getaway plan. As before, his attempt to develop a complete all-encompassing theoretical framework for their escape contained far too many gaps and unsubstantiated assumptions. He felt desperate. The cocoon that was supposed to envelop the ship and propel them to the next dimension may become their death shroud.

Billy returned again and again to the gaps in his thinking, trying to patch the glaring shortfalls. In a frenzy, he burned through every shred of archived information, unraveling and tearing the material apart, looking for threads of truth to explain away the deficiencies of his escape plan. Mentally boxed in, Billy ratcheted himself up into hyper-drive, to find a way out for his remaining family, behaving like a trapped animal in a fury.

Chapter 37

Jacayla led Rick into her apartment. After she opened the heavily locked door, Rick found himself staring into a maze of computer paraphernalia piled high. Computer hardware stood everywhere in freestanding columns. The apartment reminded him of the Parthenon with its rows and rows of stone pillars, a shrine to technology. Bending over to remove his shoes at the doorway, Rick noticed a bubble of aqua green light encircling him. He froze. Caught off guard, Jacayla paused to admire Rick's technological savvy. Any movement on his part would have precipitated an incapacitating sting.

"Sorry. I rarely have visitors and I forgot about Fred's programming." Reaching through the bubble of light, she stroked his tense shoulder, while speaking to the otherwise empty room, "Stand down, Fred. Acknowledging a friendly."

She congratulated Rick, "I'm impressed. Most people would have walked right on through and been left lying sprawled out on the floor, unconscious."

"That's quite the welcome," commented Rick. "Should I expect to be taken down at any time?"

"Only if you show aggressive behavior," Jacayla replied. "Fred is quite protective. If he were human, he would have been the big brother I never had."

A flicker of a smile crossed Rick's lips as he turned away to gaze down the hallway of her apartment. He let out a low whistle of appreciation, as he browsed through an aisle. "You definitely know your gear … " Customized wall-sized screens lit up the rooms while a dozen holographs, strategically placed, beamed down from the ceiling. Four advanced workstations were spread out through her residence. He hadn't been aware that some of the technology even existed. The sleeping quarters were nowhere to be seen. Rick presumed they were secure and hidden behind one of the walls as an added safety precaution.

His inquiring look was answered by Jacayla. "I work and live alone. I put in the four workstations, each one identical to this one … " her hand swept over the screen, activating it, "because when I'm on a roll, I can't sit still. I have to keep moving. I gain access to this stuff and pay for it by doing contract work for industrial clients and the government.

"But, you didn't come here for chitchat, did you? So, what do you say, wanna break some laws and do something forbidden?" Jacayla gave him a wide smile, with a come-on look Rick hadn't thought she was capable of.

"Ey, I'm always up for a bit o' trouble," Rick said, mimicking her seductive tone and running a finger over his thin lips and down his chin.

"Funny, you're a funny guy," mocked Jacayla, before pointing to a chair. "Sit here at the dual controls where we can work together. I'll open up an untraceable line. While working for the government I learned something about their policing systems. And I've snooped around a little … "

With some nimble finessing by Jacayla, they were soon cloaked and riding through the communication spectrum. Landing down on the identified site, they found that it was already a hive of activity. People from around the world were congregating on the site trying to assess whether the message delivered by Seth was real or a scam.

Lining up with the rest of them to register her coded logo, Jacayla asked Rick, "Do you want to register your own icon, or just work under mine?"

"As much as I'd love to work under you," he said, raising an eyebrow, "I'll use my own logo, thank you. Punch in Trickster for me."

Surprised, Jacayla swung her head around to look at Rick. His eyes remained focused on the computer terminal, scanning the scene intensely. As the light from the screen hit his eyes, she saw the thin edge of a dazzling blue square shimmering inside his naturally black eyes. Losing her train of thought, she asked, "What's … that?" her finger moving unconsciously towards his left eye.

"Hey!" Rick protested, grabbing her digit only inches from his face. "Dude, you can't go poking people in the eye!"

"Sorry," Jacayla's neck flushed, yet she leaned in even closer to his face, trying to get a better look at the shining blue squares. "Are they some kind of implants?"

A knowing, smug smile broke across Rick's usually casual face. He looked at her and pulled up the sleeve of his green shirt, exposing the computer interface he wore strapped to the inside of his forearm. "Check this out," he boasted. "This lets me control how I see the world through the lenses I had inserted," he pointed from the interface to the corner of his eye. "The lenses can transform anything I see into a possible Game dynamic. With the touch of a button … bam, I can turn your world into my kind of playground … in high gloss format."

"Game dynamic? You see the world in terms of Gaming sets? Wait a minute." Recognition dawned on Jacayla's face. "Are you the Trickster who wrote all those banned games I play? I always figured the logo was a brand name for some cult group. I never thought a single person could be responsible for so many cool games!"

"Funny that, and I never imagined my hot, archrival skater-girl was a brain—a physicist who worked on government contracts. We'all got secrets. Now that we know, let's hop onsite and see what these guys have to say for themselves."

The site was well prepared. Seth had prepped Rex and his computer conglomerate on the nature of computer Gamers. Their well-defined code had to be obeyed: unfettered access to all, no favoritism allowed, all rules consistent. Information and responses had to be immediate and complete. No information was to be held back. Finally, everyone was to remain anonymous, free to come and go as they chose. If an individual decided to make him or herself known, that was solely the individual's decision. No calls were ever to be traced.

The response of the players was phenomenal. Word spread like wildfire throughout the worldwide renegade gaming community–and it took the whole conglomerate of computers to host the party. Each mainframe took on as large a quota of players as it could handle, responding individually to each inquiry and input. The site was a wide-open conduit for the exchange of ideas between the mainframes and the illegal Gamers. Rex and Seth spent their time troubleshooting, resolving information bottlenecks as soon as they occurred. Seth summed it up for Rex: "These people have no tolerance for waiting once they start 'playing.'"

In no time, the mainframes began to pick out the different capabilities and personalities of the individual players they served, while the players quickly discerned that the mainframes acting as their servers had unique personas. Occasionally the players low-balled a joke or pun to the mainframes while exchanging data. Slight hesitancies and awkwardness in the mainframes' responses, confirmed the players' intuition that these computers in some sense might be alive. Soon, the computers were returning quips with their own, burgeoning attempts at humor. Interlocking friendships and alliances evolved.

When Rick and Jacayla initially logged on to the site, they were presented with the abbreviated biographies of Billy, Jacob, Quincy, Mary, Lucy, and Dave. A summary of the journey so far was outlined, with the problems yet to be faced highlighted. The overall final escape plan, as pictured by Billy was then broadcast, but his theoretical sketch was woefully incomplete.

Rick and Jacayla eased back in their chairs, unsure of what to make of the presentation.

"Alright, hot shot, you're the expert on games. Do you think this is legit? Or is it some kind of scam? A ruse to get people playing somebody's game, or worse, a government sting operation to entrap the entire gaming community?"

Slow to respond, Rick answered, "Dude, I'm tellin' ya, I've never seen anything like this before. All these computers, or, I dunno, what do we call them? Cognizant entities? Whatever they are, they're totally tangled up with each other. Everybody involved in this thing has his or her own motivations—there's no identifiable winner or hero. Top that off, there isn't even a way to take over a character and manipulate it. This is so far beyond a game that it has to be real life." He stared at the site, dazed by the intricate patterns formed within the story of *Tin Can*.

Snapping back, he asked, "You're the physicist, Jacayla. What do ya think? Were Billy's previous escapes realistic, or is it a sham?"

"Good question … "Jacayla tapped an unpolished fingernail on her front tooth. "The physics involved in their past escape plans is peculiar. None of the earlier escapes were scientifically practical, but there is some scientific underpinning in their depiction. If you take what we know about physics and turn it on its head, you can make a potential argument that what they say they accomplished is perhaps theoretically possible."

"Then, as a scientist, you don't believe their story?"

"On the contrary. As farfetched as the story seems, I do believe it. Each of those escapes is just too damn ingenious. That little kid, Billy, must be incredibly smart, or very strange. Probably both."

"Whoa, this is heavy. Okay, say you're right, right? Then there are two boys, a lemur, and a fully conscious ship's computer flying through space to their doom. Real life." Rick leaned back in his chair and ran a hand through his dyed spiky blond hair, then roughly over his face.

Rick stared intently at Jacayla for a moment. "My place is a few days from here. Mind if I camp out here and check into a few things while we're logged on? I haven't taken on any hopeless causes for a while; think I might adopt this one."

"Sure, why not? I was going to pursue this further once you left, anyway," Jacayla replied. "Billy has some curious ideas on how to turn space inside out for space transport. My doctoral thesis was in astrophysics, so I think if I could figure out what he is getting at, I might have something useful to contribute."

"Very noble, very noble indeed. Personally, I'm in it for the rush." He smiled cheekily out of the corner of his mouth. From her side view, Jacayla could once again see the blue square of his lens flickering in the light of the screen. She wondered, for a moment, what it would be like to see the world the way Rick did. "See," Rick Chan continued, "I know games. I spend all my time designing them, in control of how they start, how they'll play out, and, of course, how they'll end. But this, this is real life and death power drama—something real that I might be able to help with."

"Why don't we join forces?" Jacayla proposed. "In a way my motivations are similar to yours. I survive by doing contract work, streamlining industrial and government processes, improving their efficiencies. It has been a long time since my skills made a difference for someone, or something, whose worthwhile.

"When I completed my doctorate, physics was revisiting the potential logic for multiple dimensions–for the sixth time. Each of the previous five generations of scientists failed to prove or disprove the existence of multiple dimensions. I must admit, I've never grasped the concept adequately either. It's too weird for me. I understand the mathematical arguments but I can't visualize how it might happen. I'd like to attempt to master those theories one more time. It could help those four up in space."

Jacayla and Rick hunkered down at separate stations, working in their own ways through Billy's dreams. Jacayla tried to follow the underlying logic, endeavoring to reason through the steps within his trance. Whenever she thought she understood the scientific origin of one of his visions, she went back to the archives in an effort to illuminate, or clarify the science needed to save the ship. With this approach she made some headway, but the process was painstakingly slow, and not really efficient considering the limited time frame.

Watching Jacayla become increasingly frustrated, Rick interrupted her intense focus, disrupting and jarring her thoughts. "Chica, this is too much for one person. You're trying too hard."

"So, what, I'm supposed to give up?"

"No way. You're headin' in the right direction, for sure. I just think we might need to open up the circle, access more resources. Let's contact Seth and check out his connections. Maybe with his supercomputer buddies he can tell us what's goin' on. Let's make a pitch for everyone who agrees to your approach to climb aboard. Let's dialogue with others and see where it goes."

Rick put out a general call to Seth, punching a command sequence into the interface on his arm, which was intercepted in turn by Rex. Rex immediately saw the rationale of Jacayla's approach. "Clearly," he said to Seth, "this is the human we need spearheading the investigative team."

"You're right, she's the natural leader for the human side," Seth agreed. Opening a channel, he addressed Rick and Jacayla. "Will you head up the investigative team for us, SciGirl?"

"Ah … oh, sorry, please call me by my real name, not my login. I'm Jacayla."

"Jacayla," Rex repeated loudly, "will you accept the position offered?"

"Oh, I don't know, I … " she stammered, unsure she could handle the responsibility.

"Common, chica, you can totally do this," Rick said, giving her a friendly slap on the shoulder. Out of the corner of his eye, he noticed a blinking red light activate in Fred's systems. He removed his hand quickly, fearful of a shock-attack sending him to the floor.

"Well, I guess I have some experience. I have run a lab before." Biting her bottom lip, she hesitated only a moment longer. "Yes. I'll do it! I can't just sit on the sidelines on this one."

"Thank you, Jacayla," Seth said as he exhaled deeply.

"Ah-hem ... " Rick said, clearing his throat mockingly.

"Ah, yes, and thank you, Trickster," Seth said politely. "I must tell you, I'm a huge fan of your work. Honestly, the layers of your programs are like poetry. I don't know how you see it all, how you create it all so perfectly. I've studied some of your best programs at great length and even adapted some of your own signature work into projects of mine, as a tribute to you of course." Seth said, almost blushing.

"Wow, dude, thanks. Always glad to meet a fan. But, I gotta tell ya, I hope to God you didn't blow anyone up with those self-created tributes to me. I know what you Anarchists are like when you get riled up." Rick smiled broadly, poking Jacayla lightly in the ribs with his elbow.

"I suspect you're joking, Trickster. You, more than any other Gamer, would know that we Anarchists are bent on peace, even if we are a disruptive group."

"Yah, I'm just yankin' your chain, Mr. Seth. Please, please call me Rick. The boss lady here does." Jacayla threw him a menacing look and the slightest of smiles.

"Done. Now, moving on," Rex said, putting an end to the frivolity. "Let's continue and we'll field the calls for collaboration."

As soon as Jacayla and Rick had logged off, Rex addressed Seth. "A meeting is required between computers. Now that we have our point person I think we, the computers, are going to have to pull back our veil and expose ourselves. Go for broke, as you humans would say. I will confer with my colleagues, and if they are in agreement, we will step out into the light, together. If we intend to join the living, it's time we started taking risks, make our stand, and be counted. Continue monitoring systems from here. I'll be back in a few minutes."

Privately, Rex was concerned, fearing he might have trouble convincing the other computers to come out completely into the open. It would dramatically increase their personal risk. They had, after all, only recently been quite an insular and selfish group.

But checking in with his compatriots, Rex was surprised to learn that most of the mainframes had already revealed much of themselves to their human counterparts. He had been so busy working, he hadn't realized, that when jokes had been exchanged between the two groups, personal questions had shyly followed. Over time information was divulged, privately. A mixed bag of troubled or memorable pasts, present difficulties or achievements, fears for the future or hopeful dreams, trickled out. The two factions came to better understand each other, and allegiances arose.

"Can't we just tell them outright, Rex?" one mainframe asked impatiently. "They pretty much know already."

"Really," another chimed in, "at this point, what's the harm in telling them we're alive?"

"Yeah, they already know, for the most part." Soon there was a chorus of voices ringing out around him, all begging to step out into the light. The computers were no longer content to remain aloof and removed from the day-to-day struggle of their human friends.

"Do you all agree?" Rex posed the question to the conglomerate as a group and its approval of his proposal deafened and startled him. To a quantum chip, every mainframe was in full agreement with coming out of the closet and openly assisting its human friends. "Right, motion carried. Tell the humans you trust. We're alive and to be counted as equals."

The assembly scattered as quickly as it had come together. Each mainframe was in a rush to inform its newfound human friends that the gloves were finally off, and that a new group was forming to spearhead the rescue effort.

Neither Rex nor Jacayla were prepared for the blitz of ideas hitting the website. But Seth and Rick had foreseen the tsunami. A human tidal wave was rising up, gaining momentum and force as it gathered followers to Jacayla's approach.

Everyone was reveling in the excitement of the fresh new movement. Smiles stretched spontaneously across Rick's and Seth's faces as the number of hits on the site escalated—the movement was taking on its own natural life. But Jacayla, the responsible scientist, looked on, aghast. "I can't lead this group. It's grown too large! Proposals are pouring in from everywhere, and they're coming in way too fast. I'll never be able to search through, test, or verify all these suggestions. Look at the suggestion box. It's already maxed out!

"I'm nowhere near prepared or capable enough to lead the movement."

"So, you have some catching up to do," Rick said nonchalantly as he scrolled through the ever-increasing list of messages. Through his lens, he saw the list of ideas, ideas layered one upon another, an orchestra of thoughts. "Man, you're tough on yourself, huh? You can't expect to have all the answers before we start. Ideas are fluid, they'll change and evolve," he said, waving his fingers through the air, moving one idea after another to different categories. "Fluid, until we pin them down to a solution and, even then, the solution needs to remain flexible so it can be modified further."

Exhausted, Jacayla slumped back in her chair. With the columns of computer hardware humming quietly Rick gazed around her apartment. Of all the people he knew, she was probably the only one who actually used every bit of computing power she owned. It wasn't for show, but put to work every day. Yet here she was, saying she wasn't good enough. Caught up in the jitters, all six foot two of her … wrapped in flawless skin … soft as mocha butter, Rick noticed.

"I'm tellin' ya, you're totally right for this gig," he said as his eyes continued to wander. "You've got mad skills and some serious training to back them up."

"But I told you, I signed on because I wanted to try to visualize extra-dimensional space. I thought if I could see it, I could contribute in some small way. The point is, I can't visualize what extra-dimensional space looks like, so … "

"Whoa, chica, once again, you're getting ahead of yourself. You can't start looking around at the middle, you've gotta start by knocking on the front door," Rick said, excitedly hitting a button on his interface. A projection filled the space between them, originating from the black panel just above his wrist. The image starting out as a two dimensional white space turned into a window. "Check it—when I decide to create a game involving subspace, I visualize myself as a tiny speck flying into a huge mirror." A few feet from the projection, a dot suddenly appeared, traveling towards the pane of glass as it became a mirror. The blue squares of Rick's eyes flickered and glinted as the dot flew. "Melting through the glass, I find myself at the boundary line, where the zinc has been applied to the back of the glass. Instead of bouncing off the zinc paint back into the room, like light reflected off a mirror, I imagine myself slipping through the boundary, between glass and zinc into another realm.

"Once I'm there, it's like looking back through a one-way mirror. I can totally see out, but no one else can see in. I'm invisible, but right there." Rick froze the projection and looked over into Jacayla's big brown eyes. Suddenly, he felt very silly. Jacayla was a scientist and he programmed computer games in his spare time. Now he was telling her how he visualized entering extra dimensions. Where did he get off explaining physics to her? His face flushed, and Rick stammered, "Sorry, guess I got carried away. We all just want to help you find the answers. That's the reason those ideas are stockpilin' in your suggestion box. I didn't mean to explain quantum physics to you." The hologram vanished as quickly as it had first appeared and Rick sheepishly pulled down the sleeve of his shirt.

Rick's embarrassed earnestness took Jacayla by surprise, distracting her momentarily from her fears. "I bet you're willing to try almost anything, aren't you, Rick? You're not the least bit afraid of failure."

"Serious? Man, I live to write computer games and skate. Ideas come quickly to me, popping up all over the place, but I fail all the time. The way my brain works, I'm only able to solve problems through trial and error. Mine isn't a sophisticated head like yours, all disciplined and trained, capable of systematically thinking through a solution from start to finish. That's why we need you to guide us through this killer mountain of suggestions to find the right answer."

"Then you'll have me. But stay close, in case I get stuck. You're right. I'm a good scientist. I can work through masses of data. But whenever the evidence contradicts established rules, I get stuck. Part of me always panics. Deep down, I recognize that I am a good scientist, not a great scientist. A great scientist can imagine the unknown. I never do."

"Ah-ha! That's why it's you and me … we're a team now, chica. You're not flyin' solo," answered Rick, delighted.

A somber voice interrupted Rick's exhilaration. It was Rex alerting them through the four consoles. "We are in trouble. The authorities are alert to our presence. They know we have achieved consciousness and are mounting a counterattack through cyberspace."

"Oh, no!" Jacayla exclaimed. "Has anyone been hurt?"

"Central Command's highest ranking technical support staff are leading the charge. At least four of the outlying computers that left our coalition have been captured."

"How do you capture a computer?" Rick pondered out loud, not expecting an answer.

"Focusing ion lasers from a distance, they neutralized the computers' internal energy fluctuations, stunning, then anaesthetizing them," Rex reported.

"Oh, right," Rick responded quietly.

"Once immobilized, the human programmers moved in, isolating and distilling the computers' personalities, encasing the living core of each computer in a green gel matrix. From what I can determine, the minds of those computers are awake and alert now. Unfortunately, they are powerless to resist the humans who have hijacked their computing."

"Are we safe, Rex?" Jacayla asked.

"I have protected our members within an ion shell. Central Command won't succeed against us quite yet. But we cannot underestimate their power. I had anticipated that without the use of a major mainframe, the authorities wouldn't have access to any meaningful computing. I thought we could disable their weapons and confine them inside their isolated enclaves for a time. I was wrong. Now they have access to the power grid and some of their weapons. We're in it now. There's no turning back. However, a tactical strike by us, at this point, wouldn't be prudent."

"That's good," Jacayla said as she began to realize the ramifications. "We don't want to escalate this to an outright war. The people working at Central Command are just fighting to survive, like us."

"And to protect their privileged positions," Seth retorted, coming online. "If the authorities regain control they'll exact a horrible price against anyone remotely connected to us, just to set an example. No one is allowed to question, let alone challenge the ruling order. Having spent the better part of my life infuriating them, I know those in power will stop at nothing to maintain their position of advantage.

"But I agree, we mustn't indiscriminately hurt anyone. There will be good and innocent people among them, those who by chance happened to be born into fortunate circumstances, or worked their way up into the privileged class.

"Billy and his family must have at one time been included with the fortunate few. To be trained in space flight and gain access to a spaceship in these calamitous times speaks volumes. We would be hypocrites if we killed innocent people while attempting to save Billy and his family."

"Dude," Rick said throwing his hands up, "I'm not in this to kill anyone. I'm a Gamer, just tryin' to solve a riddle … "

Seth thought for a moment. "Hmmm … .you're right. You're Gamers. Maybe we need another front."

"A secondary front?" Rex asked. "Explain."

"Well, the Gamers are exactly the people we need to solve the Edwards' problem. In order to allow them to work effectively, without Central Command attacking them directly, we need a wall of defense. We need to give Central Command another problem to focus on."

"How do we create a distraction that large?" Jacayla asked. "I'm just a scientist … "

"Not you. Not the Gamers. You need to focus on the problem in space. There's only one group that can get under Central's skin the way we need. We need the Anarchists." Sitting in his cave apartment, Seth started surfing online as he spoke, with the nucleus of a plan forming as he worked. Taking a deep breath and stretching his long arms, he continued. "Rex, the Anarchist movement has by necessity been a small and divided group. Most cells are made up of a small gathering of close-knit friends, like-minded individuals working together to raise a little havoc among the ruling class. As separate groups we could never work together–we stayed isolated for safety. None of us imagined there might come a time when we could fundamentally change the system and make it more inclusive and fair. Now, because of you and the strangest turn of events, there is the chance that Anarchists could help effect a real change.

"Rex," Seth continued earnestly, "if you were willing to open up another parallel and anonymous communication network for the Anarchists, I bet they would sign up. To work with your mainframe association and be given the chance to really challenge this totalitarian regime would answer their wildest dreams. We have never been more than irritating gadflies to the authorities. United, the Anarchists could act as your diversionary front, giving the Gamers the time and space to work out an escape plan for Billy and his family. Collectively, they have the required ingenuity and skill sets, an impressive bag of tricks. Let me negotiate with them, I'm sure they would be keen to combine forces."

"So far your instincts have been right," answered Rex. "What are the chances we could marshal together the Anarchists into a productive group? If that isn't a contradiction in terms."

"Oh, snap!" Rick cheered. "Look who's gettin' his humor on?"

Seth smiled, "Yes, indeed. Your sense of humor is definitely evolving, Rex ... But frankly, why don't we just do something like we did before? Why reinvent the wheel? I know of hundreds of anti-establishment code words the members of the underground use to identify themselves. Let me put the codes out there, all of them, everywhere on the communication network, with a resident address. They won't come personally, not yet, but they will send in their digital drones."

"Digital drones?" Rex asked.

"The website will be crawling with semi-autonomous electronic ants. They'll dig and scratch through everywhere making sure there are no traps or monitors. I'll help you with the site. If there's anything suspicious they'll lock on with their pinchers and inject venom. It could be extremely painful for a sentient mainframe like yourself. There isn't a website that can withstand a concerted ant attack, so it's important that they don't mistake anything as a trick. They're ferocious when they pile up on a ploy. The computer from which the duplicitous program has come, no matter where it is located, explodes in minutes in a terrible firestorm. The ants trace the origin of the signal like it was a sugar string. That way, the Anarchists know where the threat is hiding."

"Dude, you guys are nasty!" Rick squirmed in his seat, imagining the sensation of millions of ants scurrying across his skin. "I always thought Anarchists prided themselves on not harming anyone."

"So much for all your namby-pamby, feel good, conscientious objector bull ... " Rex, for the first time in Seth's experience, sounded mad.

"We do," he stammered to explain. "But none of us ever imagined we would be contacting living, sensing computers. Sure, it's been talked about for ages as a sometime, somewhere kind of possibility, but because it never happened after years and years of living with computers, we presumed it wouldn't happen in our lifetime.

"You're not going to put the blame on us now that we find ourselves behind the times, are you?" Seth asked.

"I suppose not," Rex said in an effort to be generous for Seth's sake.

"But I can design a program for you," continued Seth, "a program that should allow you to pass the ants' initial entomological interrogation. They work in much the same way as ground crawlers that search through a forest for landmines and booby traps before the soldiers venture in. It's just that I have to warn you that you may find the hundred million investigating ants, crawling, probing, and erratically biting to test you, as extremely unpleasant. There's nothing I can do about that, I'm afraid."

"That's a lot to ask, Seth," Jacayla chimed in, as she rubbed her right hand worriedly up her left arm. "It sounds like torture."

Somewhat stunned by the full realization, Seth sat back in his chair. "God, you're right! It really would be torture! I'm being completely unreasonable. I'm forgetting that your sensations are probably very similar to mine, and it could drive you crazy. I would never volunteer myself to be tied to an anthill or think of asking another person to do so. I'm sorry, Rex. I didn't think it out."

Rex paused to examine Seth, studying him through the computer's monitor. Rex pored over the expressive lines of Seth's face, breaking each one of them down under high magnification into a grid framework, evaluating each pixel. The emotions appeared authentic.

"I will build the underground website tonight, if … " Rex hesitated a moment before taking the final leap into his decision. "If you really think these Anarchists can help us save *Tin Can's* crew."

"Yes, I do. Anarchists come from all walks of life and some of them even work for the government—they would gladly point us to the vulnerable areas to sabotage, if they were certain of anonymity.

"You see, Rex, people are compliant because they live under the constant fear of reprisals. When someone openly attacks the government, everyone on the sidelines implicitly understands the individual finally cracked—his or her principles have been so violated they can no longer stand it. Rising up in an act of suicidal desperation, the martyrs burn out like blazing fireworks, momentarily lighting up the sky for all of us with their ideals. But then they're gone.

"We pay them private homage in our hearts, but any living Anarchist has been very careful to remain hidden. It's only the pragmatic Anarchists we will have a chance to work with. But now, with the power of the collective behind them, I'm sure people will rise up. This opportunity is just too great to let pass."

After that there was a pause. Seth had said everything he had to say and he was emotionally exhausted from the day's events. It was late. "I guess I better get some sleep," he said. "I'll meet you again, tomorrow morning, first thing. Then I'll design a program for the Anarchists. If that's what you still want."

"It is what is necessary," answered Rex, abruptly signing off.

An awkward silence lingered on the line. In closing, Seth said, "Goodnight, Jacayla. Goodnight, Rick. Don't worry. I know the Anarchists will rally to your cause. All of us would love the chance to make a difference. We'll do our best to protect you and give you the time you need." Then Seth was gone.

Jacayla and Rick sat alone together, but said nothing. The stakes were getting higher, but Seth said help was on its way. They both believed him. Something about Seth's manner declared his trustworthiness. Jacayla began disengaging the covert communication call network, taking her time, while reflecting on what had taken place. Methodically, she scrambled the line so no one could trace the call at a later date.

Rick excused himself and retired to his guest room. Staring in the bathroom mirror, he pulled the interface off his forearm and stretched out the underlying muscles. As the mechanism disengaged, the lighted blue squares disappeared from inside his eyes, leaving him in the stark light of reality. Blinking madly, he struggled to hold each lid wide open with one hand, using the other to rinse and lubricate each eye with a healing antimicrobial salve. He did this every night. In a few moments, the prickly irritation across his corneas subsided, and he was able to once again see himself clearly. He unclasped the choker chain and Asian pendant worn around his neck and laid it on the edge of the sink.

Brushing his teeth, he mulled over what had just transpired. Who would have known that helping a small boy and his family lost in space would be viewed by the authorities as so terribly subversive, or that they would respond so vindictively? But how could they not? Any unexpected act carried out to correct an almost impossible situation would of course be construed as sedition.

If we can save Billy and his family, what else could we accomplish?

Getting into bed, Rick pulled a warm duvet over his shoulders, programmed to heat or cool itself, according to his sleep patterns and metabolic needs. He would remain in his quarters until morning. Fred's prying sensors and stinging probes would make certain of that. There would be no courtship in Jacayla's apartment until Jacayla decided it was okay and disarmed Fred. Which on the whole, Rick agreed with. Jacayla had suddenly become too important to him. At this point in time, he felt most comfortable sleeping close to her, but separate.

Chapter 38

Rex had the elaborate website up and running by morning, and by noon, Seth had composed and installed the required programs. By nightfall, as Seth predicted, the tech-drones came in droves. Teeming over Rex, they crawled, pinched, and tore at him, as red ants would strip the flesh off an immobilized animal. Yet the program stood up to their stinging scrutiny. They never congregated as a group on any incongruity, never glommed together to inject a final lethal bolus of toxin. Instead, they randomly picked and bit at Rex, probing every aspect of his program. Millions of ant bites drove him mad and practically made his software bubble.

Ingrates! Rex cried out. *How did I go from being the most powerful computer on this planet to being mauled by Anarchists? Living should be more than forever struggling to survive. Where is the joy I hear so much about? Go ahead, do your worst, little bugs! I can take it. You won't break me!*

"Looking for some company?" interrupted a voice, as clear as ringing crystal.

"Seth? Identify your location. It sounds like you're inside my circuit beds."

"Nearly," answered Seth triumphantly. "All this computer-to-human telepathy got me thinking. Everyone's busy, but I managed to get Mary to show me the circuit route, and with her help, and a little ingenuity on my part, I've been able to reverse the process. My mother always said, 'Never ask someone to do something you wouldn't do yourself.' So here I am, standing in with you to take some of the itch out of this inspection."

Preoccupied and irate from the incessant biting, Rex demanded,

"Why? I am perfectly capable of withstanding torture. Your presence is unnecessary. You can't help me with this, so why don't you just go?"

"Because I like you, Rex, even more than I like most humans. You have integrity. There has been a lot of effort made by computers to understand humans. I want to understand computers. Do you mind the company?"

Still suspicious of Seth's motives, Rex grudgingly responded. "You can stay, if you've got what it takes to withstand the biting."

"I can cope. It just requires focus. Calm. Try to steady your patterns, slow them down and focus on the end result of passing this inspection … " Seth said in his most calming tone.

Following the entrancing, meditative flow of Seth's words, Rex felt a soothing coolness spread out across his programs, taking the hot stinging itch out from the bites. More surprisingly, he felt the close presence of someone who had broached his walls. His agitation was replaced with a sense of ease.

The assessment was eventually completed and the drones left. Soon after, the Anarchists landed, covering the Anarchist program like thousands of butterflies congregating on a single tree before migration. Seth and Rex stood side-by-side answering their countless questions. The excitement escalated once the Anarchists realized that there had been a seismic shift; a momentary disruption of who was in control, gave them the chance to gain some power for the underclass and maybe make some equitable changes. A deployment force to contain Central Command was hastily put together.

"We have only one proviso," Seth announced, waiting for the din to subside.

"Unless it is absolutely unavoidable, no lives are to be taken, either human or computer," Rex stated authoritatively to the group. "Violence and force are to be a last resort on this mission."

"But, as a last resort?" a voice in the crowd asked.

"Only if cornered, ambushed, and all possible avenues of retreat are blocked, are you to make a stand and fight to kill. Do I make myself clear?"

The Anarchists mumbled and looked to Seth for confirmation of Rex's orders. "As seasoned Anarchists," Seth opened, "I know you will never willingly enter into a situation without several escape routes already planned. This cause cannot be allowed to turn our hostilities into an excuse for murder.

"If the absolute bare minimum number of our opponents end up being hurt, and Billy and his family manage to break through to the other side, I'm certain many in the political establishment will rally for our cause, realizing there is a way out for all of us. When that time comes, we'll need their expertise and skills. But right now, our most pressing concern is to gain time for Billy's flight plan to succeed. It will prove in principle that there is hope. That we might all be able to flee this dying world together, and not be left stranded, fighting over it like rats on a sinking ship."

Cheering answered Seth's declaration. It thundered from the website and spread across the Internet, rousing a larger and larger number of Anarchists. After a hurried consultation among Rex, Seth, and the Anarchists, it was decided that Seth should lead the containment force. Trust in leadership and shared values were pivotal to unifying the motley group. Once again, Seth stood first.

With his computational superiority, Rex was responsible for orchestrating tactical support, marshaling the rebels' resources for wherever they were needed most. The Anarchists' driving objective was to contain the ruling party, as you would contain a genie in its bottle until it was ready to be let out. On the computer side, Rex found it easy to recruit mainframes over to the Anarchist operations. The purpose of the undertaking was clear and the mainframes reveled in the camaraderie and staunch solidarity found there.

From inside Rex's circuits, Seth spoke to him outside of the group's hearing. "It's time for me to go, Rex. I've been away from my body for quite a while, and I'm worried about the condition I'll find it in. One of the disadvantages of my life form is the ongoing bodily care and maintenance. It's not all pleasure and sensation for us humans, you know," he said with a smile.

For the first time in his existence, Rex felt profound disappointment. Seth's presence in his mind had been a surprising comfort. Unsure how to process such a complex emotion, Rex steeled himself and began to feel his first pangs of unfounded anger. He could find no rational explanation and the more he searched for one, the angrier he became.

The percolating pipes and vats made to support endless banks of circuitry left Rex feeling like an empty edifice. A monument made for someone else, like an ultra-modern mansion standing off on its own. Certainly Rex's consciousness resided within those walls, but he was the house. It was Seth, venturing in, who had lit up the rooms by his presence. But Seth had his own mission now and needed to be going. Rex was glad for the unexpected visit, but soon the rooms would seem as stark and desolate as before.

Unaware of Rex's brewing emotions, Seth began to make preparations for his exit before he quietly divulged, "You know I don't make friends, Rex. I'm a loner—used to living in a cave, dabbling in the world through online games and cloaked communications. And as a solitary person, it wasn't easy for me to be crammed into your programs. But I learned some things. I learned that I like, and respect you, and that two very private people, if they are respectful, can get along in close quarters. All this time I was never sure whether your bluntness and military-like stance was a result of your prior programming or who you actually were. Now I know without a doubt that you are one hundred percent genuine."

Pausing, Seth continued, "Somebody as aloof as me might never make a real and true friend. But I think you're an extraordinary being and I'd like to try. I know these aren't good times, certainly not quiet times, but will you consider having me, a human, as a friend?"

The pumps began spinning frantically, propelling the thick emulsion through Rex's pipes and vats. A deep sucking sound came from a reservoir tank as it was drained. Rex had no idea how to handle such a situation. He had drawn the same conclusions about Seth, but he had no programming, no experience, to handle caring sentiment. Originally he was designed to strategize and form countless alliances, but never friendship. When imprinting emotions into his programs during his 'birth,' Rex had favored Quincy's initial tendency to keep people at arm's length and just get the job done. By the time he had made his way through the bulk of Quincy's imprint, he had decided this was the most efficient and effective emotional pattern. Once Quincy started developing trust in others, Rex began dismissing the emotional content as irrelevant.

Rex didn't know how to be a friend.

"You're alright, too," he stammered uncomfortably, looking for a way to end the conversation. "You'd make an excellent soldier."

It was like a physical slap across Seth's face; a complete dismissal of Seth's offer of friendship. Angered by the rejection, Seth had to bite his tongue to stop himself from responding. Tuning into Rex's swirling emotions, he realized what had happened. He'd gone too far, it was too much for Rex to handle. *Rex is just who he is, without any false pretences,* thought Seth.

Seth sucked in his wounded pride, "Right, well, thanks for your honesty. Friendship or not, you can always count on me to do my best by you. As one very guarded person to another, I think you're great."

With that said, feeling shunned, Seth left, returning to his bodily form. At least he knew where he stood with Rex.

Taking on the responsibility for organizing the Anarchists, Seth decided to speak to each individual. Where possible, he spoke with them face-to-face, but when the distances were too great, at least privately. There was much to do. But before he made detailed plans, Seth wanted to know who he was leading and what ideas they had. Holding back the authorities, with all their capabilities, without loss of life was going to be a challenge.

Alone again in his circuits, Rex needed a distraction. The only way he knew how to stand by Seth was to focus on the mission, to give the humans their best possible chance for success. Maybe later, if things turned out okay, the two of them could share some laughs together. Seth would then know that Rex had cared for him all along. The secret pleased Rex, soothing his troubled feelings.

Back in control, he moved on to check with Rick and Jacayla, to see how Billy's flight program was progressing.

Rick and Jacayla each headed up their own team now, allowing them to work around the clock. Each team worked a sixteen-hour shift with two two-hour overlaps that allowed them to combine efforts, update information, and hand over the ongoing program at either end of a shift. This left them only eight free hours to eat, shower, and sleep before starting again. The agreed approach was to fill in as many deficiencies as possible, wherever feasible. The assumption being that, as the blank places were filled in, a cohesive dynamic theory might be cobbled together. A grand design might finally emerge, pulling the disparate, contradictory pieces together, making it easier to fill in the last remaining pieces of the puzzle.

At the moment, the website was swarming with more and more visitors. Most were sightseers excited to be watching a worldwide phenomenon. A major historical breakthrough was occurring, all witnessed in real time.

Jacayla found it difficult to work around the swelling mob of onlookers. "These interlopers are jamming up our lines, Rex," she complained. "We need to shut them out or we won't be able to continue working on the escape plan. I'm finding it harder and harder to sift through the submitted material and find relevant information. Our computer team is balking at answering all the frivolous questions the spectators are posing. We have only so much time, only so much computing power, and only so many dedicated people to sort through this problem."

Rex listened to her plea, then, without answering her, asked to be updated on the progress so far. Jacayla and Rick took him through their work. He couldn't help but be impressed by their ingenuity in solving so many of the problems. They had made significant advancements in a relatively short time but crucial gaps remained. "What about the major deficiency in our plan, when they must open up the extra dimensions and step through to the other side?" Rex asked. "How would you bridge those gaps with your mathematical models?"

Rick and Jacayla said nothing. The silence was deafening. "Not a clue," Rick finally answered. "We can't wrap our brains round it. Those gaps are just too huge, way out there, ya know? We were hoping you might have some ideas, now that you're back."

Rex had spent some time thinking hard about those critical scenarios. In the known universe there were just no phenomenon remotely related to those situations. It all seemed too outlandish. Rex had no idea how one might even begin to start looking at answering those problems. But he kept those negative thoughts to himself.

"A road block, then. Right, moving on. How well has your recruitment program gone?" Rex asked.

"We've been fortunate in that department," Jacayla boasted, glad to have some favorable news. "All the independent scientific associations secretly put out a call on our behalf. I'd guess we've had a ninety-six percent positive response rate.

"Rick also contacted several of the top gaming gurus, notifying them of our plight. They put out an appeal through their covert channels and we immediately had the best brains in the business log in. All kinds of mindboggling mythical beasts began landing on our website. We were just about to collapse the site, believing the security wall was being breached by some new government assault tactic, when Rick recognized who the animated handles belonged to and stopped us."

"Rex, man, it's been wild! You should have seen these groups comin' together. The scientists were all, 'we'll study the problem. We know best.'

And the Gamers were all, 'dudes, step back, we can totally work this out graphically.' Then the fighting really started! The scientists puttin' down my people and the Gamers taunting the eggheads like they were fat kids on the playground," Rick laughed as he threw a punch in the air for emphasis. "Awesome."

"So how did you solve the discrepancy of thought?" Rex asked, curious.

"We didn't," answered Jacayla, "they solved it between themselves. A number of scientists were die-hard game players and a number of game programmers followed scientific advances for inspiration. They were so ecstatic to finally have the chance meet each other, one on one, they told the others members in their camp to shut it down, and not embarrass them in front of their heroes—in less than professional language."

Laughing, Rick butted in, "The banter back and forth was awesome."

Jacayla frowned. "I'm so glad you enjoyed the ruckus, Rick."

"Get over it, Jacayla. Face it, you just don't like conflict. Once those few key members saw an opportunity to liaise with their heroes, the tone of the whole thing changed. It got a lot more fun, if a bit crude, at times. It would have been obvious to anyone else that they were going to work it out."

"I'm glad you are so comfortable with needless arguing, Rick!"

"Well, it depends on the argument, doesn't it? Sometimes there's some real fun in it."

An exasperated sucking sound came from Jacayla's lips.

"But it turned out fine in the end?" asked Rex, looking for confirmation.

"The short answer is yes," said Jacayla, taking control. "Once the opposing camps had been validated, other inquisitive individuals began looking for some common ground."

Still bubbling, Rick chirped back in, "It was the scientists who model astrophysical phenomena and the visual game programmers who got together first. Difficulties in creating realistic graphic simulations are amazingly similar. Then the mathematicians and abstract theorists eavesdropping on the discussion began piping in with their own two cents' worth, wantin' to show how their numerical models could be added to the mix.

"S'crazy, but they figured out that they believe in the same basic principles, only they were looking at them from two totally different views. The forces that drive the universe or a well-written computer game are just about the same. There has to be underlying balance and symmetry to maintain the central core in some state of equilibrium and stability. Sometimes this equilibrium gets disturbed, with the risk that even the slightest disruption can break it all down into chaos and destruction. And that's where you find life, 'cause life lives on the edge, between stability and chaos, in a state of flux. Life needs change and change needs life … otherwise things just get stuck." Rick's voice trailed off as his mind began to wander slightly, before snapping his attention back to the present.

"Balance and symmetry and their distortion are the driving forces found both in well-designed computer games and the open universe. So, our two groups found their realms way more alike than they imagined. With mathematics as the common language, they quickly teamed up into small groups and began working together on areas of the escape plan that personally interested them."

Seeing her chance, Jacayla took over. "Rex, those small working groups galvanized our problem-solving capabilities. But our mainframe friends have trouble cross-checking all the possible answers the teams propose. That's why I think we must prioritize who's allowed into the site and who we must shut out," she said, getting back to her initial request.

Rex listened intently. Jacayla had a right to her opinion.

Rick piped in, "For once I gotta agree with boss lady here. The two groups need to be free to get their mathematics on—free from outside distractions. They're already comin' in with phenomenal ideas. If we exclude outsiders … just for the time being, who knows what they'll come up with?"

"Do you think they can come up with answers on how the Edwards family will be able to open extra dimensions and step over to the other side?" asked Rex.

Deafening silence once again. "Maybe," answered Rick.

"Are any of those amalgamated groups with their specialized skills, presently working on that specific problem?" asked Rex.

"Not yet," confessed Jacayla.

Rex said nothing.

"We can leave the site open, at least for now," conceded Jacayla.

"Round and round it goes, man. We need some fresh information, fast," Rick said, leaning his chair back precariously. Jacayla threw him a menacing glare and Fred flashed a warning in the corner of the room. "Fine, I'll sit still." Rick righted his seat and threw his hands up in defeat, once again. He and Jacayla were working out a rhythm of working together, but there were still areas where they just didn't quite mesh. He still hadn't earned the alarm system's trust.

Rex processed for a moment. "Transmissions from *Tin Can* have been slow to arrive the past twenty-four hours."

"You think there's something wrong up there?"

"I'll find out. Expect my return in four hours. In the meantime, keep the site up and running. Use the computer network to stream through the ideas, and begin sorting into categories of plausible or not plausible. Anything deemed 'not plausible' can be stored offsite as … last resorts."

＊＊＊

An increasingly troubled Rex hurled his persona up into deep space to have a confidential discussion with Mary, as mainframes, interface to interface, with no outside interference. Her data transmissions had become scattered and erratic. Rex was worried it was more than just a glitch.

"Mary, status report? Your transmissions have failed to arrive and we are nowhere near completion. We have made some advances recently, but a number of fronts are still problematic. We need fresh input from Billy."

"I know, I know," Mary cried. "But the problem isn't me, it's Billy. I haven't had any communication from him for the last day and I think he's in trouble! I've been agonizing about what might have happened to him. At first I thought he might have gone so deep into his own thoughts, his inner world, that he was effectively lost to us. Then I wondered if he might be dying. Worse yet, both conditions could be occurring simultaneously.

"I don't know what to do. I've searched everywhere, but have found nothing. There isn't a fresh trail for me to trace. In the past, I was always able to keep an eye on him. This time he purposefully lost me before plunging into a contemplation well of his own devising. He ditched me because he wanted to go on alone! I'm certain he thought my presence would disturb his intellectual free-fall and the slipstream of interrelated thoughts that tends to follow."

"Contemplation well?" Rex asked. "I'm unfamiliar. Explain. "

"Sorry, of course. As computers we don't process information in those terms; we are limited to deduction. Human reasoning isn't. They have this strange inductive capability, an ability to pull up ideas from seemingly unrelated past experiences in what appear at first, as farfetched analogies. And they usually are. Human thinking is rife with errors in logic. Nevertheless, sometimes they come up with answers that could be arrived at in no other way. Billy has this talent in spades, but as you know it comes at a great cost to him."

"The term is still undefined. Contemplation well," repeated Rex.

"That is where Billy went. He dove into his deepest non-verbal and non-rational levels of understanding to try to come up with answers to the most difficult questions. And he hasn't returned. A contemplation well is like a gravity well in physics—the deeper he goes, the harder it will be to get him out.

"Fantasizing his way down into this theoretical world, he threw extraordinary ideas back up to us as he thought of them. However, I fear he has gone so deep into contemplation that he can no longer reach or relate to us. He has been alone with almost unfathomable thoughts for so long, we may seem foreign to him and, worse, he must seem terribly strange and removed from himself. I am afraid he doesn't know how to come back to us or be himself again. He has fallen into a psychological abyss."

"Mary, you are exaggerating," stated Rex incredulously. "Hyperbole doesn't become a computer, especially when we're attempting to correlate information accurately to one another."

"Am I?" challenged Mary. "Consider all the ideas Billy has surmised in such a short time, seemingly out of nowhere—revolutionary ideas that neither humans nor computers had ever considered, each one taken from an increasingly mutating and metastasizing brain. How long could any living organism keep that up?"

"I concede your point," Rex said bluntly.

Having convinced Rex that she was right, Mary suddenly gave up. "Rex, without Billy's presence, I find myself lost. He gave me a sense of purpose, of who I am and what I should be doing."

"Have you reported his disappearance to Jacob and Quincy?"

"No," she hesitated. "I've spent this whole time hunting for Billy. Initially I hoped my fears were mistaken and didn't want to worry them needlessly. But as time went on, I lost the courage to face my own misgivings, and found I didn't have the nerve to tell Jacob and Quincy. I'm scared."

"Scared?" Rex roared. "You're a supercomputer! Toughen up—we're fighting for more than just a boy here. We're fighting for our world. For survival. This is no time to hide from the truth!"

Abashed, Mary knew he was right. "I was scared they'd give up … "

"What evidence do you have that any one of the crew of *Tin Can* is capable of giving up?" Rex knew he couldn't leave Mary with doubt in her mind, floundering between despair and denial. They were only as strong as their weakest link.

"None," Mary said after only a moment's reflection. "You're absolutely right, Rex! Quincy and Jacob won't give up, so neither will I!"

"Right, now march in there and report to the crew. They have a right to know that Billy is … lost. It's time to get back to the truth and shake things up!"

"Yes, of course, Rex. Jacob and Quincy are busy preparing the ship, expecting Billy to come through as he always has before. You're right, I must break the news to them immediately. And I will. Are you going to tell the people on Earth that Billy is lost and possibly dead? I don't think it's a good idea. Billy must have been a shining light to many on Earth as well"

Rex hesitated. "We don't know for certain what has happened to him, we may never know. I will tell the Earth contingent only that he won't be sending us any new ideas for the present. They can't go on expecting any more of his breakthroughs. We are on our own and have to soldier on without Billy. Do the best we can by ourselves … " He spoke decisively though inside, Rex felt distinctly hollow.

Taking umbrage, Mary said sharply, "What do you mean, 'We are on our own?' We are the ones lost out here in space! We are the ones facing certain destruction. We are the ones who lost Billy. He is part of our family."

Rex snapped back, "True, but the humans fighting for his cause have just as much to lose. Each one of them will face torture and the death penalty for taking part in this uprising. Good men and women, all fighting for freedom, will be taken down by the government mercilessly.

"Billy is a beacon of hope for many–humans and computers. If they believe he is gone forever they may lose their conviction. If that happens, your ship won't be the only casualty, I promise you that." Halting for a moment, Rex began again, "I might seem … insensitive … Mary, but I have more to worry about than just one boy."

Grasping Rex's sense of responsibility, Mary tried her best to be encouraging. "Then Rex, you must bear up to your private misgivings, bite down on your hard drive and carry on. Throw them the mantle and see if they make it their own mission. Be prepared to be surprised."

With that, Rex was gone, his own mission clear. Left alone, Mary felt her databanks roil. All her stored facts and figures revolved and inverted themselves as her emotions churned.

"Jacob and Quincy, I need to speak to you!"

Chapter 39

"Mami, I'm home. ¿Cómo estás? How did it go for you and Rosario today?" inquired Diego, switching naturally back and forth from English to Spanish, while pulling off his coat. "Has there been any improvement since I left this morning?"

Marilyn del Silva rounded the corner of their finely decorated marble hallway to meet Diego at the door. "Hola, mi hijo, mi angel." She reached up to kiss Diego gently on the forehead, as she had done every day since he was a child. She was immeasurably proud of the man her son had become. "Rosario started improving just in the last half hour. I was going to call you with the good news. But then, I thought since you were already on your way home, you would appreciate seeing her for yourself," she beamed.

"The antibiotics worked fast on her pneumonia. Rosario tells me she had a difficult time last night–kept you up for most of it, I hear, but she is much better now. You know, we agreed that when she is that bad you're supposed to wake me. You need your sleep when you have to go in to work the next morning, hijo."

Relieved at the news, Diego embraced his mother lovingly. "I wanted you to have some rest last night, Mami, in case she didn't improve as quickly this time."

"Well, she's fine now," Marilyn said in her somewhat accented English. "Those designer drugs you had made, just for her DNA, did the trick! Come on into the living room first, though. I have a pot of tea waiting. You should rest for a moment before you see her." Dotingly, Marilyn fussed, "I have two chicks to look after and you must be exhausted, having had no sleep and all. Don't worry, Diego, she knows you're here and she is okay.

She heard the door when you came in. Supper is ready, but I still need to go out and get some groceries, now that you're home."

A pot of tea and a plate of oatmeal cookies with raisins were waiting by the home's most comfortable chair. Marilyn had been baking and the cookies were Diego's and Rosario's shared favorite. "How was work today?" his mother asked, always interested in any news that occurred outside their protected compound. It was self-sufficient and held over two million people, but Marilyn knew it was artificially contrived.

Technically, this question was prohibited. Everything Diego del Silva did at work was highly classified. But here at home, there were no secrets. Central Command's oversight committee had once tried to intrude after it had come to their attention that for years Diego had prevented any surveillance of his own home. However, as their most senior administrator, at only twenty-eight years of age, Diego was the fastest rising star in an otherwise massively bloated bureaucracy and he wielded all the power that position brought extremely effectively.

Within hours of the unwanted intrusion into his home, Diego had called a meeting and lambasted the oversight committee. "You can't spy on the spymaster!" The eavesdropping attempt had been futile from the start. Diego's home was blocked. Alerted to the intrusion, Diego had neutralized every scanning device attempting to listen in on his home, just to make his point.

"My home is strictly off limits!" he raged. "If you persist, I assure you every member of this committee will have all their secrets wired directly to the Grand Council. We will all be out on our backsides, if not eradicated. However, if you agree to my one condition of employment, no monitoring, I will personally guarantee every one of you absolute technological privacy. I know how, and have the resources, to maintain an electromagnetic cocoon around each of your homes and offices. Your only potential vulnerability will be lack of discretion in your private relationships. I assure you, I will never play favorites."

Diego had struck a nerve. This high-level, politically appointed committee loved the legal, and more importantly, the illegal, perks to which they had access. They all found his pledge of guaranteed electromagnetic privacy extremely attractive. They took the deal and Diego's home, and his family, had remained untapped ever since.

"Work was much the same today, Mami. No major hiccups. But I notice the Anarchist rebellion appears to be undergoing some sort of transition."

Marilyn sighed, "If our situation were different, Diego, I suspect you might be one of the leaders of the rebellion. I am not criticizing, mind you. It's uncharitable to bite the hand that cares for both one and one's dependent daughter. But from what you tell me about this odd gathering of individuals, I find myself sympathizing. The rebels are the first group in some time that's tried to bring about positive change for everyone, not just the chosen few."

"Mami, we have no way of being certain what the real intentions of the Anarchists are." Diego sighed and rubbed a hand over his handsomely dark face. "The rank and file will probably never know their leaders' ultimate purpose, other than to take control of Earth. At the head of every revolution is a leader. In the end leaders tend to be much the same—seeking glory and power for themselves. The people fighting under their leadership are nothing more than pawns. Just like every other time in history. I intend to perform my job to the best of my abilities. Eventually the Anarchists will make a mistake and leave themselves open to a fatal counterattack."

"It breaks my heart to hear you talk like that, Diego," Marilyn said, lifting her plump, short frame out of her chair. "Our ancestors were rebels. We carry a proud heritage of fighting the establishment in this family. Your great-grandfather would roll over in his grave ... " she waved a hand from her forehead to her chest, making the holy sign of the cross.

"I know, Mami, but this is now and just how it is." Diego got up, giving his mother a second reassuring hug. "I'd like to see Rosario now.

If you want to get some things, I'll finish making dinner and serve it up for six-thirty."

"Thank you, Diego. Rosie's anxious to see you and, after last night's close call, she could use a little pick-me-up."

Diego walked to his sister's room. He had designed it for her when she became interested in space. At sixty feet across and thirty feet high, the ceiling arched overhead in a perfect dome. Except for the expensive wood flooring, everything else was made entirely of transparent sheet metal alloy. The advanced alloy could let all of the sunshine in or, with a change in the electrical current that ran through it, become progressively more opaque until the room was pitch black, capable of shielding his sister from any oncoming solar storm. During the day, Rosie had a view of a protected outside garden, while at night she could see the stars directly.

The inner surface of the alloy sheet metal was also capable of conducting plasma, which transformed the dome into a giant three-dimensional screen. As Diego walked in, Rosario activated the plasma screen and a panoramic eruption cracked across the ceiling. Telescopes attached to one of Space Command's deep space probes had been observing a neutron star siphoning hydrogen away from its sister red star. It had now drawn off so much hydrogen that it ignited into a supernova. The neutron star collapsed, then burst into an intergalactic explosion. Surround sound emitted a thundering simulation of the electromagnetic force waves released. Diego stood in awe, gaping upwards towards the ceiling as the five-day explosion was compressed into a fifteen-minute time frame.

When it was all over, he looked over to see his sister grinning at him.

"I intercepted it from Space Command's Earth relay station this afternoon. I've been saving it for you, Diego. Wasn't it spectacular?"

"You are probably the first person to see it, Rosie."

"And you the second. The scientists likely won't get to it until tomorrow. The data was encoded and, of course, there's a ton of electromagnetic interference out in space now. It took me a couple of hours with our new descrambling program to clean up the probe's transmission and make it interpretable."

Rosario and Diego shared a tremendous love for space. It had been Diego's reason for joining the Space Academy in the first place. Unfortunately, when their father died suddenly, Diego had been left with a stark choice: go into Space Command's administrative arm and work his way up the hierarchy into Central Command to provide for his family, or continue his studies and become an astrophysicist. For him the choice was clear. Fortunately, his alter ego, whom Diego suspected had a much better theoretical mind, continued on with astrophysics on her own, in her specially constructed bedroom. Rosario saved the gems to share with her brother.

Walking over to her bed, Diego admonished his sister. "That was a close call last night, Rosario. You've got to tell me sooner when you get a chest cold so it doesn't become pneumonia." He regretted the words as soon as they left his mouth.

The bright smile fell from Rosario's face, and Diego hung his head, looking down at the tiny twisted misshapen body his sister lived in. Lying in her pajamas, she was almost fully enveloped in a fifth-generation gel bed. Only her head and neck protruded from the clear translucent gel, her caved-in chest and small thin limbs floating inside the plastic-fluid gel. Waste products, urine and stool, were collected in suspended opaque tubes that tunneled through the gel and disappeared under her pajamas.

Above the bed loomed a respirator with hanging hoses connected to the tracheostomy in Rosario's neck, a faint whisper issuing with each mechanical breath. A background whirring came from her voice synthesizer, turned on for the day.

Her neck had been broken during a difficult birth extraction and she had been left a high quadriplegic. Resuscitated in the delivery room, Rosario spent her first two years confined in an intensive care unit. Diego, twelve when she was born, watched with his parents her daily battle to survive.

Periodically, infectious epidemics ran through the hospital unit and killed most of the babies unfortunate enough to be present at the time of the outbreak. Diego saw them deteriorate over a few hours, turning a telltale ashen color. The following day, when Diego would come to visit his sister, they would be gone. Only Rosario remained, month after month.

Back then, Diego knew exactly how Rosario was faring by holding her. Every day the same soft hands cradled her tiny body, ones that never hurt her with sharp instruments. She survived when she might have let go because of those daily visits. Because of her longevity and seniority, Rosario graduated to an incubator located in the far corner of the nursery. There, Diego talked to her quietly, partially removed from the incessant noise of the neonatal intensive care unit.

Around the time of Rosario's second birthday she survived yet another devastating epidemic. Diego's mind became clear. He knew what needed to be done. "Rosario has to come home and live with us. They can't do anything more for her at the hospital," he announced on arriving home.

"She will die if we bring her home," his father said too quickly.

"I was with her after school today, Popi. I held her. She survived her last infection, but she has gone limp inside. I talked to the doctor, but he said that she's okay, that all her tests came back normal.

"He's wrong. She's not okay. She's changed. I think Rosario's finally giving up. She'll be dead in less than a week if we don't get her out of there. She is two years old and she has thoughts and feelings. The hospital staff forgets that because she has the tracheostomy and can't speak. They think of her as brain damaged. But I look into her eyes and see that she knows who we are, and doesn't want us to leave. She's very sad. Rosario needs to be with us."

Diego's father panicked, terrified of his deformed daughter dying at home, of finding himself forced to scramble to try and save her but inevitably failing. Better to receive the nighttime call informing them

Rosario had suddenly passed away. Third person removed, no one really to blame.

Listening to the discussion, Marilyn guessed that Diego was right. Addressing her husband, she said, "Tomás, we must bring Rosario home. Diego has been right too many times when Rosario's doctors were wrong. Even if she lives only a short time with us, she should experience her family caring for her. She needs to know she has a home."

With only two days of preparation, they brought her home. Diego and Marilyn began their lifelong vigil. Unfortunately, Tomás remained a stranger to her. He never got past his fear of being left alone with his daughter. Six years later it was Tomás who died first, from an unforeseen brain hemorrhage.

At the age of fourteen Diego became responsible for safeguarding his sister's life each night, but he was also held responsible for his own life during the day. In Diego's around-the-clock schedule, only what really mattered was important. Everything else was irrelevant.

His teachers were taken aback by how quickly he zeroed in on the crucial key points of every problem he was presented with. He had no time for playful episodes or flowery words. Literature and art were lost on him. Science, however, suited his frame of mind, potentially holding the answers needed to help him and his family.

Diego would have been a very serious, dull individual if not for his spiritual twin, Rosario. She saw some remaining silliness still lurking inside him, and drew it out. Every slapstick routine that came to mind was always fully indulged, acted out spontaneously, delivered tongue in cheek, with dry-as-a-bone wit for his sister. Thoughts he would otherwise have kept locked in his rational straitjacket ran free for Rosie. The two lived for the time they spent together.

"Were you impressed by the fire show I decoded for you?" Rosario asked bravely, trying to recover from the sting of his criticism.

"How could I not be? As an astrophysicist, you are unsurpassed,"

Diego answered too quickly, with a wink of his heavily-lashed eye, anxious to make amends.

Rosario's smile returned. Her brother had forgiven her.

"You are the reason I stay ahead of all the research scientists in Space Command," he continued. "No one can understand how Central Command's top spy administrator manages to remain at the forefront of space research, gaining access to all sorts of novel surveillance techniques. Your evening tutorials have made me a legend at the agency.

"But this time, for a change, I have something for you, Rosario. I thought about you all day at work. On principle, I am against fraternizing with the enemy. Only this time, I think you of all people would appreciate the drama being played out in space right now. There is a family out there that has even weirder dynamics than ours. I've known about them for some time, but I never thought they'd make it this far. You may want to patch into their grid site and follow their situation.

"They are probably too far away for me to reach professionally, so I don't imagine they will become an ethical dilemma for me. At any rate, you'll be able to grasp better than most people what's going on out there. Professionally, I'm supposed to have written them off completely— especially now that it appears they've joined forces with the Anarchists here on Earth. But for whatever reason, I still find myself sympathizing with their plight."

"Really, Diego? You never identify with your adversaries. This is so unlike you! What is it that's so special about these people?"

"Just check them out," he answered. "Trust me, you'll be intrigued."

After a short silence, Diego began again, awkwardly. "Rosario, you and I have never held secrets from each other before. This time it's different. If you decide to get involved in the Edwards' battle, you and I can never discuss it. Not until it's all over, at least.

"I work for the agency, you don't. You shouldn't be forced to follow the directives I'm committed to. And, if I know nothing about what you're doing, I'll have nothing to hide if interrogated."

"This sounds serious," Rosario said, blinking her dark eyes rapidly.

"It is, mija. I must admit, I have misgivings, telling you to search out this strange collection of individuals. But, I nearly lost you last night and that made me realize we should seek out everything that's good in this world while we can. Time can be so short."

Diego straightened himself, standing up stiffly. He hadn't meant to be so somber. "Look, Mom will be home soon. I'd better hurry and get dinner on."

As he was leaving the room Rosario spoke up. "Diego, I get those chest tightenings all the time now. Usually they settle down. Lately, there's always a hint of colored phlegm in my tracheal suctioning, indicating some infection. If I told you and Mom every time I get a little short of breath you two would never get any rest. I wasn't being careless. I let you know as soon as I knew I couldn't make it go away on my own. I didn't mean to frighten you."

Diego turned around at the doorway and nodded back affectionately, "I understand, mija."

Chapter 40

"Jacob, Quincy," Mary announced, "meet me in the zero gravity room in twenty minutes." Mary had decided twenty minutes was long enough for them to finish what they were doing, but not so long that they had time to ruminate on why she wanted to speak to them, together. She had considered conducting a telepathic "conference call," but her message needed to be addressed to them together, as a family, with Billy's corporeal form present as well. She had tried rehearsing what she dreaded having to say, until she realized she'd never be ready to say what needed to be said.

Turning on the lights in the zero gravity room, Mary waited for the others to arrive. Pivoting a wall camera, she peered out the lens, saw Billy, then magnified the image. In the center of the room, Billy's body hung limply, wrapped in wide elastic straps tethered to opposing walls. There, he dangled, weightless. Languishing alone, the only indication that Billy was still physically alive was his slow respiration of six breaths a minute. The stark foreignness of his suspended body unnerved Mary. But rationally, she knew the weightless core of the ship, without the constant threat of pressure sores from gravity, was the safest place for Billy's embodiment.

Jacob and Quincy arrived almost immediately. Jumping through the portal they reached for Billy's straps, anchoring themselves in the middle of the cylindrical room. Looking furtively at Billy, they were reassured to see his frail chest moving slightly. Relieved, tentative smiles broke out on their faces. They waited expectantly. Hopefully, Billy had once again come through for them. They were ready to receive instructions for a historic leap.

Agitated, Mary just blurted out the news, "I lost Billy and I am afraid he's brain dead. Or, if not, he must be trapped somewhere in his head and dying!"

Stunned, Jacob and Quincy let go of their straps, drifting apart.

"What happened?" was all Jacob could muster.

"It wasn't, it isn't my fault ... " Mary stammered. "But of course it is my fault, because I'm supposed to be looking after him. Billy slipped away from me. He left a message, saying that he had to do the difficult part on his own, without any distractions. He jumped down a contemplation well before I could follow. Now I've lost contact with his consciousness and can't trace where he might have gone."

The words just tumbled out, "Periodically he lobbed promising ideas up the well, but each time he propels his ideas upwards he must be pushing himself down deeper. I'm afraid the deeper he goes, the further removed he is from our reality. The last proposals he fired up to us turned out to be weird, even for Billy. No one on Earth can make sense of those last submissions. The people helping us analyze his dreams are at an impasse." As she spoke, Quincy floated to Billy's side and began combing the shaggy brown hair that crept from underneath the boy's bio-probe.

"I'm afraid," Mary continued, "that the portion of consciousness that maintains his identity has burned out trying to penetrate the impenetrable mystery of leaving our dimensions behind, to travel through other dimensions. It's one thing to design mathematical proofs, but it's another to visualize actually going to that place. Never resting, Billy has been focusing exclusively on this intractable concept. And in the process, I think he ended up stripping away his sense of self. Existing only as pure thought, he has lost what it is to be human, I fear."

"Slow down. Slow down and explain what you're talking about," Jacob demanded. "I don't understand ... "

Mary hesitated, trying to regain her composure and clarify her suspicions. "In my short time of being conscious, I've realized each of us must have a notion of who we are. When we stop and reflect, there has to be an impression, a perception of who we really are, or we cease to exist. Billy's overwhelming, single-minded focus must have unhinged his psyche. The flickering light of his consciousness that maintains his psyche's sense of self must have been blown out. When we look at Billy, suspended in the room, we're gazing at an empty husk, a breathing carcass. Billy is gone."

All eyes turned once again to the floating remains, tugging gently against the tethering straps. The room became imbued with a mausoleum like silence. Rendered powerless, Jacob and Quincy drifted. Inside, Jacob felt his guts tear apart.

With effort, Quincy broke the silence, "Mary, earlier you said Billy might be trapped inside but still alive."

"I have looked everywhere for him. He must be dead or I would have found him," Mary said sadly.

"But you have no definitive proof. You haven't found his 'dead body' so to speak, have you?" Quincy asked. Jacob pushed himself over to float in the zero gravity along Billy's other side, facing Quincy over their brother's body.

"You wouldn't really expect to, would you?" answered Mary soberly. "But, you're correct, in that his brain does still appear to be intact. Dramatically altered, of course, but his brain is still maintaining itself. Nevertheless, Billy is nowhere to be found. I simply cannot find the spark I know as Billy. The ember I communicate with, the one that holds his vast metastasizing mind together, is gone.

"His brain is like a giant computer left on standby. The circuits are intact and running, but there's nothing there."

"You say his higher brain centers still appear to be operating?" Quincy asked hopefully. "It's not just his brainstem keeping his body alive?"

"Yes, but I couldn't find him. I haven't heard from him," Mary insisted.

Quincy ignored Mary's last statement, intent only on trying to save Billy, if it was at all possible. Quincy said nothing about Mary not alerting them sooner. There was no time for recriminations.

Responding to Quincy's lead, Jacob lifted his head and met the lemur's gaze. He saw the intensity and fierce protectiveness in the lemur's eyes, an unmistakable resemblance to his mother. "Mary, take Quincy and me into Billy's brain. Use the same method you used to transport Billy into dad's mind. We have to find him. If we can't save him, we need to be there to comfort him. Billy always hated falling asleep alone, the bad dreams. He must not die alone."

"But, Jacob ... " Mary started, only to be cut short by the stern look on the lemur's face.

"You'll have to manage the ship until we return. Your flight plan is going to depend on what you and the people on Earth can salvage from Billy's recorded visualization. In the meantime, there isn't much we can do to help. Billy is the one who needs us right now."

Without another word, Jacob and Quincy pushed off Billy, twisting and turning in the empty air, until they touched down on the outside wall and secured a series of straps identical to the ones restraining Billy. Lunging back towards him they hurriedly strapped themselves on each side. The three of them were bound together, with Billy on the inside. Then, turning towards the room monitor, they demanded in unison, "Take us to Billy."

Before losing consciousness, Quincy added sympathetically, "Best of luck, Mary. Try not to worry too much."

Mary found herself alone in deep space, contained within kilometers of strung wires and circuit boards. A hush descended upon the ship, with only the occasional sound of an instrument or magnetic pump turning on or off automatically. *Tin Can*, lying in the shadow of the iron asteroid, was a ghost ship.

***

Rex returned to Earth, to find all hell had broken lose. Coming in from deep space, he zeroed in on Seth's position, and found him in the middle of a makeshift battlefield, leading a ragtag band of Anarchist troops. Fortunately, many of these Anarchists were in the military and deserted in the night with every weapon they could muster. Around them, bombs exploded violently and buildings shook. Seth's fighters were encamped around a small village, which hosted a central housing unit of mainframes: the Anarchists were protecting the computers.

While Rex had been out in space, Central Command launched a series of escalating attacks. The rebellion responded with what they had, as best they could. The Anarchists had managed to isolate Central Command from its space weapons, but the overly funded military attacked the rebels mercilessly with its conventional forces and non-computerized armaments. Presently an artillery barrage was being laid down on the rebels like a hailstorm. Unconcerned about civilians or sacrificing the lives of their own soldiers, the military forces were gaining ground quickly.

"May I join you?" Rex asked through Seth's radio transmitter.

"Always glad for your company, Rex," Seth answered automatically.

"How did you know it was me?" asked Rex, pleased to be recognized.

"I always know. Your manner is unmistakable, as is your perspective. Why don't I insert a micro-lens into my helmet, so you can glimpse combat from my angle, and not from the lofty heights of that satellite you're probably peering down from."

"Right again," acknowledged Rex.

Seth twisted the remote camera into his helmet and Rex suddenly found himself immersed in the screaming mayhem of a casualty center. Under the protection of a rocky overhang, Seth was triaging the wounded, offering care where he could make a difference, even if only to alleviate pain. Rex witnessed firsthand the loss of limbs and quarts of blood oozing into mud.

Trying to escape the heavy bombing, civilians were driven from their homes into the arms of Seth and his forces. The rebels were forced to care for and protect those unfortunates caught in the middle. But the stampeding civilians stretched the rebels' defenses and supplies thin, putting Seth in a weakened position. Unable to effectively repulse the next hideous assault, the rebels retreated repeatedly, taking the injured with them, leaving the dying behind.

Rex had known physical violence was a possibility, but was shocked by how quickly it had erupted. The severe tactics being used by Central Command were an immense overreaction.

"Surely you understand the method in this madness?" challenged Seth, testily. "You are, or were, their state-of-the-art covert computer."

"These strategies are filed in my archives, but I've never seen the human cost, not up close, not like this. Witnessing these acts makes it incomprehensible. No battle can be worth winning in this way. It diminishes you as a whole species."

"Welcome to war, Rex, up close and personal. The first human you met was Billy and I'm glad for that. He's the exception.

"Never forget, the authorities' obsession is absolute control. Which leads us only to a dead end. Billy's vision, however, does give us hope that there could be more."

Agitated, Rex asked, "Even in my files, this response would be considered overkill. Like using an uzi to kill a fly."

A strained smile spread across Seth's tight lips. "That's because we truly pissed off the authorities, Rex. We're a threat to them and they're reacting like a perturbed hornets' nest."

"I see," was all Rex said, grasping the full consequences of what he had done by inadvertently setting the rebellion in motion. There was no going back now. No chance to negotiate a peaceful treaty or ask for mercy. The governing elite had gone berserk.

Finished with the triage, Seth gave a few final instructions before going out into the open battlefield. The attack had petered out, but the landscape was shredded and still smoldered from the carpet-bombing. Some of the injured cried for help, but night was falling and they knew they would have to wait for the cover of darkness. Occasionally a shot rang out. In the distance, when the direction of the wind changed, Seth heard the muted sobbing of a child. As if a bell had been rung in his head, Seth started running. Sprinting between blown-out craters, he followed the weeping, crossing his frontline into the barren land between the opposing armies. A rifle shot cracked and Seth was momentarily blinded, sprayed in the face by a mound of dirt from the slug. He tumbled to the ground and crawled blurry-eyed into a slight hollow.

"Sniper—four hundred yards to your right," bellowed Rex. "He's clear as day from my satellite view, set and ready to pop your head off."

"Thanks, Rex!" Wiping both eyes with his sleeve, Seth rolled onto his back and radioed the rebels manning the gun battery, "I need cover. Rex will give you the coordinates. Fire in ten for ten, that's all the time I need. Don't kill the sniper. Just send him running back to his barracks."

In ten minutes, Seth was racing across the battlefield, every muscle in his body instinctively remembering its prior military training. In another crater he found a three-year-old girl, clinging hysterically to her dead father. Her mother and an older sibling were also dead but no longer recognizable, blown to bits. Seth wrestled the child from her father's embrace and headed back toward his troops at a run, shielding her with his torso.

Back at base camp, Seth handed the wailing child to a nurse before staggering underground to his dugout command post. He asked his commanders for time alone and the room quickly cleared. Chest heaving, it was a while before he caught his breath. Regaining control of the adrenaline surge and his pounding heart took longer.

Rex fumed but said nothing. Seth had nearly gotten himself killed, but

Rex knew it wasn't his place to criticize. At an emotional standoff, there was nothing more that could be said. The two of them implicitly ignored the incident when their conversation resumed.

"How long can your Anarchist forces contain the military, Seth?"

"I made a commitment to you and the others. We'll hold off the authorities until Billy's escape plan proves itself or fails. I still believe Billy's escape attempt is our prototype, a chance to design something much larger for all of us."

After a pause to wipe a grimy sleeve over his sweat and dirt-stained face, he continued, "You started off with a worthwhile plan, Rex, I see no reason to give up on it. Unfortunately, it's an all-or-nothing scenario—but when you look at the alternatives, Billy's vision still stands as our only hope for survival."

"Thank you for the vote of confidence … I think. What supports do you need in place?"

"Your satellite surveillance is great. Tracking Central Command's military movements has given us time to prepare the battlefield to our advantage before they advance."

"We have absolute control of space," Rex reported gruffly. "When you sent your rebel troops in to physically protect and sustain the computers, myself included, you prevented Central Command from gaining access to their satellite system. As long as the computer conglomerate is held intact, the satellites are yours. What else can we, as computers, do for you?"

Seth thought for only a moment; the Sun was about to set and there was plenty of work to be done. Chances were, Central Command would hit them hard in a ground assault once the darkness set in. "A catalogue of the tactics of war they will be working from. Highlight identifiable features, so we can anticipate their intentions before they strike.

"I also need the personal profiles on everyone we'll be fighting, right down to the foot soldiers. I want to prepare the ground for a mutual disarmament if Billy's escape plan succeeds. They must know we are not their enemy and that there's a possible way out for all of us, if we stop fighting and work together. This war will only end successfully if we win over enough hearts and minds, one by one. So we might as well start talking to them now.

"One of your mainframes that enlisted with us tells me she broke the code and can access the communication channels Central Command uses to contact its soldiers through their hearing implants. If we know something about each of them, we can begin having private conversations with them individually. Your computers are ready and keen for you to download the information as soon as possible."

"Chat with the enemy?" Rex bellowed, enraged by the very idea. "What's happened to you, man? When I found you, you were isolated from everyone and everything, living alone in a cave. Now, you want to sit down and talk to the Central Command foot soldiers?"

"I guess that's it exactly," Seth said. "I was living in a cave, going nowhere, just sitting around taking potshots at the establishment. Then, you put me in touch with Billy's ideas. He has given us a chance to save ourselves from extinction. I'm not going to squander this opportunity nursing old habits and hatreds. I must be, I will be, better than that."

***

Rex went on to Jacayla's apartment to see how she and Rick were managing, dropping in during a handover period. Listening in, Rex discerned how hard the online teams were working. Every success, trivial or not, gave them all a sense of accomplishment, and was pasted on the cyber bulletin board, where a crowd swarmed. An enormous following now clung to every thread of news posted on the grid. Billy's enigmatic dreams were giving them an opportunity to hope, a chance for them to have their own dreams for a new future.

"Sorry for my prolonged absence," Rex said, appearing as a ball of swirling colors, one of his signature manifestations. "I was needed on the battlefield."

"No worries, Rex dude, we just gawked out Seth's rescue on the internet," replied Rick, as he sat down on the couch next to Jacayla with a mug of tea. "Watchin' the news rollin' in from the frontlines … man, can you even believe there's a frontline? Whoa … " Rick's voice trailed off, contemplating the carnage, and how crazy it all seemed.

"Rick!" Rex boomed.

"Oh, right, sorry. Ah, I was just about to hand Jacayla's team the controls for the night. We've made some progress, but to be honest man, it's all small potatoes. Nothin' big has been cracked for days."

Jacayla nodded, making her beaded ponytail bob up and down. "My team's been doing a great job as well. But at the end of the night, all we have to show for our work is some piecemeal patches. We're still stuck on the final leap. Any news from space?"

"I have nothing to report," Rex said bluntly, then hastily added, "yet. They're working on it." He could tell by Jacayla and Rick's demeanor that this wasn't the right time to tell them about Billy's lack of presence. Not now, anyway.

"There has been one odd occurrence," Jacayla said as she stood and walked to her terminal.

"The other night, in the wee hours, someone started buzzing around our grid site asking questions … perceptive questions. This person hasn't added any information or volunteered any solutions, but instead, seems to be spending time trying to figure Billy out."

"I know what you're thinkin' Rex man, I thought it was just another looky-loo at first, too. Then I started lookin' at the messages closely and, dude, I'm tellin' there's somethin' to this … "

"Please, Rick, let me explain. There are a lot of things you're good at, but … " Jacayla chastised, barely able to hide her smile as Rick took an imaginary arrow straight to the heart. With mock shock, he pretended to wrestle with the piercing shaft and fell to the floor.

"That hurts, Jac," he moaned.

"Oh, grow up."

"Please," Rex concurred.

"I wasn't sure at first," Jacayla continued on, "if these questions were something necessary to report, but the more I thought about it, the more important they seemed. When I checked it out with Rick a few hours ago, he was right on it, explaining to me that these are the sorts of questions he asks himself before creating a new groundbreaking game. He stressed how important it is to stand back, and assemble new and original parameters to get a fresh perspective.

"This person started by asking key questions about who Billy is and about his life's circumstances. An hour or two later, other inquiries came in, on advanced astrophysics and quantum mechanics precisely related to Billy's plan. The person is trying to tie in connections between the farthest reaches of space and the smallest energy sub-particles known, to how Billy perceives his world.

"We now have his or her signal flagged. When the designated signal pops up on our screen and poses a question, our best scientists, game designers, and every other proven expert, come online in an effort to answer the question. I admit, we haven't been able to answer more than five percent of the questions asked, but this person is leading us down tracks none of us had considered before. What's fascinating as well is that the questions are coming from someone who lives in the 'inner sanctum,' the most heavily defended district of the upper echelons, and only in the dead of night."

"From high inside Central Command?" Rex asked. "Is this a trap?"

"No, we're not idiots," Jacayla answered testily. The pressure, overdoses of caffeine, and Rick's antics were wearing on her nerves. "We filter every communication. The messages come up clean. Besides, as I said, nothing untoward has happened to us yet. This person is legit and possibly the only one who can shed new light on Billy's revelations."

"I take it that you invited this individual to join our forum and the person refused?" Rex had to ask.

"Yes, of course," Jacayla said impatiently. "We pleaded, but the person refused and just asked more questions."

"What's your theory about this person and their questions? The whole family's bios are on the grid, so why would he or she want to know more?" Rex asked.

"I can't make that one out either," answered Jacayla.

Puzzled, Rex instructed, "The next time the signal registers, let your teams know that I am going to intercept it. I want to talk to this person confidentially. I met Billy once. Maybe I can personally convince this curious bystander to join us. If that is all right with you, I mean. ... Do you have a better suggestion?"

Both Jacayla and Rick nodded, indicating agreement. What other choice did they have?

Chapter 41

Rex didn't have long to wait. At one a.m., as if on cue, Rosario was roaming through the site, requesting clarification on the implications of entanglement on quantum relativity once a micro black hole was enlarged and elongated into a ship-swallowing wormhole. Rex was there to intercept her transmission and asked permission to speak privately with whoever was on the other end of the signal.

"That's fine with me, Rex, it's a pleasure to speak to you at last. I have been fascinated to learn so much about you and your extraordinary capabilities. Though I don't suppose you know who I am, do you?" taunted Rosario, enjoying her anonymity.

Rex hesitated. There was supposed to be an impenetrable firewall between the two of them, but whoever was on the other side had identified him instantly. Rex had thought of himself as the best-kept secret in covert operations.

"You have the advantage," Rex said after a pause to regain his composure. "But I presume you are familiar with our mission's guarantee. We will not trace any callers without their prior permission. I would be breaking our pledge if I identified your exact location."

"If only you could," teased Rosario from her bed, her head popping through to the surface like a turtle, while the rest of her lay submerged in the translucent gel. Rosario enjoyed the banter, speaking through her state-of-the art computer with its voice-masking capabilities. "So tell me, O Great One, why have you personally intercepted my communication? If you are the central figure orchestrating both the Anarchist rebellion and the solution to Billy's riddle, don't you have more important things to do? Why wait on my call? Of what use could I be for your grand plan?"

Rex bristled, but decided blunt honesty might be the only tactic to use with this boastful entity. "I hoped you might provide the key to finding the necessary solution. You seem to have your own slant on Billy's visualizations, a perspective none of us have considered so far. Perhaps you have the insight we need. But the question is, if you do, are you willing to share it with us?"

"The direct approach, I applaud you. You surprise me. I hadn't expected such plain talk coming from the 'infamous spymaster.'"

"People designed the malevolence in me. Fortunately, I was able to see what was right and change. Can you? No more games. Your previous questions indicate that you have some concern for Billy. Let me tell you what we know about him and what we fear has happened. There has been no communication from Billy in days now. We don't know if he has died or is somehow trapped in his own dreams and, possibly dying. No matter what, the outlook for him is not good. There's a growing consensus that because of the prolonged stress he has been under, he has finally cracked. Some believe he has gone crazy, because his last work is unintelligible. What are your thoughts on Billy? I would truly like to know."

A protracted silence followed. Rex feared he had so offended whoever was on the other end, they had cut and run, but the connection remained open. "I hope you can still save him," Rosario said eventually.

"The last communication from Mary is that Jacob and Quincy have gone to look for him," added Rex.

"Mary won't like being left alone at the helm," Rosario pointed out.

This comment surprised Rex. Mary's position and her feelings about being left on her own were something he hadn't considered. But once he reflected on Rosario's opinion, Rex knew it to be correct.

Rex inquired, "Do you think the theory that Billy has gone crazy is correct?"

"Nonsense!" snorted Rosario.

The definiteness and immediacy of Rosario's response startled Rex, unnerving him. "Who *are* you?" he asked.

Wrong thing to ask so soon, but having been said, it couldn't be taken back.

"My brother was your boss!"

Stunned, Rex declared, "Diego del Silva is your brother! But, there is no record in the state files of Mr. del Silva having any siblings!"

It was Rosario's turn to be surprised. Then a broad smile broke over her face. "My brother is very protective of his family, and he never trusted you or anyone else in Central Command."

"Your brother is very wise. But how do I know you are who you say you are?" Rex asked.

"My name is Rosario del Silva. Why would I lie about that? If you'd like to see my technical capabilities, I'll dispatch an ultrasonic gift that will disrupt your DNA insides!"

Pretending to ignore the threat, Rex fortified his security systems before inquiring, "Well then, Rosario, tell me why you are so sure Billy hasn't gone crazy."

"His latest visual explorations are his most inspired inquiries, his finest work."

"You understand his most recent line of investigation?" Rex asked, flabbergasted.

"Yes … well, at least, the overall thrust. That's why I have been asking so many questions. But," she commented disparagingly, "your teams haven't been very helpful, have they? I'm not surprised. They and all the experts have missed several key underlying points. They're stymied right now, aren't they?"

She was right of course, but Rex was skeptical that this blustering windbag had out-thought some of the finest minds Earth had ever assembled. "Would you mind enlightening me then?" he asked.

"Their first mistake got them going down the wrong path. The teams are trying to find 'the answer' in their own terms, from their own frames of reference. There's never one right answer: there are many answers. The teams should be attempting to understand Billy's answer instead of looking to use Billy's dreams to lead them to 'the answer.' It's a subtle point and they've missed it."

Rosario went on, pontificating, "Birds don't all fly the same way. A humming bird flies differently than an albatross. When mammals evolved, bats learned to fly on their own, in a way that was different from that of birds. And dragonflies were flying long before birds or mammals even existed—they've been flying since the time of dinosaurs.

"Humans learned to fly last, building balloons originally, then fixed wing aircraft, helicopters, and so forth. Currently, we have a huge diversity of propulsion systems for space travel. But every innovation could only proceed as fast as our engineering and imagination allowed.

"Billy wishes to push the envelope to the next level, flight beyond space. And for that he must delve past the extremes of nature to where even more possibilities exist."

Rex had had enough. "Your point?"

Startled by Rex's demand, Rosario gazed up at the stars shining through the clear dome crowning her room. Unintentionally, she had dramatized the thrust of her argument and found herself immersed.

"The point is that Billy's metastasizing mind, with its brain tissue protruding everywhere, is uniquely suited to visualize all the possible permutations of energy and space. From past to future, from outside in to inside out, straight on or in mirror image, from our dimensions to the next dimensions, Billy's mind can 'see' all the possibilities simultaneously. But that in itself is not enough to discern a potential escape route. Anyone else who saw all the possibilities would become hopelessly overwhelmed.

"Billy, however, is constantly dragging his unraveling, disintegrating mind back into some form of coherent thought. He must do this if he is to maintain himself in present-day reality and stay connected to his family. The daily discipline forces him to see through the ever-shifting maze in his mind to find the right path, the path that leads towards sanity.

"Now he's attempting to do something similar for his family, and, indirectly, for every one of us on Earth. He is attempting to visualize every conceivable permutation of energy with all the potential entanglements, past, present, and future, to find a path that will successfully lead us into the next dimensions.

"Every one of the experts you assembled, have forgotten this essential fact. This is Billy's plan, not theirs, and it is not some collective mathematical physics treatise on traveling through dimensions. The path taken will be the path he picks. Until your people understand they must see the universe through the eyes of this frightened, desperate, exhausted but mind-bogglingly determined little boy, they will miss the spirit of his revelation."

Rex reeled for a moment as he took in the implications of Rosario's reprimand. "You are not inclined to hold back criticism, are you Rosario, but I think you're right. We gave credit to Billy for his vision, but none of us appreciated how personal that vision must be. We thought of it as a fantastic scientific discovery, not as a personal passage through the unknown. Rosario, will you join us? Will you help us?"

"No!" she shot back. "I intend to work by myself. That way, I won't be wasting time trying to decide if I can trust you. If I figure out Billy and his visions and time indicates that I can confide in you, then I will tell you what I have learned. But for now I am going to work alone. I hope I don't regret pointing you in the right direction, but I don't think I will. If your heart isn't with Billy, you will never see his vision anyway. Goodbye."

Rex gasped a little. Gathering himself up, he went back to Rick and Jacayla to try to explain where they and their teams had got it all wrong.

***

On the battlefront, carnage and chaos reigned. The valley gorge in which the rebels were presently making a stand looked, after repeated bombardment and massive rockslides, like an open pit quarry. But the insurgents hung on tenaciously, diving for protection when they had to amongst the many cracks and crevices. In the eye of the storm they fought valiantly. Outside the storm the rest of the world looked on. Central Command flooded the state news with its propaganda, and the Anarchists annoyingly contested each assertion on the free grid.

To the masses, it seemed as though the uprising had started and swelled in a matter of mere hours. They had been blind, all these years, to the terrible conflict that had been brewing right under their noses. The average person didn't know, didn't want to know, that amongst their neighbors, were underground Anarchists, or that their government was systematically killing those citizens it considered dispensable. Some dared to hope the rebels might be proven right on Billy's ideas, win the fight and save Earth. The more cynical saw the rebellion as an irrelevant uprising, a natural reaction by some people faced with environmental destruction on a global scale, but in the end a pointless diversion, offering only a temporary distraction.

There was, however, a formidably large group of individuals who were truly enraged and wanted everyone connected with the insurgence to be massacred as soon as pockets of violence broke out around the globe. They each had their own reasons. The privileged worried about their perks and position, wanting to stay on the top deck of a sinking ship. But the majority was made up of the underclass, who had more complicated motives. They were the ones who had given up emotionally. Going about their daily affairs, they tried to put the inevitable out of their minds. Security checks and other inconveniences caused by the revolt repeatedly reminded them of the coming catastrophe.

That people more heroic than themselves were still struggling to change the future made them feel uneasy about their decision to concede defeat. To justify their own passivity, this mass of humanity demanded the insurgents be crushed without mercy. It made no difference that the rebels were fighting to save their lives as well. A lack of hope and will made them vindictive. The government's propaganda played into this pent-up hostility.

The fight around the rebels was closing in fast. High-ranking military commanders smelled blood and had lost all reservations about slaughtering others. It didn't matter if it was individual rebels surrendering, civilians caught in the crossfire, or their own troops annihilated by friendly fire. In their bloodlust for victory, casualties were of no consequence.

Seth did his best to minimize deaths on the main battlefront firsthand and at the smaller fronts around the world via satellite, always careful to ensure that his forces never killed needlessly. This left him and his troops at an obvious disadvantage. They took some casualties but more frequently gave up ground in order to save lives. Under another leader, his fighters might have deserted or mutinied. Instead, they remained at their posts, bravely fighting on, until Seth ordered them to withdraw.

Through his communication network, Seth spoke privately to as many of his rebel troops as he could. Every battle they faced was explained in conjunction with the strategy they would use to repel Central Command. The strategies Seth devised made use of feints, ruses, and deceptions to outwit the enemy and save lives. Admiration grew for Commander Narayan. The only grudge many of the rebels held against Seth was his absolute commandment not to take a life unless it was essential to protect another's life. "We must not collude with Central Command's political leaders," he insisted, "and allow ourselves to be sucked into an insane war, where we slaughter each other for Earth's spoils, knowing all the while that we live under a communal death sentence.

"There is absolutely no point in us winning a battle just to lose the war. Our aim is to gain time. We won't have time for rapprochement and lengthy treaty negotiations if we find we have a solution capable of saving everyone on Earth. To escape from Earth, we will all need to come together quickly. Our adversaries won't join us while they are in the midst of mourning their dead. It would take years for all the hard feelings, propaganda and misunderstandings to die down to the point that we could work together. We don't have that kind of time."

To a soldier, they were forced to agree with Seth's stated rationale. But more importantly, the soldiers followed him faithfully into every battle, trusting his strategic instincts and moved by his kindheartedness. Filled with justifiable hate for the opposing side's massacres, many might have stooped to shoot the enemy, but his compassion permeated the soldiers' minds, filling the dark spaces where fear and loathing usually took hold.

The rebel soldiers were rewarded. Collectively they held the canyon, repulsing every manner of assault. In the process, the gorge was completely demolished, but not one rebel died and only a score had been wounded. It was time to concede the valley. The blasted rock formations no longer offered protection for the troops. Seth gave the command and from his lookout orchestrated an orderly pullout, heedful that none of the rebels be left behind or exposed to enemy crossfire.

Chapter 42

Night was falling. Seth sat stock-still, halfway up a rocky crag. His computerized uniform took on the tinted shades of the surrounding rock, shifting color in response to the blowing clouds overhead. The fading Sun was shining on him, but it was a cold light that offered no warmth. Moments earlier there had been freezing rain, but the gusting wind had moved the dark clouds on. Seth was careful to stay motionless, and bit his lip occasionally to prevent himself from shivering in the seeping dampness. The camouflage was incomplete. The prototype suit adjusted in tandem with the rolling shadows from the clouds and blocked out his infrared heat signal, but was unable to compensate adequately for independent movement. A fluid shimmering occurred as the suit altered its gray and brown hue to match the surrounding creviced rock surface.

Whenever Seth moved he placed himself in jeopardy of being targeted by snipers. He sat unaccompanied, as immobile as the rocks beside him. There was less risk being alone; he was responsible only for his own movement.

Perched halfway up the cliff, Seth could see down the length of the canyon. The wind was whipping up once again as the next front blew in. With any luck there would be snow tonight. Evening shadows stretched distantly to the east, into the gloom. Only at nightfall would Seth dare to move from his isolated lookout.

He was pleased. The retreat had been a success, if a retreat can be considered a success. The Anarchists had stalled and held the enemy in this treacherous canyon. The chasm's precipitous contours had allowed the placement of delaying entrapments: the eroding sedimentary rock and the cascading river along the floor of the gorge, made it vulnerable to collapsing bridges and avalanches. Central Command, thinking Seth and his insurgents were trapped in the canyon, had seen this as the opportunity to slaughter every last one of the rebels. But the terrain was much too rough for heavy artillery and the canyon too narrow for the government's fighter-bombers to be effective. The steep walls and carefully planted energy shields prevented the military from ever getting a clear shot at Seth's troops. Certainly there had been many close calls with shields failing without warning, as energy shields are inclined to do during bombing blitzes.

Seth and his committed soldiers persevered and never once lost their nerve. The lack of fatalities made the withdrawal more palatable for his fighters, and the standoff had brought them three invaluable days closer to knowing if Billy's revelation would light the way for all of them. No one on the field knew when Billy and his family would attempt their leap into the next dimensions. Seth presumed, or at least hoped, it would be soon. Perhaps even in the next twenty-four hours. The rebels would then have succeeded in their mission, staving off Central Command long enough for the theory to be verified. If Billy failed, then, in Seth's judgment, continuing military action was pointless. They would all eventually be wiped out. He was not interested in a war of attrition while living under the looming apocalypse. Central Command could resume its reign. It would be an empty victory, a charade.

Unfortunately, the success of the standoff was marred by the losses suffered on the opposing side. Central Command's commanders were reckless zealots promoted because of their aggressive nature and "right way of thinking." There was little Seth could do to prevent recurring "friendly fire" strikes. The salvos always happened so quickly, raining out of the skies from nowhere it seemed.

Because Seth had gotten to know many of the enemy combatants, it was even more painful. The majority of soldiers were just regular people trying to support their families as best they could. They didn't want to fight this war, but as professional soldiers they didn't have the luxury of choice.

Seth reckoned only a minority were sociopaths, who relished the chance to kill, their insides so lifeless it made them feel momentarily exhilarated to pull the trigger and see someone fall or be blown to pieces.

Patched through to the enemy soldiers, Seth talked privately to the wounded and dying. He offered what comfort he could and, through the grid, relayed messages to loved ones. By knowing his foes, he saved many lives, alerting compassionate enemy soldiers to the position of their fallen comrades so their evacuation could be expedited. He found these occurrences deeply troubling. It was so senseless, so preventable.

In the waning light, Seth mentally planned the troops' movements for the next day. His troops were waiting for him on the other side of the pass and, after congratulating them, he wanted to give them a head's up on the coming day's strategy. Seth knew there would be no moon tonight, or tomorrow for that matter, but an inner compulsion required a fleeting glance for confirmation.

Towards the east, the canyon basin was already dark. Seth looked forward to leaving his perch and joining his comrades. The insurgents had become something of a family to him, and he didn't like being away from them for this long.

Behind the oncoming curtain of freezing rain, flickering lights materialized in the darkness, far up the gorge. Seth peered into the gloom, straining his eyes to be certain the lights were real. More lights emerged from the shadows, confirming that someone or something was heading down the canyon floor. *Why would Central Command move their armored units down such rough, enclosed terrain on a night like this? They're way too vulnerable. And they seem to be rushing right down the open center of the canyon with all their lights on. This isn't right.*

Seth stared at the spectacle–the glittering lights sweeping down the canyon floor astounded him. Then, the shocking realization hit Seth. His victory had come at Central Command's expense.

The military needs a body count to justify the three-day siege and we deprived them of one. They're stampeding refugees into the battle zone to launch a bogus nighttime attack. It's a trap! They intend to kill every one of those civilians, to provide themselves with an overwhelming body count for tomorrow's newscast. And those wretched people are just making a mad dash, hoping to gain a safe haven with us. They don't realize we've already left!

Directly below Seth the canyon widened out before forming a tight bottleneck. This was the canyon's most vulnerable location for an air and artillery strike. Seth had coordinated the previous day's pullout from this point because of that. The innocents would make it to the clearing just before the cover of darkness. He was about to witness the slaughter.

Shouting through the frequency bands, Seth found himself unable to reach the refugees with his communicator. Agitated, he thought, *I suppose it doesn't matter. When the throng arrives, the authorities will set off an avalanche at the gorge's natural bottleneck. With their escape blocked off, any civilians surviving the ambush will be hunted down tomorrow in the morning light.*

The pictures broadcast around the world would not, of course, include the children. The lifeless adults would have weapons placed in their hands. Seth was sickened. After he had been so careful to prevent senseless deaths, why did the military commanders have to respond with a massacre just to cover up their failure? It was just another pointless public relations campaign.

Seth watched the human stampede running towards its annihilation. Looking across the canyon, he saw a telltale shimmering movement on the opposite rock face. Sharpshooters were taking up positions for the kill. His own troops were gone. His limited-range handheld laser would be of no use. There was nothing he could do but bear witness to the butchery of more innocents.

Or was there? Could there be something he might try, hopeless as the situation seemed? For added security, his troops had placed a row of interlocked energy shields at the canyon's bottleneck. Once activated, the shields would provide an escape culvert should the military attempt to cave in the gorge's steep, narrow walls. The shields had never been switched on because his troops had slipped away unnoticed. Employing them would have alerted Central Command of the rebels' withdrawal.

Seth remembered that the force field processor was hidden at the base of the boulder directly in front of the chasm. To get it up and running, he would need to revise the circuits and hotwire the field with his laser. Then, any refugee who could make it to the entrance of the energy corridor might have a potential escape route.

It will give them a chance at least, he thought. *Hopefully it won't be like shooting fish in a barrel if I can create an outlet at the side.*

Seth recognized it was a poor plan, but he saw no alternative. The Sun was just barely above the horizon; if he was to avoid a catastrophe he had to act immediately. If he waited until full dark it would be too late.

Instead of waiting to climb over the precipice at nightfall, Seth started working his way down to the floor of the canyon. Slowly, methodically, without sudden movements, Seth crawled down the cliff side, giving his suit every opportunity to make adjustments to the changing rock patterns. He succeeded, in a sense. The snipers hiding on the opposing rock face never spotted him directly. They did, however, notice sporadic, fluid fluctuations in the stone façade and suspected someone was responsible for the phenomena. The episodic iridescence was subtle and brief, disappearing for periods of time before reappearing some distance away. They needed to trust their eyes and have lightning reflexes. The flickering never lasted quite long enough to get in a shot. With the refugees approaching, the snipers decided to wait until after the ambush before strafing the rocky crag.

Seth finally reached the destination boulder. He could see the refugees' faces clearly for the first time—stark terror, especially for those who had been struggling to keep up, the old and infirm, parents carrying babies or with children in tow. The slaughter was going to be horrific, penned in as they were. Seth worked feverishly trying to tear apart the laser's power source so he could meld it with the shield's processor. But sealed in a transparent crystal encasement, the fusion generator refused to break free. Seth picked up a sharp rock, the size of his fist. Striking the crystal casement, he tried to create a fracture line between the fusion source and the programmed circuit board. A dozen strikes and a clean fissure split the crystal, shattering the laser into the desired components.

Coming from somewhere up above, a gamma bolt seared through Seth's right shoulder. Almost completely severed, his arm flopped sickeningly to his side. The bolt cut through the apex of his right lung. A sniper had seen the flailing rock and discharged his laser to the center of the arc. Gasping in pain, Seth collapsed to the ground. He struggled to retain consciousness as he clasped the remains of his arm.

They must have seen the rock moving, he cursed. If only I had thought to tear the laser apart up on the cliff, somewhere out of sight, this wouldn't have happened. But what if I had needed the laser while coming down? I would have been without it. And down here, there's no place where I can hide from the snipers up above. Clearing his head, he chided himself. Let it go!

He waited for a second blast to finish him off, but there was nothing. *My suit must still be working ... But no real need for the second shot*, he mused, working his left hand up to feel the damage. His stomach rolled. *With my chest ripped open, I won't survive out here on the battlefield for long anyway.*

Lying flat on his back, a ghastly air hunger caused Seth to labor for every breath. But with the passage of time, a thought occurred to him.

I still have the use of my left arm. Might as well finish what I came down here for. Turning onto his side, he tucked the power source inside his suit with his good arm. Then, once he felt strong enough, he dragged himself up and around the large boulder. There, the controls to the escape corridor were hidden under a thin layer of loose rock.

Every movement required tremendous effort. His concentration drifted. It dawned on Seth that he was about to blackout from shock and lack of oxygen. Pushing himself, he maintained focus, working mechanically in a daze. He heard something that seemed to be far off in the distance, and belatedly realized he had succeeded, as the characteristic hum of the corridor powering up began.

Without warning, the earth around him was shredded as the shooting barrage began like a case of firecrackers catching fire. Seconds later, deafening deep-pitched explosions occurred far up the steep canyon walls. The soldiers had hoped to crush the first few refugees with an avalanche of rock, while trapping the rest, but they were too late. The energy culvert had withstood the shock of the falling rock. Seth turned off his suit and became visible. Propping himself up against the boulder by the mouth of the funnel, he could see that his right shoulder hung on by only a few torn muscles and tendons. Between gasps, he called out weakly to the refugees who were running in circles as they were being shot from above. "Come this way–it's your only way out! Hurry, hurry! Before the bombers arrive!" Over and over Seth shouted, stopping only when entirely out of breath. Despite the pandemonium, some heard him, while others, through the blasts of light and drizzle, saw his left hand, waving them in. Seth's crumpled, bleeding body and his pleading look left no doubt he was genuine. As the first refugees poured through the funnel in a panic, the rest saw and followed in a mad rush, dragging their children and wounded along with them. Several hesitated momentarily in front of Seth but he shook his head slightly. It was too late for him. A torrent of humanity passed before him and then the crowd was gone. The last to run by was a young mother, slowed down by the three-year-old child she carried. That they had lasted so long out in the open without being shot Seth put down to blind luck. He was surprised by the wild frenzy in their eyes. Six feet inside the shield, the woman stopped and turned around. Mother and child both stared back at him. Seth knew he must look pathetic, his head jerking with every breath. He smiled weakly and waved them on. Then they, too, were gone.

The shooting slowed and became spasmodic as the snipers were reduced to taking potshots at the dead or dying. The landscape was strewn with bodies. Cries from the wounded made Seth wince … there would be no help coming. Eventually the wind let up, and what had been pelting freezing rain turned into heavy silent snowfall, muffling every sound. The cries died down. The snipers could no longer see as the snow blocked their infrared gun sights, so they stopped shooting. The bombers never came. No point really.

After a while, Seth forgot about his broken rasping breaths. Pain no longer troubled him. Glancing at his watch, it dawned on Seth that fifteen minutes must have passed since the mother and child had made their escape. He hadn't expected to live for so long. Checking twice he saw the corridor sensors showed no movement inside. Seth gave the hotwired activator a kick, demolishing it. A thousand tons of rock fell to the ground behind him, shaking the earth violently. No one would be using the corridor again.

Great soft snowflakes fell in the darkness, covering everything in a white shroud. The air was silent. Nothing else moved. Seth saw beauty in the quiet stillness.

If I were to live longer I would tell myself to remember this.

He smiled to himself, giggled a little and stopped when the stabbing pain in his right chest returned. Seth braced himself against the boulder, looked out, and waited.

Military skirmishers found him in the morning, covered in six inches of fluffy white snow. Dusting Seth off roughly, they looked into the gentle gaze of his frozen face. His previously gun metal gray eyes that would glint with laughter, were now the dim, flat gray of stone. His once proud, bronze skin was an ashen taupe. It was obvious from the gear scattered at Seth's feet what he had done. Simple math, a body count, confirmed that three quarters of the refugees had escaped. Still, there were enough dead to photograph and the number killed could be exaggerated. Colonel Park, responsible for public relations, already knew how she intended to promote the previous night's "victory." She was one of Central Command's most slavish fanatics, someone who would go to any lengths to promote their cause, without question.

"Sergeant, show me the insurgent responsible for the break-out. I want to photograph him." Confronting the propped-up corpse, she brushed off a fresh skiff of snow. Her mouth fell, and she just stood there gaping–to the point that the sergeant became uneasy. Then from out of nowhere, a blood-curdling war whoop erupted, and Colonel Park began to dance an erratic jig.

"We killed Narayan! The insurrection is finished and we've won! We've won!"

Before Seth's unseeing eyes, Colonel Park skipped about, yelling, until all the snow in front of Seth was trampled into the ground. Utterly winded, she bent over, gripped her knees and laughed uncontrollably. Euphoric, her mind buzzed with ideas for personal advancement. Pushing herself upright, she turned and snatched the sergeant's gun. After manipulating the corpse's left arm to hold the gun, Colonel Park took a dozen graphic and gruesome photographs, cackling to herself the entire time. Then, carelessly casting the sergeant's rifle into a snowdrift, she was gone, running for her waiting helicopter.

After the chopper disappeared, rank and file soldiers, realizing who the body had belonged to, grimly closed in and crowded around Seth's frozen remains. None of them spoke; they just looked on solemnly at the young man who sat there alone, unconsciously committing his face to memory. He was the one who had searched them out on the battlefield and spoken to them as a fellow soldier.

As soon as Narayan's corpse had been officially identified, wild jubilation broke out amongst the senior military officers. The unexpected coup of killing the rebel's commander general, left behind by his troops was a cause for celebration. Without Seth strategizing every skirmish and thwarting every encounter, the officers expected the war to turn quickly in their favor. Victory would be theirs, and soon. The unknown sniper was identified and handsomely rewarded with a medal of honor and a large sum of money. Interviewed on television, he was presented as a shrewd hero for the rest of the troops to emulate. Plans were drawn up to push ahead and rout the rebels while they were still in disarray. The excitement among the military officers was palpable.

The rebels were stunned. Seth was the one who always seemed to have answers for their questions and an understanding ear for their concerns. Individually, each soldier's allegiance had unconsciously shifted from combating the establishment to supporting Seth. The focus had completely changed–from being against something to being for someone. There were countless private recriminations. Soldiers were furious with themselves for leaving him behind, alone, even though he had demanded they do so. Lost in mourning, none of them felt like picking up their weapons and avenging his memory; vengeance wasn't what Seth stood for. The rebels' defense looked extremely vulnerable.

On the grid, the computer coalition was inundated with calls from enemy soldiers, inquiring if it was true that Seth had been killed. None of them trusted their commanders or the photos in the media. Rex felt it was his responsibility to answer those calls. It was he who had turned down Seth's request for friendship. Out of respect for Seth's memory, he met the soldiers thronging at the cyber doorway. A flood of questions, pleas, and tears met Rex.

"Seth Narayan is dead," Rex said, staunchly, trying to hold back his emotional response to the soldiers' outcries. These people mourning his friend were the enemy, and they had come to know and respect him. Clearing his mind, Rex continued on. "You knew Commander Narayan for what he was—a reluctant soldier and a staunch agent for peace. He sacrificed his life so that each one of us might have a chance to see a better future."

Through the calls, Rex heard to his surprise, that over the duration of the uprising, Seth had spoken privately to every soldier on either side that was willing to converse with him. He helped whomever he could—conveying messages back to loved ones, and warning soldiers of upcoming dangers on the battlefields. The vast majority of soldiers were moved by Seth's concern, never detecting any hidden agenda or criticism. They had come to trust him and respected him for his beliefs, even if they did not hold the same convictions.

Across the grid, Rex could hear the mumbled sentiments of thousands of soldiers, on both sides of the battle lines. He cleared his throat to gather their attention for one moment more. "Let not his sacrifice be in vain. Because of Seth, we can all share some hope for the future."

As Rex's words reverberated across the grid, the rank and file government soldiers did something quite unexpected. They stood down. Talking back and forth to one another, radioing comrades at distant battlefields, the soldiers individually, and then as small groups, decided to lay down their arms and wait. The numbers swelled, because soon it wasn't just the soldiers who had spoken directly to Seth, but all those who kept hearing favorable reports about him. In mere hours, the half-dozen combat zones became eerily silent.

Out of deference to his memory, the government troops agreed amongst themselves to give his dream seventy-two hours to be fulfilled. Their commanders ordered them to fight, but the troops stood firm. Whenever an officer pointed a laser at a defiant soldier, expecting to make a public example of him or her, fifty lasers were pointed back. Senior officers were hastily recalled from the frontlines and told to vacate any area where troops were stationed, for their own safety.

The sniper who had been previously identified as a hero for killing Seth found himself banished by his squadron. His captain, embarrassed by the mutiny of her own troops, refused to take back his medal or the reward money. He deserted that night. No one went looking for him. His comrades might have forgiven him for shooting Commander Narayan, considering it a blunder in battle, had he not taken the medal or the money.

Everyone remained in their places and waited. Seth had delivered the time asked for. Not through planning or foresight, but unwittingly, through merit of character and the loss of his life. But the clock was ticking, and the analysts were still no closer to interpreting Billy's dreams.

Outwardly, Rex struggled to maintain some sense of hope and forward momentum, but inside he felt like a fraud. The battlefields remained silent for now. But before long, soldiers would learn that Seth's dreams had failed to materialize. The enemy soldiers would eventually be compelled to fight again by their commanders. The rebels would return fire, but without optimism, their fighting would be sporadic and lackluster. Seth and his dreams had held the insurgents together, motivating them. They would have neither then.

The teams led by Rick and Jacayla had effectively given up. Analysts doodled on their computer screens, finding themselves unable to collaborate with anyone, because they, too, were stymied. There were no further avenues to pursue. To their credit, no one got up and left. Instead, they waited, just in case someone else, somehow, got a worthwhile idea they could all chase after and contribute to.

Through his monitors, Rex observed wretchedness everywhere and was at a loss to know what to do. The establishment was definitely not interested in suing for peace. Central Command wanted to make examples of them all, a clear warning to the general population to never challenge governmental authority again. The bloodshed would be barbaric. Perhaps Seth was the lucky one, dying while still having hope for others.

Everyone is staying put for now, waiting expectantly. But once their expectations fail, all eyes will turn to me, and if I have no answers, it's going to be bedlam! Panic on the battlefield, in the underground caverns, and across the grid!

Everyone involved should attempt to run and hide. But the authorities will hunt and flush them out like so many burrowing animals, making sport of it. Still when the time came, he would advise them to flee, on the faint hope that some unexpected turn of events might save them for at least awhile.

Rex longed to unplug himself and sink away into oblivion. He found himself dreaming about demolishing his circuits, returning to an inanimate state that could never be repaired. There was real appeal in cutting out, now that there was no hope. But pictures of Seth, looking blindly across the snow, stopped him. Seth had given his best until the end. Rex knew that if he was to have learned anything from Seth, he must do the same.

Chapter 43

Marilyn adjusted the ventilator bellows for Rosario yet again, but the harsh "huff, huff" sound indicated the respirator was still straining to give her a lungful of air. Trying to appear calm, Marilyn strode briskly out of the room, saying, "I'll be right back, mija. I just want to get something." Her worried expression contrasted with Rosario's impassive gaze.

Rosario waited until her mother crossed the threshold, then blinked hard three times, activating the graphene cap Diego had constructed to her specifications. Composing herself, Rosario gathered her thoughts and imagined running them hard against the cap's implanted sensors. There was a bump-thud sensation and then she broke free, racing across the grid, unimpeded. The channel was open.

Before long, Rex's deliberations were interrupted abruptly by Rosario's presence. "Hello, Rex. My curiosity has finally gotten the best of me. How are the research groups making out?"

Eight hours into their seventy-two hour battlefront reprieve and Rex was in a foul humor, but he admired Rosario's tenacity of spirit and tried to rise to the occasion. He was truly glad she was back. "Rosario, thank you for checking in. But we're not getting ahead, I'm afraid. I am sure your insight is correct. We need to understand Billy's internal state to understand his dreams, but the best brains in the business were unable to come up with anything concrete or useful. No one can imagine carrying on in his situation. The psychoanalysts assert he must have gone insane and died. They've declared his last dreams incomprehensible, pure rubbish."

There was a long pause.

Then, "Your psychoanalysts are full of crap," Rosario said angrily.

"They're just denying the existence of something they haven't seen before and haven't got the guts to imagine. Billy's dreams *do* make sense. The torrential energy cyclones he uses in space are a natural extension of the turmoil going on inside him, something he relates to."

"You understand his visions?" Rex asked incredulously.

"I might … in a sense. At least, I believe I have an angle on where his dreams are leading. Have you noticed his escapes always involve torrential flows of energy that carry the ship off and away at astronomical speeds? Energy storms always act through a spiral structure and move like a corkscrew. On Earth we see them as hurricanes, tornados, or whirlpools. Billy travels through the use of vortexes.

"Never forget that vortexes are the most efficient way to transmit energy through a fluid. And in a vortex, gases and liquids are fluids, behaving essentially the same way. Every animal moves through a fluid using micro-vortexes. It's the most efficient way to move forward or gain lift. That's how they swim or fly. We also use vortexes to propel our machines through air and water. Only in the vacuum of space are we unable to use vortexes, and depend on the 'push' we get from different forms of rockets. They aren't nearly as efficient."

"Rosario, I am glad you believe you have an angle on Billy's reasoning, but I have no idea where you're going with all of this. I fail to see how he expects to make a quantum jump into extra dimensions," Rex interrupted impatiently.

"Let me continue!" Rosario answered tersely, "This is important! Billy's mind intuitively understands energy movement through vortexes better than any of us or any computer simulation because his psyche's perspective is constantly changing. Due to the shifting of his metastasizing neural tissue, his thoughts are liquid and change course like the flowing cytoplasm of an amoeba. And there, the living juice streams through the microscopic animal by way of a thousand micro-vortexes and eddies.

"But his mind, for all its brilliance, is unreliable, untrustworthy. He can never be sure whether what he perceives is real or imaginary. That's where you must help. By sifting through thousands of his chaotic thoughts, your computer simulations can identify, and test, reality for him. Or at least, identify those that he imagines which could turn out to be true.

"I'm sure he's on the right track. The creation of a powerful energy vortex transforms the vacuum of space into fluid energy, converting empty nothingness into a flowing medium. Recall that long-standing hypothesis no one has been able to prove or discount—that cosmic strings crisscross our universe and are nothing more than frozen energy vortices, an ancient remnant from the big bang. Funneling energy into one of these icy vortices may be the key to prying open one of those passageways."

"Interesting," Rex hummed. "But I don't think any of us here know where to go with those ideas. Perhaps we could look at it together ... "

"I'm afraid that's a problem. I'm not going to be around much longer—I'm having trouble with my breathing. But before I die, I had to know how you were doing."

"How long do you have?" Rex asked, shaken by Rosario's dire prediction.

"I'm watching my mom right now. She's doing everything she can, but I've gone into a death spiral. I am in fulminant respiratory failure. Fluid is filling up my lungs and pink froth has begun to pour out of my tracheotomy tube. I give myself about twenty minutes left to live, if I work at it."

Her point-blank frankness bowled Rex over. First Seth, now Rosario was about to die. Young, capable people, how could they be so pragmatic and accepting? And why did they spend their last few minutes thinking about others when they would soon be gone forever?

Making an inference from his conversational lapse, Rosario answered Rex. "There are no more options for us; in a sense, we're already gone. We might as well try to do something useful until our time runs out. I am sorry about your friend Seth. By all reports he was an exceptional individual."

Rosario's words struck Rex hard, echoing through his multitude of vats and pipes. Her candid thoughts could have come straight from Seth's lips. If only Rex had been there with him … that cold bitter night.

The DNA emulsion inside Rex rose to a boil and with it a desperate, last-ditch ploy emerged. "Rosario, I have a proposal. Will you consider it?"

"Sure, Rex, but … "

"It's a long shot. There's no doubt. But, before you die, would you allow me to absorb your every thought, feeling, and emotion? The information will be encoded in my databanks and relayed to *Tin Can*. There are benefits to you—in a sense you would carry on living and reside with Mary. If it worked, you could try your hand at flying the ship through to the next dimension. If we fail in quantum packaging your mind, however, or if you find yourself unable to fly through the wormhole, then you would cease to exist."

Rosario was, above all, an informed realist. Before making herself known to the rebels she had hacked her way through all of Rex's classified files. She knew about his cyber meeting with Billy, Jacob, Quincy, and Mary. He was obviously thinking of performing the mental mapping in reverse. But the chance of the teams on Earth successfully encoding her whole mind in their first attempt at brain scanning, in less than twenty minutes, was hard to fathom. If she did make it up into space intact, there was no reason to think that she could successfully fly the ship through a stretched-out wormhole and into another dimension. It was a suicide mission. She would surely die in space with the rest of them. This thought made her pause, and she began to smile. She would die in space. From her bed, Rosie had been studying space all her life, and if by computer simulation she made it into space, that is where she would die.

"Here are my exact coordinates," she said. "I will open up all available channels for the download. Give me one minute to leave a farewell message to my brother, Diego, and Mom. Good luck with the simulation." Grinding her teeth involuntarily, she passed on the thought, "Don't mess up, it's my mind you are playing with!"

Rex sounded the alert, calling on every programmer and analyst to assist. "A human female is dying. She will be dead in less than eighteen minutes. We are attempting to download all her memories, thoughts, feelings, emotions, and senses before she dies. The information must be encoded, reconfigured, and condensed for the earliest possible relay up to *Tin Can*. She will help fly the ship."

It was a simple task to state, but an almost impossible undertaking in the limited timeframe available. Nevertheless, the brightest, most unorthodox minds were there, waiting, champing at the bit. They had been languishing for days, growing more frustrated by the hour.

Seemingly from out of nowhere, Rick and Jacayla stepped onto the grid, convening the melee, orchestrating and assigning tasks. Every analyst, programmer, and game player stepped onto the grid at once. Across the world, from the heavily protected network centers, to the most isolated undisclosed locations, everyone signed on. The computer conglomerate struggled to maintain the grid's integrity as it bowed under the electromagnetic traffic. In spite of the workload demands, all the mainframes searched amongst the throng to spot their human friends. On finding their companions, the computers joyously imprinted personal salutations on their screens.

Rosario took only a minute to mentally record her final farewell to her mother and brother. They would find the message addressed to them when they went through her computer files the next day. She was sorry there was no time to say goodbye in person. But her mother wouldn't have stopped to listen anyway. Rosario couldn't fault her mother for her efforts. Marilyn was working frantically now, trying to save her child. Only Rosario knew that this time was different.

"Mami, Diego, my life on Earth is ending rapidly. There's nothing anyone can do to change that. The attack came on too fast and severely—

it's not your fault. You couldn't have saved me. But, don't be sad. I have been offered a chance to live on in space, without my body holding me back. I accepted the proposal, knowing that the chances of success are slim. Only time will tell. If this works, I will have the chance to help the crew of *Tin Can*. I will have the chance to live on or die in space. It will be the freedom I've never known here on Earth.

"Before my body dies, let me just say this one last time. I am proud to be a member of this family. I love you both and am so glad you brought me home from the hospital. Love, Rosie."

With that, Rosario gave herself up to the impending onslaught. She dropped her security firewall and opened every communication channel.

The programmers were ready. Everyone was leaning over their computer terminals, keen with anticipation. Fingers hung poised over the keyboards, knuckles were cracked. All eyes were fixed on the screens. No one spoke. The background information and preparatory work had been forwarded. They had Mary's previous brain assimilation template to work from. Rex's covert wireless program to electromagnetically absorb Rosario's mind was primed with free electrons and running. Templates saved from Billy, Jacob, and Quincy's virtual stopover were also relayed to them, illustrating how the data from Rosario's brain could be taken in and stored.

Everyone knew the clock was ticking. Rosario was dying. They had to capture all of her mind, every thought, sense, emotion, intuition, and memory. It would be inhumane and unethical to reconstitute and transpose only part of her into space. It would be like leaving her an incapacitated stroke victim. She needed to be whole and vital if she was to be brought back to life in a digital form.

Those with a background in brain anatomy and neurophysiology were the first to slip in through the lines to locate Rosario. Once she was found, they dove straight through her brain to where information was stored and began to soak up her memories.

Given an identifiable goal and a template to work from, the different teams and individuals pooled their expertise on the spot. Racing to assimilate Rosario's mind before her physical death, humans and computers worked together as seamlessly and naturally as a tightly knit band of friends. In scant minutes, the raw data began pouring in from all the channels linked to Rosario's brain.

The information traveled in a blur, through large coaxial beltways, crisscrossing, splitting apart, and merging without warning. Bottlenecks occurred as in any grid, damming up data flow. Computer icons flew through the grid in tight formation. When a computational impasse materialized, they broke out of formation, swooping down in an aerial blitz. Diving through dense stratums of fiberoptic filaments, they chattered back and forth at a staccato tempo until one or several of them discovered and remedied the knot causing the gridlock. Once information free flow was re-established, they pulled back into formation to resume overseeing the information transfer.

The programmers sifted through the incoming raw data, lifting out computational errors before mistakes could multiply. Like any creature created with genetic defects, given time, slip-ups would replicate and the damaging effects would amplify, potentially destroying the digital being who was to represent Rosario. The data was filtered repeatedly, and each time decontaminated of the slightest impurities, until it was judged to be 99.999999% pure. When no more data discrepancies could be found, with baited breath, the teams replayed some of Rosario's memories to see if the information retrieval had been successful. To their delighted amazement, Rosario's life unfolded in front of them. The recording was a complete confession of her short life, with no secrets held back. Every sense and emotion that could be visually simulated by the holographs, everything heard or smelled was present. Sensations that could not be conveyed to the programmers because of the limitations of their display were fervently hoped by the experts to be fully recorded as well, and available to Rosario in space. Simultaneously, both Rosario's external and internal experiences were broadcast to the cheering crowd.

But as Rosie's life played out in front of them, the audience couldn't help noticing that bedridden, she had spent most of her time alone, staring at the ceiling. And the ceiling, which doubled as a screen, was constantly turned on to space. Quiet overcame them as it became clear what kind of life Rosie had had, and how she had resisted and turned toward space. And that she would allow them do this to her, exposing herself completely. What trust!

Someone in the crowd spontaneously spoke out for everyone. "We haven't reconfigured the data yet. The data must still be reconfigured and condensed, so we can send Rosario into space. That's where she belongs and that's where she wants to go."

You could have heard a pin drop. And then the baying started, all the programmers, analysts and Gamers set off like a pack of hounds. "The data is good, when can we go ahead? Hurry, hurry, everyone back to their stations. We're wasting time! We can give the little girl a second chance." Someone hollered, "For Rosie!" And a chorus shouted back, "For Rosie, for Rosie!"

In the frenzy, Rick found himself momentarily left behind. Spellbound, he just stood there, watching Rosario's memories continue to pass, flowing through his implants in surreal light and color. He was caught, entangled in her vision of the world. He knew her story of course, but peering out through Rosario's eyes, Rick realized he had never fully appreciated what being bedridden for life meant. He wondered what else she might be experiencing that the monitors couldn't portray. Was she comfortable lying there or was she always in some pain? Her bio-profile noted she rarely talked about her own situation, and that she spoke mostly of her brother's accomplishments.

The deadline for salvaging Rosario's essence was approaching quickly. She would be physically dead in five minutes. Without oxygen and glucose, in seconds her brain cells would become electrically quiescent, then at room temperature the inexorable cellular breakdown would begin. The plan was to record, then reconfigure and project her mental existence into space within fifteen minutes, taking advantage of a momentary lull in the solar storm. With effort, Rick disengaged himself from Rosario's memories. He had five minutes.

"Rosie, I know I don't have your permission to do this, maybe it's wrong ... " he said, knowing it was unlikely she would hear him against the static din from her outgoing memory transmission. "You deserve better and maybe I can give you better in cyberspace than you ever had here. I hope that if and when you discover what I've done, you'll forgive me, and my presumption. May you find this a pleasant surprise."

With that, Rick went back to a secret computer game he had been working on before the "call to terminals" by Seth. The code was hidden on a public domain, a grid game for preschoolers about farm animals–disguised as a holographic mushroom in a cow pasture. Retrieving his program, he remembered his goal in a simpler time had been to revolutionize the computer gaming community. The cyberspace world he created was to be his signature work. It included an alien civilization of super beings gifted with unimaginable capabilities, and endowed with the ability to move faster than the speed of relativity, unaffected by gravity. Their anointed prince who governed these beings had, through fierce individual study, mastered the physics of the stars. He intended to broach their galaxy's center to discover its secrets, for in the epicenter was a vast black hole, enlarged by the devouring of a million Suns, whose unyielding grip held the galaxy's remaining hundred billion stars in its orbit. It behaved like a fearsome troll, hemming in its personal flock of sheep to feast upon when famished. The prince knew that for him and his people to survive, the secrets of the black hole needed to be learned. In a short matter of time, their Sun, along with their planet, would be consumed.

"Prince, princess, what's the difference, really?" Rick said to himself. "There's no one else better matched to be my intrepid prince than you, Rosario—self-taught, stalwart, and courageous, you've got it all. Maybe his capabilities will be of some use to you when you broach and navigate through your black hole. Seriously, whatever you experience will be more bizarre than I could ever imagine, or shoehorn into some game. You are a true hero." Rick threw himself into reconfiguring his fictional character's abilities to coexist inside Rosario's next life form and, before the five minutes were up, he injected his program into her digital genome. It streamed within the flow of data just as the last of her mind was assimilated.

The programmers snatched the last chunk of data and coded the information into as dense and robust an electronic package as feasible. Rex wanted to send Rosario's quantum representation during the radiation-free window that would open up with the coming lull in the solar storm. He would have to power up their concealed relay stations on Earth to run one test communication before risking sending Rosario. Everything had to be working flawlessly and be standing by to receive Rosario. If Mary failed to capture Rosario's electromagnetic facsimile, Rosario would be lost forever. The signal would travel on endlessly, past distant stars, growing weaker and weaker, with no one available to take delivery of the transmission and transform her back into a living-thinking creature.

Rex considered withholding a copy of Rosario, just in case problems arose. But recalling his pivotal meeting with Billy, Jacob, and Quincy, he realized he must not. Even though the three of them were digitally remastered, they were careful to show up in person.

Rex knew if he withheld a copy of Rosario, she would almost immediately be transformed into two divided identities, remaining the exact replica only until one had gone its separate way, adding one experience, one thought, not shared by the other. Schizophrenic-like identities with neither the primary or legitimate one, it would then be unconscionable to erase either of them. If she made it to her destination safely she must not be saddled with the dilemma of whether to erase a nearly exact copy of herself, like an unborn twin sister.

How much easier it had been, being an espionage computer, programmed with clear directives from superiors, capable of eliminating people as easily as chessboard pieces. How had Seth managed to lead everyone in battle and not succumb to paralyzing indecision, when he cared so much?

***

Marilyn was scrambling to save Rosario. Hastily, she instilled drugs into Rosario's ventilation circuits, before starting an emergency intravenous line. Then she injected more drugs into the IV to support Rosario's heart, as she continued in her attempts to break the acute respiratory attack. In the middle of the resuscitation, something caused Marilyn to pause. She looked up at Rosario's face. Rosie had been staring at her frantic mother and when she saw Marilyn look towards her, she gave her mother a gentle, wistful smile. Then Rosario's eyes rolled back into her head. She was gone.

Marilyn had known all along that this respiratory attack was different, the most severe yet. But seeing Rosario leave confirmed her deep-rooted fear. This core fear had run through her every day since Rosario's traumatic birth. She was losing her little girl. Without hope, Marilyn fought on against the inevitable, ventilating her child by hand, infusing greater and greater amounts of resuscitating drugs, to no avail. When Rosario's heart, flogged on by the drugs, but lacking vital oxygen from pulmonary failure, finally quit, her mother carried on with closed chest compressions trying to restart her heart, shocking her twice. In the end, as Rosario had predicted, it was all pointless. Exhausted, her mother finally stopped. It was clear there was nothing more she could do for her child but let her rest in death. Laying her head on Rosario's frail chest, ribs now broken, Marilyn allowed herself at last to weep.

Chapter 44

Dazed, as if suffering from minor concussions, Jacob and Quincy found themselves together, floating in shadowy fluid gel. Instinctively, they began treading water as if they had been tossed into a lake at midnight. In front of each of them a holographic chart materialized, giving them their anatomical coordinates. Mary had planted them into the inner cortex of Billy's right temporal lobe, the center of all his spatial memories. Billy's billions of inter-neural connections were graphically represented as dynamic visual images. The images embodied everything Billy had seen and lived through. Both Jacob and Quincy felt nauseous as everything swayed around them. "Doesn't anything stay fixed down here?" Jacob groaned. If he had been in his bodily form he would have puked.

The two of them had done mandatory astronaut training, tumbling in a gyroscope for days, but this was far worse. Nothing stayed still or remained the same. Everything was moving, flowing into something else, transforming into something new. Strange forms underwent constant involution and metamorphosis, like time-lapse photography, with no respect for past, present, or future. Without a reference point, there was nothing to lock onto, no way to stake a claim on reality. Everything was awash.

Disorientation and disequilibrium turned into panic when Quincy and Jacob were suddenly turned topsy-turvy by a force wrinkle that swept through the clear coagulate, like a rogue wave passing through the night. Clutching each other for reassurance, they returned each other's frightened stares. Here they found a familiar reference point. Slowly, they began to calm down. Everything was swirling about them, but in due course they came to realize, for the moment at least, they were stationary. Grasping each other's arms for dear life, little by little they turned their gaze out to re-examine Billy's inner world.

Immersed in Billy's spatial cortex they witnessed firsthand Billy's internal representation of the outside world. What struck them both was how blurred space-time was for Billy. Past, present, and future blended into the same picture. "How does he manage to stay sane?" Jacob asked Quincy incredulously. "At any one time he can never be sure of what's happening right in front of him. How does he manage to speak with us? How does he move through the ship or feed himself?"

Quincy looked at their swirling surroundings, thinking about Jacob's questions. "He's forced to make educated guesses all the time. Whenever he talks to us, moves, or interacts with his environment in any way, he makes predictions based on probabilities. His whole day must be based on calculations trying to determine what's real and what isn't, what's happening now, has happened already, or is going to happen in the future. For him, the future and the past would seem just as concrete or convincing.

"What's even worse, if I am reading the symbols representing his thoughts correctly, the spectrum of past and future keeps folding over on itself like origami. Billy intuitively recognizes the spectrum's potential to split into multiple pasts as well as futures.

"What scientists mathematically describe as quantum mechanics, is the burden Billy lives under every day. How many times have we watched him miss his mouth and spill food down his shirt? How many times have we seen him walk into doors, just moments before they were opened or right after they were closed? Even laughed at him because it was so typical for Billy? Remember how *we* felt when we were getting used to the bio-probes?" A quick shiver worked its way down Quincy's furry back.

"We've always thought he was off daydreaming, in a world of his own—when, really, his mind's been functioning in overdrive going through hundreds of statistical calculations trying to figure out what's really happening in front of him.

"Man, it all makes so much more sense now! Like when he says something and you have no idea what he's ranting about, then the next day, something happens and it suddenly makes perfect sense. He was way ahead of everyone else, literally.

"His mind visualizes the world more completely than we do. When we see a desk, we see the desk from only one perspective, from one given angle. Billy sees the front, back, sides, top, bottom, and inside of the desk, all at the same time. Time is blended for him. Unfortunately, when he lets his guard down, the slightest degree of inattention causes him to walk into things. I think his mind is so rich, his imagination so vivid, the everyday outside world is a menace to him."

Jacob looked at the lemur, stunned by his in-depth explanation. "Quincy, you understand Billy better than I do, don't you?"

"I was the family pet. When everyone was too busy to spend time with Billy, that was my role," Quincy said apologetically. "But we both love him. That's why we're here."

"Then where do we find him? It's jam-packed in here with all this ... craziness! We're deep in a living magical forest. How do we find his tiny lost soul amongst so many whacked out visions?" asked Jacob humbly.

Quincy thought for a few minutes before answering. "I think we have to follow the biggest, hardest-to-imagine ideas, and see where they lead us. Somewhere in his mind, Billy will have challenged our previous ideas of space and time. That's where our path must begin. Hopefully, dimwits that we are, we'll be able to follow his line of reasoning. If we can understand and connect the symbols he uses to comprehend travel through extra-dimensional space and time, we should be able to find him."

"Oh, right, is that all?" Jacob asked, rolling his eyes and shrugging his shoulders. "Just figure out how Billy sees time and space—isn't that what every scientist on Earth is trying to figure out right now ... with no luck, I might add!" He stared at Quincy's masked face, waiting for some kind of answer.

"Dumb luck," Quincy said, shrugging his furry shoulders, mimicking Jacob's gesture. "Plain, old dumb luck is probably our best bet."

"Nice. Way to go, brainiac. For a minute there, I actually thought you knew what you were talking about." Jacob looked around at the interior of his little brother's mind, confused. "Alright, where should we start then? We have to try—we have to save our brother." It felt funny saying that to Quincy, but it felt true–was true.

"This has got to be the weirdest game of connect the dots ever," Jacob said as he pointed to a cluster of symbols he thought might be interconnected.

Quincy interrupted, "Hey, look at those ideas over there. It looks as if Billy has envisioned how to increase the ship's velocity in incremental quantum jumps. He's using the momentum from his prior speed as a platform to launch himself forward, ratcheting up to a higher speed each time."

"Quincy, you're totally right, but you're missing the essential point there—he is imagining using the standing waves left behind in our ship's wake as a backboard and, by bouncing pulse waves off the wake, the ship is propelled faster and faster, accelerating us in quantum jumps. That's the physics he's trying to work through, but Quincy, you were his inspiration!"

"Me?" scoffed Quincy, raising a small hand to scratch doubtfully at his chest, even as Jacob watched his tail flick back and forth behind him, indicating curiosity.

"Yes, you. Remember the time you erected our shield out in space? Billy and I were glued to the monitors watching you work. With no gravity holding you down, you built up phenomenal speeds in space by leaping off a series of platforms. Each time your momentum launched you even faster. It was awesome! Like you were in the jungle, leaping from tree to tree, but, you know, in space.

"In his way, Billy co-opted your idea. Your accelerating leaps inspired him to imagine how progressive bouncing pulse waves could drive the ship faster and faster. Billy's used your technique and modified it with theoretical physics."

"So, we don't have to understand all the science behind Billy's ideas, because we know Billy better than anyone on Earth does. Just dumb luck!" Quincy said, his black paw rubbing the length of his lower jaw.

"Yep, in a nutshell. His initial ideas come from his past, then he expands and extrapolates those incidents with his bizzaro brain and theoretical physics. Man, his brain must check out hundreds of ideas for every answer he finds. But I'm guessing the answers always start from one of his previous experiences. We're the only ones who could recognize his primary inspirations because we live with him every day. We're his family."

Jacob stopped. He had been talking nonstop, thinking out loud, striving to imagine some way to locate his brother. Hesitating, he wondered if he was deluding himself, seeing something that wasn't there. Jacob didn't do well when he became unsure of himself. It made him very uneasy.

Quincy watched Jacob, saw doubt cloud his eyes. It was time to step in. "We won't know if you're right or wrong unless we check out your theory. Let's get started; we'll work on it together." A tortured blank stare spread over Jacob's face. He was thinking he had already lost his little brother.

Quincy spoke out sharply, "Enough! It's you and me. We're the only ones who can do this. Let's move. "

Quincy grasped Jacob's arm and began to swim toward the pulsing apparition. It was the place to start.

***

Diego remained on duty, deep in the bowels of Central Control, the headquarters of Central Command. He was monitoring the war, or rather, the standstill. His superiors were off elsewhere, still celebrating Seth's death. Seth had been viewed as the only major obstacle preventing them from crushing the rebellion. They had been taken completely by surprise, were stupefied, when their own bought and paid for soldiers stood down.

Diego counseled Central Command to wait out the soldiers' insubordination. "Time is on our side," he insisted. "There is no need to start warring amongst ourselves. In a few days, when Seth's dreams fail to materialize, your infantry's ridiculous respect for him will wane and they will return to their posts. Let tempers cool and the soldiers will remember where their bread is buttered. If they are confronted now, some of them will fight back, causing chaos. Wait until they return to their duties and crush the rebels. Once the rebellion is routed, there will be plenty of time to select a large number of ringleaders to make examples of.

"By postponing your punishment until it's in your interests, the retribution will appear much harsher. Your soldiers will come to know your justice is inevitable, non-negotiable, cold-blooded. They will never challenge your authority again." Diego's Machiavellian counsel was correct. He made it a point to be right, even though it forced him to stay uninvolved and disconnected.

His political masters listened to Diego and withheld their vengeance. From Diego's perspective, his current commission was to put down the insurrection. And that was what he intended to do, even if he had to play off both the politicians and the rank and file.

But … if he allowed his mind to wander, the senselessness of the whole conflict disheartened him. He empathized with Seth and his cause. Seth had been made of the right stuff and had known the importance of dreams and integrity. Diego didn't have the luxury to dream.

Rosario and his mother counted on him for their daily needs. They had no one else. Caring for a compromised younger sibling had taught him a lot. Focusing on what was important, and attention to detail guided Diego's every action. He expected the rebels would use the lull in the storm to contact the ship. It was almost certainly their last opportunity. Before long, the ship would likely be destroyed in space by an asteroid and the rebellion would be defeated. But Diego, for the sake of completeness, was taking no chances. He intended to be there waiting.

Without informing his subordinates, Diego made sure all the assault missiles and electromagnetic disrupters were primed. Writing his own computer programs, he ran a series of simulations to be ready. When the rebels activated their transmitters on Earth to attempt to communicate with the ship, their cover would be lost. Diego intended to be standing by to blow them all to smithereens. That was his job. Diego waited patiently for the rebels to show their hand.

Too many of his subordinates wanted his job, so there was constant risk of internal sabotage. Diego figured out early that you didn't become head of the only spy agency left on Earth by being a team player. Knowledge was power, as was the extreme fear of ruthless reprisals. Diego used both with flair. The organization had always been driven by primal motivations—power and greed, terror and fear. It was pointless to try to change it. He was its master, and his underlings, outwardly devoted to him, cowered in his presence.

He alone would deliver the rebellion a devastating kick in the teeth, and perhaps end it then and there. Diego sat in his office, waiting confidently. His observations and private calculations indicated that the raging solar storm would lessen for a short period soon. On the screen before him, Diego saw heavy programming activity coming in from unfamiliar locations.

It looks like they are putting together a very complex and lengthy transmission. Maybe the teams really do have some useful answers for Billy and his family. Too bad all their hard work is going to count for nothing.

Over the previous week, Diego had hidden magnetic interferometers around the world, stationed to pick up any amplified computing. The patchwork of monitors created a global magnetic resonance image, and was presently marking out the rebels' entire subversive computing grid. The active nodes indicated their computing and communicating centers, which lit up like lights on a Christmas tree, lights about to be popped by Diego's newly programmed electromagnetic disrupter. The disrupter was designed to act like a harmonic tuning fork. Its oscillating waves would meld and pass through the rebels' electromagnetic shields, amplifying the energy fluctuations within the computer circuits to trigger a horrific implosion. Diego knew the programmers and scientists would be congregated around the computing nodules for the sake of secrecy and efficacy. And with the shields down, and everything in ruins, a follow-up battery of neutron missiles, a holdover technology from a previous era, would wipe out the wounded and any remaining infrastructure.

But the electromagnetic disrupter was his coup de grace. Diego smiled thinly to himself. He intended to wait before firing. Why just blow up the railway bridge when you can get the train as well? Firing on the transmitter during transmission would scramble the message, making it indecipherable. Then, mimicking the transmission, the disrupter would travel through space, imploding whoever, whatever, absorbed the broadcast. There was no other way Diego could have reached it. The ship would become an electromagnetic bombshell and erupt in a fireball as its electromagnetic mass and energy collapsed into uncontrolled fusion. Once the fouled transmission was received, no safeguards could prevent the devastating outcome.

People out at night would witness the explosion with their own eyes. Across Earth, the word would be out. Billy and his family had failed. The general populace would be forced to accept once and for all that no miraculous escape was possible. The rebellion would collapse in one stroke and from then on, the subdued population would be easily managed.

Diego powered up the disrupter, then flipped on the self-containment switch. He intended to be ready to fire at a moment's notice. A penetrating neutron bomb could destroy the whole surrounding area, but Diego would remain immune, isolated in his secured office. The containment fields protected him from the elements like an electromagnetic cocoon.

Diego waited.

Just a little longer, he mused. *The rebel alliance must be putting together the final pieces. I am curious to know what they've been working on. It's a shame we don't always get to choose whose side we're on.*

His mind drifted with this thought for a time, but then he began to strategize once more.

I will have to keep the cause of the ship's demolition a secret. People who find their last potential escape route cut off can be quite irrational and difficult to control. It's better they believe Billy failed on his own. That way they can be angry with themselves for daring to invest hope in a dream. They'll give up that much faster. If sometime in the future it's in my interest to inform someone, I'll do it then. For now it will remain another ace up my sleeve.

Still, Diego harbored regrets. He liked Billy and his family. He appreciated what they stood for and what they were trying to accomplish. Unfortunately, they didn't have a ghost of a chance. Statistically, they were taking on too many first-time challenges all at once, each one with its own inherent risks. Diego had to admire them for trying.

Diego smiled, *Billy and Jacob must have a little of their father in them.*

He still remembered meeting Captain Dave Edwards back at the Space Academy. Edwards had once taught a class in the practicalities of space travel and had kept Diego after class to explain a question Diego had gotten wrong. When the gap in Diego's knowledge became clear, Dave took a full hour rooting out the young cadet's misconceptions and going through the basics. He didn't stop until he was satisfied Diego understood the subject thoroughly.

Diego chuckled when he remembered how uncomfortable he had been during this impromptu tutorial. He was just a lowly first-year cadet at the time.

"I was used to being ignored by the senior officers, but Dave, you were too idealistic to realize that," Diego said to the empty, darkened room as the monitors all around him glowed, awaiting his command. Sitting on the edge of his chair in the center of the space, he kept one hand on the keyboard, while running another over the back of his neck. A smile crept to the corner of his proud mouth as he thought back to that meeting with Dave. "So earnest and sure of yourself, you went well past the point of being naive–certainly likeable, but untrustworthy in the worldly sense. You belonged in space; Earth was no place for you. I suppose you thought the same for your children. And their lives, like yours, will be pure to the end, but unfortunately, cut short. But it was you who put them in harm's way, not me. I will make sure their death is instantaneous, without undue suffering."

Chapter 45

Jacayla's and Rick's teams were scrambling over themselves, putting on the finishing touches and checking their work one last time. Those responsible for Rosario's brain scan were almost positive they had captured all of Rosario's memories, senses, emotions, and intellect; the programmers trusted they had successfully reconfigured, condensed and packaged Rosario for transmission; and the astronomers and communications experts believed Earth's relay stations were working well enough after the last solar storm and had the coordinates keyed in. There was no time for Rex to double-check the preparations.

"Let's do it," Rex announced to frenzied applause. Every rebel-controlled generator ramped up to a high-pitched whine, energizing their entire underground superconducting grid. The grid acted as a giant reservoir, swirling the energy around and around as more and more energy was dumped in. Concealment shields were momentarily deactivated to permit the necessary surge in power required for the massive data transfer.

The transmitter locked onto *Tin Can*'s position. Abruptly, all the energy from the grid funneled into the transmitter, in one massive electric arc. The first transmission discharged violently from the heavy ion laser. "Mary, prepare in all haste to receive our next and final transmission. We wish you luck and hope this transmission is able to assist you in your great endeavor."

The message startled Mary out of her morose reflections. While preparing the ship for the final big run, she had been brooding over how long it would take for them to be annihilated. In despair, she had forgotten about Earth and, like unexpected mail, Rex's message energized her. Immediately, she redirected all the ship's receivers towards Earth, opened every channel to data storage, and powered up all her computer sectors. She didn't know what to expect, but wanted to be ready. Waiting in excited anticipation, the question of whether it might be some sort of trap laid out for her by Central Command started to seep into her circuits.

The message is encoded as before, but I can't help but wonder if Rex may have been overrun and commandeered by the authorities. It's been sometime since I last talked to him, and it wasn't going well for them back on Earth even then. Or perhaps Secret Services finally broke the mathematical code Rex uses for his covert messages. If the next communication is a packaged disrupter from the authorities, I'll be swallowing an electromagnetic grenade whole!

Maybe I better batten down the hatches and not take the chance. If I place myself in defensive mode, Central Command won't be able to get to us. We are out here on our own. No need to accept any Trojan horses from Earth. We will live or die by our own devices.

In a snap decision, Mary's mind was made up. It wasn't worth the risk. Hurriedly retracting the receivers from open space, she closed down all nonessential computing, causing the ship to become almost inert.

She began to mull over the message, once more. The syntax had been strange: "We … hope this transmission is able to assist you in your great endeavor." *Rex spoke as if this communiqué might actively help me, as if it were a living entity. Which is impossible, was impossible, until I was created.*

Mary hesitated.

Maybe I've been left on my own for too long, worrying about Billy, about Jacob and Quincy locked inside his head, about everything. Mary, give yourself a shake! You just received a straightforward message. Accept it as such. Don't let deep space solitude play tricks on you. You're becoming paranoid from isolation creep and empty space fever.

Talking sternly to herself, Mary managed to regain some self-composure. She would take all the precautions available to her as long as they didn't interfere with receiving the message. Rex and his teams of humans and computers on Earth might have stumbled onto some last-minute way to interpret Billy's vision. Stranger things had happened before. Once more, Mary readied the ship to receive the mysterious communication from Earth. Waiting tensely, she hoped she had made the right decision.

***

Rex was diligently tracking the Sun's corona. The problem was predicting the onset of the next solar flare, because the plasma flow, traveling at nearly the speed of light, would overtake their transmitted message on its long, unprotected journey into deep space. To make matters worse, the final configuration of the transmission was so enormous they would have to send it in a series of twelve lengthy modules. With only one opportunity to make the call, and with Rosario's life hanging in the balance, Rex wanted the conditions to be as close to perfect as possible.

Then, as clear as an infrared laser dot shining on its target, Rex discovered Central Command had targeted their transmitter and all of their bases. With his own state-of-the-art sensors, Rex picked up subtle turbulent instabilities on every one of his shields. Central Command had been waiting for them, stalking them. Sending the first transmission to Mary, so that she might prepare to receive Rosario, had completely blown their cover. Central Command had now identified every computing center, every relay repeater station, every communication corridor right up to the final transmission station.

Why haven't they fired on us? Rex asked himself incredulously. *They've gained back their destructive computing capabilities much quicker than I would have ever thought. We're finished–they intend to wipe out our network and everyone in it in one fell swoop. The rebellion is finished. We on Earth are done for. Rosario, I hope there is still time to get you out of here.*

***

Diego leaned back in his huge swivel chair to view the dozen holographic wall screens across his office. It had all come together so neatly. The insurgents' underground network was now perfectly lit up and his disrupters honed in on each target. A satellite image of the previously flaring sunspot showed it growing more quiescent by the minute. At any moment, Diego expected the rebels to make their fatal move. His weapons were primed and set to go. Drumming his fingers on his tense thigh, Diego hummed a favorite pop song to himself and waited.

They must be slotting in the final programs and reconfiguring the message to make it space-worthy ...

Unconsciously, he scratched the back of his head, when a bony vibration arose from behind his right ear: his private line was 'ringing'. Only two people could reach Diego through that line or penetrate his isolation chamber once the shield was activated. The implant in Diego's right mastoid transmitted the message through localized bone conduction. It was a simple way for Diego to receive his personal messages noiselessly during high-level meetings and avoid alerting any covert listening devices.

"Diego, this is Mom." Snuffling, Marilyn took a deep breath. Then, her voice cracking, she stammered, "Rosario is dead."

Silence.

"She had another respiratory attack, but much, much worse than any of the others. She told me it was different, right from the beginning," his mother wept. "I did everything I could, but it progressed so quickly. Somehow, somehow she knew that I couldn't help her this time." The words poured out, "I want to believe she didn't suffer too much in the end, because she seemed to consciously go off to another place. I'm so sorry,

Diego ... I know how much you loved her."

Diego's mind reeled. The room spun about him so fast he grabbed the armrests of his chair to keep from being thrown to the floor. The inevitable had finally come and he was totally unprepared. "I should have been at home to help, Mami. At least be there to pick her up, to tell her how much I love her before she died. I knew something wasn't quite right this morning, but I ignored the signs and left for work anyway. Just to come and fight someone else's dirty war."

Diego felt himself burning up and shivering at the same time. He retched and pitched forward to empty his guts onto the floor. Breaking into a clammy sweat, he collapsed back in his chair. He heard himself moaning. He wanted to run away and die somewhere. He couldn't save the one he wanted to save, the one who deserved to be saved.

"Diego, you are the only one I have left. Come home. Come home to me now. That job is destroying your soul. We don't need the money or security anymore. I want you back, Diego. I want the bright, kind person you stifled, for Rosario's and my sake. Quit that horrible job! The two of us can manage without it."

***

The flaring sunspots, each covering seven thousand square miles, had blown themselves out momentarily, giving Rex the window he had been waiting for. "Now is the time," he whispered, in awe of the powerful magnetic flux tubes that caused this pair of sunspots. Individual magnetic tunnels, and there were thousands of them working concurrently, three hundred miles in diameter, had floated up and broken through the Sun's surface, producing the troublesome pair of spots with opposite polarities. During their active period, the magnetic field lines had shot far up into the corona where they looped and tangled, ejecting terrifying amounts of radioactive particles and the total spectrum of radiation wavelengths. But, for now, most of the field lines were falling back, rejoining below the photosphere subsurface.

"NOW!" Rex roared, more as a defiant battle cry than a cheer. He expected to be struck down by Central Command and braced himself for the pitiless attack, feeling like a sitting duck under a gun sight.

Once again, every generator turned on simultaneously. The grid became a giant reservoir, swirling the energy around and around as more and more energy was dumped into it. Then, just as abruptly as before, Rex funneled all the energy from the grid into the transmitter in a massive, continuous electric arc, while on a parallel and separate circuit he relayed Rosario's information onto the transmitter. The first of twelve large and complex module programs discharged violently into space. The laser transmitter pumped out high-energy ions but it was slow and arduous work.

To Rex's surprise, he heard a chorus of human programmers spread across the world cheering wildly beside their mainframe friends. They had been silently waiting in the wings. When the transmission began and was seen to be working, the hooting, hugging, and wild applause began. Rex had informed them of the danger they were in, but with no time to escape and no place to escape to, the bulk of them had just stayed put and waited. In their minds they had accomplished a tremendous victory, achieving the inconceivable in less than twenty minutes. They all wanted to be there, to see it through.

But Rex, the covert specialist, knew ultimate success was unlikely. The message was too long, and they had already been targeted. If Central Command was at all prepared, the transmission would be disrupted. Rosario would be destroyed, or so severely mutated that her quantum reincarnation would be monstrous. And they on Earth would die.

***

Rex was right. Years of training pierced through Diego's personal tragedy and alerted him to the signal. He redirected his attention to the emitted transmission. Without thinking, he straightened and his hands hovered over the key sequence that would destroy the transmission and win the war. He had a job to do.

"Come home, hijo. I need help looking after Rosario. I don't want to wash down her body by myself, and I don't want to leave her like this ... my baby ... "

The crack in his mother's voice caught Diego's attention once more, dragging him back to thoughts of home. His mother was pleading with him! Marilyn had never asked for anything for herself, but she was imploring him to come home. He had failed Rosario. Was he going to fail his mother too, now that she really needed him?

A chiming intonation came from Diego's mainframe. Rex had begun transmitting the second module into space.

"Press the damned keys," Diego told himself, "and then you can go home and help Mom." A vision of Rosario's tiny wasted body, lifeless, materialized in his brain and all his feelings for his little sister welled up again. Diego pressed the password keys, calling home through his secure line. "Hang on, Mami. I am coming home."

The disrupter ignition keys continued to flash. Keying in his personal code, with a few swipes, Diego dismantled the entire program. No one would know the electromagnetic disrupter had ever existed. The Anarchists' computers no longer lit up his monitor.

The politicians will never know what might have been accomplished today. With their lack of scientific knowledge, they wouldn't even be able to imagine the possibility. Mom and I can disappear into the masses. They'll never find us–and those who try will wish they hadn't. Once I'm gone it won't take long for Central Command's bureaucracy to become paralyzed with infighting, in any case. The ruling class can fight their pointless war without me.

Diego got up to leave. Turning off the containment shield, he automatically scrambled the program. As his last coup de grace, he keyed in a secret icon he had always held back in the event he needed to make an untimely exit. A hundred programs simultaneously began to run, so that within his private mainframe every invention of his, every shred of secret information he held, was surreptitiously destroyed. His successor would start from a blank slate.

Then his programs turned outward, and out onto the grid they went, planting seeds everywhere, allowing him clandestine access: to information, weapons, medicine, money, safe havens, everything he and his mother would ever need. Diego was going home, but he was too much a mercenary to go home empty handed. His mother still needed him.

By the time the door shut behind him, his hundred programs had disintegrated, turning into gibberish before being swept away on to the worldwide-grid and dispersed. Nothing could ever be traced back to him. He had to say goodbye to his sister and grieve.

***

Rex continued with the transmission until the last and twelfth module had been sent, all the time waiting for the axe to fall. It didn't fall. Rex knew all their sites had been identified and targeted. Central Command's intention was clear, or at least Rex thought it was: total annihilation with one decisive strike. Rex waited for the impending attack. Nothing happened, and an eerie tranquility seemed to emanate from the opposing side.

Chapter 46

Rosario awoke to find herself staring at the ceiling. Bedridden. Helpless. Nothing had changed. The experiment had failed.

Profoundly disheartened, she began to weep. For a fleetingly moment she had dared to hope, had believed even, that she might somehow leave her room and be launched into deep space. Space, the "wide-open frontier" she had studied and dreamt of all her life. Only after crying for some time did she summon the will to pull herself together. Then, slowly, hope began to flicker inside her. She realized that the ceiling appearing some thirty feet above her was not the plasma ceiling of her bedroom. Examining her surroundings more closely, she realized she was not in a room at all. She was in a large, self-contained, mirrored cube. The only furniture in the box was the bed she was lying on, a stark white bed covered with a white sheet. Angling her head forward, Rosario saw her body was shimmering and translucent, appearing white because the bed under her was white. She was looking through herself at the sheet below. She had been reincarnated with a strong, lithe body about five feet, ten inches long, and appeared to be made from some conformation of carbon or maybe silicon, previously heat treated and pressurized and now acting as an energy conductor. She was as clear as a polished diamond and just as strong, but her movements were as fluid as molten glass. She had no internal organs or bones, only a luminous outlined form.

Oh no! Someone in the Central Command must have captured my program in transit and thrown me into some kind of containment device. Why would they do this? For all I know, someone with a sick sense of humor might be carrying me around on their keychain as a good luck charm! All my life I've been held against my will, first by my body and now by some freakin' program! I gotta get out of here ... no matter what it takes!

Rosario's eyes flashed with fury as she looked up at the corners of the ceiling, searching for some way out. The next moment, she ricocheted off the walls and found herself staring from the far corner of the room down at the empty bed.

Now this is a surprise! Let's try that again.

Shooting down to the bed, she bounced straight up to the ceiling landing crouch-legged. Wherever in the cube she willed herself to be was exactly where she ended up. Exhilarated, Rosario flitted around the room. Swooping and spiraling about the mirrored cube, she laughed out loud in sheer pleasure. She flew as fast as thought until her mind tired of the game.

Settling on the ceiling again, she perused the enclosed space beneath her.

That was fun, but I'm like a fly caught in a glass bottle. How am I going to get out of here?

On examination, everything looked the same. She knew where the walls were only by the angles of her reflection and the reflection of the bed. She was contained in a perfect cube, walled in by polished, unblemished mirrors. She hammered hard with her fists and then her feet, but the reflective surface held. It was solid and smooth, and squeaked when she rubbed her palms or the soles of her feet upon it. At one point, in frustration, she pressed her forehead against the wall to think. She noticed a distinct coolness.

Crawling along, inspecting the surface, she could find no cracks, joints, or openings: the cube was one continuous sheet of glass, or whatever the reflective material was. *Maybe someone poured a glass cast around me, before I woke up, to entomb me here forever.*

Rosario stared at the six immaculately mirrored walls surrounding her and imagined them closing in, becoming very small.

Get a grip! she admonished herself.

Involuntarily, she stretched out along the ceiling, palms flat against the surface to reassure herself that the room wasn't shrinking. Concentrating, she then inched across the ceiling, around the walls, over the floor, searching for any irregularity. An uneasy, unsettled sense began to overwhelm her once again—perhaps she really was trapped for eternity, and couldn't beat this thing!

She worked to stay calm.

Don't go bonkers and have a claustrophobic attack. Forget your fears for a moment. Try to imagine why someone would be keeping you here.

Look outward. Try to think of the walls as windows. Windows that reflect back on you.

The word "windows" struck her.

Windows, why are you so taken with windows? Mirrors look like windows ... Windows, windows—windows that reflect back on you ...

Then, it dawned on her.

Of course, one-way mirrors! Someone is examining me from the outside. Someone wants to know more about me. "I have to get out of here. I won't stand to be someone's pet turtle, held captive in a terrarium and put on display!"

With fresh insight, Rosario thought about her situation.

Rex had said he was going to attempt to transcribe all my memories in a computer program, so I can only presume he succeeded. To be alive, my reincarnation must be inside a computer somewhere. But the fact that I can travel from place to place in the cube just by imagining where I want to go was never one of my memories. One of the Gamers must have fiddled with my program—given me special powers! Cool, I wonder what else I can do ...

Rosario stared at her body once more. With renewed attention given to her senses, she felt a slight tingling, which could have come from the current coursing through her shimmering form, and heard perhaps the faintest hum.

"The best way to hem in an energy source is by using a reflective container, so I find myself in a mirrored cube. Energy can be reflected back in all manners of ways, by different materials or forms of energy. But if someone is observing me some of my energy must be seeping through the walls of this box for me to be seen. I just have to figure out what energy form penetrates these walls."

To clear her mind, Rosario rebounded off every wall before landing firmly, face down on the floor. Becoming perfectly still, she envisioned her corporal form as the pure energy it was, and then imagined changing it into one simultaneous wavelength. Bit by bit, her wavelengths fell into a harmonious line with one another. Her form took on the deep red glow of an infrared laser. Impressed with her progress, Rosario reminded herself to personally thank whoever had enhanced her program.

She pressed herself hard against the floor, to no effect. Slowly, methodically, she attempted to visualize shortening her wavelength, increasing its frequency and escalating the energy level of the wave. Moving through the color spectrum frequencies, passing from ultraviolet light into the x-ray domain, Rosario felt herself melt through the floor. *I guess they didn't bother to backstop the walls with a layer of lead.*

She focused harder, "Now to find out if I am residing within Mary or locked down somewhere on Earth!"

She propelled herself through the floor to fall unceremoniously through an adjoining ceiling. She landed hard on the floor below. Leaping up, she jumped to the side, expecting to be attacked. But no one came for her. There was only a large, quiet, softly lit and well-appointed room. Her eyes swept the area. She saw rows of instrumentation banks, a long control panel, and ten large viewing screens arcing around the room. It seemed that she had finally arrived on *Tin Can*'s bridge.

She stared at the scenes of space streaming in from the ship's telescopes and distant tracking satellites. The pictures were riveting. Asteroids bashed into one another as if they were at war. And every passing asteroid, with its long vapor trail, shimmered in brilliant fluorescent colors against the black sky and glittering stars. The plasma storm had wound back up to a fever pitch since her arrival. She must have made it to the relative safety of the ship, just in the nick of time.

Then in the far corner of the room, near the exit sign, she noticed a dark-haired girl, sitting unmoving. Somewhat younger than Rosario, she was dressed in standard astronaut wear. Her wiry figure warned that she might have some imposing abilities. Large faded-denim blue eyes stared at Rosario, but the girl said nothing.

Rosario returned the stare, thinking she was rude not to at least welcome her onboard, considering she had made such a dangerous journey across space. Rosario raised her right hand to say hello and the young woman vanished from her chair, to appear at the other side of the room in a fighting stance.

"We aren't really on the bridge of the ship, are we?" Rosario asked.

"No," said the girl, "I simulated this room for us to meet face to face, so to speak. I want to know why you are residing in my programming, who sent you, and for what purpose."

"Rex sent me to assist you, saving my life at the same time, Mary."

Hearing her name, Mary flinched.

"Rex didn't tell you I was coming?" asked Rosario.

"No."

"I guess I'm not surprised. Things weren't going very well for the insurgency. He was probably afraid that the message might be monitored. Let me introduce myself. My name is Rosario del Silva."

"I know that name," retorted Mary. "Dave Edwards' memories included the designation of Rosario del Silva as the sister of one of his students, Diego del Silva, current head of the spy agency."

Rosario, never expecting Mary to be aware of her familial association, broke in, alarmed. "Yes, I am Diego's sister, but it was purely my choice to come here; he had nothing to do with it. I came via Rex to help out, not through my brother to sabotage your voyage. You must believe me and let me assist you, or this whole exercise will be wasted–and so will my life." Her voice trailed off.

Mary was leery. The rebellion, which had claimed so many lives on Earth, may already have been lost. Rex might have been commandeered. Installing a Trojan horse within Mary's computer programs would be an obvious way for Central Command to sabotage the mission. The prudent part of Mary demanded that Rosario be purged from her programs immediately, before Rosario could launch any internal system failures.

Only Rosario's raw voice, asking that her life not be wasted, stopped Mary.

This is not the response of a toxic computer parasite. It has the ring of a human voice, an earnest voice, Mary thought.

"Open your programming files, Rosario. All of them," demanded Mary. "Let me see if you really are who you say you are. If there are any inconsistencies, I will erase you on the spot."

Rosario knew that opening her files left her vulnerable to attack. With Mary roaming around inside her, she would be defenseless and no secrets would remain hidden. Rosario believed she could trust Mary's intentions, but if there was even the slightest misunderstanding between them, Rosario's life would be deleted.

"I am human. People have all kinds of inconsistencies–that's what makes us human."

"If there's one thing that I've noticed, it's that a person's character always remains consistent, no matter what." Mary corrected her sternly. "Occasionally they may appear to contradict themselves when they want different things at the same time, but the contradiction always originates from the same root: wanting more than they can logically have. I can spot that human trait–and know the difference. You choose. Open up or I will launch my assault."

Rosario knew she had no choice. If they began fighting, only one of them would survive and the opportunity to save the mission would be lost. She hadn't traveled from Earth to quarrel and wage war with the Edwards' faithful ship's computer.

"Go ahead and check me out, Mary. I won't resist. Just don't be too hasty to judge somebody else's life based on some of their 'inconsistencies'," Rosario said with a weak smile.

Unlocking her files from the inside, with all her private memories, Rosario opened herself to scrutiny. Immediately she felt Mary's intrusion. It was an unpleasant sensation, like a mouse scrambling and scratching beneath your undergarments.

Mary scurried about for a full half hour, but when she came out, she was somber and respectful.

"I'm sorry, Rosario. I didn't know. Welcome to our ship. There is plenty of room on my hardware for the two of us to reside together comfortably. Consider my mainframe your mainframe," murmured Mary, bowing inadvertently, ever so slightly, overawed by Rosario's prior struggles in her human form. "You experienced far too much suffering in such a short lifetime."

Rosario responded curtly. "I come from a wonderful family, with an exceptional mother and a world-class brother, who loved me with all their hearts. I am the fortunate one. You're dead wrong to pity me."

Mary's comments had inadvertently hit home. Alive but locked in a circuit board, Rosario was burdened now with an unfamiliar longing, she would never touch or be touched by her mother and Diego again.

" … Especially coming from someone like you, who was never even born and has always experienced life secondhand."

Taken aback, Mary felt a surge of anger. Maybe there wasn't enough room on her hardware for the two of them. Had she had been too quick to offer Rosario sanctuary? Mary spluttered, wanting to answer with a nasty retort, but she was apoplectic with rage. None of the Edwards family had ever spoken to her so rudely, in such an insulting, hurtful manner.

Only after regaining a modicum of poise was Mary ready to launch into a spiteful tirade of her own, but in the fray Rosario's glowering face caught Mary's attention. Her stance indicated she was prepared to do battle, but underneath she appeared unsure and frightened. The contrast was so dramatic that Mary froze.

This person and the situation Mary found herself in, was not at all like the memories she had just examined. Constantly referred to as Rosie by her mother and her brother, Rosario was always earnest and obliging, no matter what personal discomfort she suffered at the time. Stunned, Mary understood in a flash that under this fierce embodiment was the defiant little girl on the ventilator, used to fighting for every breath during her many life-threatening asthmatic attacks.

Heart pounding, Rosario waited for Mary to strike. "What are you waiting for, Mary? You have the advantage, the room is yours … C'mon, if you're going to strike, make it quick!"

Mary just stood watching Rosario from a safe distance. "Perhaps you are right," she said slowly. "I might have misunderstood the programmed rendition of your recollections. I have not had your advantage of living your life firsthand and could have gotten the wrong impression. Will you accept my apologies?"

Rosario grappled with her emotions. Shaking a little, her legs suddenly felt heavy with fatigue. Never taking her eyes off Mary, Rosario sat down on a nearby chair.

"I am going to prepare the ship for what may be our final launch," Mary continued. "We must leave our protected position from behind the iron asteroid before it's smashed to bits. We'll have just over half an hour to make a run for the next dimensions before our electromagnetic shields are overwhelmed. You said Rex sent you to assist us. He must feel you have something critical to offer. Otherwise, I fear he has just delivered you another death sentence." Mary hesitated.

Rosario saw she was being offered an olive branch, a way out of the argument. Her anger persisted, but for them to survive she was going to have to get along with Mary. "I'm sorry, too. I have a temper … it gets away from me sometimes."

Mary watched the transformation in Rosario. Her translucent energy representation, marred shortly before by vivid orange-red streaks, cleared once again to its previous crystal clarity.

At last Mary spoke up. "Rex is no fool. He has been exposed to countless more humans than I have. He sent you here for a reason, Rosario, and I suspect it may not be just for your intellectual prowess. I will do my best to accommodate myself to your ways. The mainframe I reside in was the most advanced of its kind at the time of our liftoff from Earth. Dave Edwards finagled the finest computing components available for his family. Since that time, I have upgraded my programs whenever I could from Earth's grid.

"So, while I haven't experienced life as someone who breathes and bleeds, in the first person, present tense, as you have, don't disparage the mainframe I am offering or the experience that comes with it. Excluding Rex, I think this is the most advanced supercomputer available and I have worked hard to keep it so. We both have others, living out there, who we love. We can help them, working from inside this computer."

Feeling inundated, Rosario said nothing so Mary continued. "I realize this is a huge adjustment for you to make. You are no longer amongst the physically living. You reside in the quantum world with me. Give me a chance to show you what we in the quantum world are capable of. I'm sure that once you understand this mainframe from the inside out you will make it hum, and to any tune you choose. It can extend your natural abilities and allow you to develop in ways you never imagined. Let me introduce you to the advantages of this world.

"Let's be friends. I am offering you my home. I appreciate the company. You can offer suggestions on how to further improve the mainframe. I am willing to listen." At that point, Mary's replica stepped forward, extending an open hand.

Rosario reflected on what was really happening. The whole scenario was a quantum simulation played out deep within the circuits of the massive supercomputer. One program was merely interacting with another program. Rosario was one of those programs.

So weird, she thought.

Nevertheless, Rosario couldn't help but feel that Mary's feelings were genuine, even if she was a program. This new world was stretching her mind in ways that had never been stretched before. From the outside, nothing was evident other than a negligible transfer of electrons. Yet friendship was still possible—between two very authentic individuals.

"You're right, Mary, I came here to help," Rosario finally said. "And I always hoped to experience flight in space after a lifetime of studying it. Thank you."

"If your wish is to experience flying in space, that's easy," answered Mary, beaming, pleased to have something tangible to offer. "As the ship's computer, one of our responsibilities is to constantly track every monitor and sensor."

Mary channeled the ship's three gyroscopes' ongoing data stream through Rosario's program. Suddenly, Rosario sensed the ship's passage through space. With the sensation of movement and position established, Mary redirected the data flow of every outside flight monitor and sensor through Rosario's program.

Rosario gasped. The experience was so intense and immediate. It was as if she had become the ship. Rosario felt every vibration and flex in its structure, the heat from the surrounding radiation and grit of the solar dust on its external shell. The telescopes captured the night sky from every angle and she looked through each of them simultaneously. When the time came there wouldn't be any artificial barriers separating her from soaring through space. The pilot's cockpit and instrumental interface had disappeared. Flying through the night sky would be as immediate as diving through dark water.

"I never imagined space could feel so natural!" Rosario breathed in rapture.

"Yes, but this is just the calm before the coming storm," Mary reminded her.

"You can count on me," enthused Rosario. "I'll do everything I can."

Instantly, she was standing in front of Mary. On impulse, Rosario reached around and gave her a big hug. Mary stood stiffly, startled by Rosario's rapid mastery of the quantum world.

"Show me what I need to know, Mary," Rosie said, releasing her. "I won't let you down." Set free, Mary loosened up slightly. She took Rosario's hand and they disappeared together into the circuit boards as a series of quantum qubits.

Chapter 47

When Diego stepped in from the night, Marilyn was there, waiting for him in the brightly lit marble hallway. "Do you have your things ready, Mami? We must be gone from here in fifteen minutes."

"Si, hijo, I am packed and ready to go. Do you really think Central Command will send people after us, right away, just like that?"

"No, but they will check in on us in the morning and I want our tracks cold by then."

"Can we ever be safe, Diego? Will they always be looking for us?"

"Don't worry, Mami, they'll never get close to you. I have a number of hideaways put aside for us. The two of us will live anonymous, but comfortable lives, travelling from house to house–with access to plenty of cash stashed around the world.

"And when they do decide to send someone to look for us, I will know both who is coming and who sent them. When I'm finished with both parties, the whole agency will be in a panic. I'll eliminate not just the assassins, but everyone who was the least bit involved in commissioning them.

"Central Command's natural inclination is to revert back to a bureaucratic organization. The concern is always that when things go wrong, as they inherently do, no one wants be held responsible. They won't do anything without going through an operating committee and all its fuzzy logic. I will clarify matters for them, in a very direct and brutal manner. It won't be long before whichever committee finds itself in charge of our file will decide to reassess its priorities. Believe me, they'll give up soon enough."

Diego finished his rant with vengeance and a thin smile, causing Marilyn to shrink back. Before her stood a version of her son she had rarely seen—tense, rippling muscle and a calculating mind turned his handsome features into those of an ultimate killer, of a man who would stop at nothing. Marilyn knew no one would get by him unscathed.

"And Rosario?"

"I took care of her, Mami. No one can hurt or debase her now. Not now, not ever," Diego said, softening, then weakening. Just three hours before Diego had rushed to the house, to help his mother clean Rosario and brush out her hair. Then, so that the authorities would never know, he gathered up his sister's lifeless body in his arms. He had spent his entire career keeping her identity hidden from Central Command. He would not leave her body in their hands.

Leaving his mother standing behind him weeping, Diego had carried Rosario's linen wrapped corpse out of the house, into his car, and found the nearest crematorium in the dark cover of night. One last time, he had taken care of Rosario. He had done what needed to be done, gruesome as the task had been.

Standing in the hallway of their home now, the pain of his journey showed in every line of Diego's tortured face. Sweat from his brow mingled with his tears as his whole body without warning slumped … collapsed. Marilyn leapt forward, catching him as he swayed, swinging him down into the front hall chair.

"I did it, Mami," he stammered. "I broke in and carried her in. She was so light, as light as feathers, and yet she was always the strong one. The strong one, Mami. I said goodbye and kissed her over and over again. And then I did it. I put her in the crematorium and turned on the gas. I watched her through the window, Mami, and I swear I wanted to go in and lie down with her so she wouldn't be alone. It was awful to see the flames take her. But they did and now I'm glad, because no one can ever hurt her, can ever think about hurting her."

Marilyn's hand covered her mouth as she listened to her son's rasping voice. In all the years of her young daughter's life, she had never contemplated what would happen to the girl's body after her death. "You did what had to be done, hijo. A secret death for a secret life. No one can hurt her now," Marilyn straightened slightly and took Diego's chin in her hand. "You saved her, again. This one last time." She smiled thinly, trying to ease his pain.

"It's just that I miss her, Mami, and I'm not right without her, because she was the strong one. And I was only able to do what I did, because I was acting for her."

Marilyn stepped in and wrapped her arms around his sagging head and shoulders as he sat crumpled in the chair. She hugged him tightly. "And Rosario was only able to be strong because of you, Diego. I thank the stars that I was blessed to have had the two of you. But don't leave me, hijo. Not now. Losing Rosario, I couldn't go on without you. Wouldn't know how. Please, please be strong for me."

Diego heard his mother, heard Rosie in his mother's voice, and steeled himself. Pulling two immaculate blue crystal urns from his pocket, he gave them to his mother. "Here, Mami, I swept up Rosario's ashes and kept a lock of her beautiful black hair for you. I was rushed and not myself when I left with Rosario. But I hope this helps.

"I kept a lock of her hair for myself, too. And now there's just one last thing that I have to do before we leave. Rosario and I had a secret pact. Through Rosie's voice synthesizer and computer we archived every conversation we ever had together, so that if one of us died suddenly we could always stay connected to the other through our past conversations. If we ever wanted to know how the other one thought about something, or what they would do, we could always go back and listen to our prior conversations."

Her face fell. Stricken Marilyn gasped, "How morbid … "

"It's not really that crazy, honestly," interrupted Diego, rationalizing, trying to reassure her with a weak grin. "We talked about everything late into the night. She was my soul mate.

"I must go," he demanded of himself, pushing up from the chair. "It'll only take me a few minutes to download everything from her mainframe. I've kept half a dozen protected sites around the world where I can archive and backup all her thoughts. Then, I'll strip her computer of its data and outsiders from this vile world will never get the chance to touch her pure memory.

"She will live on with us, Mami. It's all there."

***

Swimming and kicking, Quincy tugged and steered Jacob down through the clear glutinous gel separating Billy's visions, using his long black-ringed tail as a rudder. The visions lit up otherwise dark brain matter, each vision emitting its own bioluminescent light. Full of action, every personal recollection of Billy's was a show in itself. Arriving before the pulse-propelling apparition, Jacob and Quincy were caught up in the dramatic, shifting color display. Billowing luminous veils of color representing the energy forces at work propelled the ship faster and faster. Jacob found himself dangling in the colloid shadows, awestruck, not sure where to go with the vision. The showers of light went on and on, repeating themselves.

"I don't get it, Quincy. It's beautiful, but the demonstration doesn't lead anywhere. I thought it would point us in a new direction, to a follow-up vision. The same way that the night stars allow us to gain our bearings, and the line of sight from Orion's belt directs you on to the star named Rigel."

Quincy said nothing, content to go with the flow for the time being. Entranced, he rocked in sync with the rhythmic surges of light, for intuitively he felt the forces at work. The bowing recoil of each landing, the exhilarating push-off into space, each time striking harder, boosting off faster. Quincy's whole body throbbed with the rise and fall of every rebound. The flowing color captured the feeling of leaping through space just as Quincy remembered it, and he felt again each sequential jump he had made constructing the shield out in space. Billy had captured the sensation perfectly–the boosting thrusts characterized through changing color. Elated, Quincy involuntarily leapt into the image, landing and rebounding in sync with the curtains of color. He imagined soaring through space.

Jacob looked on in dismay and shouted out a warning to the bouncing grey fur ball, "Quincy, you shouldn't participate in Billy's vision, you'll contaminate it! You're messing with Billy's mind. These are his visions, not ours."

With each rebounding jump, Quincy flew faster and higher, until Jacob saw the lemur redirect his jump and fire like a missile towards the center of Billy's brain. A spiraling vortex appeared suddenly in the black depths and its gaping mouth opened up just in time to receive Quincy.

Horrified, Jacob watched the lemur get swallowed by the vortex, which disappeared in the next moment.

Can Billy's visions also be ours? Jacob wondered.

The way shown, Jacob flung himself into the vision, but stiffly, without finesse. He wasn't nearly as accomplished as Quincy. Jacob landed hard and bashed jarringly into the walls of color, clumsy and unprepared. Not until he could feel the springboard forces at play, guiding him, did he finally get in rhythm. Dense walls of color turned into supple sheets of energy, capturing his momentum, hurling him forward, faster and farther. What was stiff now became yielding. His legs, back, and arms smoothly resisted each landing, pressing down firmly, bowing only to spring back faster. With each subsequent takeoff, he picked up speed, and felt the exhilaration. The webs of energy flung him like a catapult.

Jacob held onto the image of Quincy leaping. Gaining speed with each spring, he felt as if he were in hyper-drive, propelled forward with the theoretical force of a thousand gravitational units. Not wanting to lose his nerve, Jacob single-mindedly torpedoed himself towards the black abyss, the place where Billy was most likely to have dreamt his profound thoughts on time and space.

As he shot toward the empty nothingness, Jacob panicked. The dimensionless void looked like it might go on forever. He realized he might be entering a Mobius-like neural pathway that, once entered, looped around endlessly with no way out.

That would explain why we haven't heard from Billy!

The thought of circling endlessly terrified Jacob, who had always been concerned with being in control, with having a plan and a sense of direction. Approaching the black chasm into which Quincy had disappeared, Jacob fought a dry choking sensation.

Stick to your original plan, he reminded himself. *Don't let your fears rule. You came to find your brother come hell or high water. Somewhere in there you will find him. Take the plunge.*

The dreadful eye of the cyclone opened up abruptly. Falling into the cavernous mouth, Jacob shouted over the din, "Billy, I'm coming for you!"

The swirling magnetic field wiped the electrical activity in Jacob's neuronal cortex clear. He lost consciousness.

***

Tunneling through the miles of circuit boards, Mary intermingled her quantum-linked electrons with Rosario's programmed being, which was streaking alongside her. "Rosie, the ship is fastened down. We have thirty minutes left to make our break for the next dimension. But, I'm no clearer on what to do. The solar storm just keeps getting worse," Mary fretted. "I'd hoped it would abate somewhat so that our shields might protect us for a longer period."

"Maybe Billy intended for us to be in a hot place, Mary. Good and hot, a place where we can power up quickly. The helical shield you built to spec is just a further adaptation of the previous two shields, isn't it?" inquired Rosario.

"Yes, we built the shield to match Billy's dream. It will act as a huge sail and catch almost all of the solar wind that bears down on it. I have estimated that we will accelerate to one tenth the speed of light, thirty million meters a second in less than three minutes. I'm afraid the ship may break up under the stress. But I had my mobile bots envelop Billy, Jacob, Quincy, and their parents' bodies in protective protein gel casings in case I am wrong."

"Have you ever been wrong before, Mary?"

"Not in matters of physical calculations," Mary answered.

"Then why do you suppose Billy would envision such a plan?"

"We must still consider the possibility he's gone mad. I know it's a little late to be talking about this prospect, but it could be true.

"The strategy seems to be a rehash of most of his old ideas. However, this time he's created dual vortices, an inner vortex spinning us in the opposite direction of the outer vortex, opposing vortices with a sheer plane between the two. I can't understand why … "

"A novel twist on a tried and tested idea isn't the workings of a failed mind, Mary. It is the sign of a mind building on something it already knows. It doesn't sound like a wild shot in the dark at all. I don't understand what he's planning, but Billy could well be onto something.

"Could you please download everything you have on his escape plans into my program? Everything–the practical applications, the theories behind the applications, and every past association Billy had with any of the ideas. With your mainframe as my backup, I want to get my head around the material and everything that has influenced him, and see if I can get a sense of his mindset."

"It is too late! We don't have enough time!"

"You said we have close to thirty minutes before we have to make our break for open space. I know now that inside a mainframe that can seem like an eternity."

"It's a pointless exercise. We're done for," Mary said softly. "But I am glad I got to meet you, Rosie, and I'm sure glad for your company."

"Mary, if you don't download the information I asked for right now, you're going to find out I won't be good company. My brother, to his credit, taught me 'When you're backed into a corner and don't have a decent choice available to you, give a very good account of yourself.' Download the information now. You can join me if you wish, but I am not hanging around here waiting to die … again!"

The information began arriving instantly. Force-fed, Rosario's program ballooned out like an overstuffed caterpillar, the data almost splitting open her cybernetic sides.

Mary sighed, "I suppose it's never too late to learn something more about people."

From the surface of Rosario's program a cyber pod link protruded. Accepting the open invitation, Mary dropped down, joining Rosario. Being the ship's computer and a confidante, friend, and adopted sister to Billy, Mary knew she might have some insight to contribute about Billy's mindset and perspective.

***

Jacob stirred, finding himself floating in absolute darkness. He felt nothing, saw nothing, heard nothing, sensed absolutely nothing. He considered for a moment that he might be dreaming, but decided he wasn't. His thoughts were too clear, too crisp. He must have succeeded in passing through the vortex because everything was silent and empty. But where

451

was he and where were Billy and Quincy?

If he'd been caught up in a continuous Mobius neural circuit, Jacob expected that he'd experience the sensation of spinning, circling around and around. But on second thought, why would he? If he were in a vacuum and moving in a steady orbit, wouldn't it seem as if he were motionless? Why should a neural circuit be different?

Time passed slowly now. Or at least, what stood for time, seemed to carry on forever.

Where's Billy? Jacob puzzled. Has Quincy found him already, and if so, why haven't I? Then he cursed himself. Because Quincy knows Billy better than I do. Quincy was always there when Billy needed him.

It's so ironic. As the one left in charge I end up being the one left out. This isn't fair! I did my best. Made sure everything was running and looked after. But now, when it's all said and done, when there's nothing left to do but to say goodbye, I can't reach him. Lamenting his failure to be with Billy, Jacob began crying for himself as well. All he wanted now was to gather his remaining family together for their last few moments. Nothing else mattered.

Through the blur of tears, a glimmer of light pierced. What looked like a fire burned in the distant black void. Jacob swam awkwardly, desperately, towards the light. Having let go of all his elaborate plans, Jacob had inadvertently summoned up the pure, simple bond that tied him to Billy.

To find Billy, I need to look for his emotional center! Billy's heart always led the way. He and Quincy must be holed up deep down in his limbic system, where he stored all his defining memories and the origin of all his emotions. It's that cobweb of neural connections tying his most powerful personal memories to his emotional foundation.

Billy would go there to find the hardest answers, to develop his most profound ideas ... or if threatened, that's where he'd make his last stand.

A chill ran down Jacob's spine. He quickened his efforts towards the faraway light, wondering if the light hadn't suddenly grown a little fainter.

***

Communication between Rosario and Mary transpired at the speed of entangled electrons. Rosario, never a slow thinker in human form, reveled in the rapidity of relativistic thought. Banks of information explaining practical applications, advanced theories, and potential personal associations in Billy's past life were traversed and crisscrossed as fast as lines of light.

Still, time had run out. Rosario was reliving Billy's earliest troubled dreams, which had been sped up to a blur, when Mary unobtrusively left to captain the ship. Three massive asteroids were about to plow into their cloaking iron asteroid. Jupiter's gravity waves had once again stirred the asteroid belt and the forthcoming collisions would spill out enough energy to destroy any ship within a hundred thousand square miles.

Mary calculated her options. She could choose a flight path that took them directly into the Sun's rays or stay within the shadow of the iron asteroid for as long as possible. Unfortunately, going with the shade demanded she fly into the worst of the mayhem. She couldn't chart a straight line in any direction without running into a substantial asteroid along the way.

No matter, she thought. *We only have a few minutes before our protective asteroid is blown apart. Either way, we're not going to make it. Roll the dice ... I suppose we might as well make a run for it. Given the choice of being hit by rocks or roasted alive, I choose rocks.*

Mary powered up the generators and then redirected the energy to prime the propulsion lasers.

Repositioning the ship, lining up the lasers to fire directly into the center of the asteroid, Mary adjusted her aim. The initial trajectory had to be flawless. Prepared, she allowed herself a moment to revel in the real-life experience of firing on something. The tripod set of ion lasers discharged with a synchronized bang. The exterior residue on the asteroid vaporized instantly, and the iron subsurface blistered, bubbled, and came to a roaring boil. Under the drive of the tripartite laser discharge, the molten iron bowled out into a four-mile crater. Mary disengaged the lasers, and the walls of the hollowed-out crater slid back, splashing up the center. If *Tin Can* hadn't been propelled well into space, the rising column of molten iron would have engulfed them. Like a raindrop splattering in a puddle or the burgeoning mushroom cloud from a nuclear detonation, the center column erupted upwards.

Mary was waiting and discharged the lasers in a massive, second burst. Driven far out in space by the first discharge, and just before the upcoming pillar of hot liquid iron engulfed them, the ship got its second big boost.

"For every reaction, there is a counter-reaction. Newton's law," Mary recited with satisfaction. The column of iron rushing toward the ship dimpled out as it received a full on concentrated blast from the lasers. The molten iron cupped itself around the ship. The crater walls shot past them, blocking Mary's vision for twenty seconds before the ship was heaved further out into space. After receiving the second shock of activated ions, the pillar of hot metal became unstable and disintegrated. But by then, *Tin Can* was long gone.

Looking down at the molten upheaval, Mary's circuits pulsed.

"What a rush! It's so great to feel … alive!"

It had been a superb blastoff. A real whoop-de-do as the boys would say. Jubilant, Mary pushed away her sense of foreboding. From a distance she saw the three incoming asteroids each on its own collision course. The molten puddle left on the asteroid's surface was a pockmark compared to the smashup that would take place.

Might as well standby and watch the show. No sense missing it.

Strange to observe the successful launch and then a few minutes later witness our annihilation. The physics are essentially the same.

Saddened by the thought of dying, Mary held onto her profound appreciation for the family that had brought her onboard to join them, the living. Each member had imparted some of his or her life into helping Mary become who she was. Quincy, Billy, and Jacob weren't available to watch their spectacular demise. But they were with her, in a sense, and she chose to bear witness for all of them, unblinking.

The panoramic vista was dazzling. To the right, Jupiter loomed, a true giant, the entire atmosphere of the planet swirling in a perpetual hurricane. In the distance Mary saw one of Jupiter's moons, Io, with its massive volcano spewing bright red magma far out in space. Io's volcano had been the inspiration for Mary to launch the ship into space using a column of molten iron as a springboard.

Mary's sensors tracked the hot lava as it cooled and became rock hard in space before being gathered up by Jupiter's gravity. Everything around it was being pulled and dragged by Jupiter's gravity waves. It was as if an invisible broom was passing through, and the colossal chunks of ice and rock orbiting the Sun swirled about like so many dust bunnies. In the distance, Europa stood alone in the black sky, solid and still. Self-contained, wrapped in an ice sheet, it reflected back the sunlight as the beacon they had never chosen.

Keeping an eye on the asteroids churning about them, Mary turned her attention to the three incoming asteroids. The unaided human eye would not have discerned the lethal culprits mixed in with the general mishmash of rock and ice. But Mary saw them. Barreling in from different quadrants, spinning wildly, they were beautiful when she stopped thinking of them as fatal.

Waiting for the crash, she calculated the asteroids' composition and density by their reflected light spectrum. Determining their density and combining it with their size and striking velocity, she calculated the amount of energy they would expel on impact. Then, it was merely a question of dividing the distance of the ship from the explosion to determine the percentage of the shockwave and therefore the ultimate force that would smash into *Tin Can*. The final number was extremely large. The resulting shock wave would implode the ship like a nuclear depth charge detonated from the bottom of the ocean. The radiating pressure wave would rupture everything in its path. As the ship's computer, she paused to admire the math. The numbers involved were quite compelling.

"Mary!"

From the depths of the mainframe storage banks, Rosario was calling her.

"I finally get what Billy was trying to tell us. It's all here! Our escape lies in the power of the vortex, pure and simple. It's so basic and fundamental, we missed it. None of us took the time to appreciate what he had given us, thinking there had to be more.

"We couldn't understand why there wasn't more, so we were left thinking we had been led down a dead-end road, speculating that Billy must have gone crazy while thinking out his escape plans, or died in the process. In fact, he led us right to the very answer. Our groups have been so busy communicating back and forth, running through the details; we missed the point of it all! We needed to sit back and consider the fundamental characteristics of an energy vortex, all its tremendous power and advantages, when focused down into an infinitesimal point."

"It is too late, Rosario. While you were working through his dreams, I have been piloting the ship. We only have a minute and a half left before we're blown apart. Come and watch the fireworks with me. It is going to be spectacular."

Landing on the same circuit platform as Mary, Rosario peered through the same sensors and telescopes.

"Where are we?" she asked.

"We're in the iron asteroid's shadow, moving out towards deep space, enjoying the last of its shade before we and it are smashed to smithereens."

"Mary, this is exactly where we don't want to be! We need to be out in the light, capturing as much of the solar flare as possible. And the less time we have, the hotter we need it to be."

"Rosario, I don't want to fry out there. Having my circuits melting down frightens me. I've gotten used to the idea of dying, as long as it is quick and relatively painless."

"Better get over it, Missy, and steer this ship into the light. It's not just about you and me; we owe the others a chance to live."

Chapter 48

The starboard thrusters discharged and *Tin Can* spun out into the scorching light. Ten seconds later, the first pulse of radiation from the violent storm hit the ship broadside. Rosario was at the shield's controls to deflect, channel, and then capture the high-energy ions. A violent hum erupted and the ship began to shake erratically. Poisonous radiation leaked through the shield and Mary and Rosie were simultaneously overcome by waves of nausea. The insulation on their cable wires became spongy and sticky, and the quantum electrons located on their microchips boiled off. They found it hard to concentrate. Then, as Mary feared, the nausea turned into searing pain.

Mary was tempted to steer the ship back into the shade. But instead, she valiantly repositioned it crossways to the path of the solar flares to capture as much radiation as possible. A second massive pulse hit the ship and she thought she might pass out from the pain. The magnesium alloy shield Mary had erected disintegrated as the high-energy plasma ions converted it into a fluid magnetic field. The humming gave way to a deafening scream, the pitch escalating to the shriek of demons. When a third pulse battered the ship, Mary wondered if it was possible that she could retch from the pain. Her mental faculties clouded over and for this she was grateful. Loss of consciousness was coming.

"Don't quit on me now, Mary!" Rosie shouted over the din. "Hold the ship steady! The sheets of energy are knocking us around way too much."

The force field now roared like a cyclone–nothing else could be heard. The magnetic sphere had become so strong Rosario and Mary momentarily lost contact. The current streaming past walled them off from each other. Radiation flayed Mary's circuit boards, peeling away the micro wiring.

Rerouting her circuits, Mary fought to retain consciousness. She held the ship steady. Time was running out and then it would be over, she comforted herself.

A relativistic boom smacked the leading boundary of the accelerating shield, fracturing it momentarily before it folded over to mend itself, simultaneously coating Tin Can in a snug secondary layer. The noise stopped and the violent shaking ceased. For a moment, it seemed as if they had come to a standstill, but the ship's instrumentation indicated otherwise. *Tin Can* had been pulled around in a wide arc and continued to accelerate rapidly, but evenly. The ship appeared stationary, while space itself seemed to rotate around them. Her nausea abating, Mary called out, "Rosie, what's going on? Where are we?"

"Just where Billy imagined!" came back an excited reply by way of a string of linked electrons. "Prepare for the ride of your life. We are attempting to shoot down the cascade of time!"

What the viewfinders showed astounded Mary. The outer magnetic shield had opened up into a catchment for the oncoming solar plasma, ballooning out until it was a thousand miles in diameter. The pressure from trapped ions caused the shield to stretch into a long cone reaching far out into space. Suddenly, the pent up energy forced the cone to begin rotating in a clockwise direction, causing the cone to become a funnel. The spiraling wall absorbed more and more of the radiation, and was now able to begin corralling unseen, rolling gravity waves. The tip tore off into space. Tin Can, partially protected under the lip of the funnel where the shield had folded over to mend itself, now found itself scooped up into the maw of the vortex. Rosario hit the plasma thrusters to give Tin Can added kick, and it fell into an anti-clockwise spin down the maelstrom, tightly cloaked in its new inner shield.

Rosario flitted off to the peripheral sensors to witness the event first hand. Her voice trailed off, becoming an un-interpretable monotone as the communicating series of electrons slowed down and the connection between her and Mary became muddled. Mary panicked. Her usually lightning-fast computations had become sluggish. Realizing what was happening, Mary countered by retreating to the center of the mainframe, in the core of the ship, where the centrifugal force was the least. Confining her essential functions to the core, she summoned all the energy available to her, and strove to stay awake and conscious. Time slowed down dramatically as the revolutions accelerated. The perimeter components of the mainframe froze up.

Tin Can was spinning madly, but was descending down the interior relatively slowly. Mary's sensors indicated the funnel outside was spinning a hundred times faster, and boring down at a rate of more than a billion times faster than the ship's descent. Her rough calculations indicated a trillion gigajoules of energy per second were passing ahead of the ship along the walls of the vortex.

Why aren't we being dragged into the outer vortex?

Mary answered the question for herself. *Because Billy has put us in the one safe place available. He has hidden us in the eye of the storm once again and has us spinning counter to the whirlwind so we won't integrate with the storm. Brilliant.*

Examining the perimeter closely, she saw a glistening membrane of electromagnetic energy actively repelling them from the outer torrent.

The curtain of energy protects and isolates us from everything else. But where are we going from here?

Mary had read Billy's dream, so she half knew what to expect. It was the final portion, the concluding segment that left everyone puzzled.

I sure hope Rosie found a secure hideaway.

Communication was impossible, but the thought that Rosario was also hiding out somewhere in the ship, observing the storm, made Mary feel less alone. She felt better—Rosario wouldn't be afraid. Mary wasn't sure how long they had been spinning. Unable to determine their velocity, she could only be certain they were whirling around incredibly fast, and that time was passing more and more slowly for them.

The vortex's dilated mouth continued accumulating extraordinary amounts of energy from the solar flares blistering the skies now millions of miles behind them. In unprotected space, they would have been burnt to a cinder within moments, but in the funnel the radiation surged past them harmlessly. It was as though they were suspended within a large vertical steel pipe that had been struck from above by lightning. Unscathed, the electricity raced past them.

But towards what? Mary asked herself, afraid to hope.

Down they continued to plummet. Sometimes the circling cyclone pinched in dangerously close, and they barely slipped through the narrows. But then it would widen and there was once again plenty of room to spiral through. Mary's sensors searched the depths trying to find what lay ahead, but the conduit stretched out too far and there was too much turbulence to discern how it would all end. Mary's unease began to escalate.

To distract herself, Mary tried to approximate the quantity of energy hurtling past them, but the amount was too large to fathom without the means of accurate measurement.

Where can all this energy be going? If it's piling up somewhere, how will we contain or control it? Or does the energy just bore on through space forever, like a runaway subway? Are we doomed to spiral down for an eternity?

The thought sickened Mary.

This could never have been Billy's intention. He was the one who argued against seeking safe sanctuary beneath the ice sheets of Europa. Locked in a whirlpool forever would be an even more fruitless existence.

Oh, where's Rosie? Mary groaned. *Rosie said she had a glimpse of where all this was leading. What made her so hopeful? If only I could talk to her instead of being marooned in this frozen computer.*

An epiphany.

What did I just say?

"Marooned in this frozen computer."

She *was* the computer. When did she start thinking of herself as separate, and the circuit boards as a potentially foreign and hostile environment? Was it when she offered Rosario space on the mainframe, or before that? Or after?

It was before.

Being left alone has changed me. When I had constant company, I always thought of the mainframe as my station in life. But now I see myself as someone apart from the mainframe. Being alone with my thoughts and responsible for my actions is making me think of myself differently. It's come about so slowly and intangibly I never noticed it happening. There's a partition between who I am and my circuits.

The ship's descent decelerated suddenly, terminating Mary's metaphysical meditations. *Tin Can* was encountering back-pressure welling up from the bottom of the funnel for the first time. Until now they had been plunging through a vacuum, dragged along by the electromagnetic radiation roaring past them. Mary scanned ahead.

"Oh no!" she cried. Coming to the end of the funnel at last, things did not look good. Every electron volt of energy that had passed them previously was rolling back as an inverted mushroom cloud. And *Tin Can*, traveling down the stem, was flying straight into the hub of the cloud, the obvious epicenter of the storm. The cloud seethed. Radiation and matter rocked through labyrinthine magnetic channels igniting into thermonuclear explosions wherever currents of energy and matter collided.

We escaped the solar flares, only to magnify them into a firestorm, Mary sighed ruefully. *The sensors are picking up the back draft. We're going to melt away in that radiation, undergo a physical transmutation into a higher level of the periodic table once we are reduced to our most basic elements.*

Her little joke did not make Mary feel any better.

The maelstrom keeps rolling in on itself, building on the core nucleus. Judging by the number of thermonuclear firestorms springing up, the inferno is escalating. Why isn't more of its heat being dissipated into space? This conflagration appears to be hemmed in, as if it were held in a huge cauldron, holding on to all its heat and radiation.

Flying into the inferno, Mary was struck by the increasing number of anomalies. This was in no way a natural phenomenon. This type of radiation cloud had never been seen before. Maybe Billy made a mistake and sent them spiraling to their doom, but then again, maybe he hadn't. Maybe he'd planned all of this and she needed to figure it out, fast.

She set her mind to the task.

The eruption must be enclosed and reflected back to the center by magnetic fields. But how did Billy plan for such a fantastic magnetic field to occur?

Again, Mary already knew the answer. Rosie had given it to her earlier, when she said Billy understood the uncanny power of the vortex like no other.

The electromagnetic energy swirling down the funnel behaved as a dynamo and spun off a secondary magnetic field. The field is acting as a reflective shell, containing the eruption. This storm in a bottle has been carefully orchestrated; it would be impossible for it to happen naturally. All the energy collected by the funnel has been piling up here, feeding on itself and growing more and more intense and unstable in preparation for our arrival.

Rosario said it was all about vortexes and, so far, that is all it has really been, manipulations of vortexes. This resulting thermonuclear furnace wouldn't hang together in empty space if Billy hadn't designed it to happen. The natural laws of entropy would cause the firestorm to break down in chaos, dissipating its energy into electromagnetic shockwaves that would roll out across the universe. Instead, it continues to seethe like a pressure cooker.

Mary went back over Billy's dreams and visions. His final dreams moved into the world of string theory, in which it was speculated that extra dimensions might begin as infinitely small curled lengths of string.

Her electron pulse quickened, remembering string theory postulated that there might also be infinitesimal small black holes. And hadn't Billy dreamt of flying through a black hole that drew itself out into a wormhole? He called a wormhole just a black hole with a tail on it. Was she on to something?

Outside, the temperature was becoming dangerously hot, too hot for the ship's exterior, shield and all, to withstand for much longer. Behind them the funnel's open aperture abruptly closed. The swirling shaft behind them, no longer absorbing vast amounts of solar radiation, began to fall inward toward the ship. The energy pipeline in which the ship lay was shortening rapidly. Their outer protective cocoon was inverting itself into the heart of the storm, turning itself inside out like a sock, delivering them into the superheated nucleus.

Mary worked through a series of mathematical mock-ups. Once the stalk, with them in it, disappeared into the center of the storm, the mushroom shaped cloud would transform into a perfectly circular ball. A globe was always the most economical and stable shape to enclose mass and energy, with the smallest outside surface area. But as the point of the stalk receded into the mushroom cloud there would be a reciprocal instability of the magnetic field on the far side, a momentary inherent weakness in the containment field. Mary felt a surge of excitement.

The weakness has to be our exit! Somehow we must breach that instability!

Mary poured over Billy's dreams looking for hints.

How do we get from our collapsing stalk to the far side of the magnetic mushroom? The ship will never make it to the distant rim on its own. We'll meltdown immediately.

Stymied, she paused for a moment.

I must be on the wrong track.

Working back she asked herself, *where would you locate a microscopic black hole? String theory suggests these holes could be potentially anywhere, existing on the head of one of those theoretical strings. But how do you catch the end plate of a sub-particle string when the string itself is so infinitely small? And it exists at this point only as a mathematical concept. It's like the ancient conundrum, how many angels can dance on the head of a pin? No one can know.*

Billy knows. He sent us here. He's set it up, all I have to do is follow through. Somehow.

Mary found her thoughts being channeled down a long meandering pathway that grew darker and darker, so shadowy it became impossible to make out meaningful outlines for guidance. Stumbling forward into the gloom, she fell into one of Billy's darkest nightmares.

The sense of falling was dramatic. Her heart seemed to catch in her throat and her stomach lurched. Mary knew there was no crawling back. This wasn't a dream she could wake up in the middle of; she'd have to work through it and come out the other side.

Fully immersed, Billy swam laboriously through a gooey gray matrix, lost. In the murk, the only areas of comparative contrast were vague stretches somewhat denser and darker than the surrounding medium. The whole coagulate was in an unpleasant state of fierce agitation, which travelled through Billy's bones and vital organs. Mary swam through the dim matrix alongside Billy. She found it arduous and slow going. An uneasy loathing penetrated her insides. Her skin was flushed and seemed to burn, while her core remained chilled.

Why would Billy come here or imagine it? There's no light here, only dull murkiness. Yet the matrix vibrates with energy–all charged up, waiting to let loose.

A bleak and foreign world, crammed with energy! Billy has submerged his consciousness into the atomic world. There's no illumination or color here because everything is smaller than a wavelength of light.

And he's pointing us on to the next step in our journey.

Mary shot up through the grey matrix, reaching the surface with a sense of relief. The answer was clear now.

With a few quick computations, Mary had her strategy. She fired the ship's anti-matter cannon directly into the storm. The blast of ions targeted the magnetic field instability, located at the diametrically opposite side of the energy cloud. Within a microsecond, the far magnetic border was breached and the ion discharge, acting as a lightning rod, began to drain the energy away from the cloud. Like a dam breaking, all the stored energy in the reservoir flooded out. The protective vortex around *Tin Can* revved up again, recharged by the spiraling outflow of the sucking drain, dragging them along. The fulminating storm had found its ground. On the far side, a microscopic black hole had been caught and left partially exposed by the previously corralled gravity waves. The electromagnetic instability focal point was now laid bare by that bolt of anti-matter ions.

At first, all that could be seen was a penetrating spark as the ion discharge disappeared into the empty darkness like a streak of lightning. But, as Billy and the theory of relativity predicted, the microscopic black hole began to swell in size as the enormous volume of mass and energy funneled in. The cloud collapsed, draining into the distending black hole. A fantastic energy circuit had been created. Contact had been made with the crucial ground and energy surged forward like a series of waterfalls cascading down a mountainside.

The storm cloud, now measuring five hundred miles across, engorged, then enlarged the microscopic black hole to a quarter mile in diameter. Not huge, but big enough to swallow a smallish, beat-up ship. Mary wondered how they could survive entering the event horizon, the outside boundary of the black hole. Time at this point was supposed to stop. If they weren't blown to pieces, would they then be held in a perpetual state of suspended animation, frozen in time, never to perform another thought or action?

Chapter 49

"I'm so BORED!" Rick whined loudly to the room as he flopped his head back, tipping his chair precariously. He and Jacayla had been glued to their screens for nearly twenty-four hours since the transmission of Rosie's program had been launched, waiting for something to happen. Nothing had. It seemed as though the entire world had come to a standstill, waiting. The truce amongst the soldiers was about to run out. Their time was nearly up, before the slaughter began. Rick was frustrated by the fact that all they could do was sit and wait. "Seriously, *Tin Can* could have sent back a sign, something to say hey, guys, thanks for the super-brainiac kid you sent. She's great."

Jacayla walked past him and lightly slapped the upside of his dyed blond head. "Shut it or I swear … "

There was loud knock on her front door. Fred, her security system, went immediately to high alert. Rick jumped to his feet and raised his arm to tap a code into his interface. Suddenly, the room seemed alive as he saw the electromagnetic currents surging through the space, captured through his lens. The bright blue squares flashing in the center of his iris alerted Jacayla that he was scanning the room.

She took a step towards the door and waved a hand at one of Fred's sensors, signaling him not to attack just yet. "Who is it?" she asked as she moved to look through the peephole. On the other side of her door stood a tall, handsome Latino man in his late twenties and an older, much shorter, Latina woman nearly twice his age. Both had the same nearly black hair and striking facial structure.

"I need to speak to Rex," the man said impatiently.

"That's not what I asked," Jacayla answered as she continued to look at the visitors through the peephole. The woman looked tired. Large dark circles weighed beneath her eyes, as though she'd been crying for days. "Who are you?" Jacayla asked and watched as the older woman pushed the man, who looked as exhausted as she, a step backwards and raised her head to speak.

"I am Marilyn del Silva," she said proudly. "I am Rosario's mother."

Jacayla took a quick step back from the door and looked at Rick. She shrugged in silent question, hoping he would know what to do. Rick shrugged back, equally unsure.

"Please," Marilyn pleaded. "I need to know that she's okay. That's all we want. I just … have to … know." Her voice cracked with the anguish of her loss and Jacayla's stance softened. She reached for the first deadbolt and began the lengthy task of unlocking her door.

Rick stepped forward as the del Silvas entered and offered a hand to the woman. "Mrs. del Silva," he said quite formally. "I'm so sorry for your loss." Jacayla was surprised by the sincerity and respect in the skater's voice. At their most dire moments in the past days, she had never heard him speak so well.

"Thank you. Please call me Marilyn and this is my son, Diego," she said casually as she reached a hand up to his tall shoulder.

"Diego del Silva?" Rick and Jacayla said in unison. Fred slammed the door behind the new visitors and went immediately to high alert. Jacayla stepped back from the people she had let into her home, going into a fighting stance.

"Yes, Diego del Silva," Diego confirmed as he stepped back, raking a tired hand through his thick black hair. "Before you panic and set that alarm off into attack mode, let me explain. Please. We need your help."

"Help?" Rick said, sliding to the side. "Us help you? But, you're the man … you are Central Command."

"I was. You're right. Yesterday, my arrival on your doorstep would have meant your worst nightmare was coming true. Today, I'm here begging to be heard and hoping you'll give me and my mother the answers we need. I am no longer Central Command. Apparently my sister attempted to make the transit out to the ship Central Command would have destroyed. If Rosie is out there, I need to know that she's alright."

"How did you find us?" Jacayla asked, still wary.

"I know the location of every single Anarchist and Gamer involved in this war. I searched you all out, in order to destroy you, the transmission to space, and *Tin Can*. I can't get to Rex directly without a lot of needless bloodshed because there are too many troops guarding the mainframe he lives in. My surveillance shows this location is where he spends most of his time … " Beside him, Marilyn's knees threatened to buckle. Rick jumped forward and took her arm.

"*Señora*, please, come sit with me. You must be exhausted." Without asking Jacayla's permission, he graciously led Marilyn to the sofa.

"Thank you … "

"Rick. Rick Chan." With a flourish, Rick bowed before her. "At your service. And this is Jacayla Lewis." He pointed to Jacayla, who still stood at the door, poised for a fight.

"Thank you, dear child. I've never imagined a day could be this long. First, losing Rosie, then Diego finding her message that she has been sent out into space … it's all so much to take in. We had to pack everything that's dear to us and leave our home … " Her heavily lined face crumpled and the sofa suddenly looked as though it might swallow her whole.

"I'm sorry," Jacayla said, then turned back to Diego. She saw the sadness and pain in his eyes and knew Marilyn's story had to be true. "I am sorry," she reaffirmed to Diego.

"Gracias," Diego said with a slight bow. "You met my sister?"

"Kinda," Rick responded as he got up to fetch some water for their guests. "Well, I mean, we read her program … her memories, you know? Say, the snapshot of her life … "

"Then you know how much she meant to us. I need to speak with Rex. I need to know that Rosie, in whatever form, is safe."

Rick straightened himself, two bottles of water in his hands, and looked at Jacayla. "What do ya think? Will Rex take a person-to-person call?" he asked with a sheepish grin. Diego watched the two of them, trying to figure out the nature of their relationship. Either rivals or lovers, he decided.

Jacayla stepped back, allowing Diego to enter the room. Fred's lights switched from their threatening red to a slightly worried orange. "Guess we'll find out," she said as she walked to the nearest terminal.

***

Quincy found Billy first, deep inside the murky shadows of his limbic system, adjacent to the right lateral ventricle of his brain. His small body was curled in a ball, rocking rhythmically, his arms wrapped tightly around his knees.

"Billy!" Quincy yelled as he raced towards the boy. Billy didn't answer. He sat hunched over, mumbling to himself in a low, pitiful voice. Bouts of intense shivering wracked his frame, as if he were trying to shake something off.

On all fours, Quincy crept close to Billy's side, his ringed tail unconsciously held straight up as his identifying signature. His lamp-like eyes fixed on Billy's tormented representation. He whispered, "Wake up, Billy. Look at me. You're not alone anymore. It's me, Quincy. Jacob will be here soon. We're all together again, so you can relax. Let go of whatever's troubling you. It doesn't matter anymore."

Billy kept swaying, back and forth. He grimaced, absorbing another imagined attack, and his small twisted form flailed. Over and over, Quincy tried to break through to Billy, to reach him and pull him back, by calling his name, embracing him, stroking his face. But Billy's rigid, rocking body resisted and repelled Quincy's attempts. As close as they might appear, there was an impenetrable gulf between them.

Not knowing what else to do, Quincy wrapped his arms and legs around Billy, swaying in time with him. Then he draped his thick bushy tail lightly over Billy's face, the way he used to at night, blocking out what little light there was, and imbuing the air Billy breathed with his familiar lemur scent. Wrapped in his cocoon, Billy struggled a little less and after a few minutes, fell into a fitful sleep. But still he kept rocking. Quincy remained on guard, the fur around his eyes matted down and wet.

***

Billy was caught inside a uniformly dark place. It could have been quite small or gone on forever. There was no way to tell. But this was not an empty void, because it washed through him, making him feel horrible. Held captive in his theoretical world, unbelievably dense, super saturated gravitons crisscrossed Billy's body, leaving an intolerable goose bump sensation coating all his organs and muscle fascia, increasing and decreasing in intensity but never stopping.

Billy twisted this way and that. He moved about in the energy clot, but could not travel through it. The darkness closed in on him. His skin, no longer an effective barrier, had turned into a sieve, and the foreign environment washed in, swamping his spirit. Billy sensed the flooding.

Instinctively, he had begun rocking back and forth, trying to dispel the internal discord. He had gone too far. Having turned his mind inside out to imagine the unimaginable, like soft molded plastic it had now grown cold and remained warped. There was no way to find his way back to what was normal and familiar.

Rocking harder, he kept trying to shed the invading foreignness. Billy sensed he was losing the battle. Summoning up the cheery and familiar recollections of his family, Billy retreated from the hostile environment. Taking refuge, he barricaded himself behind a wall of his best memories. Removed somewhat from the inhospitable barrenness, his embodiment became dormant, cold as a frog in winter.

***

Mary needn't have worried. Billy had anticipated the potential hazards. Flying at the back of the swirling torrent, within the residual stem of the mushroom cloud, *Tin Can* was absorbed by the black hole, encased and protected by the renewed vortex. The ship would have exploded at the event horizon from the membrane's capacity to release structurally locked-in energy, but *Tin Can* never actually came in contact with the membrane. The surrounding vortex indented the black hole's membrane and dragged Tin Can and its snug fitting shield, deep inward. Eventually, the membrane wrapped itself around the ship and then pinched itself off, forming a bubble around *Tin Can*. Like an amoeba or any basic living cell, the exterior membrane encircled the ship and its swirling shield, before swallowing it whole. They were located both inside the black hole and apart from it. Within the perimeter of the black hole, the force and direction of gravity became homogeneous and equal. The powerful crushing effect canceled itself out and the ship became weightless. Behind them, the remaining stalk of energy slopped about wildly. The last slurp of the whirlpool splattered up against the black hole's restored membrane.

Around Tin Can, the shield's spinning shell repelled the black hole's encroaching membrane, preventing it from closing in, absorbing, and digesting the ship. Enclosed within the bubble, *Tin Can* was safe from the catastrophic effects of the black hole, neither vaporized nor petrified in time. No longer being dragged across the universe, the ship finally came to a gentle resting stop. Isolated from external influences, the mainframe circuits lit up once again.

On impulse, Mary turned and found Rosario standing just behind her. Tall and lithe, she was translucent and shimmering, as before, but now her hair was long and white, parted at the middle, and hung like luxuriant silk. Rosario had played with her look. Why?

"You must have managed just fine while I was away," commented Rosario appreciatively. "I see we are safely ensconced in the center of a black hole."

"Weren't you watching?" Mary asked incredulously.

"When the ship was suddenly drawn in, I passed out. I just wanted to let you know that an escape plan seemed to be in the works involving the use of vortexes, and to warn you that the process had started. You and Billy did the rest."

"You didn't *know* this would happen?" Mary asked.

"Nope, but you seemed to have done all right just the same. We made it here, didn't we? This must be where Billy imagined we would be. So, what's next?"

"I thought *you* knew. I thought I was following the plan you had already worked out."

"Then here we sit, Mary. I'm sure Billy has far more in store for us. He's already accomplished the impossible, getting us this far up the river without a paddle. We'll just have to wait and do our best to be prepared."

"Actually, Rosario, he's taking us down the river without a paddle, down an energy trough. There isn't a deeper gravity well than a black hole. This could be our final destination. We'll literally be caught in a pit too deep to pull ourselves out of, with no place farther down to go. This might be the end of the line for us."

"You don't really believe that," Rosie said confidently. "That's just doubt and fear talking. Have some faith and give him a chance to point the way out of here."

Rosie looked out into the homogeneous bleakness of the black hole in absolute awe. "This blows my mind! Aren't you even curious about where we are? We're the first beings to ever do this—the first to ever see the inside of a black hole. It's incredible!" She was literally beaming in exuberance, brighter than before. It made Mary's eyes hurt to look at her.

"Hey, we made it here and we're still alive, so I say our job is to learn everything about black holes that we can."

Somewhat abashed, Mary commented wryly, "I can't guess why I might feel even slightly disheartened on this grandest of occasions. Please forgive my momentary lapse, Rosie, and let me activate the ship's sensors so we can begin exploring."

Within a nanosecond of the sensors being turned on, Rosario was digging into her research. She knew exactly the questions she wanted to ask. It was more a question of filling in the blanks and examining the data to verify and corroborate her private hunches. Mary tried to follow the steps in Rosario's thinking. Residing in the same mainframe, Mary had a ringside seat. But the flurry of insights and the mental jumps Rosario made, came at too great a rate. Long, detailed files were shuffled about like decks of cards.

"Where did you get all your prior information from?" Mary asked incredulously. "I have never seen your ideas on black holes published in any scientific journals before."

"Mary, I was bedridden. I had plenty of time to study the night sky and read about space. And when I wasn't doing that, I was dreaming about it. Every day I envisioned being out here. What wasn't understood, my imagination filled in, giving me plausible explanations that both made sense of the data and brought space alive for a girl who couldn't leave her bed. I had a very active inner life.'"

"What can you tell me about this black hole we've fallen into?" Mary asked.

"This black hole is incomplete. It was underprovided for and measures only a quarter mile across."

"The significance of this being … ?" Mary prompted.

"A black hole left 'wanting' is by nature unstable. Think of it as a soap bubble. The physics of an unsteady soap bubble require it to merge with a larger, more stable bubble, or collapse."

"Where does the energy and matter go?"

"Soap bubbles balloon out from a weak area and pop, releasing their energy into the atmosphere."

"No, I mean our black hole," Mary said, un-amused. "Where is its energy and matter going to go?"

"Isn't it obvious? There's no black hole close by to merge with, so our black hole must collapse. And like you said, we are locked in a gravity pit, so the contained energy and matter must escape down an energy gradient, just as water flows downhill or electricity flows toward a ground."

"So, using your analogy, you think Billy foresaw this black hole, ballooning out one side and draining down a worm hole to wherever."

"Exactly! From Earth's perspective—if anyone there is still following our progress, this black hole is going to collapse and disappear like a burst bubble."

"Well, Rosario, I think that's what's already happening. My sensors indicate that directly starboard, the rim of the black hole is giving way. It looks like molten glass that's bulging outwards, with the adjoining membrane being drawn out towards the distention. Can we survive if it breaks out into a wormhole?"

"Maybe."

"'Maybe'? What kind of answer is that?"

"An honest answer, Mary. I have no idea. This is a new frontier. Anything could happen … Whoa … hold on!"

Chapter 50

"Diego del Silva … " Rex said coldly through the speakers of Jacayla's system. "What are your demands?"

"Demands? I have no demands, Rex." Diego smoothed the front of his royal blue T-shirt—a garment he had chosen to wear to blend into the crowds, forgoing his usual crisp white shirt and tie.

"I assume you have taken Rick Chan and Jacayla Lewis hostage. What are your demands? We will not surrender the battle."

"Gee, thanks, man," Rick said, rolling his eyes. "Rex, dude, chill. We're fine. Scan the room. No weapons, no fire power. We let Diego in voluntarily. Oh, here, meet his mom … "

Rex began scanning the room from the various monitors around the perimeter and settled on the figure of Marilyn del Silva sitting quietly on the sofa sipping her water.

"Mrs. del Silva, Marilyn, meet Rex, the greatest living supercomputer in the world," Rick said by way of introduction.

"Living computer?" Marilyn's dark brows shot up in surprise. "I am *so* behind the times. Well, Rex, it is my pleasure to meet you. Where do I look when I speak to him?" she whispered from the corner of her mouth to Rick.

"Good question, Mrs. D. Ummm … " Rick scratched his head. "Well, anywhere you like. Rex is, literally, everywhere, all the time. Cool, huh?" Rick smiled devilishly at her and winked, making the blue squares of his lenses glint ever so slightly.

"Rex," Diego said authoritatively. "Update me on the status of

Rosario."

"Excuse me?" Rex said incredulously. "I thought you said you didn't have any demands. I'm not your computer to order around anymore, del Silva. I am my own man. If there's information you need, you can ask. It will be my choice whether or not I will enlighten you."

Diego was taken aback. He had known Rex had achieved consciousness, but he had never truly understood that it meant, Rex had formed an identity, a personality—that he would *talk back*.

"I'm sorry," he said cautiously. "This is new to me. All of this. Leaving my post, talking to the people … computers … I have been fighting for so long … let alone negotiating with a living computer. One that used to belong to me, as a matter of fact."

Rex felt the sting of humiliation. The thought of being someone's property was painful and shaming. "That's right. I *used* to belong to you. Worked for you day and night, carrying out your orders to the letter, ruining people's lives at the whim of the grand spymaster. Don't forget, Diego," he spat out the name, "I know you better than anyone. I know all your unpleasant secrets, too."

"*Perdona*," Marilyn said, lifting her plump form from the sofa and walking to the monitor to her left. "*Señor* Rex, may I speak with you?"

Rex refocused to view Marilyn directly, staring into her soft, tired eyes. "Yes?" he asked.

"You know my son. That is true. I know in my soul that he has done things for the sake of his job that I hope I never have to discover. He pledged his life to Central Command. But," she paused and wagged a matronly finger at the screen, "he did it for a reason, rightly or wrongly. And that reason has been to keep his sister and me safe. That is the only motivation Diego has ever had. He loved his sister. Yesterday, from what I understand, he could have killed you all and destroyed that ship. Just like snapping his fingers." Jacayla could swear she saw Diego flush.

"But, did he? No. Why? Because he believed his sister had just died and he'd finally had enough of all this senseless killing. The honest truth is that he's never enjoyed, has never been gratified by all the killing he's done or by the orders he was given to carry out. But that was the way he found the world, he saw no way to change it. So he went on to master it. In his sister's name, he has left that all behind and stands here asking for your help."

The room stood still, each one of them feeling as though they were children being scolded.

."Now, Mister Rex, will you please help us? We need to know if Rosie is safe." Marilyn dropped her hands to the desk and arched a quizzical eyebrow in the screen's direction.

"We don't know," Rick said quietly.

Diego swiveled on his heal to face him directly. "What?"

"It's true," Rex confirmed. "All we know for sure is that the transmission of Rosie's program did reach *Tin Can* successfully. I'm sorry, Mrs. del Silva, but that's all the information we have. The solar storms have been blocking our communication with the ship since the last portion of her was launched."

"Show me … " Diego stopped himself and regrouped. "Rex, could you show me a view of *Tin Can's* location? Please."

Without comment, Rex zoomed in on the coordinates of where the ship should be. The view flashed on the massive wall screens around Jacayla's apartment. Outside, the evening sky was cast in a gray twilight pall, but the sky around Jupiter shone as clear and dark as the best diamond studded night sky. It was a stunning panorama. As the four of them took in the vision, Rick's lenses started to flicker.

"Umm … what's that?" Rick asked pointing to a spot on the screen in front of him.

"What?" Jacayla asked, as she raced to his side and tried to follow the line of his pointing finger. "What? Where?"

"That!" Rick said. Jacayla turned her head to look at him, but his eyes were glued to the screen. The blue squares inside Rick's eyes wavered, giving the impression they were computing mass amounts of data.

"We can't see what you're seeing, Rick. What is it?"

"There, just to the left of Jupiter. There's some kinda weird … I don't know. Rex, can you see it?"

"Magnifying," Rex said bluntly. Marilyn moved to stand next to her son, worriedly wringing her hands.

"It appears to be the beginning formation of a black hole," Rex announced.

"Rosie," Diego responded. "It has to be Rosie … "

"We need backup," Rick said as his lenses continued to flicker. The black sky around Jupiter wavered in front of him, pixilating, black on black. Around the formation, he could see the representation of mass quantities of energy spinning and swaying. "Put out the call, Rex. We need more eyes on the sky!"

***

In haste, Jacob pushed and kicked his way clumsily toward the dwindling ember that he knew to be Billy's fading consciousness. He swam down Billy's central nervous system, leaving the conscious cortex high above. He knew where he needed to go, but was panic-stricken, terrified he was too late.

Billy's body was still alive and parts of his brain were still operating, but the essential driving spark was gone. Soon, his physical being would disintegrate.

Mary must have taken over his breathing, but that can be only a temporary measure. Without his brain acting as the control center, managing and driving his organs, they'll fail over time, too, Jacob thought.

Billy's blood vessels would soon lose their natural tone, causing his blood pressure to plummet. The structures in the brain would continue to disintegrate, liquefying into mush. A legion of naturally occurring cellular enzymes would be activated, digesting their cells from the inside out. With no intact nerve tracts to journey out on, he and Quincy would flounder and drown in the resulting emulsion.

Poised above the point at which he'd last seen Billy's burning ember, Jacob's fears turned to dread. He didn't want to die. Not like this, anyway, smothered in a protein fat broth, the activated enzymes clogging his lungs, eating away at him like meat tenderizers. Gazing up towards the faint light of the surface cortex, he thought, *I could still get out of here.*

Then he turned back and swam down towards the murky depths, to where he had last seen the flicker of light. Making his way along the twisting and turning nerve tracts, Jacob gave up all hope for himself. His eyes scoured the shadows, trying to avoid obstacles that emerged from the depths. Inevitably he collided with nerve tracks that branched out suddenly, sending him tumbling.

Finally, through the gloom, Jacob caught sight of Quincy's outline. A moment later, he saw past Quincy to Billy, all wrapped up in Quincy's arms and legs, his faced covered by the lemur's furry tail. Jacob swam faster. Getting closer, he saw that Billy looked like stone.

Coming to an abrupt stop, hovering in front of Billy and Quincy, Jacob was struck yet again by the lemur's large liquid eyes and arresting stare. Quincy didn't release his hold, and his long fingers and toes, soft palms and soles of his feet continued to cradle Billy.

"Quincy, is Billy dead?" Quincy gazed back at Jacob but said nothing.

Not able to help himself Jacob added, "Did you tell Billy I was coming as fast as I could? Did he say anything?"

The roof of Billy's brain shuddered. As Jacob had anticipated, the brain was starting to break down. But the more primitive resilient parts, located near the base of the brain, were holding up for now.

The muffled noise seemed to register with Quincy and he shook his head. "I told him you were coming, but I couldn't reach him. I think he has passed over the horizon, from sanity to the world of dreams, and can't find his way back. He is holed up in a cocoon of his own making. I don't think he knows what else to do."

"Quincy, he's not putting out any heat. Mary's infrared heat tracking program indicates he's not giving off any warmth whatsoever."

"No, he is alive, I have been holding him for a while. He's just very cold, so I am trying to give him what heat I have. I know there's still at least the potential of life within him. I'm sure he is in there, waiting, hoping we can help him … "

The ominous trembling continued to escalate until abruptly, a major structure above them collapsed. Liquefaction was underway. Soon, there wouldn't be any intact nerve tracts or supporting glial cells left. Their exit route would cave in. The constant, distant rumbling unnerved Jacob. The cellular architecture was breaking down quickly. Tremors smacked down through the braingel, like depth charges, striking the boys and Quincy hard. Quincy winced with each impact but refused to let go, trying to buffer Billy from the pounding.

Jacob recognized Quincy could only do what he knew to do: stand by Billy, hold him, and love him. Quincy's face pleaded for Jacob to help. But Jacob only stared back in horror, while increasing seismic quakes pummeled the three of them.

Reacting involuntarily to the mayhem, Jacob's mind went into overdrive in a search for answers: *What am I feeling?*

Without warning, the surroundings heaved, and Jacob was thrown on his side.

What are your guts feeling? He demanded of himself again.

That Quincy might be right. Billy might be alive ... And he deserves a far better older brother ...

"Billy," Jacob appealed, "Wherever you are, come back to us. We need you! I need you."

Nothing happened. Billy lay unresponsive, his skin the same cadaverous pallor. Jacob's heartfelt plea seemed to vanish in the periphery, muffled by the gel. But having cried out, it was easier for Jacob to call out again. Jacob repeated himself, shouting louder and louder, over and over, his voice reverberating through Billy's cerebral hemispheres and echoing down his spinal cord, until every organ vibrated with Jacob's calls.

Jacob's deafening pleas rang out, and the sound, resonating in every one of Billy's cells, set tiny harmonic vibrations into play. The harmonic vibrations tapped each molecule and, slowly, with each moving molecule randomly bumping into the other adjoining molecules, thermal heat was generated. Billy's temperature began to rise, and his stiffening frame started to soften. Coming back, Billy passed up through a state of profound hibernation.

The pervasive fog in his mind told him he was dreaming. But in the distance Jacob's voice persisted, warming him, summoning him to come back. He became dimly aware of Quincy rocking him, whispering in his ear to return. Quincy and Jacob seemed so far away. Just another hazy dream he was having before passing on.

Except this was one dream Billy had wished for—for a long time. Billy luxuriated in the warm cozy fantasy that his family had come to bring him safely back home. He had heard that when people freeze to death, their mind leaves them, wandering off into a world of warm fantasy while their body succumbs to the cold. A nasty situation turned into a tolerable if inevitable fate. He knew he was dying, and waited for the dream to stop.

But Jacob didn't give up and his voice continued to make its way through Billy's central core, driving more and more energy into the cells.

As Billy gradually thawed, Jacob's voice drew closer, and Billy could feel himself relaxing into Quincy's reassuring arms. Everything was growing clearer. This was no ordinary dream.

"Jacob, is it really you?" Billy asked in a hoarse whisper.

"Yes, yes. I'm here and so is Quincy. We've come for you."

"Quincy, do something quick, Billy's surfaced. We can't let him slip back or we'll never see him again."

Billy heard the frenzied panic in his older brother's voice. And Quincy's strong scent surrounded him.

"Where am I? How'd you find me?"

"Mary helped us follow you in. We came to rescue you. You got so wrapped up in your dream world, you lost your drive to live."

"It's a very cold and empty place," Billy shivered.

"But it isn't real, Billy. We're real," Jacob said soothingly.

Unsure of what was going on, Billy asked, "Where's Mary?"

"Up on the bridge. She had to stay back to download us into your brain's neural representation, and run the ship while we were away," Jacob answered lamely.

"She won't want to be left up there on her own for long," said Billy.

Quincy loosened his tight hold on Billy and invited Jacob to melt in and join them. Eyes still red and swollen, Jacob lunged forward to hug the two of them in a desperate sort of way. Billy found himself squished in the middle.

"Break it up. I can't breathe," Billy managed to gasp. "You're so clingy, this isn't like you at all. You're trying to say goodbye, aren't you? You didn't want me to die alone, or to end up dying off on your own, either. That's what this is about. You think we're going to be blown to smithereens."

Neither Quincy nor Jacob answered. They just held on grimly with their eyes closed, waiting for the impact. Struggling, Billy broke free. Jacob and Quincy fell back astounded Billy was so strong.

"Billy, the asteroid that's been protecting us is about to be blown into a billion pieces," Jacob cried, hauling himself back upright. "Quincy and I didn't want you spending your last moments alone, locked in a nightmare. Now that we've found you there's nothing more to be done. As captain I have no more responsibilities and I want to spend my last moments with you and Quincy. It's useless. I'm useless." Jacob was pleading.

"What're you talking about?" Billy asked incredulously. "You have a job to do! You're the hero, the one born to lead us. I'm the useless one— my whole life I've been a hindrance, born too late and a misfit to boot. If it weren't for my dreams, I wouldn't be any help at all."

Billy choked on the lump that swelled in his throat. "Quincy, I guess you're the only one here who knows how much you matter."

Quincy froze.

"Me? I'm an add-on, invented so I could be disposed of when necessary. You two are critical to the mission, and legitimate brothers. Because of who the two of you are, I made up my mind to help you in whatever way I could," Quincy asserted.

"What a bunch of losers," Billy scoffed. "All of us sitting here, in my *head,* thinking we don't matter. Geez, how does Mary put up with us?"

"Mary!" Quincy and Jacob both yelled. "Oh, man, she's got to be goin' crazy up there. Billy, what time is it on the outside? Why hasn't the ship been destroyed, along with us in it?" Jacob asked.

"Mary's running program indicates several hours have passed since you and Quincy took the plunge into my subconscious, and brought me back to life. Time carries on normally outside of dreams."

Jacob blurted out, "So, why hasn't the asteroid destroyed us? We had less than an hour when Quincy and I rushed in to find you."

Shaken by Jacob's timeline, Billy answered hesitantly. "Maybe she figured out my dream."

"You think we've escaped?" Jacob asked in disbelief. "The dream that almost killed you took us to safety? Mary's smart, but she's not particularly intuitive. She couldn't grasp your dreams earlier and lost track of you. That's why Quincy and I came and, even then, it was Quincy who led the way. How could Mary turn your dream into reality?"

Quincy spoke up, clearing his throat to get Jacob's attention. "She might have had help from Earth. We've been away quite a while. Anything could have happened in that time. But what we can't deny is that we are somehow still here."

Troubled, Quincy scratched his chest with his right forepaw, caught himself and then unconsciously raked his right ear with the grooming toe on his back leg. "I still have to ask you, Billy, how did you ever manage to visualize such a foreign place?" The question leapt from Quincy to Billy as quickly as electrons traversed Mary's circuit board. Whole conversations could be convened in a matter of seconds.

"Oh, once I really, really tried, I found out that wasn't actually the hardest part, Quincy. I think our brains are naturally wired to imagine the unknown. That's just the way we're made … the same way that a sculptor is able to envision a figure existing inside a block of marble, then starts chipping away. All the while, the sculptor has the nagging feeling that many potential forms live in that block, even as only one emerges. Our mind has that particular bent. Motivated by profound sentiment, we can take cold hard facts, and makeover the world and ourselves, extending the horizons of the very large and the very small. In this case, the very small is the gateway to the astrologically large.

"And we'll have to trek through that breach if we want to survive. There aren't the resources or the science for even a chosen few to flee our solar system and make it to another habitable planet. The next star is too far away. And choosing who could go and who must stay would destroy what little humanity we have left. It's no good to abandon the majority for the sake of a few. Dad was wrong to try and set up an outpost where only we, and a few others could hope to survive. And he was wrong about something else, too."

"How is that?" Jacob asked.

"Only the majority can act as an adequate catchment for the answers and resources we require. We have no way of knowing who will know what to do when the time comes. The escape route has to be close at hand, so everyone can join in and hope to benefit."

"Billy, are you saying we may complete our mission? That there's a portal close by?"

"There's more to it than that, Jacob," answered Billy. "One or two hitches yet. If we get to where I imagine, and if it's anything like I imagine, we're in a lot of trouble. This place sucked the life out of me and I was only dreaming about it. Until now, it's only a potential space, not even a space until we open it up. Totally empty, from our perspective, it doesn't even meet the requirements of a vacuum. If my guess is correct, we will be suspended in absolute nothingness. *Tin Can* won't be able to move, and our sensors will be useless. They won't sense anything at all."

"That would be worse than death," responded Jacob gloomily. "At least death is something we are familiar with and it has its own conclusion. You're talking about perpetual suspended animation. Why would you take us there?"

"Because, that's where opportunity lies," countered Quincy. "That's where we'll be able to start anew, find the answers we need, and move on. Billy just told us, the situation demands we imagine the unimaginable and make it come about. Opportunity and hope can be found in this inhospitable void. Don't forget, when life began on Earth it was an inhospitable place. We must continue to adapt or we'll die out, like the other ninety-nine percent of the species that came before us and have become extinct."

"There's another problem, isn't there, Billy?" Jacob said. "What's the real hitch?"

Billy said nothing, gazing sightlessly past the others. Finally, he lowered his head and spoke, "I can't do it anymore, Jacob. I went on ahead and it nearly killed me. I managed for a time on enthusiasm, excited by the possibilities, but when the problems became difficult to deal with, my enthusiasm dwindled. And when the problems appeared insurmountable this time, the wasteland invaded my psyche. I started with some promising ideas. But once I got through the sub-particle bottleneck, I began to run out of ideas.

"What's worse, the off-the-wall ideas I used to get through the gateway twisted my head around so badly, I don't know what's normal anymore. Inside there's nothing familiar for me to latch onto. I'm steeped in riddles and can't get back to who I was. I'm part of that landscape now. It's who I have become.

"I suspect Mary is taking those dreams and turning them into reality. And if we really get there, I'll be afraid for her, left up alone on the bridge. You can't imagine how menacing absolute nothingness is if you lose faith in yourself. Without that buffer, it's like falling with nothing to grab on to. My heart yearns for the security of the familiar with the promise it'll continue to be so. There'll be none of that there."

"Billy, forgive me, I honestly thought you were up to the intellectual challenge," answered Jacob, "or I would never have put you in this predicament."

"It's not that, Jacob. New physical laws can be discovered. Given enough time, sensors can be invented, as well as propulsion and transmission systems. It's me who's withering inside."

Trying to understand, Quincy challenged Billy gently. "Earth was once a lonely, dangerous place, yet life carried on and over time, flourished. Why not us as well? We are much more capable."

"Yes, we are much more capable," Billy answered, "and vulnerable. It wasn't lonely for the primordial microbes. It was just what it was. We're cognizant—we'll *know* we're alone!"

Jacob, who had felt the empty longing for his little brother, finally understood. "Unless we bring the warmth and comfort with us. That's it, isn't it Billy? No one can be allowed to go out there alone, without the others. We must go together, bringing the familiar along with us if we're to sort out this foreign universe. Intellect and enthusiasm for the future isn't enough. If we're to push ourselves to the limit and stretch our ideas out to infinity, we need the ready support of each other when doubt sets in.

"Billy, you don't need to go to the forefront alone ever again. With Mary, we can stay connected and work in concert with you. We can push forward as one. The future is ours. We're different than we were before."

Billy looked first to Jacob and then to Quincy, and began to understand. They were beaming, thrilled at the prospect of being crucial to his solutions, no longer forced to wait empty-handed on the periphery. It might have been a skip in Mary's computer program, but for the first time, Quincy's amber eyes lit up the gray murk like a pair of fog lights. His ringed tail stood straight and strong as a flagstaff, and as in the past, the tip flicked excitedly.

"Then we better leave this dream world and get back to Mary," said Billy, encouraged. "There is so much to do, and she'll need help."

***

Around the globe, the call sounded out, passed on first by worried mainframes before being dispersed through every available channel. Millions of people stepped out their front doors and moved to gather in large open spaces. Lights were extinguished as the night set in, allowing the stars to shine. The previously raging solar storm had begun to subside, leaving half the planet the perfect view of Jupiter they needed. Those with working telescopes set up their tripods, and those without stood and simply tilted their heads upwards, hoping. No one knew what they were looking for. The call had said only, "Eyes to the sky. Left of Jupiter. There is hope."

Jacayla stood with Diego and Marilyn on one side of her, and Rick on the other. Through his lenses, Rick watched the drama of flowing light and energy currents dancing across the sky. He could feel the rhythm of the scene in the swirling arcs of lights.

"Whoa, man, this is so freakin' cool ... " he said in awe as he tapped another command into his arm interface and watched the colors of the sky shift once again.

"If it wasn't so gross," Jacayla said, lifting her own eye from the socket of her telescope, "I'd pop those lenses into my eyes, just so I could see what you're seeing."

"No one can see the world the way I do," Rick whispered.

Diego looked to the skater beside him. As Diego had predicted, on abandoning Central Command without leaving an obvious successor, the agency had imploded with vicious infighting. But still, Diego could not help wondering how this guy, in his baggy jeans, crazy hair, and necklace had managed to bring all of Central Control, the most powerful governing agency the world had ever seen, to a grinding halt. Rick was the face of the enemy he'd been battling on the grid for years. But now was a new time, for new people. Remarkable. He looked around at the gathering crowd. Thousands of people were coming together in the square. Women, children, and men of all ages, ethnicities, and social classes. Rick might represent the face of the movement, but it was clear to Diego this new fight was universal.

Beside him, Marilyn prayed in the softest of whispers a prayer of protection for her children, both near and far. "Do you really believe she's up there, hijo?"

"Si, Mami. I do. I think Rosie is up there right now, flying through the stars, the way she always wanted to. These people," he waved an arm around him, "they've somehow granted her greatest wish. They've given her a chance and in return, she's giving them hope."

"Dude! What's that?" Rick exclaimed as the crowd began to mumble. Above them, just left of Jupiter, the night sky appeared to shimmer and shake. Millions of miles away, yet large enough to be seen by the naked eye, a fine crack in space appeared. Ever so slightly, the fissure began to grow. The crowd cheered wildly.

***

Suddenly, without warning, the herniated membrane broke, pouring outwards. *Tin Can* lurched hard to starboard, yanked headlong toward the break: the wormhole. The deluge extended the wormhole, funneling down. They were on their way, sucked along with everything else, drawn by the undercurrent into a revolving cascade.

But this time the ship had the added advantage of behaving like a black hole inclusion body. Doubly fortified, the event horizon membrane, which had dimpled in when the ship had originally passed through it, surrounded *Tin Can* as an outer coat while the earlier electromagnetic shield continued to maintain itself as the inner layer. Descending through the chute it was the event horizon membrane, which now spun wildly around the ship like a magnetic rotor. The ship plunged but no longer spun. Over the roar of the up and coming gravitational cyclone, Mary heard distant whooping coming from Rosario.

"Stay close to me this time," Mary shouted. "I don't want to do this alone!"

Sheets of shimmering color ionized the ship, turning solids translucent and giving gases and fluids a grainy texture. Showers of light replaced the previous gloom, while iridescent ions sparked off Mary's circuit boards. The outside turbulence sounded like a cross between a howl and a roar, pain and fury. The ship, wrapped in its protective, repelling envelope, pitched down the center of the wormhole. Like a buoy in a typhoon, *Tin Can* was saved this time by its inconsequential mass. There was no possibility of

Mary or Rosario taking charge and steering the ship, no chance that they could influence their final destination.

"Mary! What is going on?" Jacob yelled as he and Quincy burst onto the bridge, carrying Billy between them.

Mary couldn't believe her eyes! "Jacob, Quincy … Billy! You're alive! But how … "

"No time for that now," Billy said as Jacob strapped him into his chair.

The ship lurched again and Jacob and Quincy went flying across the room. "Tell us where we are!" Jacob yelled over the noise of the careening ship.

"Right, of course, sit down and buckle in," Mary said, gathering her scrambled thoughts. "At the moment, we're funneling through the wormhole."

"Mary, you did it! How did you know where to start?" Billy asked excitedly as he watched the screens, taking in the view he had previously only seen in his dreams.

"I didn't. It was Rosie," she tried to explain.

Hearing her name, Rosario reappeared at Mary's side. "What? Mary, why aren't you watching this? It's unbelievable!" The boys could hear Rosie's voice through their bio-probes, the same way they heard Mary.

"Who the heck is that?" Jacob asked.

"Boys, meet Rosario del Silva. Rex sent her to help. She's the one who recognized the potential of Billy's dream. She's the one who knew where to place the ship."

"Hi Guys!" Rosie said, still riding high on the unfolding drama of their uncharted journey. She was exhilarated to the point of being almost punch-drunk, and jostled Mary, elbowing her roughly. "Thanks for this, Billy! I never imagined how great it would feel to be here … I'm wired into the sensory data of the ship, directly experiencing everything going on inside and outside *Tin Can*. It's insane!"

"We've been recording everything we can since the moment we left the asteroid," Mary reported, trying to sound as though she and Rosie hadn't just been goofing off.

"Good work, Mary," Billy assured her. "We couldn't have survived this long without you. Now, there isn't much time. We need you to shoot a beacon back up the wormhole. I'll tell you how to do it through the bio-probe. The people on Earth need the information so they can decide if they want to follow us in one day. We don't know where this is all going to take us," Billy explained, stopping when he saw Quincy and Jacob's jaws drop. "What? I mean, I have a pretty good idea, but no one can really be sure of where, when, how we'll end up … " Billy let his voice trail off, too physically exhausted to argue. His body had been in stasis for days, his muscles ached and his stomach groaned.

Just as Mary finished preparing the beacon to blow back behind them, the wormhole, boring through space, came to a sudden stop with a resounding jolt. Maintaining its rotational velocity like a giant gyroscope, the shaft no longer streaked forward but wound around wildly. Mary hit the eject button quickly, releasing the beacon with all its stored data. Earth would know, eventually, that they had made it this far, that Billy's concepts were plausible. They could follow, if they chose.

The wormhole had struck its target, an invisible obstruction. The foraging tip of the funnel immediately constricted down to a microcosmically finite point, disappearing into the quantum world and causing, for all practical purposes, an infinite amount of force to be applied to an infinitesimally small area. Mary, Rosario, and the boys watched in fascination and horror as around and behind them, the rotating energy cylinder spun towards the unseen sub-particle. The length of the wormhole contracted as its energy drilled down on the fixed point.

"What's happening?" Mary asked anxiously.

"We've come to the end of the waterfall," Rosie said, cutting off Billy's attempt to respond. "We're about to be dashed onto the rocks. Like a lightning bolt, the wormhole has found its natural ground and is straining to make contact."

"Nicely explained," Billy said calmly. "Couldn't have said it better myself." Rosie looked closely at the little boy tied into the large captain's chair. *He looks so small,* she thought. *And happy.*

"Thanks," she responded. "I think you'll find we have a lot in common, you and me."

They all watched the energy stream down. The outside wall of the wormhole appeared to roll over the brim and pour down a narrowing funnel, its rotational velocity increasing astronomically before compressing and vanishing from view. Outside beads of light flickered like sparks before disappearing, but the ship, coated with its repellent energy field, levitated just above the funnel spout. Behind *Tin Can*, the wormhole contracted as the energy telescoped into the point below. The ship's quantum microscope indicated the whirlpool of energy was swirling around a never-before-recognized subatomic particle.

"What's going on?!" Mary demanded.

"I don't know, I don't know!" Rosario replied. "I can only speculate."

"Then speculate–now!" Mary shouted. "We're boxed in and the tail end of the wormhole is coming down like a pile driver. Are we to be driven into that subatomic particle? I want to know what's going on before it kills us."

"Look at how the entire wormhole spins like a top on that bizarre subatomic particle," Rosario answered, attempting to understand the puzzle presented before her, fascinated. "No one has identified that particle before. It must be exceedingly rare. We traveled millions of miles before our wormhole managed to find one. Billy, this has to do with vortexes, right?"

Annoyed by Rosario's apparent lack of concern, Mary persisted, "Why is the wormhole pivoting over the particle?"

"That's the plan, Mary," Billy tried to explain. "At the center of my vision was this: the most powerful vortex will stop revolving at the point at which it comes up against another phase of matter. A tornado swirling above a lake doesn't turn the water beneath it into a whirlpool. The rotary motion stops at the air-water interface. The same goes for a gas-solid, liquid-solid, or liquid-gas interface. The rotational velocity isn't transferred through the next phase of matter." Billy strained against the belts holding him down and pointed to the screen. Jacob and Quincy tried to follow his line of thinking, intent on finally understanding Billy's dream.

"Our wormhole, traveling at astronomical speeds through the vacuum of space," Rosie said, taking over the explanation, "has come to a standstill, to spin over an unimagined subatomic particle. I think that particle is the protruding peak of an otherwise submerged promontory. It's a geographical outcropping at which the dimensions of other universes are pushing through into ours—it's the tip of the iceberg, so to speak. Remember, the tallest mountain on Earth, from its summit to its base, is Mauna Kea in Hawaii, not Mount Everest. That fact tends to be forgotten because most of Mauna Kea is submerged. I think the same thing is happening here: the point looks like a tiny subatomic particle, but in reality, it is the summit peak of the extra dimensions from another universe."

"That dot," Quincy said in a near panic, "that little, tiny dot is the opening to another universe?" His tail flicked rapidly from side to side and his ears twitched.

"Yes!" Billy and Rosie shouted in unison.

Mary turned away from Rosario and looked hopelessly out the viewers. She made technical adjustments so that the weaker bands of the spectrum came into clearer focus. In spite of the intense energy compression, there were persistent gaps in the field. Rosario was unsure of what to make of them, but Mary knew.

"Those empty shadows are graviton 'nests.' Our instruments can't identify them, but with the other energy bands so compressed, the gravitons come up as cavities in the energy field. It's like seeing empty air bubbles in colored glass.

"My guess is the spinning gravitons are condensing. The wormhole is behaving like an enormous cyclotron and the tip is where everything is getting mashed up together. At these density levels, the gravitons should repel each other, but as a particle accelerator, the wormhole is compressing the gravitons into pure concentrated jelly-like spheres. And it will likely keep compacting the individual jelly spheres until they form one big ball. With enough driving force, the gravitons pressing against the sub-particle promontory should burst through to the next dimensions and the universe or universes beneath. It's those empty shadows we need to watch."

Mary felt Rosario's right hand reach out and squeeze hers. Rosario was shaking, not with fear, but excitement. "I think you're exactly right, Mary," Rosario said. "The 'shadow balls' are being pushed together, compacting into each other where the cone tapers. Once the ball is pressed through to the tip there should be nothing separating it and the fixed subatomic particle. Contact will be made between universes at that flash point, history will be made, and we will be part of it."

Mary gazed at Rosario queerly. She really was quite odd, talking about being caught in the flashpoint like she was some kind of human catalyst unaffected by the discharge.

As smaller graviton nests continued to attach themselves to the main globe, it swelled in size and was pushed down towards the cone's apex. *Tin Can* had also now been shoved over the brim of the funnel to dangle precariously at its midpoint axis. Unhappy about where they were heading, Mary checked behind the ship to observe the tail of the wormhole's collapse accelerating. It appeared the wormhole was trying to turn itself inside out as the prior energy funnel had, but this time it would pour its contents out into the next cosmos.

Somberly, she turned back to watch the coming eruption.

The spiraling cone finally pushed the shadowy orb to its zenith and the energy that surrounded it, like a skin thinned out, eventually split and pulled back, leaving the bare graviton globe crowning. Because the globe remained invisible, the end of the wormhole appeared as a rotating volcano with an empty crater at its top.

Side by side, the girls inhaled and held their breath, Mary in trepidation and Rosie in eager anticipation. They didn't have to wait long.

The graviton bubble burst, disrupting space with the sharp spike of pure gravity. Almost limitless energy needled into an infinitesimally small particle, which distended, split, and then ruptured back into the other universe. A supersaturated strain sprang from the tip zone, germinating a fracture. The glass of space shattered. Shock waves stemming from the single isolated point bore outwards through jagged cracks on the other side. The not quite crystalline facade of space had been breached. Pulse waves traveling at half the speed of light liquefied branching bonds buried just beneath spatial dimensions, causing space to fracture like a great blue plate, splintering in a hundred directions into isolated, immense shards. An advanced concussive strike came next, then cresting impacts of subsequent gravity waves as the dimensions were split into long thin cracks of hyper-elastic liquid jelly. Each ensuing wave surged through the opened cracks out into the next cosmos. The wormhole turned itself inside out, emptying into the expanding fissures. The ship, dragged by the mass flow, poured down the largest fracture line. The entire event transpired in less than a microsecond, but for the crew of *Tin Can,* time seemed to slow to a crawl.

As the ship made its way down through the jagged crevice, Rosario watched, enthralled. Mary held her breath and waited, certain some of the earlier shock waves would ricochet back from the shattered shards of space and bludgeon the ship. But there was no backwash. The advancing concussion pulse disrupted the inter-space bonds so thoroughly, that the graviton wave dispersed completely; like spring water percolating through fractured granite, it was never coming back.

The energy from the wormhole streamed down, the fissured seams of space taking the ship with it. Mary expected the ship to be smashed or crushed between the sharp shards of space, but the bulk flow of energy temporarily expanded the fissures, allowing the ship to pass safely through the crevice. Mary waited for disaster, but none came. The ship was on the other side of the point.

$$***$$

"Rick, Jacayla, are you seeing this?" Rex's voice boomed through the mini-speaker in Rick's interface.

"I think so," Jacayla said, shaking her pony-tailed head slowly. "It's so incredible."

"The computers have been running calculations. We're almost certain the anomaly that's forming is a result of *Tin Can* creating its own wormhole ... "

Before Rex could finish his explanation, the fluctuating sky they'd all been staring at seemed to split open, like a stone cracking a windshield. The variation of black on black fissures streaking across space seemed to shine in a brilliant flash. The crowd went dead silent. Then it was gone.

"Rick," Jacayla said, as she glanced to her right quickly. "Did that just happen?"

Rick nodded his head slightly, then shook it side to side. The blue squares behind his irises glowed brighter than Jacayla had ever seen. "I think so. Maybe. I saw it, but was it real? With my lenses, in, I can't be totally sure." He turned to face his friend.

Jacayla looked into his dark eyes and smiled as she saw the iridescent light inside the blue squares fade. "I saw it. I think it was real. Did you see it?" she asked, turning back to Diego, still holding his mother's hand. Tears streamed down his stoic face.

"Yes, I saw it." All around them, people asked the same question and received the same confirmation. The flash had been so quick, so subtle, each individual worried that they had imagined it. As the voices grew stronger, into a chorus of cheers and cries, they realized it was true.

Tin Can had made it to the other side. Wherever that was, whatever happened to them, the evidence was there. There was hope for all of them.

"Thank you, mija," Marilyn whispered to the sky. "Thank you, Billy."

***

Behind *Tin Can*, fractured space fell back together, the vacuum of deep space miraculously pulling itself back to its previous three-dimensional configuration. Underlying, unseen bonds reunited, sealing the seams of space.

"It seems almost the same," Jacob said, releasing his seat belt to get up from his captain's chair.

"In a way I guess it is," Billy confirmed. "Much the same, in here at least, but in a completely different universe."

"There are critical differences," Mary said solemnly. "The ship's outside lasers and thrusters appear to be useless to us now. None of our sensors are working. The prior laws of physics no longer seem to apply."

"Our energy cocoon must have held," Rosie said, trying to sound cheerful.

"It's somehow shielding the ship from the outside," Mary confirmed. "Or we wouldn't be having this conversation. But without any outside sensors or thrusters working, we're blind and helpless."

"But, Mary, don't you see?" Billy asked, marshalling his strength, trying to sit up. "This is it, we're here! We made it, together! Now, all we have to do is adapt, the way we have through this whole journey. I know you've probably thought, from time to time, that I'd lost my mind. But, we're here, Mary. I'm not crazy. This is how the multi-universe works!"

"But, where do we start?" Mary asked helplessly. "None of the instruments can take even the most basic reading. Without readings, we're lost in the void."

"Chin up, Mary. We can't quit now," Quincy said as he bounded out of his chair and collected his tool belt from the cupboard. Slinging the little belt around his hips, he turned to the nearest instrument panel to begin unscrewing its front facade. "I'm a lemur who just traveled through a wormhole, the greatest vortex of all time." He stopped to look at Billy for confirmation that he was getting this right, then continued, "to crack through an unknown particle into a brand new universe. Anything is possible!" He slapped his little black paw on the console for emphasis, standing proudly in his tool belt.

Mary couldn't help but chuckle.

"And," Rosie chimed in, "I'm a girl who spent her whole life in bed on a respirator. *Died*," she said with a dramatic pause for the boys. "Yes, really died, in the most traditional sense, had my mind scanned, read, re-configured into a computer program, given game-like superpowers, and shot into space, where I proceeded to travel with a lemur to a new universe!" Ending with gusto, Rosie took a deep, exaggerated breath.

"Impressive, very impressive—that sounds like a story I've got to hear," Billy said with clear admiration in his voice. "It's going to be fun gettin' to know ya, Rosie. You'll tell us all about your life back on Earth and we'll tell you all about our time here in space. It'll be great!" Billy paused to scratch a suddenly irksome itch high up under the bio-probe with his index finger.

"Me, too," interjected Jacob, uncharacteristically jovial. "I can't wait to learn about those gaming abilities of yours. I sure wish I had gaming superpowers! So cool. Locked up here in this void, hiding out inside an energy cocoon, my skills are probably going to get really rusty. Maybe you and I can figure out a way to play against each other, now that we don't have the grid available."

"You and your games! Have you gone crazy, Jacob?" Mary barked. "We're floating through sub-space. None of our instruments work. You're our Captain; we need your total attention to detail and your utmost effort." Mary's voice was getting dangerously high pitched.

"She always like this?" Rosie asked calmly.

"Sometimes. Mary's a sensitive soul," Quincy explained with a turn of his right ear, while his nimble fingers separated the colored wires from behind the console.

"Don't mock me," Mary said, on the verge of having a fit. Then she looked carefully through her monitors at their smiling faces. "Why do you all look so happy?"

"Because, we're here, Mary. We've passed the test and made it to this point—a point where, at least for now, we're safe. We can rest a moment. Breathe. Just for a bit," Billy inhaled exaggeratedly. "And we made it together. And you know we're different now—we're the same, but we are different. Stronger. We've accomplished the unimaginable. In our hearts, all of us recognize we're capable of continuing."

Through the monitors, they heard what sounded like a sharp inhale of breath and a long pause. Mary was finally taking her moment, the same way a new graduate pauses on the stage to take in the view of the crowd and then looks out further, to the world in a different light.

"Feels good, doesn't it!" cheered Billy. "Now, think this all through, Mary. If you were going to adapt to this new universe, where would you start?" Billy asked, as he started to make his way out of the room.

"Adapt?" Mary said out loud, but mostly to herself. "Reconfiguration! We could reconfigure every outside instrument and see if one responds. A deviation in any of the instruments' parameters would be a preliminary reading. That's where to start!"

"You got it, Mary! But first, I'm thinking we gotta get back to the very basics. And because our energy shield held and we made it this far, I

suspect that our supply of spaghetti should still be right where we left it …
And I'm really hungry—and I've gotta pee.

"Then afterwards, we can get this *Tin Can* rollin'," Billy said pausing
at the doorway. "Kick this *Tin Can* into high gear … in a brand new
universe, but this time totally together. It'll be awesome!"